Joanna Courtney's first litera[...] prize at primary school and f[...] be a novelist. She was always r[...] up stories for her brother and [...] was when she took a degree in English literature at Cambridge, specialising in medieval literature, that she discovered a passion for ancient history that would define her writing.

Joanna began writing professionally in the sparse hours available between raising two stepchildren and two more of her own, primarily writing shorter fiction for the women's magazines. As the children grew, went to school and eventually left home, however, her time expanded and she started writing novels. Her first series, The Queens of the Conquest, is about the women married to the men fighting to be King of England in 1066. Her second traces the real stories behind three of Shakespeare's most compelling, but least realistic heroines – Lady Macbeth, Ofelia and Cordelia.

It was whilst researching Cordelia, a tribal leader in middle England c500 BC, that she realised Cleopatra, a famous 'ancient' queen, ruled far later than Cordelia, coming to her throne in 52 BC, and a new idea was born – to explore the stories of three vital women, living and ruling in the vibrant and heated world around the Eastern Mediterranean in the years either side of the birth of Christ. With *Salome* and *Magdala* to come, *Cleopatra & Julius* is the first of this series.

Get in touch with Joanna on Facebook:
/joannacourtneyauthor; Twitter: **@joannacourtney1**;
or via her website: **www.joannacourtney.com**.

ALSO BY JOANNA COURTNEY

Shakespeare's Queens series

Blood Queen
Fire Queen
Iron Queen

Cleopatra and Julius

CLEOPATRA
& JULIUS

JOANNA COURTNEY

PIATKUS

PIATKUS

First published in Australia and New Zealand in 2023 by Piatkus
This paperback edition published in Great Britain in 2024 by Piatkus

1 3 5 7 9 10 8 6 4 2

A CIP catalogue record for this book
is available from the British Library.

ISBN: 978-0-349-43297-7

Typeset in Baskerville by M Rules

Printed and bound in Great Britain by
Clays Ltd, Elcograf S.p.A.

Papers used by Piatkus are from well-managed forests
and other responsible sources.

Piatkus
An imprint of
Little, Brown Book Group
Carmelite House
50 Victoria Embankment
London EC4Y 0DZ

An Hachette UK Company
www.hachette.co.uk

www.littlebrown.co.uk

For Johanna, with love.
You are the strongest, bravest woman I know.
Not to mention the best dancer!

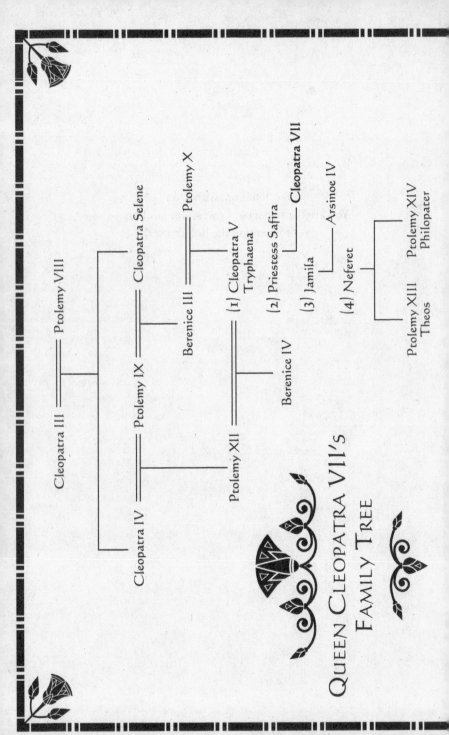

QUEEN CLEOPATRA VII's FAMILY TREE

Cleopatra III ══ Ptolemy VIII

Cleopatra IV ══ Ptolemy IX ══ Cleopatra Selene ══ Ptolemy X

Berenice III

Ptolemy XII ══ (1) Cleopatra V Tryphaena

Berenice IV

Cleopatra VII

(2) Priestess Safira

(3) Jamila ── Arsinoe IV

(4) Neferet

Ptolemy XIII Theos

Ptolemy XIV Philopater

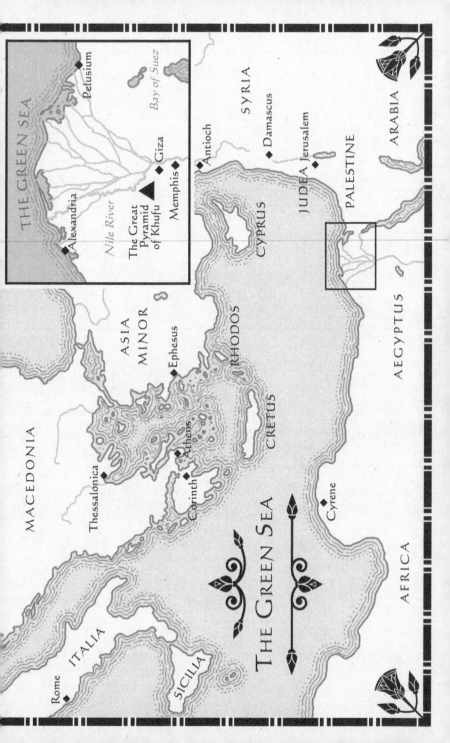

PART ONE

Alexandria, 56 BC

Chapter One

'People of Alexandria, all hail, your future rulers – Princesses Berenice, Cleopatra and Arsinoë, and Princes Ptolemy-Theos and Ptolemy-Philopater: the Sibling-loving gods.'

'Pah!' Berenice spat over the roar of the crowd. 'By Isis' arse, I'll never love those bastard boys.'

'Berenice, hush!'

Cleopatra, standing on the royal platform between her two sisters, looked nervously across the cheering people on the Canopic Way. The vast street, the centrepiece of Alexander the Great's favoured city, ran from the Temple to the sea and was wide enough to take eight carriages abreast, but today it was packed with people. Everyone had turned out for the presentation of the new royal baby and, no doubt, to make the most of the wine that would soon run from the fountains in celebration. The Alexandrians were in the mood to love their royals but their mood could turn on a golden deben and there was no point giving them cause for discontent.

'Why should I hush?' Berenice demanded. 'You should hate those damned boys too.'

The eldest of the royals turned her gimlet eyes on Cleopatra.

3

The only one of them born to King Ptolemy XII's true sister-wife Cleopatra-Tryphaena, Berenice had a statuesque magnificence that was emphasised today by a clinging gold dress, the jewelled collar of the heir, and a righteous fury to match.

'They're just babies,' Cleopatra protested, looking down the platform to four-year-old Ptolemy-Theos, sat stolidly in a golden chair, and baby Ptolemy-Philopater in the arms of his proud concubine mother, Neferet, whilst Queen Tryphaena glowered beyond.

'They're boys!' Berenice spat the word onto the marble platform where it glistened a moment before evaporating in the ferocious sun creeping beneath the silken canopy.

'Does it matter?'

Berenice glared at her, hawk-like beneath her royal headdress.

'Does it matter?! What sort of a fool are you? It *should not* matter, sister dear. It should be an irrelevance. Clearly *I* am the heir and clearly *I* am the one most fit to rule, right, Arsinoë?'

'Of course, Berenice,' their younger sister said sweetly. 'You are every inch a queen already.'

Berenice preened, then shot Arsinoë a suspicious glance. The youngest princess, although only twelve, was already showing all the signs of a delicate beauty as great as Jamila, her celebrated concubine mother – and all Jamila's calculated charm as well. Berenice chose to take her at her word.

'I am. And only need Father to die to take my true place.'

'Berenice!'

'Ideally before those bastard princes grow much more.'

Cleopatra's head was reeling at Berenice's reckless words. They were on the royal platform, before the whole of Alexandria, with their father, the king, just a few steps away. He was too busy waving to the crowd to pay any attention to his daughters but there were others around. Potheinos, the narrow-eyed vizier for one, and Charmion, keeper of the princesses, for another. Responsible for their day-to-day nurturing, she was the closest thing any of them had to a true mother and was tender in her care – and stern in her discipline. Cleopatra glanced nervously across but, although Charmion's intent stare told her the older woman knew exactly what was being said, she was at the lowly end of the platform and could not challenge them. Not yet at least.

'Why so fast, Berenice?' Arsinoë was asking.

'Because, fool girl, due to a huge injustice in Egyptian law' – this word, too, sizzled fat and wet onto the marble – 'when they reach fourteen, that mewling newborn and his podgy wretch of an older brother, will stand above me in the line of rule.' She gestured contemptuously to the baby as King Ptolemy took him in his hands and raised him above his head like a trophy in a chariot race. 'Look at the damned people cheering that weak bundle of limbs, when I am stood here in royal glory. It is surely the mind that counts in a ruler, not what's between his legs?'

Cleopatra frowned, considering this. She'd been raised, with her royal sisters, to prepare for rule. Accidents happened, especially in the Ptolemaic family where people regularly met early ends despite the best medical care in the known world, but she had not truly considered the order of precedence before.

'You think you should remain heir even when Ptolemy-Theos comes of age, Berenice?'

Berenice threw her hands to the skies.

'Gods be praised, she works it out! I thought you were meant to be clever, Petra, with your fancy books and your fifty languages.'

'Not fifty, Berenice. Egyptian is only my thirteenth—'

'Egyptian!' Her elder sister stared down at her in horror. 'Why on earth are you learning Egyptian?'

'It is the language of our country, Sister.'

'It is the language of the peasants, *Sister*, and therefore below your royal dignity – if you had any. It's a good thing that Father has me because you'd be a useless heir, forever running off down the Museon to chat to scholars when you should be learning how to rule.'

'The scholars tell me the history of Egypt. That is important.'

'If you wish to rule over the tombs. The people are *alive*, Cleopatra – look.'

She gestured across the Canopic Way where, already, the crowd was restless with the ceremony and looking to the fountains, waiting for them to gush ruby-red wine. Alexandria was a city bursting with nations. There were a hundred more languages spoken here than Cleopatra could ever hope to learn. Jews worked shoulder to shoulder with Namibians, Syrians, Cypriots and Ethiopians. Traders sailed in from every land within a thousand miles, their ships docking in either the shining harbour on the Green Sea side, or the busy inland port on Lake Mareotis, leading down the Nile into the heart of Africa. It made this surely the most vibrant city in the known world, but also the most unpredictable. Cleopatra could see that King Ptolemy would do well to signal the fountains to flow, but first the new 'Sibling-loving' god must be blessed.

The High Priest stepped forward, imposing in his ceremonial garb, and the people stilled. Berenice bowed her head in a show of reverence that hid her words from all but her two sisters.

'You rule *people*, Petra, not ideas. There is nothing to be gained by burying yourself in learning. Or in worship, whatever your priestly mother might think.'

Cleopatra's fists clenched at the jibe. Before them, the High Priest was chanting, his voice amplified by his conical headdress so that it rang out across the heads of the people and all the way down to the Green Sea.

'Mother is given to Isis,' she hissed.

It was a glory of which she was proud. The Priestess Safira was from the much-revered line of the High Priests of Ptah further up the blessed Nile at Memphis. She'd been dedicated to the service of Isis at a young age but when several babies had failed to inhabit Queen Tryphaena's womb after Berenice, the king had been granted use of her sacred body. Once Cleopatra had been born, Safira had returned to serve the Goddess and Cleopatra knew her only as a shadow.

'Your mother is more devoted to Isis than to you,' Berenice sneered.

'Of course she is,' Cleopatra shot back. 'As are we all. Isis is the Earth mother, the giver and protector of life. We owe Her our absolute duty and it is a joy to me that my mother is granted a place at her high altar.'

'Not high enough to be seen from Alexandria,' Berenice sneered, waving to the glorious monuments of the capital – the Serapeum holding Alexander's tomb, the vast palace complex, and the giant Pharos lighthouse, acknowledged wonder of the world.

'There is more to Egypt than Alexandria,' Cleopatra said tightly.

Berenice gave a shrill cackle, barely covered by the High Priest's chant even as it reached its apogee.

'You think so, sister? That proves your stupidity. Alexandria *is* Egypt. The hinterland is only there to provide us with grain and history.'

Cleopatra gasped. It was true that the elegant capital city was where most of the country's communication and trade went on but Upper Egypt, with its temples and pyramids, was what gave the country its prestige and the riches it needed to keep that high.

'If that is what you believe, Berenice, you are not fit to be Egypt's queen.'

Berenice gave a low growl.

'If that is what you believe, Petra, then *you* are not fit. You think people worry about a bunch of old monuments these days? You think the ravenous Romans care that we had kings and culture long before their little nation was even thought of?'

'Yes!' Cleopatra said defiantly. 'That culture is what sets us apart. It's what underpins Egypt in ways that the likes of the Romans will never understand.'

'The Romans kill cats,' Arsinoë whispered, pressing in close.

'Exactly,' Cleopatra agreed.

Just two months ago they'd watched from one of the myriad

royal balconies as the mob had set upon a Roman envoy who'd carelessly kicked a cat aside, little knowing the febrile creatures were sacred in Egypt. The enraged people had torn him limb from limb and Cleopatra could still hear his screams, still picture the animal fury on their faces as his blood had splattered across them in a fierce red arc. That's how important culture was. Berenice, however, gave a sly smile.

'That man will be the first of many to die. The Romans have devoured their way around the coast and Egypt is alone in resisting their disgusting locust march. They have their eyes on taking Cyprus from us, you know, and if they succeed, they will come for Alexandria and all your precious hinterland with it. You think that not understanding our "culture" will stop the march of their damned armies, Petra?'

'If I have anything to do with it,' Cleopatra said fiercely.

'You?!' Berenice gave her high-pitched laugh again. 'Little priestly you with your tiny dark-skinned body and your backwater mother and your peasant's tongue?'

'Berenice, enough.' The voice was low but firm and they turned to see Charmion had edged around the platform and was standing behind them. 'I brought you up to stand shoulder to shoulder with your royal sisters, not tear each other apart before the very crowd here to adulate you.'

Cleopatra hung her head.

'Sorry, Charmion. We were just discussing precedence.'

'Precedence?' Charmion's eyes narrowed. 'You *know* who has precedence, do you not?'

Her eyes flashed challengingly along the line of her royal charges.

'Isis,' Cleopatra supplied, head still low.

'Isis,' Charmion confirmed, gesturing to the great Temple behind them. 'Isis and the other gods who do you the good grace to inhabit your royal bodies and permit you to rule.'

Berenice ground her teeth so loudly that the scrape of them echoed off the marble columns.

'Then tell me, Charmion, why they choose to inhabit men's bodies above ours?'

She gestured contemptuously to the wailing baby and his toddler brother, kicking petulantly at his golden chair just along the great platform. Charmion leaned in.

'In truth, I do not believe they do. Many of Egypt's most successful rulers have been queens. Look at Hatsheput. Look at Nefertiti, Ahhotep and Cleopatra II. They achieved great things for this country and you girls can too.'

'But these boys of Father's, these tiny Ptolemies . . .'

'Are young yet, Berenice. We cannot know the intentions of the gods and should not presume to try. All you can do is to be the best you can be so that if they come calling, you are ready.'

'Maybe it is not enough to wait for them to call,' Berenice shot back as the priest, thankfully, wound up his chanting. 'Maybe, sometimes, you need to knock on their door.'

Cleopatra glanced nervously to Arsinoë and saw her littlest, prettiest sister looking up at Berenice, drinking this in. She glanced to the two princes, fed up with adulation and ready only for milk and cuddles. Then she looked to her portly father as he finally gave the signal to Sosigenes, the brilliant royal engineer, to turn the wheel that would let the wine flow.

It burst from the pipes like the richest, darkest blood and, as the Alexandrians dived ravenously upon it, she was grateful to be ushered back to the palace. If she was lucky, Berenice would be distracted by the many visiting lords and princes, and Arsinoë by her own reflection in the myriad pools within the lush grounds, and she would be able to escape to the scholars of the Museon and relax at last. Being a goddess was hard work and there was much to ponder on, not the least how Berenice planned to secure her throne and what that meant for the royal siblings she was sworn before the whole city to love.

Chapter Two

'And finally, Princess, a gift from your sacred mother.'

Mardion gestured to the shining ebony doors at the end of the grand chamber and guards stepped forward to open them. Cleopatra leaned eagerly forward on the throne. It was her fourteenth birthday and, to Berenice's ill-disguised disgust, she had been granted the privilege of sitting on her father's golden seat as her gifts were presented.

There had been many as rulers sought to curry favour with the richest country in the Greek world. Cleopatra was surrounded by golden chains, bejewelled cups, soft furs and rolls of the finest fabrics. Some had been more unusual. She was especially pleased with the manuscript of the *Iliad* presented by the scholars of the renowned library here in Alexandria, and with the giraffe sent from Ethiopia, which was currently eating hay in the outer courtyard. The gift from her priestly mother, however, was always the one she treasured the most.

The doors slid back to reveal a young woman, tall and slim, with skin the colour of honey, a golden collar emphasising a stunningly long neck, and a protrusion of curls worn proudly around her head in a dark cloud. Cleopatra heard whispers ripple across the gathered courtiers, but the woman's dark eyes fixed on Cleopatra and she began to walk towards her with such grace and poise that even the most determined gossips were silenced. When she reached the throne, she knelt and prostrated herself, bowing three times with unhurried reverence, before rising with the same fluid grace and giving a quiet smile.

'I am Eiras, Princess Cleopatra, sent to serve you by your gracious mother, the Priestess Safira, devotee of Isis in the Great Temple of Ptah.'

Cleopatra's heart clenched at her mother's name and she looked in wonder at the proxy-companion she had sent her.

'And I thought your hair was unruly, sister,' Berenice scoffed at her side. Cleopatra threw her a contemptuous look and rose to offer her hand to the new arrival.

'Welcome, Eiras. I am honoured to accept your service. Where are you from?'

'The land the gods forgot,' Berenice snickered but Eiras ignored her too and focused on Cleopatra.

'I am from the lands where the Nile begins.'

'A fine homeland indeed, for does not the Nile bring us everything that is fertile and strong?'

Eiras bowed her head in acknowledgement and around the room the courtiers hastily did the same. Beyond the grand chamber, a gong rung out, low and sonorous, as if sounding a blessing on the great river – though in truth it was simply calling the royal household to their midday meal. It meant Cleopatra's brief reign on her father's throne was over but she cared not, for it also meant she was released to enjoy her gifts before the celebratory dinner this evening and could get to know Eiras alone. King Ptolemy waved a hand to dismiss the crowd, pressing Cleopatra's shoulder as she rose before sliding firmly back onto his throne behind her.

'Happy birthday, my gecko.'

He always called her that. Berenice taunted her as 'little lizard' but Cleopatra cared not, for her father had told her that geckos were nimble and sharp-witted and clever. He loved her lizard tongue that could already speak twelve languages and, if she could only master tricky Egyptian, would soon speak thirteen. He loved her glossy onyx hair, apparently so like her mother's, and he loved the questions she always showered him with when they got rare time alone.

'My clever little gecko,' he would say, doing his best to answer her queries on the nature of kingship, though he ruled more by force of entertainment than philosophy. The courtiers called him 'Auletes' – the flute-player – for his love of music and dance but he said simply that a happy country was a peaceful country. Cleopatra could understand the point but thought perhaps it was more that a peaceful country was a happy one. They all knew the Romans were snapping at their heels and she feared musicians would be little defence if the red and gold armies landed in Alexandria's elegant harbour. But it was her birthday and such concerns were for another time.

'Come,' she said, taking Eiras' hand, 'let me show you where you'll be living.'

The courtiers dropped to their knees as she headed down the chamber, Eiras at her shoulder with Berenice chuntering indignantly behind. Arsinoë, well trained, held her own place at the rear of their procession until they were through the ebony doors, then instantly skipped forward, staring up at Eiras.

'You have so much hair.'

Eiras smiled.

'Where I come from, hair is to be celebrated not hidden.'

Cleopatra saw Berenice put a self-conscious hand to her gauze-covered locks, held in place by her diadem, the deceptively simple white ribbon that they all wore as the symbol of royal power. She smiled.

'Are you truly from where the Nile begins?' she asked Eiras, shepherding her around the vast fountain, gushing water from gilded statues of seahorses, and west towards the women's quarters. Eiras did not even look at the riches around her, but kept her eyes on her new mistress.

'I am.'

'Have you seen her birthing place?'

She shook her head.

'No one has. It is the Goddess' mystery from whence she conjures the great waters and anyone who has gone to try and penetrate it has never come back.'

Arsinoë gasped.

'Killed?'

Eiras shrugged.

'Taken up, perhaps? Maybe those brave souls live in ecstasy with the Goddess but I, for one, am happy with this life, especially now I am here with the Princess Cleopatra.'

Cleopatra felt herself blush under the girl's steady gaze and was glad when Mardion, their eunuch, bounced into the women's quarters.

'Look at you!' He turned a circle around Eiras, openly scrutinising her. 'This long neck, this honeyed skin, this glorious hair! You are truly the most handsome woman I have ever laid eyes on.'

Cleopatra was astonished to see a blush lighten Eiras' cheeks.

'I was selected from many by the Priestess Safira to please her daughter,' she said quietly.

'And you do!' Cleopatra told her. 'Don't embarrass her, Mardion.'

The eunuch shrugged easily. Given to the royal family as a small boy and fully castrated long before he grew to manhood, he was still short and round well into his twentieth year, with skin as smooth as a baby's and a childish bounce to his step. After the troubling presentation-ceremony for Ptolemy-Philopater, Cleopatra had asked what it was about the penis that made this royal baby higher than those without and he'd just laughed and said he'd lost the power of his far too long ago to answer but didn't seem to have suffered without it.

'In losing two little flaps of flesh, Princess,' he'd said cheerily, 'I gained a palace, so who am I to complain – or to comment on their worth.'

Cleopatra had supposed he spoke true but it hadn't answered her questions and few others seemed keen to engage in the debate. Sosigenes, the royal engineer based at the Museon, the renowned centre of research in the heart of the palace complex, had told her ancient wisdom held that a man's brain was superior but even as he'd said it, he'd grimaced at the unscientific nature of the proclamation and suggested she take it to the philosophers. She must do that soon but today was a day for joy not philosophy and she was glad of Mardion's enthusiasm for her new companion.

'How old are you?' she asked Eiras.

'Fifteen, Princess.'

'You are very tall.'

Cleopatra looked at her enviously. Berenice was as tall as a man and carried her height with imperial pride. Arsinoë too, had recently grown, her body as lithe and elegant as a giraffe's, and Cleopatra had no idea why Isis had not chosen to bless her with similar royal stature.

'It is not the size of your body that counts, but of your soul.'

Berenice, feeding herself apricots from a couch, gave a bark of a laugh.

'Your mother has sent you a walking platitude, Petra,' she scoffed. 'Try asking a Roman army the size of their soul and see how far that gets you.'

Cleopatra turned her back firmly on Berenice and led Eiras over to a secluded alcove.

'You have been with my mother?' she asked eagerly. She knew Safira could not leave the Temple but she still missed the shape of a mother in her life. Berenice had imperious Tryphaena and Arsinoë beautiful Jamila and, whilst both women were too busy to spend much time with their daughters, they were at least here in Alexandria.

'The Priestess Safira sends you her most fond love and bid me tell you she prays daily to Isis for your health and good fortune. She asks that, now you are of age, you journey to Memphis to see her.'

'Yes!' Cleopatra snatched at this. Her father took the vast royal barge up the Nile at least once a year to see his subjects in Upper Egypt and surely now that she was fourteen, she would be allowed to accompany him. She would ask tonight at the feast. He always granted a birthday request and this would be hers – the chance to see the Temple and her sacred mother. Her body thrummed with excitement.

'Do you speak Egyptian?' she asked Eiras.

'I do, Princess.'

'Perfect! I need help mastering its coils.'

'And I would be honoured to give it.'

From across the room Berenice groaned.

'This is all we need,' she said to Arsinoë, who'd crept closer to curl tentative fingers into Eiras' cloud of hair. 'Peasant-speak in the palace. Ridiculous!'

Cleopatra opened her mouth to contradict her sister but caught sight of Eiras' calm smile and resisted.

'What do you like to do with your time, Eiras?' she asked instead.

'If it pleases you, I like potions.'

Arsinoë leapt back as if stung and Berenice sat up with new interest.

'Potions?' Cleopatra asked, alarmed.

'Oh, nothing that will cause harm. I am interested in the plants in Isis' rich garden and the properties which can be mixed to help cure ailments – to heal wounds, cure fevers, help women in child-birth and older people when their joints ache.' Cleopatra stared at her, fascinated, and she went on. 'I confess I am also interested in how they can make skin smoother, hair glossier, lips redder.'

Berenice was suddenly all ears.

'You have potions that can do that?' she asked.

Eiras grinned.

'That and much more. I can show you, if you'd like?'

'Yes please.'

Eiras went to a chest that had clearly been delivered whilst the princesses were in the great chamber, opened it up, and took out a large wooden box, carved around the sides with blossoming vines. Unlocking it with a key from a golden chain around her neck, she began lifting out calcite jars and glass pots, setting them in a careful line across a side table.

'Would you like to take a seat?' She gestured to a chair and, as her sisters drew close, Cleopatra sank onto it. She eyed the potions nervously but her mother had sent this girl, so she must surely be trusted and she sat tightly as Eiras untied her diadem and ran her fingers through her hair. It caught in the knots that always seemed to twist so easily into it and Cleopatra jerked away.

'Apologies, Princess. We will soon have these out.'

Eiras cracked the seal on a jar and a smell of jasmine and lotus blossom filled the room, as if the plants themselves had sent tendrils shooting around their feet. Cleopatra closed her eyes as Eiras began working the scented oil into her dark locks and within minutes her long fingers were passing through it as easily as if her stubborn hair was oil itself. She opened her eyes to see that Berenice had drawn closer, fascinated, and now Eiras was twisting and curling, teasing her hair into immaculate ringlets around her face. Arsinoë clapped and as Eiras replaced her diadem, Mardion ran to fetch the big bronze mirror. Cleopatra dared to look and saw her long, boyish face, framed with soft curls that drew attention from her sharp chin and straight nose, focusing it instead on her eucalyptus-green eyes.

'Your mother has sent you a magician,' Berenice breathed and her envy was the best birthday present of all.

Chapter Three

That night Cleopatra walked into the banqueting rooms, head held high and glossy curls tumbling from beneath the royal sun disc that she was permitted to wear for her special feast. The hall looked especially fine, with a thousand candles sparkling off the gold-coated rafters and sending the ceiling murals flickering as if they were alive. The light shone in the pure marble walls, winked from the tortoiseshell inlays, and danced in the bejewelled dining couches so that the whole place seemed alive with colour.

It was packed with the great men and women of Alexandria, plus many foreign dignitaries, and for once Cleopatra enjoyed their gaze as they rose from their coloured couches to bow. She was a vessel of the Goddess and tonight, with Eiras' skilful aid, she felt a worthy one. Her new companion had applied the kohl that everyone wore to shade their eyes from glare and ward off infections, but with a sweeping upward line at the edges that made Cleopatra look pleasingly feline. She had mixed ground copper with the malachite usually used for eye colour to give a blue sparkle and had applied several layers of red ochre to her lips so that they stood out in darkest red. Cleopatra knew her features were not nearly as well arranged as Berenice's or Arsinoë's but at least now they were striking.

Spotting the Parthian ambassador, she touched her fingers to the beautiful collar he had brought from his master with a nod that made him beam. His pleasure gave her further confidence and she paused to speak to several other dignitaries in their own languages, enjoying the challenge of matching their faces to their native tongues. Berenice growled in impatience, and, amused, Cleopatra paused to ask Sosigenes, the chief palace engineer, about the year-clock he had shown her just the other day. It was a thing of beauty, with thirty-seven wheels that ticked round in a steady motion, their tiny teeth interlocking with the next so that they all turned in different sizes and motions.

'This one here ticks off minutes in a day,' he had shown her, 'and this one hours – twenty-four for each turn of the moon. This one pinpoints the Ides and Calends of each moonturn, and this vital one indicates how far those lunar turns are getting out of sync with the solar ones so that we can insert enough extra days to keep the calendar aligned with the seasons. It's quite simple really.'

It had not looked simple to Cleopatra but it had stayed with her. Sosigenes was a lean man with hair the colour of desert sand in moonlight and alert eyes that lit up when he talked of his myriad inventions and she was determined to learn more from him. Especially when it made her sister cross.

A glance back told her that Arsinoë was quite content letting every man kiss her delicately proffered hand, but Berenice was always happiest on the platform and radiated almost palpable fury. She was always simmering these days, hissing in corners with sly men and women and going on about the threat of the Romans and whether their father was up to withstanding it. Cleopatra thought it beneath the precious royal dignity she was always going on about and was glad to make her wait.

Beyond the hall she could hear the rumble of the Alexandrian crowd. To mark her birthing day, the king had sent platters of pastries and barrels of wine into the streets and many were gathered beyond the gates. After the meal, she would be taken onto the foremost balcony and presented to them and she knew their scrutiny would be greater than that inside the banqueting hall. She hoped Eiras' magic hair potion held her curls that long. The mob had been simmering as much as Berenice recently and she wanted nothing to spoil her coming of age.

Finally, she took her place on the couch at King Ptolemy's side and he waved his beloved musicians to play as servers came in with the first dish of Nile fish roasted with cinnamon and figs. Berenice reclined with Queen Tryphaena on the couch to their left, and Arsinoë with Jamila to the right. Neferet, mother of the two little Ptolemies, was just beyond, but at least the princes were safely in their nursery where they could not, for now, upset the precarious balance of the royal family. Charmion and Mardion stood behind and Eiras settled herself quietly at Cleopatra's feet.

'That is a fine gift from your lovely mother,' Auletes said to Cleopatra, gesturing so carelessly to Eiras that fish flesh from their shared platter dropped into her magnificent curls. Cleopatra hastily plucked it out.

'Eiras is wonderful, yes.'

'Your mother is well?'

'So I am told.'

'A lovely woman. So poised, so sweet-tempered, so gorgeously ripe and ... ' He stopped himself and gave Cleopatra a lopsided grin. 'She was a fine concubine. I miss her.'

His voice had dropped conspiratorially and Cleopatra glanced to his gathered wives, glad to see neither was listening in.

'I do too, Father. I was wondering if next time you take the royal barge up the Nile—'

She was cut off by a skirmish at the back of the chamber.

'Whatever is the matter?' King Ptolemy demanded.

A guard came forward, red-cheeked.

'There is a messenger seeking admittance, your majesty. We have told him it is the princess's birthing day feast and you are not to be disturbed but he insists that his missive is of the utmost importance.'

Auletes glanced to Cleopatra.

'Do you mind?'

Cleopatra hesitated but Berenice was already sitting up.

'Of course she does not, Father. Business is business, right, Princess?'

Cleopatra had to nod her agreement, though she could hear the murmur in the street notching up a level and disliked the feel of this intrusion. The guard grabbed a skinny young man by the elbow and propelled him roughly forward. He bowed so low his nose almost touched the floor and Cleopatra had to suppress a laugh but it was short-lived for Auletes was reading the missive and his face was darkening to almost the same purple as his richly embroidered tunic.

'What is it, Father?' she stuttered. 'What's happened?'

The whole room held its breath as he turned to her.

'It's Cyprus,' he said, shock shaking his voice. 'The Romans have taken Cyprus.'

Uproar.

Courtiers leaped to their feet, howling indignation. Auletes sank onto his couch and Neferet ran to tend him, leaving Berenice to snatch the missive from his limp hand and read it through. Cleopatra watched as her sister absorbed the news and a familiar dark gleam appeared in her eyes. She looked around at her father's advisors as they clamoured for information and then cocked her head, feline like, to listen to the mob beyond. Glancing to Tryphaena, she gave a sharp nod and her mother slipped from the room, unnoticed by any save Cleopatra. Before she could do anything about it, however, Berenice held up a hand. The room fell quiet before her.

'It is my sad duty to announce that the Romans have indeed seized our beloved Cyprus. They came upon the island by stealth and overwhelmed the guard. They seized my beloved uncle,

Ptolemy of Cyprus, in his bed and demanded his submission. What could he do?'

She looked around the guests, hand spread wide. They murmured uncertainly.

'He did not submit!' Berenice cried triumphantly and the noise grew. 'They offered him a paltry place as a priest at the Temple of Aphrodite – a valued role, of course, but a mean offering for a royal prince, carrying the gods within him. He turned it down and, when they tried to force him, my noble uncle chose . . . ' She paused dramatically and the crowd of high-born men and women crushed forward like savages. 'He chose to submit to his own sword rather than demean himself beneath a Roman master.'

A shocked gasp ran around the room and then someone cheered and suddenly it was a mass of shouting. Auletes stumbled to his feet and looked around, dazed.

'He is a hero!' Berenice called and the word 'hero' came back again and again. The noise on the street beyond rose and Cleopatra tensed. The Alexandrian mob went after drama like a dog after a fresh bone.

'Berenice, please – we need calm.'

'We need action,' Berenice shot back, her voice determinedly loud. 'We need to raise the navy and sail on Cyprus. We need to seize her back and send the upstart Romans packing before they come knocking on Alexandria's doors too.'

The dinner guests roared their approval. They pressed forward around the royal platform, fish and figs kicked to the floor and trampled like battlefield carnage into the pretty mosaic.

'Wait,' Auletes protested faintly. 'That is not what the missive says. There is only a small army on the island to escort a group of envoys. My brother has fallen on his sword, may the gods bless him, but he was always prone to over-reaction.'

No one heard him. Everyone in that room, Cleopatra knew, was 'prone to over-reaction' and their blood was up.

'Order the navy, Father,' she urged him. 'Stand up and order the navy loud and clear, or you may not get out of this alive.'

He looked at her, disbelieving.

'This is my palace, gecko, my throne. This is my food, my family, my musicians.'

But it seemed he was under threat from the Romans before their armies were anywhere near Alexandria, or at least under threat from his daughter. Berenice was standing tall and magnificent at the front of the platform, the birthday feast pushed aside. Cleopatra remembered her talking of knocking on the gods' door; was this what she was doing now? For a moment she admired her elder sister's nerve, but then the ebony doors flung back as a rabble of street men and women surged into the room and suddenly the nobles' whining press for information looked like children begging for a new toy.

Berenice lifted her hand, pointed one long finger at her father and said, loud and clear: 'He will not fight.'

'That's not true,' Auletes gasped. 'That's not what I said. I just said that we should wait, that ... '

But the mob never wanted to wait and they surged forward, waving eating knives like swords.

'Come, Princess!' Eiras tugged her off the platform and out of the small back door through which Tryphaena had slid earlier. Had she gone to let in the mob? Was that what Berenice's nod to her mother had meant? Were they sacrificing Auletes to make a bid for power? And on her birthday too.

I never even got to ask if I could sail up the Nile, she thought forlornly, then saw the foolishness of her concerns. Mardion was ahead of her, half-dragging a bewildered old man and she realised with a start that it was her father, his royal body sagging like that of the poorest peasant as he was bundled out the back of his own palace.

'Berenice!' she called. Arsinoë was clinging onto their elder sister's gown as if it were a life-raft and Cleopatra pulled out of Eiras' grasp and ran to her too. 'Berenice.'

'What do you want, little lizard?'

'I want to stay with you.'

'With me? In Alexandria? What about your precious Egypt? What about your beloved mother and her brave representatives?' She indicated two men scurrying for a side door, arms wrapped over the heads, then suddenly bent down and shoved her face into Cleopatra's own. 'Do you denounce Ptolemy-Auletes as king, Princess Cleopatra?'

'What? No! Why would ... ?'

'Do you acknowledge me as your queen?'

Cleopatra looked at her in horror.

'Queen? You?'

'Me, little sister. Do you acknowledge me?'

'*I* do,' Arsinoë was piping, her beautiful eyes appealingly wide. 'I do, Berry.'

Berenice beamed at her.

'Good girl. Wise girl. So, little lizard?'

Cleopatra shook her head.

'You can't do this, Berenice. You can't just ... '

'Listen, Petra.' Berenice grabbed her golden collar and pulled her chokingly close. 'We are women, set at a disadvantage from the start. You must see the adulation sent the way of the bastard princes. You must see the unfairness of our system however ancient and "cultured". Those great queens Charmion spoke of – Nefertiti and Ahhotep and Cleopatra II – did not rule by sitting prettily on their throne and being nice. This is my chance and I'm going to take it. Are you with me?'

'Not like this.' It was happening too fast. She needed time to think but with the crowd baying for blood, time was the one thing she did not have. She glanced to the back door and saw Charmion, her kindly eyes looking with horror upon the carnage in the royal hall. 'Not like this,' she repeated.

Berenice shook her head then, pulling back, gave her a sudden, violent shove.

'Seize her,' she shouted. 'Seize the traitor.'

'Berenice, no!'

But Berenice's face had hardened and she turned away, Arsinoë still clutching her golden skirts. Guards closed in on Cleopatra and she squirmed to avoid them. Hands closed around her and she struggled to fight them off before a warm, familiar voice said, 'I've got you, Cleopatra. This way.'

'Charmion.'

The older lady enfolded her in her thick arms and lifted her bodily from the chamber. Outside, Mardion was waiting, fear etched across his normally happy face and Eiras at his shoulder. The mob were howling and already a number of them were spilling out of the banqueting hall and running helter-skelter around the palace grounds, high on stolen power. A large man with a scythe lurched towards them and, grabbing Cleopatra's hand, Mardion ran, ducking around the pretty maze of low hedges and darting for an alcove at the far side. He knew the palace inside out and they soon had the advantage on their pursuer but Cleopatra felt her heart thudding in her chest and fear shaking her legs.

So many times she had run around this beautiful complex playing games with Arsinoë and Berenice, but the games, it seemed, were ended and she followed the eunuch without hesitation when he yanked her into a dark tunnel. It wound beneath the earth, under rough, dripping bricks, and came out at the far end of the docks. Dusk was falling and the sea sparkled in disorientating shades of pink and orange before her tunnel-dimmed vision. She swayed and felt someone put an arm around her. Eiras.

'It's not usually like this,' she managed to her new companion. Eiras smiled grimly and dragged her after Mardion who was running down the furthest dock towards an anonymous-looking ship. She stopped dead. 'What's that?'

'That,' Mardion said darkly, 'is your only chance. On board, Princess.'

'But it's so dark and, and dirty.'

'On board!'

His voice rose in panic and looking back, Cleopatra saw a handful of men running their way.

'I'm a princess,' she protested. 'I carry Isis within—'

'Now!'

Cleopatra heard the urgency in Mardion's high voice and, swallowing down her every royal instinct, she made for the gangplank, Eiras in tow. Sailors pulled her roughly on deck, yanked the plank up behind her and unfurled the sails. In the depths of the boat, oars were poked out of holes and began digging through the water, clumsily at first but with increasing rhythm.

Stop, Cleopatra wanted to shout; this was too fast, too confusing. Mardion had melted back into the tunnels and she was alone at sea.

'Where's Father?'

'Here, gecko,' a weary voice said and she turned to see him sitting on a hessian sack.

She looked aghast at the King of Egypt, sat amongst the grain like a peasant, then turned frantically back to Alexandria. The mob had reached the dock and were lobbing flaming torches after them, but they were just too late. The brands fell into the sea with a hiss and turned to harmless flotsam in the water, but there was no doubting their intent and Cleopatra felt her every royal fibre fizz with horror at the hatred thrown her way.

She stared up at the huge Pharos as they passed out of the harbour entrance. It stared impassively back, the height of a hundred men in three grand tiers, first square, then octagonal and finally circular. In a giant cage on the top, a great fire was kept forever lit and reflected by mirrors of Chinese steel across the dark seas beyond the harbour. Travellers said you could see it three whole days out at sea and it seemed Cleopatra was going to find out if that was true.

'Where are we going, Father?' she asked, her voice shaking in the rougher water.

The reply did little to steady her.

'Cyprus,' Auletes said. 'We are going to take on the Romans on Cyprus.'

Berenice had wanted a fight and now she had one but with the royals on opposing sides, Cleopatra dreaded where it might end.

Chapter Four

MARCH 56 BC

'Land! Princess, look – there is land!'

Cleopatra sat up, wiping sleep from her salt-encrusted eyes, and peered blearily across the thankfully still seas. She felt as if she'd been living in this boat forever. They'd fled Alexandria the day before the full moon of the Ides of February and it was now past the sliver of the Calends and into March. Her father, it emerged, had kept this unassuming craft as an escape boat and had it laden with treasure but you couldn't eat gold so she'd been surviving on salt fish and dried dates and was heartily sick of them.

She was a princess, a goddess; she should not have to live like this. Her stomach ached, her throat was parched, her hair hung around her face in scraggy lumps and she'd long since pulled off her white diadem, furious at its inability to protect her from these indignities. At last, though, the torment might be coming to an end for small puffs of cloud were hanging on the horizon in the damp morning air and below them, clearer all the time, was what had to be Cyprus. She leaped up, running to the prow to see more clearly.

'We've made it. We've truly made it.'

'That's Paphos, Princess,' the gruff captain said. 'Nice place. Very smart. Amazing wine and the richest olive oil you'll ever taste.'

He licked his chapped lips and Cleopatra's mouth watered in anticipation.

'Do they have decent baths?' she asked, tugging on skirts that were so watermarked she looked dressed in the sea itself. 'I cannot meet the people of Cyprus like this.'

'There's a lovely bathhouse, yes, and a half-decent port to land the old girl in.' The captain patted the side of the ship and then gave a rueful grimace. 'If they let us, that is.'

Cleopatra's empty stomach tightened with more than hunger pangs. They had escaped Alexandria but were they sailing into greater danger? Had they put up with dried fish and salt water simply to be seized the moment they landed? She shivered and Eiras put a warm arm around her shoulders.

'We will be quite safe. Your father is a friend of the Romans, remember?'

Cleopatra groaned. How could she forget? It was all King Ptolemy had talked about as one long sea-hour had rolled into another. Had he not supported the Romans in their fight against the Seleucids six years ago? Had he not entertained Pompey the Great in lavish style on his Parthian campaign? Had he not been formally sworn in as a friend and ally of the Roman people just last year?

'They will back me, Cleopatra,' he'd told her over and over, as relentless as the waves. 'Pompey the Great assured me of his support and now it is time for him to honour his promises.'

Cleopatra wasn't sure that Roman promises were good for much, however 'great' the man. From all she'd heard of the rapacious nation, their promises, with their friendship, lasted as long as it suited them. Surely, though, a king and a princess would not be hurt on their own island?

Former island, she corrected herself grimly, taking in Cyprus as it grew larger before them. Paphos looked almost as flat as

Alexandria, and the harbour, although nowhere near the same scale, was reassuringly flanked by a large seawall to keep the docks safe from storms and invaders – though not, it seemed, Roman ones.

'How did they not stop them?' she wondered aloud and, hearing a snort, turned to see her father at her shoulder.

'Paphos is a city of trade. I imagine the fools mistook war boats for merchant ones and simply let them into the docks. My brother was a gracious ruler of this pretty island but not, perhaps, a wise one.'

Cleopatra looked askance at her father.

'You think he failed?'

Ptolemy shrugged.

'Do you not?'

He pointed up the small rise behind the harbour and Cleopatra saw the outline of men across the horizon. They was no mistaking the bulk of the figures or the outline of spears at their sides: Romans.

'Are you sure this is wise, Father?' she asked, eyeing the narrow harbour entrance – and exit.

'Of course,' he said breezily. 'The Romans are my friends.'

Cleopatra had no reason to doubt him but fleeing the Alexandrian mob in fear of her life and living out of a barrel for two weeks had eroded her confidence in her father's godlike power and she retreated nervously to the bows with Eiras as the captain guided their ship up to one of three long docks. The low sun was casting a golden light across the warm sandstone buildings of the small city. People were beginning to bustle around, loading and unloading goods, and Cleopatra relaxed slightly. Above the first line of buildings, white marble walls marked a Ptolemaic palace and to the north she could see porticoes and temples against the horizon. The gods were strong here and would surely protect her?

They docked with a small bump and much throwing of ropes but no one came to see who they were and no soldiers appeared to threaten them. Never before had Cleopatra arrived anywhere without a flurry of attendants rushing to tend to her every need, and she stepped uncertainly onto the wooden boards with just Eiras at her side. No one turned. No one hailed her. She just stood there in her bedraggled dress, free to do as she wished. It was most disorientating.

'Where do we go, Father?'

Ptolemy, too, looked disconcerted at the lack of welcoming committee but drew himself up and waved his handful of servants forward.

'To the palace,' he declared. The servants looked uncertainly at one another and Ptolemy's brow creased. 'A litter! Now!'

The men looked around but no litter had been packed on the escape boat and everyone in Paphos harbour was busy about their own affairs. One of them dashed into the city and Cleopatra stood awkwardly at her father's side until he finally returned with two curious locals and a rough-looking litter.

Ptolemy's lip curled but he stepped into it as regally as if it were draped in purple and waved the bearers on. Cleopatra was left to walk behind, her legs unsteady from so long at sea and her dress rough against them. She had never felt more conspicuous and yet still no one paid her a second glance. Did they not know who she was? She felt almost naked without her rich clothing and fine jewels, and tugged awkwardly at her golden collar, wishing she'd thought to order it polished as they came into port. But they were approaching the palace and surely here, at last, they would receive their due.

The tall gates were closed. One of the king's men went uncertainly up to their blank bulk and knocked. Nothing. He knocked again and there was a small sound from behind before they creaked open a crack and two men edged out. Cleopatra stared. They were dressed in scarlet tunics, topped with leather-banded kilts and golden breastplates that flashed so brightly in the sun she could scarce make out their faces, hidden beneath scarlet-topped helmets. The little she could see was not friendly.

'Yes?'

'King Ptolemy of Egypt is here. And Princess Cleopatra.'

Cleopatra took a step forward and the two Romans looked at her down noses longer than her own.

'Are you sure this is a princess?' one of them asked, his lip curled in amusement.

Fury shot through Cleopatra and she stepped closer, thrusting her shoulders back to show off the collar the King of Parthia had gifted her just two weeks ago. It might be sea-tarnished but it was still gold – real gold, not the gaudy plate of their uniforms.

'We are sure,' she said in Greek, adding it in Latin. The soldier's lip uncurled.

'Of course. Apologies. That is . . . I'll, er, fetch someone.'

The pair disappeared inside and the gates closed again. Cleopatra looked to her father in disbelief but he was sat back in the litter, eyes closed, and it was Eiras who guided her to a marble plinth where they sat in the increasingly hot sun until, at last, the gate cranked open again.

'You can come in,' the guard said, standing back but leaving only a sliver of an entrance, not wide enough for the poor litter in which the king was sat.

'Open up,' Ptolemy demanded furiously.

'I cannot. Security.'

'Security, *your majesty*,' Ptolemy corrected him furiously.

The guard shifted.

'We, er, we do not recognise royalty in the Republic.'

Cleopatra stared at him in astonishment. Did not recognise royalty? What sort of a barbaric people were these Romans? The opening remained only wide enough for a single person and in the end King Ptolemy had to clamber out of his litter and walk in on foot, turning sideways to get his luxurious bulk through.

'You,' he said to the guard once they were all inside the complex, 'are an insolent upstart. If Pompey the Great – my *good friend* Pompey the Great – can recognise my kingship, then surely you can manage it?'

31

The man turned white and looked at the ground.

'I'll take you to the waiting chamber.'

'Waiting?' Ptolemy spluttered but the two men were already off, marching in rigid time, and the royal party could only follow.

Cleopatra found herself in an opulent courtyard, rich with green plants, a fountain plashing at the centre of an elegant marble seating area. Taking a seat on one of the pleasingly cool benches, she looked around for refreshment but there were no servers in sight.

'Is there anyone here?' she asked her father.

'Oh, someone's here all right,' he growled. 'But they are doing their best to impose their paltry authority in the meanest of ways. Typical bloody Romans.'

The 'my friends' aspect of the Romans seemed to have been rapidly dropped from her father's speech and Cleopatra felt her throat tighten as she looked around the deserted courtyard. She was thirsty, her stomach was rumbling and she really needed the latrine. She felt tears prickle and blinked them crossly away. If there were games being played here then she could play them too.

It was Eiras who lost her temper first.

'This is just plain rudeness,' she shouted, leaping up. 'Even the poorest home would welcome travellers with a little refreshment, not to mention simple politeness. Are Romans even poorer than they?'

Her words echoed around the courtyard and were absorbed uselessly into the marble porticoes.

'Perhaps they are busy,' Cleopatra said nervously.

'Perhaps they are miserable barbarians,' came the tight reply but someone must have heard her rage for there was a rustling at the back of the courtyard and a man appeared.

He was not a soldier, for he was dressed in the toga Cleopatra had seen Roman envoys wear in Alexandria – a curious garment made of far more fabric than needed and wrapped around the wearer in a complex set of folds that seemed designed to fall apart at any moment. Deep purple-red stripes around the edge and on the tunic beneath denoted magisterial authority. It was a much-prized status symbol in the petty Republic but to Cleopatra it just looked uncomfortable.

The man stood before them, unspeaking, and she took him in. He was in his middle twenties, tall and stockily built with sandy-coloured hair and fine cheekbones. Cleopatra supposed he was handsome, but his cloud-grey eyes assessed her as if she were a bug and she drew herself up as tall as she could, determined to show him the Goddess within.

'Marcus Junius Brutus,' he introduced himself.

'King Ptolemy XII of Egypt,' her father said tightly. 'And my daughter, Princess Cleopatra.'

Marcus Junius Brutus gave them both a small nod. Cleopatra saw the muscles stand out on his neck and assumed he was exerting himself to resist obeisance. How exhausting for him.

'We are here,' Ptolemy went on, his voice icy, 'for the body of my brother, dead at Roman hands.'

'Dead at his own hand,' Brutus said calmly. 'He was offered an honourable position as High Priest of Aphrodite but chose to take his own life instead. A shame.'

'A tragedy!'

Brutus gave a curious little tilt of his head.

'A coward's way out.'

Ptolemy made a dark, choking sound.

'You force my royal brother from his position as ruler of this island, humiliate him with a lowly priesthood, and then condemn him for his honourable suicide? How dare you!'

'I do not mean to condemn the *man*,' Brutus said easily. 'Merely the act. Philosophically it is an interesting debate whether suicide is a noble act. Personally, I believe—'

Ptolemy put up a hand.

'I do not give a rat's arse what you personally believe, Marcus Junius Brutus. This is not a philosophical exercise but my broth-er's life.'

Brutus blinked, surprised.

'It is both,' he said. 'There is something to be learned philosophically in every situation, is there not?'

Ptolemy rolled his eyes.

'Who is in charge here?'

Brutus shifted.

'I am.'

'Nonsense.' Ptolemy waved a dismissive hand. 'You are far too young. Romans don't let anyone in charge of anything until they are halfway to the grave. So, Marcus Junius Brutus, who is in charge here?'

'My uncle,' Brutus conceded, looking so like a toddler caught with another child's toy that Cleopatra almost laughed. He glanced her way, then snapped his eyes back to Ptolemy. 'Marcus Portias Cato.'

'Cato!' Ptolemy gave a hoarse laugh. 'That explains everything.' He turned to Cleopatra. 'Cato is the most rigid of the rigid Romans. He keeps his morals as tight as his belt and his words as dry as the desert.'

Brutus looked furious.

'That is not true. My uncle is a brilliant, principled, honest man.'

'As I said,' Ptolemy agreed, turning away from him with a dismissive wave, 'beware a man of "principles", daughter, for they will matter to him more than anything – more than manners, more than sense, more than even those they love.'

'That is not true,' Brutus exploded again, tugging on his sandy hair and looking around the courtyard for rescue. He found none.

'Principles,' Ptolemy went on blithely, 'work like a rod in a man's back, making him unbending.'

'Strong,' Brutus said.

'Fragile,' Ptolemy shot back. 'It is the straightest trees who fall first in a storm.'

Brutus had gone pink with fury and Cleopatra tugged uneasily on her father's arm.

'This is not a philosophical exercise, Father,' she reminded him.

Ptolemy frowned at her but, to her surprise, Marcus Junius Brutus burst out laughing. It transformed his face, softening the rigid lines and bringing light to his grey eyes.

'You are right, Princess,' he agreed, with the slightest of involuntary bows. 'Let me fetch you some refreshment and then, perhaps, my uncle will be free of his many duties to receive you.'

Cleopatra inclined her head and sat herself down again with as much grace as she could muster. These fools may not 'recognise royalty' but she did not need their paltry recognition; she just needed her country back and all would be well.

Chapter Five

Two hours later, they were still sat in the courtyard. A latrine had, at least, been provided, as had ice-clear water, rich wine and cured meats. When it had become clear that the mysterious Cato would not be calling them in a hurry, Cleopatra and Eiras had taken the time to bathe as best they could in a handbasin. Although Cleopatra's dress was still unavoidably salty, her skin was clear, and Eiras had wrapped her hair into a loose bun at her neck and washed and restored her white diadem. She'd even polished up her golden collar so that it shone in the sunlight pouring into the centre of the lush courtyard. Still, though, no one came.

Eventually Brutus reappeared, his large body toddler-awkward again as he cleared his throat and announced, 'My uncle will see you now.'

'Here?' Ptolemy asked.

'Er, no.' Brutus looked at the mosaic on the floor, apparently studying its every whorl. 'Within,' he eventually managed and dipped back into the palace, leaving them to follow unattended.

'This really is the height of rudeness,' Ptolemy muttered. 'Wait until I see Pompey. Wait until I tell him how this jumped-up intellectual treated us. Wait . . . ' He stopped dead in the doorway through which Brutus had just passed. 'No.'

'Ptolemy of Egypt,' said a voice, thin but unwavering. 'Do come in.'

'No,' Ptolemy said again and put a hand on the doorframe to steady himself.

Alarmed, Cleopatra peered inside. The putrid stench hit her first and it was a moment before her watering eyes could find purchase in the fly-infested little room to see a small man, toga hitched around his waist, sitting on an open latrine as if it were a throne. It seemed that there *were* new heights to this Cato's rudeness and she recoiled with a shocked gasp.

'Uncle ...' she heard Brutus say but he was waved into silence and stood, head bowed, as Cato waved them forward.

'I am a king,' Ptolemy cried.

'Not here.' Cato's face crumpled in unmistakable concentration and a fresh smell cut through the must of the existing stench.

'My daughter ...'

'Can choose where she stands. I have been about important business all morning and have not had time for my ablutions until now.'

He smiled nastily, delighted to consign them to unimportant business, and screwed his face up again. Cleopatra watched with astonished horror. This was Roman hospitality? This was the way of the people who were conquering the known world? The envoys she had known in Alexandria talked pompously of 'civilising nations' but if this was their concept of civilisation then the nations in their forced care were in a sorry state indeed. Her heart ached for poor Cyprus and she feared for Egypt, standing proudly alone against these crude barbarians.

'Has he no dignity?' she whispered to his father.

Ptolemy sighed.

'He has principles, remember, gecko. Admirable is it not?' He took several steps forward and Cleopatra watched admiringly as he squared up before the strange Roman governor – a small man, as far as she could tell from his hunched position, with pale skin and dark hair cut in a severe line across his forehead, as if

37

underscoring his mind. 'I come, Cato, to ask you to return Cyprus to the Egyptian people, to whom it rightfully belongs.'

'Why would I do that? The Republic has annexed this island for its own protection and I am charged with its governance, a duty I take very seriously.'

He reached for a stick sitting in a bucket at his side and lifted it, looking vaguely at the spongey tip before reaching back with it to wipe himself. Cleopatra covered her eyes; had the man no shame?

'You have wrongfully and unlawfully seized a land granted to me by Rome when it formally ratified me just last year as a Friend and Ally of the Roman people,' Ptolemy asserted.

Cato gave a sly smile.

'True. And as that ally, you will surely understand that all land within the protection of the Republic is held in common. I do not own this fair island, Ptolemy; I merely govern it for the good of everyone.'

'As was my brother doing before you drove him to his grave.'

'A shame that,' Cato said lightly, bringing the sponge-topped stick back out and examining it dispassionately. 'He seemed a decent man, if impetuous. It is only land; not worth a life surely?'

Cleopatra saw her father dig his feet into the rough ground and felt for him.

'You owe him respect,' she burst out furiously. 'If not as a prince, at least as a ruler. At least as a *man*.'

Cato peered curiously at her. 'You will allow that?' he asked Ptolemy.

Ptolemy looked round.

'Allow what, Cato? Allow my royal daughter to speak her opinion? Why not?'

He gave a thin laugh.

'She is a woman.'

'She is a princess.'

Cato rolled his eyes.

'Not this again. We are getting nowhere. You have come to ask for Cyprus back; I am not going to give you it. Are we done?'

'No! I demand a hearing.'

'Do you indeed? By whom?'

'By Rome, by the senate who made me promises etched in ink that is barely dry upon the papyrus.'

'Ah.' Cato seemed to ponder this, but only as carefully as he had studied his own ordure. 'You see, I am merely an instrument of the Republic. If you wish to address your complaint to the senate then you must climb its hallowed steps. If you want a hearing by Rome, Ptolemy of Egypt, then you must, I fear, go to Rome.'

'Rome?' Cleopatra gasped. She looked back down the long corridor to the pretty courtyard and the sea beyond. Somewhere across that, Alexandria sparkled, already far too far away for her liking. 'We cannot go to Rome.'

But Ptolemy was squaring his great bulk before the thin-faced man on the latrine.

'I *shall* go to Rome and I *shall* address myself to those in the senate who understand the ways of the world better than a jumped-up lawyer with an overstretched opinion of himself. I hope you have enjoyed your moment of petty humiliation, Marcus Portias Cato, because it will not come again. You will accommodate myself and my household whilst we provision ourselves, as is our right beneath your precious Roman constitution, and you will send news to your beloved city of our imminent arrival. I will have Cyprus from you, I swear, and then I will be back to rub your smug face in that precious shit of yours. Good day.'

He stalked from the room and Cleopatra hurried in his wake.

'Where are we going, Father?' she asked as he made for the gates and his paltry litter beyond.

'Back to the ship.'

'No!' Cleopatra's heart quailed. She hated that ship.

'And on to Rome.'

She swallowed.

'Am I ... am I coming?'

'Unless you wish to face your sister's armies?'

Cleopatra remembered the furious faces of the mob, the hands reaching for her sacred person, the burning torches flung at her with evil intent. She remembered Berenice's eyes boring into her own and her cruel shout: 'Seize the traitor.'

'I do not.'

'Then yes, daughter, you are coming to Rome. You like learning, do you not? Well, get ready for the precious Republic and the greatest education of your life so far.'

Chapter Six

My dearest Charmion,

Rome – what can I say? It's so ... disappointing. I don't know what I expected, especially after our rude reception on Cyprus, but truly I hoped Cato was just a poor example of a Roman. When I got to the city itself, I was sure I would see what makes these people so great, but it is the reverse. Rome is exactly the sort of city I can see that tight-arsed boor of a man springing from.

It has energy, certainly. The place buzzes but that's mainly because its citizens are so crammed in. Truly, I've never seen so many people living in so small a place. Buildings are put up on top of other buildings, temples perch on the shoulders of villas, statues lean drunkenly against walls. It is ridiculously cramped and they do not even have street lights, so at night they stumble around like fools.

The other day I saw a building fall down. It just crumbled to dust and imploded in a terrible rumble of bricks. There were people falling into the wreckage like as much masonry – women and children screaming as they were toppled out of their houses six storeys above the street and smashed to their deaths. And the Romans? They just tutted and stepped around the writhing mess until someone came with brooms

41

to sweep up, carefully picking out whole bricks to use again but casting the bodies aside. These people, Charmion, believe they are civilising the world but, truly, they are barbarians.

The streets of Rome are crooked and so narrow you can barely fit the smallest cart down them so that they seem always to be blocked with muleteers screaming furiously at one another in their funny stop-start Latin. Everyone in Rome is impatient and no wonder, for they live like animals, penned in together. There is no space to breathe, no openness to soothe the soul.

This is all because the city is built between seven hills. Nonsense, I know. What sort of planners did they have when they picked this place? Could they not have found a plain to lay it out with space and order? But no! They love their little hills and the top of each one has been claimed by the rich for their fancy villas so they can physically look down on the rest – as if status came from geography! I think of our beautiful palace, my dear Charmion, and laugh at what they take for grandeur. I would ship every one of them to Alexandria to show them true elegance, save that I fear they would never want to go back and the last thing we need is a load of Romans strutting down the Canopic Way.

This place is so full of its own importance but it is like a tiny cockerel strutting amongst ostriches. Its first kings trod this paltry bit of the earth just 700 years ago. Imagine! And only seven of them reigned before some Roman called Lucius Junius Brutus kicked them out. They have his statue on the hill alongside those of the kings he got rid of, as if they are all friends together! But that's Rome for you – a city of endless contradictions.

I am not – you will not believe this – allowed inside the city itself. Why? Not because I am a foreigner, for there are plenty of them selling dubious wares in Rome's streets. Not because I am a woman, though they do have strange ideas about keeping females in their houses. No, it is because I am royal! They have an actual boundary, marked out with rough white stones, and no monarch is allowed to cross it. Imagine! I am determined to check their precious constitution for myself if I can

42

*find anything as useful as a library, so that I can actually see this
strange city before I, pray Isis, head for home.*

*Our host, Pompey, who is called the Great (though when I think
of our own glorious Alexander, it seems impossible that this boorish
Roman could claim the same title) seems eager to lead an army on
Egypt and confident of victory. I worry about the price he will exact of
us, but Father insists that I am not to concern myself with it, for Egypt
has more gold than the whole Roman Republic. I think not so much
of money as of a far greater debt of obligation, but what can we do?
The gods have thrown us into this strange city and we must make the
most of it.*

Yours,
Petra

'There – you look like a princess again!'

Eiras sat back with a satisfied smile and held out the looking-
glass to Cleopatra. She peered into it and ran a contented hand
down her smooth curls, then touched her fingertips to her freshly
laundered diadem. The rigours of her terrible journey to Rome
had, it seemed, aged her pleasingly and Eiras' skilful painting had
perfectly enhanced the new sharpness in her cheekbones and brow.
Her companion was not happy with the cosmetics she'd been able
to draw together on short notice but had done her best. Roman
women liked their faces boringly bland and the darker shades of
kohl and brighter compounds for eyeshadows had been impossible
to track down, but she had at least found red ochre and used it with
skill on Cleopatra's lips and cheeks. Satisfied, she drew in a deep
breath, luxuriating in the rose petal fragrance from her bath, the
softness of the cushions on her seat and the silken fabric of her robe.
They had been in Pompey's house for two days and it was, praise
Isis, every bit as comfortable as she had been promised, with just
one problem.

'Do I really have to wear that?' she asked, gesturing to the dress
hanging nearby.

It was kind of Pompey's wife, an eager, open-faced young woman called Julia, to lend her clothes until she could purchase a new wardrobe, but the Roman woman had far bigger bones than Cleopatra and far coarser taste in fabrics, and she winced in antic-ipation of the rough linen against her skin.

'We will find dressmakers very soon,' Eiras assured her. 'Someone in this city must know how to make finer clothes than these.'

'They better do, or Isis will truly desert me. I have put Her through enough already without dressing her like some mer-chant's wife.'

'Hush!' Eiras cautioned. 'Julia will hear you. And Pompey is not, you know, a merchant, but a great general and an esteemed politician.'

'Then he should buy his wife better clothes.'

But she had little choice bar staying in her room forever, so she rose and let Eiras dress her. The gown was, at least, a pretty shade of blue and, once Eiras had put stitches into clever places, it did not make her look quite so much a sack of cotton as it might.

'It will do,' she sighed, forcing herself to be positive. 'Come, Eiras. Julia has invited some women to the villa this morning, so at least we may have good company. And they may know a decent dressmaker too.'

Eiras smiled and offered her arm and Cleopatra took it and headed into the main hallway of Pompey's villa, an apparently grand home that barely measured up to a side-wings of her own palace. Not that she had said so. She was having to learn tact and it was exhausting but perhaps, with a group of high-born women, she could relax again.

Pompey was in the hallway with Ptolemy, his voice booming around the tight walls.

'Fret not, Sire, fret not, I have the senate eating out of my hand and will soon secure the troops to see you home. You are, after all, a friend and ally of the Roman people and we owe you a duty of care.'

He puffed out his chest and gave Ptolemy a hearty pat on the back that almost sent him sprawling. The man was heading into his latter years but was still tall, with the legs and shoulders of an ox. His belly, Cleopatra noticed, was sagging and the carefully styled quiff on his broad brow was thinner than was ideal to carry the amount of oil needed to keep it high, but he was still clearly a man of strength and, it was to be hoped, power.

'I knew I could count on you,' King Ptolemy said once he was steady again. He waved Cleopatra eagerly over. 'I told my daughter, did I not, Cleopatra, that Pompey the Great would come through for me. I told her we were friends and that you had assured me, at my own table, that you would be my supporter if I ever I needed it.'

'I did, I did, I did. And it does honour to my own ancestry to fulfil that pledge.'

Pompey gestured back to the dark death masks of his ancestors leering out from glass cases along the wall, and smiled benevolently at first Ptolemy and then Cleopatra. It did not suit him any more than the folds of toga that bunched around his large body. Cleopatra suspected he was happier in uniform and, sure enough, he added now, 'It will be good to be back on campaign,' and looked happily into the middle-distance, as if already seeing battlefields carved across the walls of his Roman villa.

'Won't it be dangerous?' Julia, his wife, asked, clasping at his arm.

He turned to her, a look of surprising tenderness crossing his heavy features.

'Not at all, my love. I have the best armies in the world and these days I command from the rear. Let the youngsters seeking glory wield their swords in the first wave, as I once did.'

His chest puffed out again and Julia gazed dotingly up at him. Cleopatra watched curiously. Pompey was over fifty and Julia just eighteen so that they seemed far more like father and daughter, save for the burning way they looked at one another.

'I'm sure you will be wonderful,' Julia said.

Pompey nodded complacently.

'I know the East, my dear. And I know Alexandria. We have

legions stationed in Syria that can be marched round in no time. We'll have you back on the throne before the year turns, King Ptolemy.'

Cleopatra hoped he was right. Already she was weary of Rome and the thought of a whole summer here was enough to turn her stomach.

'I'll head to the senate shortly,' Pompey assured them. 'Will you come, my dear?'

'Oh, I'd love to, Gnaeus,' Julia said, 'but Calpurnia is here.'

'Women's business,' Pompey said with a wink at Ptolemy and patted her hand.

Julia let go of her grip on her husband and turned, instead, to take Cleopatra's arm. It was most familiar of her but Cleopatra steeled herself not to complain for no one here seemed to understand how to treat royalty and she could not, she supposed, condemn them for their unfortunate ignorance.

'Calpurnia is married to my father, you know,' Julia told her happily, guiding her into the ladies' parlour. 'We are all but sisters.'

'Your father is . . . ?'

'Julius Caesar. He's a brilliant man, is he not, Calpurnia?'

A skinny, tight-lipped young woman stood up and nodded primly. 'Brilliant.'

'How nice for you,' Cleopatra said mildly, though her mind was racing. If this Caesar was so brilliant, might he be able to help her if Pompey could not? 'Will I meet him?'

'If only!' Calpurnia sighed dramatically.

'My father is off conquering Gaul,' Julia told her. 'He's been at it for ages, poor man. They're fearfully wild, you know. They have a lot of hair and live in very cold climates and drink wine without watering it down!'

'Shocking,' Cleopatra said obligingly but it did not seem the scariest quality in an enemy. 'Does that not make them rather easy to fight?'

Julia frowned.

'Oh no! They're very fierce. No match for a Roman army, of course—'

'Of course,' Calpurnia murmured, like a simpering Greek chorus.

'But very fierce. Julius has been brilliant.'

'Brilliant.'

Cleopatra glanced to Eiras, who'd followed her into the parlour, and was amused to see her companion struggling to control her mirth at these earnest Romans. Mind you, if this was the level of their conversation, it did not bode well for the morning's entertainment.

'I had a letter from your father this morning,' Calpurnia told Julia, patting at her bosom and pulling out a small, slightly sweaty scroll.

Julia leaned in eagerly.

'How is he? Is he well? Is he sleeping? He's not a good sleeper, you know.'

'Oh, I know,' Calpurnia agreed. 'He is often up out of our bed before the dawn comes. It's his mind; it whirs constantly. I consider it my marital duty to distract him as best as I can.'

They giggled together and Cleopatra bit at the inside of her lip to stop herself snapping at their silliness.

'He speaks mainly of me,' Calpurnia was twittering on. 'He asks if I am well, if I am in ... in full health.' Her voice quavered and she placed a fluttering hand on her belly. 'Sadly, I am,' she said and Julia gave her a quick squeeze.

'Me too,' she said mournfully. 'However hard I try.'

Cleopatra squinted at them in confusion and Eiras leaned in.

'I think they would like to be with child, Princess.'

Cleopatra groaned. So many women were obsessed with having babies, as if it was all they were good for. She was thankful to be a princess, enough in her own right without needing to produce new humans to justify her existence. She shifted awkwardly as the two women dabbed at each other's tears and was hugely relieved when one of Pompey's richly clad serving men appeared.

'The Lady Porcia,' he announced.

47

'Ah,' Julia said.

Cleopatra saw her hostess compose her kindly features into a smile of welcome and looked curiously at the woman who entered. She was young but she carried a child on her slim hip. The boy was fretful, his face puckered in bad temper, but Porcia held him like a badge of pride.

'Porcia. How wonderful to see you.' Julia did her best but her soft voice lacked the enthusiasm of her words.

'You too, Julia dear. I thought you might like to see little Marcus. You could hold him, perhaps. It helps, you know.'

She shoved the mewling child at Julia, who took him, startled, and awkwardly rocked him but he was not impressed and let out a loud wail. Porcia gave an audible sigh and waved her serving lady forward. The baby was duly removed and Porcia sat herself on the couch from which Julia had just risen and looked around.

'It's not as nice here as your central villa, is it?' she remarked.

'But larger,' Julia countered, 'and suitable for our guest.'

She indicated Cleopatra and Porcia's eyes turned to her, as sharp as a hunting hawk's.

'Ah yes, the Egyptian "Princess".' The word dripped from her tongue and she sat forward, openly scrutinising Cleopatra. 'You're very small,' she concluded eventually. 'And very dark.'

'I am as you see,' Cleopatra said quietly.

She recognised something of Berenice in this Porcia and knew better than to rise to her baiting. Porcia's eyes narrowed.

'And you are here, I believe, because you have been thrown out of your country.'

'My father has,' Cleopatra agreed carefully. 'And I am here to support him.'

'And are doing that very well,' Julia said.

Cleopatra smiled at her hostess gratefully but Porcia did not even glance her way.

'A good job that you are more dutiful than your older sister – for now at least.'

'For always,' Cleopatra flared hotly.

Porcia raised an eyebrow.

'Sweet. And unusual. Familial loyalty is not, I believe, a character trait readily found in the Ptolemies.'

A fleeting image of them all being presented to Alexandria as the 'sibling-loving gods' flashed into Cleopatra's mind. Berenice had been so angry that day and clearly already planning the coup of Cleopatra's ruined birthday. Not that this snooty Roman needed to know that.

'I am flattered you have studied our history,' she said evenly.

'I was taught it by my own father – as an example of how not to rule.'

Cleopatra sucked in her breath and Julia half rose.

'There is no need to be rude, Porcia.'

'Not rude, merely factual. Royalty is a deeply flawed system.'

'As is a republic,' Cleopatra shot back.

'Oh no.' Porcia drew herself up tall. 'A republic is a perfect system.'

'In that case, it must be the men running it who are flawed.'

Porcia gasped and two spots of colour flared on her sharp cheekbones.

'My father said royals were insolent.'

Cleopatra rose.

'Your father must, then, be very crass to believe that all royals can be categorised in a single way. And it is you who has come here, to my hostess' house and attacked her guest – that, surely is greater insolence than me simply engaging in the debate you initiated?'

Porcia looked stunned, then her eyes narrowed.

'My father is one of the most intelligent men in all Rome – as you should know.'

'I should?'

Her smile turned to a sneer.

'I believe you have met him. He is governor of Cyprus and working hard to bring what he writes to me is a very decadent island into a decent state.'

49

It all fell into place. Cleopatra looked at the young woman and saw something of the stern-faced Cato's features beneath her carefully arranged hair. There was no doubting that she had absorbed her father's republican fervour, not to mention his sense of superiority and unforgiveable rudeness.

'Please,' Julia said, flapping between them. 'This is no place for politics. We are women. Let us talk of women's things.'

Cleopatra looked at her and for a moment thought that perhaps she would prefer sparring with Porcia to 'women's things' but her hostess was genuinely distressed, so she offered her most demure smile and said, 'That would be lovely.'

Porcia snorted but Calpurnia was quick to back up her friend.

'Are you married, Cleopatra?' she asked, her voice carefully modulated to cut through the tension in the grand room.

Cleopatra laughed.

'I am only fourteen.'

Calpurnia shrugged.

'Many girls marry earlier than that.'

'I am fourteen,' Porcia put in, 'and I've been married to my dear Bibulus for two years and have a son.'

'To go with the adult ones he already has from his first marriage,' Calpurnia sniped.

'Things happen to sons,' Porcia said easily. 'A man can never have too many.'

She darted a sly look at the other two who pointedly ignored her.

'I don't want a husband,' Cleopatra said, 'not yet.'

They all looked shocked.

'You have to have a husband.' Julia looked at the others. 'We all have husbands.'

Cleopatra chose not to point out that that these male appendages seemed to have blocked off anything of interest from their lives. It was not their fault, she supposed, that they had been brought up in a less enlightened society than she.

'I am too busy training to rule,' she told them. 'I learn the workings of government, the needs of the country, the finer points of trade. Royalty may be a "flawed system"—' she threw a dark look Porcia's way '—but it is one that relies upon highly trained leaders who understand the country and its needs inside out and that is what I must become.'

'*You?*' Porcia sneered. 'But you're a girl?'

'So? You underestimate yourself, Porcia. Do not women run households?'

'Of course.'

'And is not a country simply a larger version of a household?'

'Well, now—'

'It seems to me that women are perfectly equipped to rule and, as the system of royalty is thankfully intelligent enough to allow it, I intend to do so, be that alone or with a consort.'

'But you have brothers?' Calpurnia asked, looking nervously at Porcia whose eyes had narrowed again.

'I have brothers,' Cleopatra agreed. 'Two. But they are young so who knows when I will be called upon. And even if one of them ascends to the throne I will most likely do so too.'

'How?'

'As his wife, of course.'

Julia and Calpurnia gasped and clutched at each other, eyes wide in delicious horror.

'You will marry your brother?'

Cleopatra shrugged.

'It is usual.'

'And you will . . . will have babies with him?'

Again the women exchanged giggles; this was getting tiresome.

'If the gods will it,' she told them with the last shreds of her patience. 'We are their vessels so our bodies are in their gift.'

Calpurnia stared but it was Porcia who spoke, leaning so far forward that she looked like to topple off the couch at any moment.

'You believe you are a goddess?'

'No,' Cleopatra said, gritting her teeth. 'I believe – I *know* – that

I carry a piece of the Goddess within me. I am her representative on earth, or one of them.'

Porcia threw her hands up.

'The arrogance!' she declaimed loudly.

'It is not arrogance,' Cleopatra snapped at her, 'just fact.'

'You assume you are above everyone else.'

'And you do not?!'

Julia leaped up.

'Right. Lovely as this has been, ladies, I believe my husband is leaving for the city in a moment and I am keen to accompany him and show Rome to my guest.'

Cleopatra looked at her hostess in surprise but Julia's chin was set and there was little Porcia could do but rise too.

'Your guest is not allowed into Rome.'

Cleopatra went to Julia's side.

'Your city does not have goddesses?' she asked Porcia. 'Strange, considering how you shove temples into every corner.'

'Our city does not have *royals* – they poison the air.'

'Oh dear. In Alexandria the air is so much more robust. Perhaps it is the fresh sea breezes from our famous harbour, or the gracious width of our streets, or perhaps it is simply the tolerance of our people.'

'Please!' Julia looked desperately flustered and, riled as Cleopatra was by the patronising visitor, she bit her tongue for her hostess' sake.

'Thankfully,' she said to Porcia, 'I have found time whilst sitting arrogantly around, to consult your precious constitution. It's a shame Rome doesn't have a library. We have a wonderful one in Alexandria, you know – the finest in the Greek world – but at least Julia's husband keeps a decent study with copies of the key documents of your finely ordered republic. The Latin is a little overworked, but it states clearly that *reigning* royalty is not allowed within the Pomerium. I do not reign.'

'Neither does your precious father,' Porcia snapped and then realised the implications of that and flushed furiously. 'Fine,' she said to Julia. 'Take your pet princess into Rome. Show her the Senate, where true governance takes place, and perhaps she will understand why we are conquering the world whilst her precious family scraps amongst itself. I am too busy to linger anyway. My son needs me.'

She flung this last at Julia like a dart and was gone, calling her serving woman to heel with the baby still bleating crossly in her arms. The cries faded and, finally, were gone.

'Well, that was fun,' Calpurnia said.

'She's a poisonous cow,' Julia muttered, 'parading around with her high-handed opinions and her damned baby.'

The last came out on a sob and Calpurnia flung her arms around her friend.

'You'll have a baby, Julia, I know you will. No couple I know loves each other like you and Gnaeus and the gods will bless that love with fruit.'

'Fruit that ripens?' Julia asked, her voice shaky with palpable fear.

'Of course. Just be patient and take care of yourself. At least your husband is here in your bed. How am I meant to conceive with mine rampaging across Gaul?'

Julia hugged her back and Cleopatra watched curiously. When the pair seemed, finally, to smile again she seized her chance.

'Are we really going into Rome?'

Julia looked at her, wiped away a tear and then smiled.

'I don't see why not.'

Chapter Seven

Pompey led the way, chest puffed out and purple-edged toga flapping in the spring breeze. It was growing warm in Rome and their party, like all others, clung to the shade that was offered by the crush of buildings narrowing the streets to mere alleyways. Cleopatra thought longingly of the Canopic Way, strung on either side with the eponymous silken canopies that offered strolling Alexandrians pastel-tinted shade at all points, but she was grateful to get this far and stepped keenly past the funny run of stones marking Rome's precious border.

She was eager to see the Forum of which everyone talked with such awe and, to be fair, when they turned into the vast courtyard, flanked on all sides by porticoed buildings and dominated by a platform in the centre, she was impressed. Here, at least, was a sense of proportion and order. Here was some style and space. It was not a patch on the Alexandrian Courts of Justice, set on a circular, many-stepped platform at the heart of far-reaching groves of acacia, fig and tamarisk trees, but it wasn't bad for Rome.

The only problem was that most of it was filled with groups of men jostling to be heard. Many were stood on makeshift platforms, raising their voices above those of their neighbours to gather a greater audience. There was much throwing back of heads and casting out of arms as orators fought for attention and Cleopatra tried not to giggle at their florid style. She had been taught the finer points of rhetoric and understood the need for inflection and emphasis but in Egypt they preferred a more pared-back style, keeping their theatricals for the awe of a religious ceremony rather than their own aggrandisement.

They made slow progress. Pompey stopped endlessly to shake the hands of men and to ostentatiously accept the petitions pressed into his hands by the people who gathered around them.

'See how they flock to him,' Julia said fondly.

To Cleopatra it looked a sparse group but she smiled agreement and turned her eyes to the senate building. Inside there, Pompey would present her father's petition for troops to back his return to the throne, so she could only pray that he was as great as his name implied.

At that moment, however, there was a disturbance in the far corner of the Forum. The crowds turned to watch as a young man bounded in on a beautiful white horse, trapped out in silver livery that sparkled almost mythically in the sunshine. Cleopatra felt Julia stiffen at her side as he came their way, followed by the sort of crowd that Cleopatra would definitely call a 'flock', and headed by three intriguing women.

The first wore a dress of Chinese silk so fine that you could see every inch of her lithe body beneath it, the second was in blood red and carried a hawk on her arm, and the third and eldest wore a necklace of the largest pearls Cleopatra had ever seen nestling on her ample bosom. With them was a girl about her own age who caught her eye and gave her an open, easy grin and, for the first time since fleeing Egypt, Cleopatra felt she had seen people worthy of her company.

'Who are *they*?' she breathed.

'The Claudii,' Julia groaned.

'The Claudii?'

'One of the oldest, richest families in Rome. And one of the most decadent, irresponsible and self-seeking besides. They are self-styled *Populares.*'

'Populares?'

'Liberals, full of plans to improve the lives of the people, though it's all conceit and attention-seeking as you could find no group with lives less like the poor. That one there, that Clodius—' she spat out his name as if it were a maggot in her food '—got himself adopted by a Plebeian family last year so that he could stand as People's Tribune and has been lording it over Rome ever since.'

Cleopatra absorbed the flood of technical terms, filing them for analysis later as she prayed that these sparkling people were coming to introduce themselves. Their leader, however, did not seem to even notice her as his eyes fixed on Pompey, then on Julia behind him. He smiled a slow, sensual smile.

'Ah, Pompey the Great!' He lifted his little finger, waggling it as he said the word 'great' and the crowd jeered delightedly. 'And your beautiful wife. I'm surprised you could tear yourselves out of your love-nest to join the humble crowd at the Forum.'

Cleopatra saw Pompey's neck flush to a dark purple and his ox-shoulders tense.

'I am here to do the people's business, as always,' he said stiffly.

Again, the easy smile from Clodius.

'I suppose it makes a change from doing your wife.'

Pompey visibly shook with rage.

'I am blessed in my wife,' he asserted as Julia hung onto his arm. 'She is beautiful, wise and very well connected.' Cleopatra wasn't so sure about the first two, but had to admire Pompey's confidence.

'Of course,' Clodius agreed, his eyes sparkling as more and more people drew round. 'I'm sure Julius Caesar is grateful that you are looking after his daughter so well whilst he is off conquering Gaul.'

This was accompanied by a lewd thrust of the hips that had the crowd jeering delightedly again.

'I am here to do the people's business,' Pompey re-asserted but his words were lost.

His ox-shoulders sunk in on themselves and he ran an anxious hand through his careful quiff, sending it wafting sideways. Cleopatra looked enviously at the Claudii, her eyes drawn once again to the women. The one in the see-through dress looked so like Clodius that she must be his sister and the woman in red was perhaps his wife. Did that make the older woman his mother? There was no time to speculate, for now Clodius had noted her.

'Ah ha, is this the Egyptian Princess I have heard so much of?' He leaped from his horse and bowed low before her. 'Princess Cleopatra, I am at your service.' The crowd gasped at this show of royal respect and Clodius grinned round. 'Surely a man is allowed to bow to a beautiful woman?'

Cleopatra drew herself up tall as he ostentatiously kissed her hand, but felt horribly self-conscious in her borrowed dress. She was used to such adulation at home but had known nothing like it here in Rome and was not convinced of Clodius' sincerity.

'You're a lucky man, General,' he said to Pompey, 'with two beauties in your house.' And then he dropped her hand and leaped back onto his horse, wheeling it around to face his gang. 'What's the name of the sex-mad general?' he cried.

'Pompey!' they roared back.

'Who prefers the sheets to the speaker's platform?'

'Pompey!'

'Who . . . '

But Cleopatra was pulled away before she could catch the next accusation, Pompey pushing through the crowd, Julia dragging Cleopatra in his wake. She glanced back at the bright group.

'The Claudii,' she breathed.

'Are trouble,' Julia snapped.

Cleopatra liked the sound of that.

'In what way?'

'They seduce people.'

Cleopatra liked the sound of that even more. She looked at Julia curiously as they reached the relative space at the edge of the forum.

'Any people in particular?' Julia coloured. 'You?'

'No! Goodness no, not me. But I've seen first-hand . . . '

She stopped herself.

'Your father!'

'Come away. Now!'

Julia was flustered enough to have forgotten her perfect manners; Cleopatra must be right. She looked back at the three eye-catching women.

'With which of them? The elder one with the pearls?'

Julia's flinch told her she'd hit the mark.

'Lady Servilia is not actually a Claudii,' she said stiffly, 'just friends with the damned family. They are all rude, unpleasant and puffed up with their own importance.'

Cleopatra looked at the magnificent pearls, nestling on an equally magnificent bosom, and then upwards into an open, handsome face. The Lady Servilia was looking straight at her and, to her delight, she winked.

'Cleopatra,' Julia snapped. 'We must go.'

Cleopatra spun round, furious at being ordered about but then she saw her hostess, red in the face and plucking anxiously at a wisp of hair that had escaped from her demure headdress, and reminded herself of the infernal rules of politeness Charmion had ever pressed upon her. With a last glance at Servilia, she turned and followed Julia back through the rickety streets, back over the damned Pomerium and back into Pompey's gloomy villa. But the Claudii felt like a precious slice of the East in the heart of Rome and already she wanted to know more.

Chapter Eight

MAY 56 BC

Cleopatra heard low voices coming from her father's rooms and marched inside to find King Ptolemy sitting opposite two men she hadn't seen before. The first was tall with a long face and greying hair. The second was too hunched over a wax tablet to see clearly but she sensed him looking curiously at her from beneath a shaggily dark brow, and stared back. He looked down again immediately.

'I didn't know you had company, Father.'

'Merchants,' Ptolemy said dismissively and the tall man tensed.

'Bankers,' he corrected imperiously. 'And you invited us here, your majesty.'

'Of course, of course. And I am delighted to see you, Rabirius.' Ptolemy looked shiftily to Cleopatra. 'Did you want something, my dear?'

'Why do you need bankers, Father?'

He gave a self-conscious laugh.

'Invasions do not fund themselves.'

Her throat tightened.

'I thought we brought treasure with us on the ship?'

'Of course, of course. We did. Plenty of it.'

'But not enough?'

The tall man – Rabirius – smiled thinly.

'Armies are costly, Princess.'

'But effective,' the younger man added drily.

'And what price a throne?' Rabirius added.

'I don't know,' Cleopatra shot at him. 'I assume that is what you are here to tell us?'

Ptolemy frowned at her. 'Did you want something, Cleopatra?'

'A new dress would be good.'

'As I told you,' Rabirius said imperiously, 'we are not merchants but—'

To everyone's surprise his young assistant interrupted him. 'I know a dressmaker.'

'Leviticus!' Rabirius reprimanded but Ptolemy put up a hand.

'This is good news. My poor daughter is stuck in borrowed gowns when she should have the finery worthy of the heir to the Egyptian throne.'

'Heir?' Cleopatra gasped.

Ptolemy shrugged.

'Well, of course. I'm hardly going to keep Berenice at my side once I wrest my throne back off her, am I? You will be queen after me, Cleopatra, and you should dress appropriately.'

'Yes, Father,' she stuttered, trying to grasp the import of this, but Ptolemy was already waving to Leviticus.

'Take her to this dressmaker.'

'Me, your majesty?'

'Of course you. It can hardly be me, can it?'

'Er no. Of course not. That is, I'd be delighted to. When would—'

'Now,' Ptolemy ordered. 'Take her now. She has waited long enough.'

Leviticus looked to his boss who gave a reluctant nod of agreement. He leaped up, gathering his papers eagerly into his satchel.

'It would be my honour, your majesty.' He looked to Cleopatra and bit his lip. 'That is, of course, if the Princess is willing and—'

'I'm willing,' Cleopatra confirmed. 'More than willing – as long as this dressmaker is good.'

'Oh, she's good. She's the best.'

'Perfect.'

Cleopatra held out her hand for an escort but he just looked at it in confusion. 'Your arm, Leviticus.'

'Of course. Sorry. I didn't dare presume . . . ' He glanced back at his boss, but seeing him already deep in his numbers, shook his dark curls vigorously and drew himself up tall, offering his arm with new elegance. 'Allow me, Princess.'

She took it gladly as Eiras came running to join them.

'This is Leviticus, Eiras.'

'Levi, please, Princess. Everyone calls me Levi.'

'Very well. Levi is going to find us fine dresses.'

'The finest in the world,' he confirmed, 'for Egypt's heir.'

Eiras looked at Cleopatra.

'It's official?'

Cleopatra looked back.

'You expected it?'

'Of course. Did you not?'

'I . . .'

She should have done, of course – she was meant to be the intelligent one – but it was still a shock to have it stated so clearly.

'You will be a wonderful queen,' Eiras said, beaming at her. 'And now, let's shop!'

Levi led them round the usual twist of Roman streets and then, to Cleopatra's surprise, steered them into a large square. It lacked the elegance of an Alexandrian one but was, at least, planted with pleasant trees and shrubs and littered with benches on which men and women were chatting happily in the dappled sun, many in the dark costumes of Judaism.

'You are Jewish?' Cleopatra asked Levi.

'I am, Princess, as are my dressmaking friends. Is that a problem?'

'Oh no. Not at all. We have many Jews in Alexandria. A resourceful people. Very good with money.'

'And with a needle, Princess. In here please.'

He opened a small wooden door and stood back to let her step through. Inside, a gaggle of women worked at long tables on an array of fabrics worthy of an Eastern market. A number were labouring at the dull linen the conservative Roman housewives favoured, but Cleopatra caught glimpses of gauzes and silks in a rainbow of colours, and her spirits lifted.

'It's a treasure house,' she said to Eiras.

'And run by a jewel,' Levi said. 'Maria – come quickly, I have a fine customer for you.'

A tiny, dark-haired woman scurried across, pins stuck from her dress like a porcupine and a tape measure for a scarf. She clapped her hands.

'Such a beautiful one too, Levi.'

'This is the Princess Cleopatra.'

Maria gasped.

'A princess, forced to wear such, such ...' Her fingers darted to Cleopatra's skirts and she rubbed the fabric with disdain. 'You poor, poor dear. Do not fret, Maria will soon have you clad as befits your station. This way, this way ...'

Cleopatra glanced delightedly to Eiras as Maria and Levi ushered her between the women towards the bright fabrics at the rear. It was like stepping into sunshine and she passed a happy morning choosing fabrics and explaining styles. Maria was quick-witted and imaginative and sketched beautiful dresses onto wax tablets, promising to send the work to the very top of the queue. Cleopatra ordered gowns for Eiras too and was just debating whether she should have her fifth creation in azure or rose when the door swung open and a familiar figure walked in.

'The Princess Cleopatra, if I'm not much mistaken.' Cleopatra gazed at the glamorous woman who had stood behind Clodius at the Forum and who she had longed to meet. Isis, it seemed, had brought her here. 'I'm Clodia Metelli and I'm impressed you've found the finest dressmaker in Rome.'

'And not a moment too soon,' Cleopatra said.

'I did notice your dress didn't seem quite as . . . regal as I'd have expected.'

'It was Julia's.'

'Ah! Poor you.' Women had gathered around Clodia who was unselfconsciously disrobing as Maria flicked her fingers for a gown to be brought across. 'You must be going mad with boredom around pompous Pompey and his cow-eyed wife.'

Cleopatra glanced at Eiras and they both bit back a laugh at the accurate description.

'Julia has been very kind to me,' she said carefully.

'I'm glad to hear it. Julia is a very kind woman, if not blessed in her husband.'

'She does not seem to feel so.'

Clodia raised an eyebrow as she stood unselfconsciously naked before them.

'So, she and Pompey the Not-so-Great truly are "in love"?'

Cleopatra frowned.

'Is that a bad thing?'

Clodia shook her beautiful head, the rest of her perfectly still as Maria slid the gown on.

'Of course not. I love being in love. I'm forever falling for people – such a delicious sensation, is it not? Oh, you won't know yet, bless you, but you will. You have the shape of a woman who knows how to love.'

'I do?'

'You do.'

'And that is a good thing?'

'It is.'

'But not in Julia?'

Clodia laughed again.

'You're a sharp little creature. It is perfectly fine in Julia and

I am being mean-spirited. She is a good woman with a very clever father.'

'Julius Caesar? Do you know him?'

'Of course. Who doesn't? He's the sort of man you don't miss when he walks into a room – and that you'd happily walk out of it with.'

She winked and Cleopatra gaped.

'Have you . . . ?'

'Not me, no. I'd love to but Servilia would kill me.'

'Servilia?' Cleopatra remembered the lady of the pearls and the wink. 'I would like to meet her.'

'That can be arranged.'

Clodia's dress was in place now and she stepped back and looked at herself appraisingly in the mirror. Cleopatra gaped at the deep yellow robe, slashed sideways across the middle to reveal a honed belly and the curvaceous edges of luscious breasts.

'I see little point in modesty,' Clodia said, following Cleopatra's eyes.

'You look amazing,' was all she could manage.

'Thank you. I enjoy clothes.'

'That seems unusual in Rome.'

Clodia let out a fluid laugh.

'Sadly, yes. Is it different in Alexandria?'

'Oh yes!'

'Then I hope to visit one day but for now I will have to make do with scandalising everyone here. Cato is, sadly, returning from Cyprus around the Ides of June and Servilia is planning a party.'

'Why would she do that?'

'The poor woman is his half-sister.' Cleopatra gaped at her for she could not imagine two creatures less alike. 'And Brutus, who is out there as his assistant, is her much-treasured son, and therefore Cato's nephew. Welcome to Rome, Princess – everyone is interrelated and Servilia, above us all, knows how to make the most of that. Cato has influence, sadly, and she is best placed to . . .

manipulate it. As for me, I just hope to shock him. Do you think it will work?'

She jutted out one exposed hip and Cleopatra laughed.

'Admirably.'

'Excellent. Thank you, Maria,' she said to the dressmaker, 'it's perfect. Are you finished with the Princess?'

'We must only make a choice of fabric for the final gown, my lady.'

She held up the two silks and Clodia laughed.

'The azure, of course. Rose is far too demure for an Eastern princess, right, Cleopatra?'

'I supp—'

Good. If we are done here, can I treat you to a glass of wine?'

'Now?'

'Yes.'

'Where?'

'In my home. A few of my family and friends are gathering to eat today and I know they are eager to meet you, if that appeals?'

Cleopatra smiled. It most certainly did.

❖

Stepping into a Claudii house was like moving through a portal from the square-lined, over-stuffed Rome to which Cleopatra had grown wearily accustomed into another, brighter world. Her heart swelled in recognition and she turned to Eiras to share a happy smile. The villa entrance was much like any other whitewashed archway in this city, but just a few steps within, the space widened out into a courtyard tiled with vibrant mosaics and run around with richly frescoed walls and exotically carved columns. Lush plants grew from giant pots and light poured in from the central space in the roof and through coloured glass in the walls, creating even more colour. It was a sensuous paradise and Cleopatra spun slowly, letting it sink joyously into her Eastern soul.

Clodia drew Cleopatra further into the room, summoning a

server and thrusting a silver cup of wine into her hand. A rush of spices wafted into her nose from the ruby-red liquid and when she took a tentative sip, her mouth filled with the tastes of home.

'That's delicious.'

'We have only one body, Princess – best to fill it with good things. And good men.'

Clodia laughed wickedly and the dark-eyed woman who'd been with her in the forum appeared at her side, wrapping an arm around her exposed waist.

'I see you have invited a young guest to corrupt, Clodia?'

'To educate, Fulvia.'

'She does not need your education; she has Isis within her.'

'Does she?' Clodia leaned down, pressing her beautiful face closer to Cleopatra's. 'Do you?'

'So I am told,' Cleopatra said awkwardly.

'Wonderful! Lucky you. Do you know, Princess, if I am ever in a tricky situation—'

'Which is often,' Fulvia put in drily.

'—then I ask myself,' Clodia continued blithely, 'what would Isis do? It's an excellent guide, I find. But you – you *are* Isis.'

'No, no. I merely carry her spark within me.'

'Same thing. Lucky you. I told you, you have the shape to love, and such amazing eyes. I love this dark liner, and these bright colours on the lids.'

Cleopatra glanced to Eiras. Her friend had assiduously tracked down both kohl and malachite in the darker reaches of Rome and she was grateful.

'Eiras is a magician with cosmetics.'

'Then, Eiras, I hope you will work your magic on me?'

'It would be my honour,' Eiras agreed shyly.

'Marvellous! Now, Catullus, darling, come and meet the Princess Cleopatra. She is a very goddess.'

'No, I . . .'

A small, bright-eyed man appeared, throwing his hands up and letting stream so many floral praises in both Greek and Latin that she felt drowning in language.

'Poets,' Clodia laughed, 'don't you adore them?!'

'I pray so every day,' Catullus said, running a hand around her waist and up over the curve of her breast. Clodia did not even flinch and it was a second man who hurried over and swatted his hand away.

'Not before the Princess, you barbarian.'

'She'll understand. She is Isis.'

'I'm not Isis,' Cleopatra protested. 'That is . . . '

'Pleasure to meet you, Princess,' the new man said. 'And your lovely companion.'

His eyes went to Eiras, still at Cleopatra's shoulder, and Cleopatra drew her closer.

'This is Eiras.'

'Eiras.' He ran her name over his tongue as if it were honey. 'The poet Cinna at your service, my lady.' Eiras blushed prettily and he reached for her hand. 'May I show you around the villa?'

'Oh no,' Eiras said. 'I couldn't leave my mistress.'

'Of course you could,' Cleopatra said. 'I'm quite happy.'

'Fret not,' Fulvia assured her. 'I will take care of the Princess. I wish her to meet my niece and ward. Claudia!'

Someone else came skittering into the room and Cleopatra saw it was the girl from the forum. She went eagerly forward to meet her and Eiras, released, allowed herself to be led away by her poet.

'Hello,' the girl said easily. 'You're Cleopatra.'

'Princess Cleopatra,' Fulvia corrected.

'Right, yes. Pleased to meet you, Princess Cleopatra.'

She stuck out a hand and, surprised, Cleopatra took it. She was used to people bowing and the hearty shake the girl offered was new, but not unpleasant.

'Claudia?' she asked. 'Are your family all called that?'

'We are,' she agreed with a grimace. 'We're the Claudii, you see – though Clodia and Clodius have changed to the pleb spelling because they think it makes them seem approachable.'

Cleopatra glanced across to Clodia, teasing Catullus in a corner, and was not sure that being "approachable" worried her one bit.

'Pleb?' she queried.

'Plebians – people. As opposed to nobles. The *Optimates* are very hung up on it. They think the nobles are the only ones who can do anything. Call themselves the "*Boni*", for Jupiter's sake – the "Good men" – as if everyone else is bad. Clodius says it's arrogant and backward and not in the spirit of the Republic. They don't like that!' She grinned wickedly. 'He's a noble, of course, but he got himself adopted by some lovely plebs last year, just to annoy the *Boni*. It worked too!'

'Is Pompey a *Boni*?'

'He is these days. He started out fiery but he's too paunchy and dull for rebellion now.'

'And Cato?'

Claudia rolled her eyes.

'You know Cato?' Cleopatra nodded grimly. 'Poor you. We hate him. Clodius says he's everything that's bad about Rome.'

'He was the first Roman I met,' Cleopatra confided.

'No! Where?'

'On the latrine.'

'Impossible!'

'Truly. We went to Cyprus to talk with him and he received us sitting on the latrine.'

Claudia's hands went to her mouth.

'He's such a barbarian. And as for his wretched daughter, she's so far up her plump backside that it's a miracle she can walk straight. Have you met Porcia?'

'I'm afraid so. She hates me because I'm royal.'

'Which is just stupid, right? She should get to know you before she hates you.'

'Erm, right,' Cleopatra stuttered and Claudia laughed merrily and took her arm.

'I think being a princess must be amazing. Come – sit down and tell me all about it. What's Alexandria like? Do you have a palace? Do you have eunuchs?'

The questions kept on coming and Cleopatra reclined gladly on a plush couch and made the most of finally being back where people understood her worth.

'Everyone has to bow to you?' Claudia asked.

'Not the king, my father, nor the queen, my stepmother, nor my elder sister, Berenice, who is ahead of me in precedence. That is, she *was* ahead of me until . . . '

She stuttered to a halt, confused suddenly.

'Until?' Claudia pushed.

'Until she stole the throne,' someone provided crisply and Cleopatra looked up to see the Lady Servilia standing in the doorway.

'Your elder sister stole your father's throne?' Claudia gasped. 'Jupiter's toes, I bet you hate her, don't you?'

Cleopatra's head spun. Did she? She supposed she must. In many ways she'd always hated her imperious older sister, but she'd loved her too. Now, it seemed that if they ever got back home, she would take her place.'

'I . . . ' she tried but felt her lip wobble embarrassingly.

'You poor dear.'

Servilia swept across the room, sat on the couch at Cleopatra's side and, without a moment's hesitation, pulled her into her arms. Cleopatra stiffened at the intrusion but Servilia's arms were so strong, her bosom so soft, and her confident care so very like Charmion's, that she gave in to the embrace. And oh, it felt so welcome.

'I don't hate her,' she said. 'I can't hate her. We're the sibling-loving gods. We . . . '

'Hush now,' Servilia said kindly. 'Some things are too complicated for words, Princess, especially when it comes to families. Right now, the most important thing is to care for you.'

Rarely had any words been more welcome. Cleopatra leaned fully into Servilia's arms and felt herself relax for possibly the first time since that damned messenger had interrupted her birthday feast three long months before. She would get back to Alexandria, whatever it took, but at least for now she had found an oasis in Rome.

Chapter Nine

Princess,

*I pray this reaches you in Rome. Rome! It is so far away
and sounds such a terrible place. I hope they are looking after
you. I hope they are treating you with respect and care. I hope
you are safe. Certainly, you are safer there than you would be
in Alexandria. I have sent this missive with a trader I trust but
Berenice has eyes everywhere and I can only hope it gets through
safely. How goes the petitioning? Every day when I rise, I look
hopefully to the horizon praying to see ships bringing you and your
royal father back to us, but every day I see only the merchants
and traders and scholarly travellers that always cross beneath the
Pharos' protective gaze.*

*Bring a large army, sweet one, for Berenice has her claws so firmly
into the throne that it will take great might to wrest it from her. Even
the mob are beginning to regret following their new queen for although
she dazzles in ceremonies and rituals, she is taxing them hard
and they are feeling the pinch of her parsimony whilst she parades
its benefits.*

She has married, at last. It was suggested she take the elder of the Ptolemies as her brother-husband, as is tradition, but she refused and, besides, Neferet was halfway into Palestine with them. She is not as stupid as she looks, that one. A veritable stream of men were brought for Berenice's approval, including Aulus Gabinius, the Roman Governor of Syria, but all were turned away save one poor unfortunate who was invited into her bed and found strangled the next day. The mourning period was not long.

She has finally settled on Archelaus, a Greek claiming to be a son of the King of Pontus though the branches of that family tree are wobbly at best. No matter, he comes with money and a martial bearing and he is fortifying Alexandria as if we were at war. It means more taxes for the people and less chance of restoration for your father if you stay away too long. I am told Aulus Gabinius is furious and swearing revenge. He has Roman armies at his command, just over the borders, and is keen to raise them against the woman who slighted him. All he needs is permission from the senate ...

Yours in hope.

The letter was not signed but Cleopatra knew it was from Charmion and read it over and over, its warmth stealing through her, so much softer than the hot summer sun that was currently turning Rome into a cesspit.

'All he needs is permission from the senate,' she read out to Eiras, grinding her teeth in frustration. How simple Charmion made it sound. How simple it *should* be, but Clodius was playing games with Pompey and blocked any motion to invade Egypt.

'Do you not want me to get my home back?' Cleopatra had dared to ask him two weeks ago when she'd been with Claudia and he'd come dancing in, high on some new victory against his arch-rival.

'Nope,' he'd said gaily. 'I like having you here. Rome needs jewels like you, Princess. You make the city so much less dull.'

He'd winked cheerfully at her, and then three large men, covered in scars and tattoos, had arrived and he'd rushed them into his private rooms. He'd recently resurrected some ancient institution called the *collegia* – unions of men from shared trades, meeting to discuss and protect their own rights. He'd explained to Cleopatra that it was vital for the poorer people to have someone to speak for them and that had made sense, but mainly Clodius seemed to encourage them to fight.

To counter him, Pompey had brought in his own gang leader, a black-haired Roman called Milo, who was fighting fire with fire. Cleopatra had been used to the mercurial Alexandrian mob, but this was another level. Reports of street brawls came in all the time, with casualties both within the armed gangs and of passers-by unlucky enough to be caught in their quarrels.

'Why does Clodius do it?' Cleopatra had asked Claudia at a heart-breaking report of a mother and child crushed in the latest brawl.

Claudia had shrugged.

'Because if he can break the grasp of the *Optimates* on the city it will be better for everyone in the long run.'

'But not in the short term.'

'No.'

The power struggles consumed the city and, in the meantime, there was no question of an army for Egypt, whatever Charmion said. Cleopatra folded up her precious letter and sighed.

'Perhaps I could talk to the senate myself?'

'As a woman!' Eiras mock-gasped. 'You know what the Romans feel about women speaking in their precious democracy.'

Cleopatra rolled her eyes.

'I know. And yet, behind the scenes, the women run it all. Servilia has senators coming to ask her advice every single time I'm there. I swear she knows everyone in Rome, Eiras, and they all listen to her. She is more a queen here than Berenice is in Alexandria; she just rules from the wings.'

'Then perhaps she can tell them to let this Aulus Gabinius invade Egypt?'

Cleopatra sighed.

'She's trying but she says it takes time. She says you have to get men's egos out of the way before their brains can kick in and that is a slow process.'

Eiras grinned.

'Servilia seems a wise woman. And talking of her . . . ' She rose and glanced at the sundial outside the window. 'I'd say it's time to start your hair for her reception, Princess.'

Cleopatra groaned.

'Do we have to go, Eiras?'

Eiras cocked her beautiful head on one side, her myriad curls glistening in the sunlight.

'You do not *have* to do anything, Princess, but Servilia will be disappointed if you're not there.'

Cleopatra groaned again but pushed herself up to prepare. Cato was back in Rome and tonight, on the new moon of the Ides, Servilia was holding a grand reception to welcome him and her precious son, Brutus. She had personally delivered Ptolemy and Cleopatra's invitation the other day and, as she was taking a big risk inviting Egyptian royals, Cleopatra could not let her down by staying away. Pompey was pointedly not invited and Julia had admitted that he'd had Servilia's husband – Brutus' father – executed a few years ago. She'd been dutifully insistent that he'd only been obeying orders but it was clear that missing out on such a key social event was paining her and she'd begged Cleopatra to bring back a full report.

'Thank Isis Maria's gowns have arrived,' Eiras said, opening the wardrobe that now bulged with a rainbow of glorious dresses. 'Something fabulous is needed to show that toilet-toad, Cato, how you thrive in his precious city. Be sure to let him see how many friends you have and perhaps he will back the provision of troops just to get rid of you.'

Cleopatra gave a low laugh but saw the sense of Eiras' words and allowed herself to be primped and preened into the azure gown

Clodia had chosen. She chose a necklet and earrings of her largest pearls and encouraged Eiras to paint her eyes in brightest blue and silver – a woman's armour for the battle ahead – before going to fetch her father. The once grand king was unbecomingly excited at the chance of a party and she had to hurry him past a dark-eyed Pompey as they left.

It was not a long ride to Servilia's house, but the royal litter had to pass the front door and head around the back. The house stood just outside the Pomerium but the front portico was along its line so Clodius had come up with an amusingly ridiculous process by which the king would enter via a carefully erected set of steps over the high back wall. Now, Ptolemy stood at the base of the structure and frowned up at it.

'I will break my royal neck climbing those.'

Cleopatra patted his arm. She could hear a buzz of conversation from within and was eager to join the crowd.

'It is quite safe, Father. Here, I'll go first.'

She took the steps lightly and paused at the top to look down on the assembled guests. Many were in the courtyard, juggling togas with wine glasses and squinting in the high sun, unwilling to retreat beneath the canopies and miss the spectacle of Egypt's portly exiled king arriving over the wall. All eyes turned her way and she forced herself to stand still, revelling in the azure silk as it rippled around her legs in a welcome breeze.

Catching sight of Clodia Metelli looking approvingly at her, she remembered her advice the first time they had met: 'I always ask myself "What would Isis do?"' Cleopatra knew that Isis would take the gaze of the crowd so she held her position a little longer, using the time to work out the most dignified way to get down the steep steps. She managed it without falling and Eiras came next, looking as beautiful as the finest statue in a clinging white gown, her hair a gloriously dark cloud against the fierce sky. Cinna came rushing forward.

'Is she not the most magnificent thing you have ever seen?'

he proclaimed, prostrating himself extravagantly beneath the lowest step. 'Tread on me, Goddess,' he demanded and Eiras, to Cleopatra's delight, did just that, stepping lightly on his back and down to the paved courtyard as if such adulation was her due.

The crowd cheered and looked eagerly upwards as Ptolemy's bulky form reached the top. He hesitated, steadying himself, then the sight of the party-goers below proved too much and he took the first eager step down to join them. At that moment, however, someone stalked into the garden, demanding 'What's all this?' in a loud, thin voice.

Everyone jumped and Ptolemy lost his footing and bumped down the last three steps, rolling into the scrawny figure of Cato and knocking him flying. The crowd gasped and Clodius led a rousing cheer that was swiftly crushed by Servilia sweeping between the men and helping them to their feet. They stood between her like fighters in a bout, save that neither had won. Cato glared at Ptolemy, who glared back. The crowd pressed in and Cleopatra saw Servilia give a quietly satisfied smile – her party would be talked about now, for sure.

'You'd have thought a trained monarch would be able to arrive with dignity,' she heard a whiney voice say and didn't need to look round to know it was Porcia.

'Or a Roman senator to stand his ground,' she said lightly.

'Have you not gone home yet,' Porcia growled in her ear. 'Oh no, you can't without Roman help.'

'We are simply offering the Republic a chance to aid a country with riches it cannot even dream of.'

'Oh, don't worry, we have other ways of finding gold. I hear tell Julius Caesar has made it deep into Gaul.'

'A land known for its culture, sophistication and strong beers,' Cleopatra sneered.

'He is talking of penetrating the mystery land of Britannia, whose shores, we are told, are lined with pearls.'

Cleopatra fingered the rope of the prized stones around her neck.

'And guarded by scaly-tailed monsters and giant men dressed in furs. Personally, I prefer my pearls from Persia, from whence my country has been importing them for the last three thousand years, but I'm sure your precious general knows what he is doing heading north.'

'I don't know, Cleopatra – ask your gracious hostess, his daughter.'

'Julia is not here, as you well know, Porcia.'

'Because her husband killed Servilia's.'

'Porcia!' Claudia berated her, bobbing up between them. 'That is hardly a kind topic of conversation in this house.' Porcia glanced around, looking almost ashamed, and Claudia strung an arm through Cleopatra's. 'You should ask Servilia your question, Petra, as she so graciously warms Caesar's bed and is reputed to have been gifted the largest pearl in all Rome by him. Let's go over, shall we?'

'In a moment, Claudie,' Cleopatra told her affectionately but Claudia was jumping up and down impatiently.

'No, now! *He's* with her – look!'

Her eyes had taken on a strange new light and Cleopatra tried to see who'd excited her interest but the crowd was thick and there was no way of distinguishing one be-toga-ed Roman from another.

'Who's with her?'

'Brutus, of course. Is he not handsome? Come on!'

She tugged Cleopatra towards Servilia, and Cleopatra saw that Brutus – the man who had done his best to mitigate his Uncle Cato's rudeness on Cyprus – was standing at her side. Servilia was talking away to him, her hands patting at his chest and reaching up to smooth a blond curl from his brow, as if she could not get enough of her returned son. And she was not the only one. Guests were clamouring to shake his hand and it was clear that this was a young man on the rise.

'Wouldn't you love to run your hands through those curls,'

Claudia said in a dramatic whisper. 'Jupiter, I have to find my Aunt Fulvia!'

She took an abrupt about-turn and Cleopatra was pulled the other way as Claudia sought out Fulvia, handsome as ever in a near-black gown that stood starkly against the washed-out pastels of the other Roman women.

'Fulvia,' Claudia said, grabbing her hands, 'Brutus is here.' She sent her urgent looks and Fulvia smiled.

'I assumed he would be, Claudie, with this being his homecoming reception.'

'You said you'd, you know, talk to Servilia.'

'I will. Indeed, I already have, but all in good time. You are young yet.'

'I am nearly fifteen and plenty ready to marry, especially if it is to Brutus.'

She gestured towards the young man, who was talking earnestly with a group of elderly senators. Cleopatra could see why Claudia might be eager for the match but wasn't convinced that Brutus, with his abstract philosophising, would be the ideal companion for her lively friend. She stood back as Fulvia guided Claudia into the group and was pleased to see Brutus smile at her with genuine warmth. It looked as if she might get her heart's desire – and a very influential husband into the bargain. Cleopatra watched them thoughtfully but then became aware of an equally interesting conversation between Eiras and Cinna nearby.

'I was to be dedicated to Isis,' Cleopatra heard her companion saying.

'Dedicated to her?'

'To serve in her shrine at the Temple of Ptah – like your vestals here in Rome.'

'You were to commit your body to the Goddess? As a virgin? Forever?' Cinna was aghast.

'For thirty years,' Eiras agreed calmly. 'But then I was chosen by the Priestess Safira to be sent to Princess Cleopatra and my destiny changed.'

'Praise Isis!' he said, then cleared his throat awkwardly. 'So, to be clear, you are not, er, dedicated . . . ?'

'I am not.'

Eiras' voice sparkled with teasing laughter and Cleopatra could not help but smile too. Cinna popped up wherever they went these days and Cleopatra imagined he must lurk the streets for hours, waiting to find them. She was glad for her companion. Eiras was newly sixteen and ready for marriage and Cleopatra's only fear was that she would lose her from her service if she chose to stay in Rome when – if – they marched back to Egypt.

The uncomfortable thought was cut off by a server banging on a gong and Cato stepping up onto the platform erected for King Ptolemy's arrival. If there was an irony in that, he did not choose to see it and waited, thin arms raised as everyone turned his way.

'Men and women of Rome, it is good to be amongst you all once more.' This was met with a polite round of applause and Cato smiled graciously. 'I return from Cyprus pleased to say that my governorship of the island has been modestly successful.'

He swept a hand sideways and servers whipped a cloth from a trestle table. The crowd gasped as the light from several artfully placed torches fell on a mound of golden cups, platters and chains. Sitting atop them was the crown of Cyprus, a beautiful twisted gold diadem, studded with rubies and emeralds and fronted with the sun-disc of Isis. Cleopatra's hands flew to her mouth and Cato, spotting her, could not disguise his smirk.

'Behold – the riches of a decadent monarchy brought here to fund the working of true government.'

'But . . . ' Cleopatra started, then felt Eiras' step close, her hand stroking her back in soothing curves, and stopped. She looked nervously around for her father and was relieved to see he'd absented himself.

'I was not sure, before this posting, of the value of taking far-flung lands,' Cato droned on. 'I feared that campaigns, especially to the luxurious East, were stretching our beloved Republic into places which might only erode its purity.' Cleopatra gave a strangled yelp and Eiras' hand stroked harder across her back. 'But I have learned much on Cyprus and am now convinced that taking Roman ways and values further afield can only benefit the world. Indeed, I am convinced that it is our duty to take our advanced notions of governance and order to less civilised nations.'

'Less civilised,' Cleopatra choked. 'This from a city that is tearing itself apart with gang warfare, that draws some sort of prohibitive ring around its heart, and only permits its precious citizenship to those who fit a pre-ordained mould.'

'But whose leaders do not throw their own fathers and sisters to the mob, or have their husbands murdered, or their people taxed to fund their own banquets.' Porcia stepped close and pressed her thin face into Cleopatra's own. 'Is *that* civilised, Princess?'

So Egyptian news had reached Rome by other routes than Charmion's smuggled letter. Cleopatra swallowed down bile.

'That, Porcia, is an aberration that my father and I are working hard to correct – if only Rome would do so too. But perhaps now your precious uncle is so keen on civilising the East, he will see his way clear to backing our return.'

'As vassals to Rome, perhaps, but my father will never condone *royalty.*'

She spat out the word in a way that reminded Cleopatra uncomfortably of Berenice's scorn for her baby half-brothers six endless moonturns ago. The tangles of power were, it seemed, complicated in every city.

'So, I thank you all again,' Cato was, thankfully, concluding, 'for welcoming myself and my honourable nephew back to Rome.'

There was a notably more enthusiastic response to mention of Brutus and all eyes turned to where he was standing, tall and imposing, at Servilia's side. Claudia was on his arm in a clear statement of allegiance and now Clodius bounced up to ostentatiously welcome him into the Claudii fold. Pompey was notable only by his absence and Cleopatra was beginning to wonder if her father had backed the wrong horse. She must learn from Servilia and play her own game – starting with an invitation to what was bound to be the biggest wedding this summer.

Chapter Ten

JULY 56 BC

Baiae was the most beautiful place Cleopatra had ever seen – after Alexandria, of course – and she blessed Isis that she had made it here for the wedding. Ptolemy had gone to Ephesus for the summer to pray to the gods for restoration, and Pompey had not been happy at the idea of her coming to the seaside resort alone. He'd insisted Baiae was for 'reprobates' and she'd be better off in his own retreat in the Alban hills. Cleopatra had panicked, but then reminded herself of how Servilia dealt with senators and looked down demurely.

'I just fear upsetting my poor friend Claudia by refusing the invitation,' she'd said breathlessly and had even squeezed out a sorrowful tear. Pompey had shuffled uncomfortably and snapped his fingers for a handkerchief and finally said he supposed 'a mere girl' could not create much bother. Cleopatra had kissed his hand and blessed him and started babbling about gowns and flowers so that he'd hurried away, leaving her in happy possession of the permission she'd so desired.

Now she stood on the clifftop, getting her breath back from the early morning walks that had become her and Eiras' new habit, and feasting her eyes on the sparkle of the Green Sea. A little boat was in the middle of the harbour, casting rose petals across the water to honour today's grand wedding and already the scent was catching headily on the air.

'The Romans call it Mare Nostrum, you know,' Cleopatra said to Eiras. 'Our sea! How arrogant they are!'

'Insecure, perhaps, Princess?'

Cleopatra laughed.

'You are too kind, Eiras. It is love blinding you.'

'It is not!'

'Is not love, or is not blinding you?'

Eiras shook her head ruefully.

'You're too clever with words for me, Princess.'

'This from the girl courting a poet!'

'Cinna does write beautifully.'

'And on such intellectual matters . . .'

Her friend flushed. Cinna, Catullus and their fellows wrote guttural, earthy poems about the sensuality of the body. Cleopatra had been absorbing their work and had learned much about the mysteries between men and women. Not just the mechanics – for who had not seen that in the streets of a steamy night? – but the passions that drove them. They seemed a great thrill, though a great danger too and watching Catullus trail after Clodia, in equal parts entranced and enslaved, she thought a wise woman would avoid them if at all possible. Not that today was the day for such mean thoughts.

'We should get back to Claudie.'

She indicated the huge villa at the centre of the beautiful seafront promenade below.

All the houses in Baiae were built in white marble with vast gardens and courtyards, sewn with exotic plants and dotted with fountains, statues and gazebos for the shade and comfort of the inhabitants. None, though, were as grand as the Claudii's, especially today. Already it was alive with hundreds of staff preparing

83

for the grand ceremony and when they reached the gates, they had to thread their way between a mass of deliveries. The only dampener on the happy scene was Cato, stood in the shade of a palm tree watching with disdain.

'I've no idea why Servilia wants that damned man here,' Cleopatra muttered to Eiras.

'He is her brother, Princess.'

'*Half*-brother. And as like to her as a sewer rat to a giraffe.'

'And yet, she is fond of him.'

Cleopatra had to begrudgingly admit that was true.

'Cato isn't as bad as he seems,' Servilia had told her the other day. 'He's just very passionate about republican values and that can make him seem a little . . . '

'Inhuman?' Cleopatra had suggested.

'Inflexible,' Servilia had corrected. 'And there is some sense, you know, in a system where leaders are elected. Not that I dislike royalty – I'm sure you'll make a wonderful queen – but it seems fair that the people should get to choose.'

'The people,' Cleopatra had queried, 'or the "good" people?'

She'd been learning about the Roman political system in the hope of finding a loop in it to get Aulus Gabinius the permission he needed to launch his armies from Syria, and could see how their precious voting system was skewed. The rich had the most votes and were allowed to cast them first, so that the ordinary man in the crumbling streets had little say. That was true in Alexandria as well, of course, but at least the Ptolemies did not pretend to listen.

'*All* people,' Servilia had insisted, 'that's what Julius would say at least.'

'Julius Caesar? He is a Populares.'

'Oh yes, of the most genuine kind.'

'And Brutus?'

'My poor son is confused,' she'd admitted. 'He feels the weight of his ancestry.'

'His father . . . ?'

'Is a painful loss, but I think more of his ancient forebears. We are descended, you know, from Lucius Junius Brutus, the man who threw out the original tyrant kings and established the Republic.'

'Ah.' Cleopatra sighed. 'That makes a lot of sense.'

'Rome's constitution means a lot to my son but sometimes he thinks about things too deeply. He can see the other side of any argument and takes himself on long, painful walks around all aspects of it. He does a lot of muttering.' She'd done a neat impression of earnest Brutus talking away to himself that had made Cleopatra laugh, then added, 'Claudia will be good for him. She will bring out his sunnier side.'

Certainly here in Baiae, Brutus seemed relaxed, ditching the deep debates in which he could usually be seen around the Forum and taking to the sea, proving himself a skilful sailor in the many races, cheered on by his bride-to-be. At evening events, too, he had lost the usual tight set of his broad shoulders and laughed often, his handsome features lighting up far more with this new joy than his usual brooding quiet. And today he would marry.

Claudia reached for Eiras' arm and guided her into the vast central hall, set at the front of the villa with balconies and columns framing a stunning view of the great bay. A host of servants were putting up garlands and silks around the frescoed walls and steam was pouring from the kitchens at the back, wafting out on a rush of shouts and clatters that reminded Cleopatra sharply of home. Mardion had often snuck her into the kitchens when she was hungry as a child and the cacophony of busy food prep felt achingly familiar.

She shook off the rush of melancholy. Today was her dear friend's wedding and she would not be anywhere else but here, so she pushed on through to Claudia's rooms.

'Petra! Eiras! Oh, thank Isis – my hair is a total and utter disaster. It will never go into the tutulus.'

Claudia pulled frantic hands through her honey-coloured locks. They looked beautiful to Cleopatra but were certainly some way

85

from the complex crown of twists and braids that Roman tradition dictated for brides. Eiras rushed forward.

'Your hair is little dry, that's all. It's the salt and the heat. Fret not, I have the perfect thing. If you just sit yourself here, I'll soon have you sorted out.'

Cleopatra saw her friend's shoulders visibly relax and went to sit next to her as Eiras rushed for her basket of potions. Claudia clasped her hands.

'I'm going to be a wife!'

Cleopatra smiled. In truth, tying yourself to another person, especially one with more power, did not seem, to her, a cause for much celebration but if Claudia was happy then so was she, and she set herself to enjoy the day.

❖

The heady scent of rose petals on water filled the air as the Claudii gathered at the Altar to Venus set on the open side of the hall, fluttering around their youngest member like colourful butterflies. Clodia dazzled in a gown made of layers of silk in shifting shades of yellow and orange so that she seemed to dance like fire when she moved. Clodius was in a toga daringly coloured in a shade of burned umber instead of the regulation white, and Fulvia was stunning in her favourite red. It was not, Cleopatra gathered from several comments, the usual way with weddings where Romans more normally all wore the same, but the Claudii never worried about what was usual.

Claudia, in pretty contrast, was dressed in a simple white tunic and woollen belt, fastened with great ceremony by Fulvia in the 'knot of Hercules' that could apparently only be undone by her groom. To Cleopatra it looked easy enough to unravel but it was all part of the ritual and Claudia was so overwhelmed at the thought of Brutus untying her that it was probably best it was not too tricky. A pale-yellow veil and her tutulus crown of twisted hair and flowers, expertly fixed by Eiras, completed her outfit. The tableau was so beautiful that Cleopatra was shocked when the groom's party burst in, marauded between the guests with feral whoops, and seized his bride.

'What on earth?' she gasped, until she noticed Claudia's eyes alight with joy and saw how carefully staged this abduction was.

Madness! Cleopatra could not begin to imagine how she would respect a husband who treated her this way. She thought of Egyptian weddings, held in sacred temples, deep with mysticism and time-honoured ritual, and shook her head at the coarseness of even the richest of the Romans.

'It's not very becoming for poor Brutus, is it?' she heard a tight voice say behind her and craned her neck to see Porcia – of course. Ostentatiously clutching the bulge of her second child, the catty young woman was talking to her husband, Bibulus, a man who was everything Cleopatra would have wished for her – old, fat and quite without charm.

'He looks happy enough,' Bibulus remarked mildly as Brutus swept his new wife into his arms.

'Of course he is now,' Porcia muttered sourly. 'Wait until he tires of her in his bed and he will regret allying himself to this giddy lot.'

'Or maybe,' Cleopatra could not resist turning around to say, 'he will thank his lucky stars every single night for sending him a wife who knows how to bring joy into his life. Unlike some.'

Porcia gave an indignant squeak and Bibulus was taken by a fit of coughing. Cleopatra turned back to the front as the ceremony was concluded and the bride and groom kissed.

'Well said,' Eiras muttered in her ear.

'She'll hate me now.'

'She hates you already.'

'I suppose it's refreshing. It gets so tiring being worshipped all the time.' Eiras laughed but with the ceremony over, Cinna was approaching and, as her eyes were pulled inexorably towards him, Cleopatra nudged her. 'As you should know.'

Her friend flushed in that becoming way Cleopatra loved, her honeyed skin lightening in pink patches beneath her vivid eyes, making them shine even more clearly. She teased Eiras often about her poet but looking at her before Venus' altar suddenly made it all seem more serious.

'Do you love him?' she asked.

'I love *you*, Princess.'

'That's very kind, but it's not what I asked.'

Eiras shifted.

'It matters little. I was chosen by your blessed mother to serve you and that is what I shall do.'

Cleopatra looked her up and down. The musicians were starting to play and Cinna was hovering but he'd sensed heat in their conversation and held back. She took Eiras' hands.

'I thank you for it, truly. I would never want to lose you, Eiras, but I do not require *all* of you.'

Eiras blinked.

'You mean . . . '

'I mean that if you wished to join with Cinna, then you would have my blessing.'

'Truly?'

'It is not my place to stand between you, though if you could see your way to staying in my service, I would be very grateful.'

'Cinna says he'd love to see Egypt,' Eiras burst out. 'Cinna says that he has long dreamed of visiting Alexandria, that he hears it is the most inspirational place in the world.'

'Which it is.'

'He says that he is sick of the restrictions of the Republic and would willingly embrace a freer, more cosmopolitan world. He says he yearns for the East – for history and culture and a people who embrace their own sensuality. He says he would follow me to the ends of the earth.'

She clamped her mouth shut but Cleopatra smiled to see her enthusiasm. Eiras was usually so calm and composed that this torrent of words was like a gift – a little piece of her true self Cleopatra did not usually get to see.

'I hope,' she said, squeezing her hands, 'that he will need to go no further than Egypt, but he would certainly be welcome – if we ever get back there ourselves.'

'Oh, we will!' Eiras seemed to have risen even taller than usual. 'We *will* get back. You do not deserve to be in Rome where they know not how to value you.'

'But where someone, at least, has learned to value *you*. Someone who is, I believe, waiting ...'

She nodded over to the hovering poet and Eiras lit up further. She grabbed Cleopatra in a sudden hug then, embarrassed, pulled back and patted at her shoulders as if afraid she had sullied her. Cleopatra pulled her firmly into another, longer hug.

'Now, go!'

Eiras needed no further urging. She turned and almost ran to Cinna, who seized her hands and pulled her towards the musicians. Dancing was frowned upon in Rome, especially for men, but they were in Baiae now, in the house of the Claudii, and Eiras and Cinna were not alone on the mosaic-ed dancefloor.

'That was kind, Cleopatra.'

She looked around to find Servilia at her side. For such a voluptuous woman, she moved with astonishing grace.

'I want her to be happy.'

'Which is kind, especially in a queen.'

'Princess. And why should we be any more or less kind?'

'I'm sorry. Please. I didn't mean anything, save that the reputation of some monarchs have preceded you.'

'And the history of your glorious senators is pure and perfect, is it?'

Servilia held up her hands.

'A very fair point. Truly, I'm sorry. I was trying to be nice.'

'It did not work as well as it might have done.'

'No.' Servilia gave her a rueful grimace. 'I grow old and less sharp than I was.'

Cleopatra saw small lines of sadness around her gorgeous eyes and clasped at her hand.

89

'You are not old, Servilia. You are beautiful.'

Servilia looked down at her and, to her astonishment, Cleopatra saw a tear gleam in her eye before she blinked it fiercely away.

'Don't mind me – weddings aren't my strong point.'

Cleopatra squeezed her hand.

'You miss him.'

Servilia jumped.

'What?'

'Julius Caesar – you miss him.'

Servilia looked anxiously around but everyone was too busy crowding in to talk to the bride and groom to pay them any attention.

'I am too old to "miss" a man,' she said primly.

Cleopatra frowned.

'I would have thought you'd miss someone more as you got older and were at your own hearth more often.'

Servilia winced.

'You, Princess, are far too astute for such a young woman. I confess, there are times, especially in the winter, when I would like a man to stoke my fire – and I do not even mean the way the poets would have it – but there is only one man I would choose and that cannot be. Even if he were in Rome, which he never is, he would be at his wife's hearth and not mine.'

'Why did you not marry?'

'Our fates never aligned. We might have done, when we were younger, but we were never free at the same time and then . . . ' She gave a heavy sigh. 'I am past childbearing, Cleopatra, and Julius yearns for a son. He has only Julia, you know, and for a man as great as he to leave no one to carry his name is a deep pain. He married Calpurnia in the hope of an heir but . . . '

They both glanced across to where Calpurnia was watching Porcia, her eyes fixed on the other woman's swollen belly with painful envy. Servilia looked pointedly away.

'It is not Calpurnia's fault. How can a woman conceive when

her husband is not in her bed? And it seems that Julius wants Gaul even more than he wants a son.'

She shrugged but Cleopatra saw the pain beneath and knew that Calpurnia was not the only one who had lost out to these coveted Gaulish lands.

'Marriage seems to me a troubling institution,' she said. Servilia looked down at her, a curious look on her beautiful face, and then suddenly she laughed and gestured to where Claudia and Brutus were dancing together, their eyes fixed only on each other.

'There is rarely fun without trouble, Princess. But perhaps, in your position, you will be spared its coils. Though be warned – it is not marriage that tangles a woman, but love.'

She looked out to the sea as if she could draw Julius Caesar home with her thoughts and Cleopatra watched her curiously and longed to meet the mysterious man who seemed, even from such a distance, to reach into every part of Rome.

'My only love is Egypt,' she said firmly.

Servilia pulled her eyes from the sea.

'Lucky you.'

'Hardly! I am as separate from her as you are from—'

'Then we must change that.'

Cleopatra blinked.

'Sorry?'

The older lady's eyes had gained their usual sharp focus and now she nodded firmly to herself.

'I have been lax, I apologise.'

'Servilia, you—'

'It is true. I have been so caught up in this wedding that I have not thought of wider concerns but it is done now and done well so I shall take up your cause. Come the autumn, Princess, when we are all back in Rome, we shall take action.'

Cleopatra looked at her in delight.

'I confess I was hoping Brutus . . .'

Servilia waved this away.

'Oh, we don't need Brutus. I have plenty of ideas. But for now, come – let us enjoy today!'

And at last Cleopatra thought she truly would. Let all these doting couples have each other, for she had a greater partner in Egypt and surely, with Servilia's help, she would be back in her sparkling arms before the year was done.

Chapter Eleven

'Can I trouble you to ...?'

'Would you like to consider ...?'

Cleopatra ground her teeth as yet another pompous senator marched past, brushing away the leaflet she proffered as if it advertised hair pomade or virility treatment. A few had stopped hopefully but, seeing that she was not offering the sort of services they clearly looked for in a woman, had hurried on again. This was not Servilia's finest idea.

'Make them see your plight,' she'd suggested. 'Appeal to their manly instincts to save a poor young woman from exile. Everyone in Rome thinks king and queens are mythical horrors, like dragons or gorgons, so the sight of a beautiful young woman might confuse them long enough to make them think again. Oh, and be sure you mention Egypt's gold. If there's one thing a Roman senator likes more than a pretty female, it's gold.'

Cleopatra had commissioned the leaflets at great cost from another of Levi's enterprising friends in the Jewish quarter. They exhorted the Romans, in bold lettering, to right an injustice, extend their influence in the East, and earn their city riches, and Pompey had been furious when he'd seen them this morning.

'Oooohh!' he'd cried, like a wounded animal, actually clutching his hand to his heart as if Cleopatra had stuck a spear between his ribs.

'I just thought they might help,' she'd said, shocked.

'You thought that these ... populist rags might do more for your cause than the support of I, Pompey the Great? You thought senators would sooner read your golden lettering than listen to my careful speeches? For nearly a year you have lived at my charity. My wife has nurtured you as a friend and treated you with care, even when you turned down her invitation to the hills to go and carouse with the bloody Claudii, who make it their greatest joy to torment me. And now this! It is treachery, Cleopatra. Treachery!'

'I didn't mean ...'

But he'd gone, stalking out, leaving Julia to wring her hands and cast her cow eyes balefully on Cleopatra.

'Just because we do not wear see-through dresses, throw roses on the sea and parade around as if we own Rome, does not mean we are dull, you know. Pompey has been working very hard for you and your father and this is how you repay him?'

'I just thought I'd help.'

Julia had sniffed.

'Well, go and think it somewhere else, will you? Gnaeus is upset and if Gnaeus is upset, *I* am upset.'

There had seemed little else to do but get on with it. Servilia had told her she would choose a propitious day for distributing the leaflets and would help her to do so, but Cleopatra was tired of waiting for other people, so she'd taken Eiras and headed out. What a mistake that had been.

A few drops were starting to fall from the low clouds gathered over the city and she shivered. She was weary and embarrassed and had a low ache in her belly that must surely be hunger, save that it felt more like sickness. All she really wanted was to go back to Julia and ask her forgiveness, and perhaps a hot bath, but that would be embarrassing too. Drawing in a deep breath, she forced her chin up once more.

'Help a lost young woman,' she tried, stepping in front of an ageing senator as he hurried across the Forum.

He stopped.

'To do what?'

'To reclaim her country.'

'Which country?'

'Egypt, Sir. I am—'

'The Princess Cleopatra. I heard you were here.' He looked her up and down. 'You're not as grand as I'd expected.'

'Because my throne has been stolen from me.'

'Careless.'

'Not careless, Sir, but robbed. It is a great injustice and one the Romans are perfectly placed to help right. You have legions in Syria ready to strike at a simple word from the senate.'

'But why would they?'

'Because my father was sworn in as a friend and ally of the Roman people. And because it will be good for Rome to have Egypt in her debt should she need assistance in times to come.'

'Rome? Need assistance? Never!' He leaned in, jowls wobbling. 'I can give you a bed, Princess, if that's what you lack.'

She drew herself up tall.

'No thank you. I need political intelligence, not mindless lust.'

'Suit yourself.'

And off he went, sweeping his toga over his arm as he laboured up the steps into the damned senate house without a backward glance. This was impossible.

Cleopatra looked around for Eiras. She'd had enough. Rome was packed out with everyone returning from their summer retreats to get back to business, but no one wanted to listen to a displaced royal. The skies were darkening rapidly, clearing the forum fast and as someone bashed into her, sending her spinning, she felt tears prick and stamped her foot furiously. She was a princess, she had the Goddess in her soul; she was not here to scrabble to be heard like a commoner.

'Eiras!'

To her fury, her companion was huddled up in the shelter of a column with Cinna, her leaflets dangling, forgotten, in her hand. The pair had announced their engagement the day after Claudia's wedding but wished to marry in Egypt so were still mooning around each other. Normally Cleopatra thought it was sweet but not today. She stormed across, blinking rain from her eyes.

'For all the good we're doing here, we might as well head home,' she said sharply. 'Then you can at least gaze into each other's eyes in comfort at the villa. Come.'

She stalked off down the road and Eiras hurried guiltily after her but at that moment a noise from a side street heralded the arrival of Milo and his gang of thugs. Cleopatra's heart raced as, from behind her a Clodian group also strolled in, walking with the exaggerated swagger of midday wine and with their meaty hands on the well-sharpened daggers at their belts. Cleopatra turned to get back to Eiras, but Clodius' group exploded forward, cutting her off from her friend. A heavy hand fell on her shoulder, fingers digging into the flesh, and someone plucked a leaflet from her hands.

'A petition, how sweet. You must be the Princess Cleopatra. Exotic little thing, aren't you? Got the Goddess inside you, Clodius says.'

'She can have *me* inside her,' one of the others called coarsely.

Cleopatra looked furiously around and, to her huge relief, spotted Clodius himself riding up behind his thugs on his beautiful white horse.

'Clodius!' she called, but his eyes were fixed on the leader of the other group.

'Let her go,' Eiras shouted furiously but the thug's grip only tightened.

'Clodius!' Cleopatra called again, her voice shrill.

He glanced her way and leaped from his horse, but it was Milo, his opposite number, who spoke.

'The Princess is Pompey's special guest, and you will let her go.'

Cleopatra looked to him, relief flooding through her, at least until she noticed the deep fissure of a scar across her cheek and missing left eye. *This* was to be her saviour?

'For you, Milo?' her captor demanded. 'Why should I?'

In answer Milo whipped a dagger from his belt, the long, thin blade shining in the rain that was now falling hard upon them. His opponent let go of Cleopatra's shoulder to grab for his own weapon and she looked a third time to Clodius. Surely he would stop this? Surely he would protect her? But he was intent only on the fight and, throwing the damned leaflets to the ground, she fled, ducking down the alley from which Milo's men had come.

It wasn't a street she recognised and she hesitated a moment but at the sound of blade on blade, she ran on. Better chance the unknown people ahead than the known thugs behind. Her shoulder throbbed where the man's fingers had clawed into her flesh, the ache in her belly had turned to sharp pain, and her heart beat so fast she could feel it hammering in her throat but still she ran.

'Whoah there! What's a pretty thing like you doing careening down the street?'

A man put out hands to stop her but she pushed him away and ducked sideways. She had no idea where in Rome's jumble of streets she was now but she was, at least, alone and as the alley opened out into an almost gracious little square, she paused to catch her breath. Her whole body ached and she felt the tears that had threatened earlier bite at the edges of her eyes. She wanted to be home – not Pompey's stark-lined villa with the creepy masks of his ancestors along the walls but her real home in Alexandria. She wanted her lush, open rooms and her own bed and, above all else, she wanted Charmion.

'I wish I'd never come,' she burst out on a sob. 'I wish I'd just told Berenice she was wonderful, proclaimed her as queen and been allowed to stay. I wish ...'

Her words dried up in her throat as she caught sight of her gown. It had twisted as she'd run and now she saw that her skirts were marked with blood. Had one of the daggers caught her without her noticing? Was she bleeding? If so, where was the wound? And would she die of it here in a dark corner of a foreign city with no one to even hold her as she breathed her last?

She pictured Clodius' face, creased with delight as he'd drawn his dagger on Milo. He'd thought nothing of Cleopatra, paid her no attention. The man of extravagant bows and praises had been replaced by something far baser, and Cleopatra could not believe she had placed such trust in the reverence he'd seemed to have for royalty. The Claudii, much as she loved them, had reverence for nothing, including themselves. She'd been a fool and now she was in danger.

For a moment the horror threatened to overwhelm her but as she reached for a tree to steady herself and felt the coarse bark against her palm, she realised she was still here, still standing and no more blood seemed to be pouring from her. She drew in deep breaths and told herself to be calm. She had never been so thoroughly uncared for but she had herself and she had the Goddess within and she could find safety.

'What would Isis do?' she asked herself, looking around, and realised she recognised this square. If she just cut across it and around the corner, she would be at Servilia's door.

'Servilia!' Suddenly she was up again, careening down the street and hammering on the familiar front door. 'Servilia! Let me in, please.'

The door slid open and a servant looked down at her.

'Princess Cleopatra?'

She almost swooned with relief at being recognised and stumbled inside, sinking gratefully onto a stool as another servant ran for his mistress. Footsteps sounded from within and suddenly there was Servilia.

'Cleopatra! Oh, my poor dear, look at you. What on earth has happened?'

At her kind voice, the tears fell. Cleopatra batted crossly at them but they were not to be denied now that she was safe and all she managed to gasp out was 'gangs' and 'fight', 'Clodius' and 'lost'.

Servilia gathered her into her arms and Cleopatra fell into the embrace. She had yearned for Charmion and whilst this elegant, sensual Roman was not quite her dear nursemaid, she felt every bit as soft and kind and Cleopatra cried harder.

'Come inside.'

Servilia half led, half carried her through to a cosy side room. A fire burned in an ornamented brazier and the couches were twice as large and soft as any at Pompey's villa.

'You're very kind,' Cleopatra managed as she was wrapped in a blanket and plied with warmed wine and the world started to feel a little more normal again. 'Oh, but I'm bleeding.'

She leaped up from the couch, terrified of staining the rich fabric.

'You are wounded?'

'I'm not sure. I didn't think so but there is blood on the back of my dress.'

The older woman looked at her curiously.

'Do you hurt anywhere?' she asked gently.

'Only here.' She pressed at her stomach. 'But that is more of an ache than the pain of a cut.'

Servilia gave her a kindly smile.

'It sounds like it might be your monthly bleed, Cleopatra?'

'My what?!'

'Ah.' Servilia put warm hands on her shoulders and pushed her gently back down. 'Welcome to womanhood, my dear.'

'Womanhood?' Cleopatra stuttered. This – blood and pain and tears – this was womanhood?

'Fun, isn't it?' Servilia said drily. 'But there is nothing to worry about. It is simply that your womb has decided it is time to flower.'

'Well, it picked a very inconvenient day to do it,' Cleopatra grumbled and Servilia burst out laughing.

'You'll get used to that too. Now come, I think a bath is in order and then I shall sort you out with a fresh gown and some pads.'

'Pads?' Cleopatra asked uncertainly and Servilia laughed again, though less heartily this time.

'Where is your mother, my poor dear?'

'In Egypt,' Cleopatra sighed. 'Deep in my homeland of Egypt.'

How she wished she could be with her now. She remembered Eiras telling Cinna about her life as a devotee in her mother's temple at Memphis and swore that she must ask her more about it when she got back to Pompey's villa – and that she must insist on visiting there if, no, *when*, they got home. She thought, with a new twinge, of the leaflets she had ditched in her panic. They would be trodden into the rain and dirt now, lost to some petty Roman brawl. The only upside was that Julia would be pleased. She clutched at Servilia.

'I've been handing out your leaflets.'

'Today? Alone? Oh, Cleopatra, I told you I would go with you.'

'I know. I'm sorry. I got impatient. And I thought I could do it alone. I thought it might be better that way.'

'Rome is not safe, sweet one.'

'I see that now.' She groaned. 'I've been so stupid, Servilia. I thought being a princess made me special. I thought Isis would keep me safe. I thought other people would want me protected and happy, but why should they? I'm *not* special. And Isis will only stay within me as long as I am a fine vessel for her, just as the people will only want me to rule if I prove myself worthy.'

'Cleopatra, you do not need to do this.'

Cleopatra pulled back.

'Oh, but I do. When those gangs were facing each other, I

assumed that, once they knew who I was, they would treat me with respect but if anything it was the reverse. And they are not alone – Cato thinks I am worse for being royal; Porcia too.'

'Porcia is not a kind person, Princess.'

'But she is sharp. She sees the world as it is, whereas I see it only as I want it to be. I wanted Rome for what she could do for me. I sought out the Claudii to offer me comfort and amusement whilst I expected Pompey to get me the troops we need. I have assumed people were put on earth to serve me, whereas in truth, if I ever wish to be a good ruler, I need to work out how to serve *them*.'

'Well, yes, but . . .'

'But what is the point if I am never going to get back to Egypt anyway? Why should, should . . .'

But Cleopatra could say no more, for sobs were tangling up her words and she curled in on her aching belly and let them take her.

'Oh, Cleopatra,' she heard Servilia say, 'you are too hard on yourself. You are learning still.'

'I am learning that I'm not fit to rule. You would not find Berenice whimpering like a baby.'

'And you would not, perhaps, find Berenice thinking about what it is to rule either. Your curiosity, Cleopatra, your desire to know more, to consider all you see – that is your strength, not your weakness. The only way to improve is to make mistakes.'

Cleopatra groaned.

'Then I must be much improved indeed!'

Servilia gave a soft chuckle.

'Come,' she said, 'let me get you that bath and then I will take you back to Julia myself. I think you will find her in a good mood.'

'Why? Because I am cast down.'

'No. For the same reason that *I* am in a good mood.' Cleopatra peeled her hands away from her red eyes and looked at Servilia. She could see concern for herself in the older lady's grey eyes but something else, something like excitement. 'Julius is coming! Julius Caesar is coming back to Italy and if you want a man to show you how to rule, he is it. Power with compassion, that's the key. Now – bath!'

Power with compassion, Cleopatra thought as her kind friend summoned servants. Pompey, perhaps, had compassion for her and her father but no power to turn it into action. Clodius had power, but, it turned out, no compassion to use it for good. She had been trying to find a middle ground and failed but here, perhaps, was a way out for them all. She just prayed this Caesar lived up to expectations for she had learned much in Rome and she swore she would use it for the good of her people if only she could find a way back to them.

Chapter Twelve

Lucca. Cleopatra pulled up her horse to look down the lush river valley to the bright-orange roofs that told her they were finally close to the curious town that was their destination. Julius Caesar, as a serving provincial governor, was not allowed back into Rome without resigning his 'imperium', despite the fact he was due to stand as Consul with Pompey next year. He had therefore come to Lucca to meet his ally, with the result that the whole of Rome had emptied up the Via Francigena to be there too. It was a classic piece of Roman nonsense but at least it meant Cleopatra got to travel more of Italia.

She had not, she realised now, seen hills before. She knew temple mounds, of course, and the seven hills that hampered Rome's town-planning, but they were nothing like the endless tree-covered rises and falls of the Etruscan countryside. She wasn't quite sure what to make of them. Brought up amongst the sharply defined lines and brutally fierce colours of city life, she found the rolling curves and soothing shades of green a little underwhelming but the air was certainly fresher and her horse was a fine beast, keen to be given his head, so the journey had been invigorating. Plus, now that they drew close to Lucca, she could see crowds to match those in Rome and looked forward to being amongst them once more.

There had been a lot of time to think on horseback and little of it had been comfortable. She'd sat down with Julia after her brush with the gangs in the forum and apologised for any offence. Her kindly hostess had been gracious in her acceptance and, as Servilia had anticipated, too excited about her father's return to worry anyway. It had been a further lesson in how little the world revolved around Cleopatra and whilst it had been a relief at that moment, it had made for uncomfortable musings on the road north to Lucca.

If Cleopatra wanted to rule Egypt, she would have to win her country back and, more than that, she would have to win it over. Her time in Rome had been one of unprecedented discomfort but also unprecedented freedom, and she'd seen far more of the world than she'd ever done within the golden walls of her palace. She'd seen how a crowd could turn, not just from on a balcony, but from within its ranks. She'd seen how a man – or woman – could influence opinion with charisma and style and also how empty that was if not backed up with sound judgement and care. She felt wiser now than when she'd first ridden into Rome and she yearned for a chance to prove herself. First, though, they needed approval for Aulus Gabinius' troops and Servilia assured her Julius Caesar was the man who could help secure it. Cleopatra was certainly going to ask.

'My father writes that he is keen to meet you,' Julia had told her, waving Julius Caesar's precious missive like a flag.

'My father and I?' she'd asked, for King Ptolemy was back from Ephesus and eager for company.

'Just you. He knows your father already and is always more interested in what is to come than what is here already.'

Cleopatra had taken that little nugget to dwell on. It had held two interesting elements: that a good ruler must look to the future; and that this Caesar saw that future in her. Or, at least, he was prepared to. She must make the most of that.

Their party was dropping down to the river and turning to head into Lucca. It was a small town, contained between typically square walls, but with all of Rome descending upon it, its usual order had been burst apart and tents were pitched in every available space to house those unlucky enough not to have secured lodgings. Pompey, of course, had a central villa and Cleopatra steered her horse tight behind his as his standard-bearers cleared a route through the crowds. Everyone turned to stare and Cleopatra pushed back her shoulders, grateful for the elegant travelling dress Maria had made for her.

She tried not to look longingly over to where Servilia was travelling with Claudia, Brutus and the rest of the Claudii. All three nights of the journey, their Pompeian group had sat in the quiet corners of the taverns whilst the Claudii had held centre stage but, whilst Cleopatra had talked politely to them, she had refused to defect to the wilder group. That lesson was learned.

Instead, she looked for her father and saw him taking his time through the crowd, waving as if he were the one they had all come to see, and indeed they were cheering wildly. He must have stopped to change for he was wearing the richly embroidered purple tunic she'd not seen him in since the night they'd fled Alexandria and an extravagant Pharaonic crown that must have been part of the treasure on his ship. To Cleopatra it looked ridiculously archaic but the naïve Romans weren't to know that and Ptolemy was clearly delighted to be wearing royal garb once more.

They processed up the central street of Lucca, every door open for the inhabitants to gape at the noble arrivals. Ahead, Cleopatra could see a small but gracious Forum, set with open-sided tents to shade Caesar and Pompey in their debate. Many trestle tables were stacked around the edges ready for feasting following the anticipated success of the talks, and servers hovered nervously between the main tent and the closed-off one beyond, which must house the kitchens.

'Surely the talks are not starting immediately?' Cleopatra heard Julia say to Pompey.

'Apparently so,' he shot back. 'I am told Julius has to return to his precious Gauls with all speed so there is no time to waste. Is my hair in place?'

He patted nervously at his stiff quiff and Julia reached up and took his hand with great tenderness.

'You look magnificent, husband.'

His shoulders visibly relaxed and he leaned over to kiss her. A few men jeered him but he ignored them and, for once, Cleopatra was impressed by her host.

'Where is Father?' Julia whispered to Pompey.

'Waiting to make an entrance, no doubt,' was the scornful reply, as if Pompey himself had not just paraded up the main street.

He swung himself out of his saddle, helped Julia down, and then strode forward to take up his place on one of the two couches, reclining awkwardly alone as the crowd gathered. Cleopatra felt someone squeeze at her waist and turned to see Claudia wriggling in next to her.

'Julius is not here yet, I see,' she said. 'Funny that, Servilia disappeared a while back too.'

'No!' Cleopatra stared at her. 'You don't think . . . ?'

'Wouldn't put it past him.'

'Poor Calpurnia,' Cleopatra said, gesturing to Caesar's wife, stood demurely behind the empty couch.

'Foolish Calpurnia. You have to seize your chances in life if you ask me.'

'But surely Caesar would not keep all these people waiting just whilst he . . . you know?'

Claudia gave a low chuckle.

'Oh, I'd say he would. He's quite the showman is Julius, and quite the lover too. This is a chance to do both. Ah, but here he is now.'

Cleopatra heard a low murmur at the back of the crowd, growing rapidly as a man strode through them in the uniform of an active general, and she eagerly took him in. Julius Caesar was of average height and stature, with a thin nose, high brow and balding hair. Nothing about him was remarkable and yet he walked as if he owned the earth and looked about as if every inch of it was fascinating. His limbs rippled with taut muscle and he radiated energy, as if he had come from a restful few weeks in Baiae rather than a three-year campaign in some of the toughest territory known to man. A fading scar across one cheek told of battles recently past and his hand, if you looked closely, hovered constantly above his dagger hilt, but his smile was broad and he paused to address so many people as he made for his supposed ally that it seemed he might never reach him.

'It's very good to see you,' Cleopatra heard him say over and over, each time with the right name and a quiet enquiry about the health of a family member, the progress of a trade, or a matter of personal business. Eventually he stopped by King Ptolemy, offered his hand and inclined his head, half bow, half nod.

'I am sorry to hear of your troubles,' he said, graciously oblique.

'My ungrateful daughter has stolen my throne,' Ptolemy replied baldly, 'and left me an exile.'

'And your people without the benefit of your rule.'

Ptolemy blinked, as if it was the first time this had occurred to him, but recovered swiftly.

'Quite. They suffer beneath her unjust yoke and need me back, and my heir besides.'

He gestured to Cleopatra and Caesar turned fluidly towards her, taking her hand in his own and dropping a kiss upon it.

'Princess Cleopatra, you are very welcome in Italia. I trust my daughter has been looking after you?'

'Most kindly.'

'Good. And you have made friends in Rome?'

Cleopatra felt as if his eyes were boring straight into her, noting her treacherous preference for the glamorous Claudii.

'Everyone has been very good to me,' she managed.

'Everyone?' His left eyebrow lifted and Cleopatra felt herself smile despite her nerves.

'Almost everyone,' she corrected. 'Some people do not feel that royalty has any place in the Republic.'

'Some people,' he countered immediately, 'have not seen enough of the world beyond it to understand other cultures and respect them as they deserve.'

Cleopatra stared at him, delighted, and could not help her eyes sliding towards Porcia, standing pleasingly open-mouthed with the obnoxious Cato. Caesar's eyes followed her own and he smiled more widely.

'Travel, Princess,' he said loudly. 'It does us all good. There are many horizons on this earth and it can be sadly limiting to see only one. The roofs of Rome are not, I fear, as fine as I once thought before I left their confines – though it is always, of course, good to come home.'

'I wouldn't know,' Cleopatra said, 'though I should like to.'

'I'm sure. What would you like best about returning to Egypt?'

Cleopatra blinked. It was a good question and one she would have liked time to consider but Caesar was in Lucca for only a few days and was unlikely to have so much as another minute for an exiled princess.

'I would like,' she said carefully, 'to apply the learning I have made in Rome.'

'Which is?'

'Which is that to rule a people you have to listen. I do not believe my sister, Berenice, has ever listened to anything other than the drum of her own ambition. To be fair, I could have been the same, but I know now that there is a greater tune and I want a chance to hear its notes.'

Caesar looked her up and down curiously.

'A royal Populares, fascinating.'

'Good royals are always Populares,' she shot back. 'How else will they be popular?'

It was a pun on the Latin and he smiled at it.

'You speak well, Princess. Egypt has a worthy heir. So, how can I help?'

'Troops,' Ptolemy said.

'Could you be more specific?'

Cleopatra spoke before her father could blunder in again. 'Aulus Gabinius has troops in Syria who are ready to march on Alexandria if the senate permits it. Your gracious ally Pompey has been working for that permission but he needs . . . backing.'

'I see. A good job, then, that I am here for talks with my "gracious ally" and that we will, assuming a successful conclusion to those talks, be stepping into power together.'

'Power with compassion.' The words were out before she could stop them and again he looked at her curiously. She flushed. 'It is how Servilia told me you ruled.'

'Is it indeed? Well, she is a very astute woman so I take that as a fine compliment. And a fine standard to live up to.'

'For us both.'

Again the smile.

'For us both, indeed. Let me do what I can, Princess. I am told Alexandria's horizon is one of the finest and it deserves to be presided over by someone whose bearing can do it justice.'

He dropped another kiss on her hand and then he was gone, on through the crowd to join Pompey, leaving Cleopatra staring. Her whole body felt jolted, as if lightning had struck, and she could only pray it had – and that it would scorch her way back to Egypt. She was ready now. Ready to rule.

Chapter Thirteen

FEBRUARY 55 BC

My dearest Charmion,

We have done it. At last we have done it. I can say little more, as you will understand, but know only this – that I hope to see you and Mardion again, I hope to see Alexandria again, I hope to see the palace again. I have been too long away and I swear my very blood is starting to thin without Egyptian air.

It is down to one man – Julius Caesar. There is something of the East in him, I swear, for although he is as ruthless as any Roman, he has more charm, culture, and interest in the world beyond the Republic than any of the others. I saw him for only two days before he was called back to Gaul, but I watched him intently and I swear he never rests. He strides around a room if he is in debate and when he is not, he is always heading out to see things and meet people. Even when couched to eat, he is forever turning this way and that and his eyes follow everything that is going on. His mind must never stop and I have heard both his wife and daughter say that he sleeps little. Perhaps that is why he has so many women in and out of his bed – he needs more active ways to rest than most.

Pompey, of course, is claiming he has secured us what we need but if

110

that were the case, we could have been home within months of leaving instead of standing as guests to Rome all year. No, it is Caesar who swept in to convince the senate and Rabirius, the banker, who has provided the funds to allow the Syrian governor, Aulus Gabinius, to aid our cause. My sister is going to rue the day she turned down that particular suitor.

Burn this letter, Charmion, and speak of it to no one, but be joyous. Order the finest dishes from the kitchen and I will surely be there to enjoy them with you.

All love,
Petra

Cleopatra swayed in yet another desert wind and put a hand beneath her veil to rub sand from her stinging eyes. Her bottom ached from the saddle, her back was sore from sleeping on rough pallets, and she was permanently hungry as the supply caravan had been hit by pirates, and soldiers needed feeding before princesses. If she had learned a lesson about the precariousness of royalty in Rome, this was another about war. It was not, it turned out, the glorious pursuit of victory that the after-dinner poets would have you believe, but an endless round of discomfort, pain and fear.

'That's Alexandria, Princess.' Cleopatra peered through the veil at the lieutenant before her, struggling to remember his name, but appreciating his eager vigour. 'Over there – can you see it? It's Alexandria. We're taking you home, Princess!'

Tears stung at the precious word and she peered across the plains. She could just about discern the outlines of roofs but it was too far away yet to recognise any of the beloved buildings. She would have to trust him.

'Thank you, er . . .'

'Mark Antony, Princess.'

'Of course.'

The tears had cleared the sand from her eyes and she could see him more clearly now. He had the rugged body of most of the senior soldiers but an unusual amount of blond curls peeking from beneath his helmet, and surprisingly kindly eyes. It was this man, she remembered, who had stopped her father from massacring the inhabitants of the outpost city of Pelusium when they had taken it two days ago.

'They will love you for your mercy,' he had told King Ptolemy. 'And will praise the gods for restoring you to your throne.'

And support you staying there, had been the unspoken implication. Pelusium had fallen easily, surprised by the Roman ambush, but they would have had time to send messengers to Alexandria and Berenice's troops would be waiting outside the capital.

'There will be a battle?' she asked.

'Inevitably, Princess. But we will win it.'

'How do you know?'

'Because we always win our battles. We are well trained, well equipped and well led.'

'But not well fed,' Cleopatra pointed out.

Mark Antony grimaced.

'True but hunger will only sharpen the men's need to get into the city.'

Cleopatra shuddered. Another thing this march had shown her was the tough ruthlessness of the Roman legions. Here, truly, was the sharp end of the Republic – not the pompous politicians with their philosophical ideas about choice but the hardened, disciplined front line, prepared to cut and kick and claw their way to victory. Most of these men would never wear a toga, many of them would never step over Rome's precious Pomerium. They were fighting for personal gain – for wages and bonuses, for farmland in Italia at the end of their service and, above all, for loot in the lands their masters conquered. And her father was inviting them into Alexandria.

'When?' she asked.

'Tomorrow. Gabinius wishes to hit hard and fast before they have too long to dig in.'

Cleopatra had a vivid picture of Alexandrian men digging into the soft sand, preparing to defend their homes and hated that it had come to this. If – *when* – her father was restored and Berenice banished, they must work for peace and prosperity. They must reduce the taxes her sister had forced on the people and help them to live well. A glance across to the royal tent being set up nearby, however, told her that such clemency would be hard to achieve for there, sat alongside her father, was the banker Rabirius.

King Ptolemy was in debt to the Jew to the tune of 10,000 sesterces. He had not wanted to tell her the sums but Levi had suggested in his quiet way that if Cleopatra was to be Ptolemy's heir, she needed to know the whole scope of royal business so he'd reluctantly given in. He need not have worried – it was a sum too vast for Cleopatra to grasp, larger than all the profit from the fertile Egyptian cornlands in one and maybe even two years. She feared that, far from reducing the taxes that were keeping Berenice's rule on a convenient knife-edge, they would have to increase them and that would not be popular.

Cleopatra shook herself. Now was not the time to fret about the economics of rule. Berenice was still holding sway in the beautiful royal palace that should be her home whilst she was in a half-built tent with nothing but desert-grit in her stomach. They had come this far and there was no choice but to finish or be finished.

'Thank you,' she said to Mark Antony, and he bowed low and went off to arrange his troops for the final fight.

She looked around for Eiras but she'd gone with Cinna to try and find water. She had, as always, been an oasis of calm on the long trip from Rome, both for Cleopatra and for her betrothed who was finding army life harder, perhaps, than either of them. Watching Cinna prod at blisters, leap from bugs, and miserably try to pick sand from his food had been amusing enough to alleviate Cleopatra's own suffering, and Eiras teased him mercilessly.

'You have to live to write, my darling,' she'd say.

'This sort of living,' he would grumble back, 'can only inspire verse that a man can – and *should* – wipe his arse with.'

Following Eiras to the ends of the earth was, it seemed, not as romantic as Cinna had envisioned, but he stumbled along with the rest of them, and she prayed that he would feel it had all been worth it to get into the Museon, the library, and the blessed Pharos of beautiful Alexandria.

'Tomorrow,' she murmured, her heart thudding. She had been weeks on the road from Rome but tomorrow, one way or another, their journey would end. She swallowed, her throat drier from fear than from sand.

'Water, Princess?'

Levi stepped up, proffering a bulging skin and Cleopatra took it eagerly.

'Where did you get that?'

He pulled a face.

'There is room for a banker's powers even in an army on the march, Princess.'

'You bribed someone?'

He gave a rueful nod.

'This skinny body was not made to fight, but this funny brain is more efficient. It's not a very glorious way to operate, but it works.'

Cleopatra gratefully gulped down water before re-screwing the lid and returning the skin to the young Jew.

'It does. And a man must surely make the most of the skills he has?'

'I believe so, though I confess I sometimes wish my skills were theirs.'

He indicated a group of soldiers, gathered around whilst two of their party wrestled exuberantly with each other. Cleopatra shook her head.

'Take it from someone small and weak, Levi, it is better to have brains.'

'You are very kind, Princess, but you are a woman – you are not expected to have strength or brains, so to have any of either is a weapon indeed.'

She laughed.

'You have no idea how strong a woman needs to be.'

'Oh, I think I do.' It was said very low and when she looked at Levi, she could see his fingers twitching nervously at his tunic.

'Are you well, Levi? It must be hard for you, so far from home.'

His head sprung up.

'Oh no, that is not hard at all. My mother . . . Let's just say that she most certainly wants me to be more like those men.'

They both looked as one of them threw the other into the dirt with a loud whump and his fellows cheered.

'Are you sure?' Cleopatra asked.

'Oh yes. She tells me so all the time. "Why can't you be more like Mucia's son, Levi? Have you seen all his muscles"; "Why can't you join the army, Levi? That's a proper way to earn money"; "Why can't you marry Sofia and give me lots of lovely grandchildren, Levi, like a real man?"'

His delicate features creased in pain and Cleopatra put out a tentative hand.

'Is that why you came to Egypt?'

'To avoid being a real man?'

'No! To avoid your mother. I wouldn't blame you. Families can be hard work. Look at mine – my own sister kicked me out of my home and it's taking ten thousand Roman troops to make her take me back.'

Levi let out a bark of a laugh.

'Oh Princess, I didn't know you were so funny.'

'Hilarious,' she muttered and he hit a hand to his head.

'I'm sorry. I didn't mean to mock, truly. Your situation is awful but you have certainly made me feel better and I thank you for it.'

'What was she like, this Sofia?'

'A nag – like my mother.'

'Then you are best away from her, as I was best away from Berenice.'

She glanced nervously to the horizon. The winds had died down as evening fell and now she could see the roofs Mark Antony had pointed out to her, shining enticingly golden against the setting sun. Alexandria! What was Berenice doing? Was she looking her way, readying to kill? And what about Charmion and Mardion? Were they obediently serving the impostor queen whilst all the time watching for Cleopatra's return? She prayed so.

'I will look forward to seeing *your* home, Princess,' Levi said. 'This Egypt seems a wondrous place.'

She beamed gratefully at him.

'It is, Levi. It truly is. Someone told me recently that travel does us all good. "There are many horizons on this earth," he said, "and it can be sadly limiting to see only one."'

'He was a wise man,' Levi said and turned his eyes, with hers, to the sun dropping fast and bright over Alexandria's glorious horizon.

❖

The city, in the end, fell faster than Cleopatra could have dreamed. Perhaps the Alexandrian troops had not the heart to fight their own king, or perhaps the Roman ones were just too good. Either way, they fell back within an hour of the first swords clashing and messengers came running to Cleopatra saying she should prepare to enter in triumph.

King Ptolemy was already with the troops, dressed up in armour to pretend to lead the fight, though Cleopatra had clearly been able to see his great bulk hovering at the rear as the lines collided outside the city walls. A bit of her despised him for not being prepared to risk so much as a swordcut to win his own throne, and she vowed, as Eiras hastened to make her presentable for her people, that if she ever had to fight for her own place, she would do it from the front.

'They don't make armour small enough,' Eiras told her crisply.

'They do if I commission it,' she retorted. 'If they can make me a necklace, they can make me a breastplate.'

Eiras tutted but Mark Antony was arriving, his golden curls

sweaty as he swept his helmet off to bow, but otherwise no evidence of harm.

'May I escort you into Alexandria, Princess?' he asked and Cleopatra's heart thudded against her unarmoured breast at the thought of her beloved city.

'You may,' she agreed and let him boost her into the saddle of the brave white horse that had carried her across the barren plains and would now see her up the Canopic Way in glory.

She prayed that she and King Ptolemy would not be booed but the people, as mercurial as ever, cheered them down the central street as if they'd been weeping for their return and had not chased them from the city with pitchforks raised. Cleopatra tried not to judge. It had been a long year and, besides, with fearsome Roman soldiers lining the way, they would have been foolish to do otherwise. Everyone must protect their own interests and she reminded herself again of her vow to listen to her people's needs. Even Berenice, she supposed, had simply been trying to stop their baby half-brothers from taking her birthright.

Berenice. Cleopatra shuddered at the thought of facing her and hoped her sister had followed their own example and fled out of the back, taking a ship past the Pharos to safety in some other land. But no, she remembered Gabinius had sent two galleons to cut off the harbour and as she glanced over to the glorious, sweeping lines of the gracious docks, she could see them bobbing menacingly in the centre of the water. It was an ominous sight but there was no time to dwell on it for, as she came towards the top of the Canopic Way, there was a scuffle ahead and she heard Berenice's furious scream. Two burly soldiers had her royal sister by the arms and were dragging her, kicking and spitting, out of the palace gates to stand before King Ptolemy, who sat high on his horse, his armour glinting and his eyes dark. Berenice thrust her head up high.

'Father.'

'You're no daughter of mine,' Ptolemy spat. 'You stole the throne. You stole it from me, the gods-appointed ruler, and you stole it from the country, who deserve a ruler who rules for their profit not her own.'

Cleopatra shifted on her horse. In all his rages, she'd not once heard her father bewail the fate of his people, but the premise was correct.

'You left, Father,' Berenice bit out.

'I was driven away in fear of my life, and well you know it.' The crowd jeered, delighted at the conflict. 'You bribed my guards, manipulated my people and stole my throne – and now you will pay. String her up.'

The jeers stuttered. The people looked nervously to one another, the guards either side of Berenice froze. Cleopatra stared at her father, unable to believe what she'd heard.

'String her up!' he said again, his voice icily certain.

'Father,' Cleopatra started, but he put up an imperious hand.

'The lowliest peasant is hung for theft, so why not this woman, whose crimes are far greater and have dragged the entire country into their coils? String. Her. Up.'

Berenice's confidence drained from her as officials went running for a gibbet, eager to be seen to do the returning king's bidding,

'Petra, please,' she called, her grey eyes imploring. 'Help me, sister.'

Sister! The word seemed to snag on Berenice's tongue and all Cleopatra could see was her face last year, when she'd refused to swear her in as queen. 'Seize her,' she'd shouted, shoving Cleopatra towards the baying mob. 'Seize the traitor.'

'You did not help me, Berenice.'

'And have regretted it every day.'

Cleopatra yearned to believe her. From the moment of her birth, Berenice had been there, stepping ahead of her in royal trains, showing her the way. But Berenice's way was no longer her own and a year in exile had sharpened her ideas of the truest rule.

'If you had regretted it, Berenice, you could have sent for me. I would have come. I would have come from Cyprus and I would have come from Rome, but you never sent. Only Charmion wrote. Only Charmion cared what had happened to me.'

'Charmion wrote to you?'

Berenice's face crinkled in fury and Cleopatra knew then that there had been no regret, no moment of missing her little sister, no time for anything but her own advancement.

'Traitor,' she hissed and stepped back, taking Eiras' arm for support, as she'd done on that hideous day when she'd fled the palace a long year ago.

A group of men were dragging a gibbet onto the platform before the palace, rough and stained with the blood and sweat of a hundred common criminals. Berenice fought furiously, twisting her statuesque body away from the noose so that her golden dress sparkled in protest. Never had anyone so glittering been dragged to so ignominious a death, and the soldiers hesitated. She wore the heir's bejewelled collar, clearly unwilling to secede even the succession, and it would surely catch on the rope. One of them fumbled awkwardly with the catch as Berenice writhed beneath his thick soldier's fingers.

'Undo it,' Ptolemy said to Cleopatra.

'Me?!'

Watching her sister die was one thing, all but placing the noose around her neck another.

'It needs a woman's fingers,' Ptolemy said, as if this were a party not an execution.

Berenice stood suddenly still.

'Yes, come on, Cleopatra, sister, princess – come and take your prize.'

She thrust her long neck forward mockingly. Out of the corner of her eye, Cleopatra saw a wonderfully familiar figure emerge from the palace, clutching the chubby arm of another.

'Charmion,' she whispered. 'Mardion.'

Their eyes lit up as they saw her but then flickered to the gibbet and filled with dismay. Cleopatra spotted Arsinoë cowering behind them and remembered nights in the nursery, all three sisters crowded around Charmion to hear tales and legends and snippets of palace gossip.

Power with compassion, Servilia's voice said in her head and she shook it firmly.

'No, Father.'

'No?! Come, Petra, if you are to be heir, you must learn to be strong. This woman was happy to let you die at the hands of the mob. Do you remember what they did to that Roman foolish enough to kick a cat? They tore him limb from limb.' He pulled his horse round to press his face into hers. 'That could have been you. Berenice would have stood and watched, then wiped your blood from her face and ordered wine to her new throne. Does that not burn inside you?'

Cleopatra swallowed. It hurt, for sure, but it did not 'burn'. All had been confusion that night, and all was far, far too clear now.

'I would send Berenice into exile,' she said to Ptolemy, low-voiced.

'Then you would be a fool, for she would escape and return to haunt you. Undo the collar.'

Cleopatra's cheeks stung with mortification but on this one she was certain.

'No, Father.'

Berenice's eyes lit up and she gave a sudden, hard jerk, wrenching free of one of her captors. The other held her firm, however, and now a slim figure slipped from a horse at Cleopatra's side, took the five steps up to the captured queen and, standing before her to look straight into her eyes, reached her hands around and unhooked the collar instantly.

'Cleopatra is worth ten of you,' Eiras told Berenice in a firm, loud voice and then she turned and walked back down to Cleopatra, the heir's collar held before her.

Cinna ran out adoringly and placed an arm tight around Eiras' shoulders. She leaned into him a moment but was instantly tall again as she reached Cleopatra and offered the collar. Cleopatra slipped out of her saddle to meet her and so missed the moment when Berenice's beautiful face was shoved into the noose and it was hitched high. When she looked back, her sister was dangling, slim legs kicking out, no longer in protest but in pain. Her grey eyes turned stormy not with fury but with fear and the crowd held its breath until finally, on an exhausted hiss, she went still.

'Leave her there,' Ptolemy snarled. 'And send the rest of her cabal after her. For now, people of Alexandria, I present you with my heir, Princess Cleopatra.'

He led her onto the platform in front of Berenice's corpse, took her hand and lifted it high. Cleopatra glanced again to Charmion and Mardion and longed to run into their arms and hide away but she had vowed to be a good ruler and that was not about personal comfort but about working for your people. She forced herself to steady her legs and step forward, out of the shadow of Berenice's swinging body, to smile down at the Alexandrians. A year in exile had taught her the value of power; an hour back had taught her its price. Neither were lessons she intended to forget.

PART TWO

Alexandria, 52 BC

Chapter Fourteen

'You will be queen, Cleopatra.'

'Not yet, Father.'

'Before the day is out. Ra comes to lead me to the underworld and we must talk.'

King Ptolemy reached out a hand, grey and wasted with whatever illness had been eating at his substantial flesh for months, and grasped Cleopatra's own. She felt the grip, chill but determined and shivered. She had known this time would come, had been all but ruling in her father's stead for weeks, but now that it was here, she felt the moment fill her soul with awe, as if Isis were swelling within her.

'Come closer, please,' Ptolemy rasped. 'The gods have dimmed my sight ready for my great journey and I can scarce see the one who will shoulder my earthly burden.'

Cleopatra felt emotion choke at her throat. Sadness at the loss of her father, yes, but also an aching awareness of a shift in time, a turning of the page of history – to one that she would now occupy more fully.

If I were in Rome tomorrow, she found herself thinking absently, *I would not be allowed within the Pomerium.*

She shook her head crossly. She was *not* in Rome and had no intention of ever again being in Rome so what did it matter? She looked around the opulent bedchamber that would soon be hers and felt a rush of power that both shocked and delighted her. Her father's vizier, the desert-weasel Potheinos, hovered close by but even he dared not approach the royal bedside at this sacred time. Ptolemy's hands tightened around hers.

'Listen carefully, daughter. You are my heir until your brother comes of age, or beyond if you have the strength to keep him at bay.' She gaped and he gave her a wizened wink. 'Come, we both know you are the best equipped to rule Egypt. You pay the most attention to the world, Cleopatra, and in return it will pay the most attention to you.'

'Father, you—'

'Listen! We have not much time. You understand Egypt, the whole of Egypt, not just this fickle city at its head. It is a gift from your beautiful mother and you must use it wisely. You are my gecko, remember – my nimble, sharp-witted, clever little gecko and you will need all those wits now.'

'I can do it, Father.'

'You can. But it is hard. Rome, as you know, is a greedy beast and if it senses one moment of weakness from Egypt, it will pounce. We are the only country in the Mediterranean that has resisted the march of the Empire and it will take all your strength to resist it still.'

'I know that, Father. I have seen it first-hand.'

'And that will stand you in good stead, but it is not only the enemy without that you must fear. Treachery comes easily to the Eastern soul, daughter. You must watch for there will be snakes waiting to pounce, both outside the palace and within its golden walls. You must tread the path of your rule firmly, but with care.'

'I will, Father, I swear it. I will listen to the people and I will work for their good.'

'And you will watch for the snakes?'

'I will. And I have others around me to watch for them too.'

He nodded, his brow creasing in pain as he fought the tug of Ra on his soul.

'Know who you can trust, daughter. It will save you much pain.'

'I have Charmion, Father, and Mardion. I have Eiras and Cinna, Sosigenes and Levi.'

'The Jew?'

'He is a good man. Did he not warn us that the people were going to turn on us because of Rabirius?'

Her father had made Rabirius his chancellor – a condition of the funds that had secured his return – but the Roman had been ruthless in collecting his dues. Cleopatra had fretted about the hardship for the people but it was Levi who had come to her last year, telling her that he had picked up rumblings amongst the mob that might, with just a little stirring, turn into ever-simmering rebellion.

'What would you advise my father to do, Levi?' she'd asked.

'Oh, I would not presume to advise the king, Princess.'

'But if you *were* to.'

'Then I would suggest he send Rabirius back to Rome and collect the taxes in a quieter, more prolonged way so as not to bring suffering on his people, whose genuine delight in his return may be muted by their struggles.'

It had been beautifully put and Cleopatra had thanked him.

'I would not see you in danger, Princess,' he'd said earnestly and she thanked Isis, when Rabirius had been despatched, that Levi had chosen to stay. He had become firm friends with Charmion and Mardion as well as the royal engineer Sosigenes and on their advice she had appointed him her financial advisor. He had served her well and if this was truly the moment she was to step up and be queen, she would make him her chancellor.

'Those are good people,' Ptolemy said, though it was clear the effort of speaking was draining the last of his strength. 'But they are servants, not family.'

She frowned.

'I have Arsinoë.'

'You do,' he agreed on a small sigh. 'She will be your heir now. See her married, Cleopatra, to a man you can trust, for she is like honey to them.'

Arsinoë had pleaded herself innocent of all treason on her father's return and, aged just thirteen, it had been hard to condemn her of anything more than a younger sister's fondness. At sixteen, however, she had grown into a true beauty and attracted much attention. Where Cleopatra's nose was long and sharp, Arsinoë's was elegantly sculpted; where Cleopatra's brow was heavy, Arsinoë's was smooth and high; and where Cleopatra's skin was nut-dark, Arsinoë's was amber-bright. Even Eiras' skilful painting could not compete.

Arsinoë was taller too, her limbs long and lithe beneath the linen sheaths she wore with an increasingly high slit. The moment she entered a room, a crowd would develop around her, all male. It wasn't her fault, Cleopatra supposed, but she did little to discourage it and was horribly indiscreet. Only the other day Cleopatra had come across her talking in private with Achillas, the head of the Alexandrian army and a man with a wife and children in Giza. Not that it had seemed to bother Arsinoë who'd been batting her long eyelashes and fiddling with the amulet nestled between her annoyingly ample breasts, his eyes following hungrily as if he might climb right in between them.

'Arsinoë! Where are your maids?' Cleopatra had demanded.

The girl had turned lazily.

'I am quite safe, Sister. Achillas is head of the whole army, so what harm could possibly come to me in his company?'

The flirtatious tone had made it clear that she knew exactly what harm could come to her and would welcome it. Cleopatra had been forced to take her firmly by the arm and lead her back to the women's chambers, her charge looking coyly over her shoulder at the general. It had made Cleopatra feel old and dull. She'd thought of Clodia's maxim – What would Isis do? – and had a feeling Isis would have let the girl enjoy herself. Or maybe not. Isis was a goddess. She understood the needs of the flesh, yes, but also the duties of a ruler. Arsinoë must marry for the good of her country – and the good of her queen.

'I will see it done, Father,' she promised.

His grip tightened and he yanked her down, so close that she could smell the rot of death on his breath.

'She is not the only one, Petra. The country needs you to marry your brother.'

'But Father, he is only seven and—'

'And it is tradition. I am sorry but it is so and it is a condition of my will.' His eyes drilled into hers with dark intensity. 'They wanted me to write you out,' he whispered. 'Potheinos wanted me to make Ptolemy-Theos king, but I refused. I insisted upon you, Cleopatra, so see you justify my choice. Now, I want you—'

But what he wanted of her was lost in a hacking cough. His hand dropped from hers and went convulsively to his throat. Doctors rushed in, but it was no good. His eyes fixed imploringly on hers as his last breaths failed him and, with a jerk, he fell back on his pillows and was gone from the world. The doctors looked down, frozen a moment, and then, as one, turned and dropped to their knees before her.

'All hail, Cleopatra, Queen of Alexandria and Egypt.'

'Wait!' Fast as a cobra's strike, Potheinos was there. His eyes swept the room, taking in the dead king and the kneeling medics. 'Nothing can be declared until the will has been formally read. I have a copy in my chamber. Achillas!'

The doors flung wide open and the head of the royal army came rushing in, but swift on his heels were Charmion and Mardion, the rest of the court intimates spilling in after as news shot around the palace. Cleopatra looked at them all, stunned.

'Fetch Ptolemy-Theos,' she heard Potheinos hiss to Achillas, and she knew she was in some sort of danger here but her head was too clogged with her father's death to be sure what form it was taking.

Charmion stepped forward, her hands clasped demurely over her large bosom and her voice loud and firm, brooking no opposition.

'The official will is, of course, kept in the sanctuary of the Serapeum, beneath the tomb of the blessed Alexander. It must be released by the priests and brought in state to the palace to be publicly read, as it has been since the ruling of Ptolemy I. Mardion, you would perhaps go with Achillas to see custom correctly followed?'

'Of course.'

Mardion came forward, his smooth face the picture of innocence but his large body bristling with purpose. Potheinos stepped in front of him.

'On whose authority does this eunuch operate?' he sneered.

Now it was Cleopatra's turn to step forward.

'On the authority of my vizier, Potheinos.'

He looked at her in confusion.

'I am your vizier.'

She smiled.

'You were my father's vizier and I thank you for that service, but my father is dead now and I appoint Charmion as mine.'

'A female vizier?'

'For a female queen, yes.'

'You are not yet queen, Cleopatra.'

'Not until the will is read, no, so perhaps we should get on and fetch it. Mardion?'

He bowed.

'Of course. Come, Achillas, let us walk together. And perhaps we should take a guard? The king's will is a sacred document to be protected at all costs.'

Cleopatra saw Achillas exchange a furious look with Potheinos but there was little they could do and she blessed Charmion for her foresight. The will would presumably dictate the wishes the dead king had just expressed to her and not the ones Potheinos felt he should have ordered, but even so she found herself holding her breath as Charmion shepherded the rapidly growing party into the hall, leaving Ptolemy's body to the care of the embalmers.

'You are sure, my Queen,' she whispered to her as they went, 'about making me . . . ?'

'My vizier? Very sure, Charmion. You have been my truest help and I will need all your skills now.'

'They are few, my Queen, but they are, of course, at your service.'

'Not queen yet,' Cleopatra reminded her but Charmion just smiled.

Word had spread through the city and the crowds flocked behind Mardion and Achillas as they escorted the royal will from the Serapeum to be read in the very hall in which Berenice had staged her coup four years ago and Cleopatra had been forced to flee for her life on the heels of her royal father.

Today, that father's will, read out by a furious Potheinos, pronounced her as Queen Cleopatra VI. Charmion ordered copies distributed throughout the land and Potheinos had to lead her out before the people to announce the new order for Egypt. Cleopatra stood, with Ptolemy-Theos on one side, Arsinoë on the other, and little Ptolemy-Philopater sucking his thumb in front, and knew it was her time to lead the sibling-loving gods. She just prayed to Isis within that she could do a better job than Berenice.

Chapter Fifteen

Cleopatra,

I miss you so. It's not the same without my dear friend to chat to, though I imagine you would be too busy to chat with a little old governor's wife like me now that you are Queen of Egypt. Queen! It sounds so grand, which is to say, it is so grand. But, then, you always radiated something special. Was that the Goddess inside you, do you think? Is she still there? Does she get bigger now that you are officially crowned? Sorry — you must think me very stupid but, as you well know, we don't have queens in Rome so I am quite the ignoramus on the subject.

Not that I am in Rome anymore. Did anyone tell you? Brutus is Governor of Cilicia this year so we are living in a divine little place called Tarsus, just up the coast from you in Alexandria, or so it looks on the maps, though Brutus tells me it is still some days' sail, which is a shame as it would be wonderful to visit. I love it here. It's so much prettier than Rome, though quiet. I would like to hold parties worthy of my family but Brutus says we are in a position of responsibility and must not be seen to be too extravagant. He can be such a spoilsport sometimes.

Mind you, I am told we are best off away from Rome for there was chaos at the latest elections. Clodius and Milo raised their gangs again and then stupid Clodius went and got himself stabbed to death and Fulvia paraded his slashed body around the forum in protest and everything got even more heated. It all comes from poor Julia dying in childbirth, bless her soul. She was the glue that held Caesar and Pompey together. A cow-eyed, simpering sort of glue, to be sure, but a glue all the same and now the two men bicker over everything and the city is divided with them.

I swear Pompey is jealous because Julius is hailed a hero for making it onto the dark shores of Britannia. He sent reports back describing the fierce blue-painted people and the wild countryside in the most lurid detail and everyone devoured them. It quite put Pompey's stupid big nose out of joint and now they are fighting again because Julius wants to be consul next year and Pompey doesn't want him to, or some such thing. You know politics has never been my strong point.

Brutus says I am slow-witted, which is probably true. He says it kindly, but I think it irritates him, especially because I cannot even produce a child. I have tried all the tricks Clodia recommended, though I fear I am not quite flexible enough to do some of them justice and I felt very stupid with honey in my ... well, you know, but nothing is working. What do women do in Egypt? I feel sure you must have the answers and this poor, barren Roman needs them for I would so love a baby. And so would Brutus.

Write soon, your majesty (is that right?)

All my love,
Claudia

Cleopatra smiled as she clutched Claudia's scrawl of a scroll to her chest, picturing her friend's perky features and hearing her voice as vividly as if she were here speaking the letter into her ear. Save that if she were here, she would be horrified at what Cleopatra was about to endure.

'Marry *him*?' Cleopatra could imagine her saying. 'But he's your brother! And he's only eight. And, besides, he's an irritating, snotty little brat.'

'You're so right, Claudie,' she said out loud and Eiras leaned forward from where she was twisting her hair into an elaborate knot.

'Did you say something, my queen?'

Cleopatra sighed.

'Nothing of importance. Eiras, do you know any cures for infertility?'

'You are not thinking of—'

'No, no, no. Not with my brother. It is not for me but for Claudia, whose womb is proving reluctant.'

'Poor woman. I believe the oil of poppy seeds can help. I could make some for you?'

'That would be wonderful. Claudia deserves to be happy.' Pictures leaped into her mind of the day of her friend's wedding in Baiae four summers ago. She could see the roses on the water, the altar set up before the beautiful bay, Claudia fretting over her hair, desperate to look beautiful for the groom she loved. It would not be the same for Cleopatra.

'Oh Eiras, I cannot wait to get this day over with.'

Eiras stroked comforting fingers down her neck and across her shoulders, gently kneading at the tension within them.

'Think of it as just another ceremony, Princess. We all know that the marriage is for show only. You are not going to be bedded with your brother, nor to form any sort of true partnership.'

'So what is the point of this sham?' Cleopatra ground her teeth in frustration. Eiras' wedding to Cinna had been beautiful – far quieter than today's grand ceremony, but rich with a love that had sparkled more than any gold. She envied her. 'I'm all for the Egyptian traditions, but perhaps it's time to move on from this one. I need a true husband to give Egypt an heir.'

'An heir who would secure the throne.'

'Exactly! I'm stuck, Eiras.'

'You're eighteen, my queen. There's plenty of time. Let us focus on ruling Egypt for things are unsettled around the Green Sea.'

Cleopatra looked curiously at her in the mirror.

'In what way?'

'Rome brawls with itself constantly. Cinna's poet friends write and even they are distracted from eulogising over women by the dissension on the streets. There has been talk of . . . ' she leaned in to whisper, 'civil war.'

'No!' Cleopatra spun round to stare at her friend. 'Rome would not do that to itself.'

'You think Egypt the only country foolish enough to fight over who is in charge?'

'Of course not, but in Rome no one person is in charge. Is that not the point of their damned republic?'

Eiras gave a dark laugh.

'In theory, my queen, yes, but in practice, as we both know, the men at the top carry all in their wake. This time there are two men wanting to be at the top and their wakes are colliding into a big wave that may sweep across the whole city.'

Cleopatra squinted at her.

'You've been around poets too long, Eiras, though I fear you are right. Well, perhaps it will keep them too busy to come bothering us for we have problems of our own.' She looked to Charmion. 'How is the Nile?'

'This is hardly the day to concern yourself with the Nile, my queen.'

'This is precisely the day to concern myself with it. I cannot be Egypt's queen without Isis pouring her blessings on us. So, how is the Nile?'

Her vizier shifted.

'The inundation is slow to begin.'

Cleopatra put her head in her hands.

'Today is the Ides of August so we are already ten days past the rising of Serius. That means the inundation is long overdue. Where is it up to?'

Charmion swallowed.

'Thirteen cubits, my queen.'

'Thirteen! If it stays that way, it means starvation for half our people.'

'Two thirds,' Charmion mumbled.

'Sorry.'

'Records tell us that below fourteen cubits means around two thirds of our people will not have enough grain to last to the next harvest.'

Cleopatra leaped up.

'What does this say? Isis cannot approve of my marriage. She cannot be happy with it.'

'Is that what she's telling you?'

Both women looked intently at Cleopatra and she strode to the window-opening to avoid their searching gazes for if Isis was within her, she could not feel Her, nor hear Her voice. 'What would Isis do?' Clodia had said to her, but with the sort of blithe insouciance of a woman who only ever asked the Goddess' opinion on choice of clothing or lovers. Cleopatra was expected to translate Her wishes for a whole country, but she could hear nothing over the roar of courtiers, priests and people.

She looked out at the guests gathering on the steps of the glorious Theatre of Dionysus in their brightest finery. All the top scholars from the Museon were here, all the richest and most influential people in Alexandria, all the ambassadors from countries vital to Egypt, all the priests of the most important temples, including those of her mother's at Memphis.

'We cannot back out of the marriage now,' she said firmly. 'The ceremony must go ahead and we must take the chance to talk to as many of our gracious guests as possible for we will need allies going forward. As for the inundations – what grain do we have in the royal granaries?'

'Plenty, my queen. Harvests have been good these last years and, as your father was kind enough to put me in charge of supplies,

I have ordered surplus sealed in jars for such times as these may turn out to be.'

Cleopatra turned back to her vizier.

'You, Charmion, are a marvel and I will see you well rewarded.'

'Egypt living in prosperity is all the reward I need, as long as they know that it is to you they owe their salvation and not to that slimy toad Potheinos.'

Cleopatra laughed. Potheinos had created himself the position of Vizier-to-the-King and Charmion's hatred for the man trying to set himself against her was, if possible, even greater than her own. She delighted in besting him whenever possible and it seemed that today might be one of those days.

'I will see the grain relief announced,' she said, 'and be sure it is credited to those who have worked for it. Now, come – it is time for me to take a groom.' She pulled a face but then Eiras held up a mirror and she saw herself painted and dressed as the Goddess incarnate and smiled. The lines of kohl were more dramatic than ever and for this, her show of a wedding day, Eiras had mixed powdered gold into both her eyeshadow and the ochre dust along her cheekbones to make her shine like the sun. 'You are a marvel too, Eiras.'

Eiras gave a modest smile.

'Let's see that eight-year-old brat of a boy try and draw the eyes of the crowd standing next to you, my queen!'

Cleopatra nodded and set her head high as she moved towards the door to face the crowds. She was not so much marrying her brother today, as her country. This ceremony would cement her on her throne and make her strong enough to stand against enemies both beyond her borders and within. That should be more than enough for any woman.

Chapter Sixteen

Queen Cleopatra

Greetings to your gracious majesty from Lady Servilia, your admirer and, I hope, your friend. I trust Egypt prospers and know that you will do your best for the country that is honoured to have you rule over it. I remember you so vividly as a scared young girl chased into my home by the gangs of Rome. You were badly shaken but still ready to put your head up and reflect on what the experience meant for you.

'I have assumed people were put on earth to serve me,' you said that day, 'whereas in truth, if I ever wish to be a good ruler, I need to work out how to serve them.'

It was an astute observation at just fourteen and I can only imagine the woman you must have grown into now you have a chance to serve those people as their queen. Egypt is lucky – luckier than Rome, who tears herself apart daily. Julius wishes to return to stand as consul for next year, but Pompey is accusing him of war crimes against the Gauls (war crimes; imagine, after all he has done for the Empire!) and if he crosses the Pomerium, he will be arrested. It is a nonsense that deprives the city of a worthy ruler, and myself of much-needed company.

Perhaps I will visit you, Queen. The East, you know, holds a

fascination for us Romans. We are hungry for its riches and seduced
by its glamour though we rarely, it seems to me, understand its dangers.
The Governor of Syria, a fine young man called Cassius, has been
battling to repel an invasion by the dreaded Parthians. I am told it was
a brave campaign indeed for they are fierce horsemen with vicious long
bows that can shoot arrows into the enemy from an impossible distance.

Cassius was hailed as a hero but then who should turn up?
Bibulus! You remember Porcia's husband? He is a man not favoured
physically by the gods but audacious in pursuit of his own advantage.
He was arriving to take over from Cassius as governor and his
ridiculously enormous guard came across a detachment of fleeing
Parthians, sent them packing (hardly a tricky task seeing as they were
already destitute), and had the good fortune to find one of our stolen
Eagle standards hidden in the bottom of their packs.

Next thing Cassius knew, Bibulus was sending it off to Rome
and claiming to have single-handedly routed the Parthians and saved
Roman dignity in the East. The cheek of the man! Apparently he
arrived in Antioch wobbly with smugness and Porcia has been utterly
impossible, telling the whole court they have come to 'save them' and
setting herself up as some sort of queen. It is laughable, Cleopatra,
given her supposed republican sentiments, how swiftly she has adopted
the trappings of royalty. She has not, I think, learned the lessons that
you did here in Rome and I bless you in your rule and wish you the joy
of wielding power with compassion.

With very best wishes,
Servilia

'No.'

The refusal came out louder than Cleopatra had intended and
the roomful of courtiers and petitioners turned from their idle
chatter to stare. She touched her fingers to Servilia's letter, tucked
into the cushion of her throne, wishing she could bury herself in it
again but the harvest must be sorted.

'No?' Potheinos countered, every bit as loud. 'You will not

sanction King Ptolemy-Theos' generous proposal to ensure that all grain is shipped direct to Alexandria for the preservation of her dear people?'

A stir went round the room. Cleopatra glared at Potheinos.

'And the death of the rest of the population of Egypt,' she said curtly.

Potheinos gave a mock sigh.

'Any loss of life is, of course, tragic, but if there must be losses, then surely it is better that we lose simple peasants with few skills rather than the learned people working day and night to keep the country running smoothly?'

A murmur of agreement ran round the room full of 'learned' people. Cleopatra touched Servilia's letter again and fought to hold onto her patience. Power with compassion, she reminded herself, and rose to face the desert-weasel Vizier-to-the-King.

'Those simple peasants farm the grain, Potheinos. Without them, no one eats.'

'Anyone can farm grain.'

'Not if they are dead.'

This time Cleopatra had some murmurs of support. Potheinos' eyes narrowed.

'Not all of them will be lost and there is, after all, less grain to harvest anyway as Isis did not see fit to bless this, the first year of your reign, with her sacred tears.'

'Perhaps,' Cleopatra countered, 'Isis was so happy at this, the first year of *our* reign,' she gestured to her brother, sat amongst silken cushions, playing with a fluffed-up cat and paying not the slightest attention to the exchange, 'that she had few tears to shed. She will cry again, as she always does, but in the meantime it would surely be more efficient to let our citizens in Upper Egypt eat the grain from the fields whilst we in Lower Egypt eat the grain that has been stored here for just such an emergency.'

'You would make Alexandrians eat old grain?'

Noses wrinkled and Cleopatra glared at all her spoilt courtiers.

She knew she was running the risk of offending the volatile city mob, who had little capacity to see beyond their own marble walls. Already she had heard them muttering against her, stirred up by Potheinos' shadowy army of serpents. But she had sworn to listen to her people – *all* her people – and she must stick to what was right.

'I would offer Alexandrians the grain that my vizier has, with great foresight, stored for their benefit. It is, of course, up to them whether they wish to accept the gift.'

'But . . .'

Levi stepped forward. 'There is little point, surely, in wasting the country's resources by shipping one set of grain up the Nile, only for it to cross with another set going down?'

Potheinos glowered.

'How would you know, Jew? You cannot possibly understand Egypt.'

'But I can understand basic economics and as Chancellor this falls firmly within my remit. The cost of the ships will be an added burden to your people, which you surely do not want?'

Potheinos opened his mouth to answer but even he could not find a way to refute such clear logic. Cleopatra smiled at Levi. Her newly appointed chancellor was proving increasingly useful as he got to grips with the tangles of Egyptian bureaucracy. All trade and agriculture was controlled from the palace, seed being issued from the royal barns and the harvest collated in them so that tax could be accurately collected from every farmer and trader along the route. Levi had been astonished at the complexity of the system and had spent hours with Sosigenes working it all out, but he was rapidly getting to grips with it – and ironing out some of the unnecessary twists as well.

'Thank you, Levi,' she said. 'See it done, please, Charmion.'

Charmion bowed and brought forward a papyri for Cleopatra to inscribe the decree.

'You would issue this order now?' Potheinos demanded shrilly. 'On your own authority?'

'On our joint authority, as always.'

'King Ptolemy does not agree,' Potheinos spluttered but Cleopatra was already before her brother with the paper.

'Sign this please, Ptolemy.'

'Why?'

'Because if you do, you can have my share of the rosewater cream at dinner tonight.'

He took the quill and lazily scrawled his signature before Potheinos could find any valid way to stop him. Cleopatra retook her throne and smiled sweetly at him.

'I'm so glad this is sorted. And you must agree that it is excellent that Charmion saw fit to secure supplies. Imagine if we had simply bartered them away to foreign lands in exchange for political favours.'

'Political favours we could now call in by demanding grain.'

Cleopatra shook her head.

'From where, Potheinos? There is a shortage of grain across the East, as you would know if you talked to all the wise ambassadors in our court as I do.'

Potheinos glowered. He spoke only Greek and whilst most of the countries bordering the Green Sea favoured that language, those further afield preferred their own. Interpreters could be found but they were costly and unreliable, usually so scared of their employers that they translated everything in their favour, which was of little practical use. The only sure way was to learn their languages yourself but that Potheinos was far too lazy to do.

'You speak in tongues,' he said petulantly.

'I speak in *their* tongues,' Cleopatra corrected him. 'And write in their languages.'

Potheinos' dark eyes gleamed suddenly.

'You write? To whom?'

'To anyone of diplomatic interest to Egypt. To ambassadors and rulers and friends.'

'And all these letters go through the court for approval, do they?'

'All official ones, yes.'

'And unofficial ones?'

Again she touched her fingers to Servilia's letter, feeling its quiet power run through her.

'Those are just to other women,' she said with a casual wave of her hand. 'Trifles. Talk of babies and gowns, no more. And if I pick up snippets of information along the way, then it is mere idle gossip, of no interest to sensible men.'

Potheinos shifted and she knew she had him. He loved to parade her femininity as evidence of her weak nature and poor grasp of vital issues, so he could scarcely contradict her when she claimed it herself, even if he knew as keenly as she the value of that 'idle gossip' in keeping up with events across the world. Rome, it seemed, was in uproar and she prayed to Isis every day that it would keep them from her own shores.

'Now,' she said, turning to the queue of petitioners, 'who is next?'

A man stepped forward and dropped to one knee before her.

'I come, Queen Cleopatra, to seek audience with you for my masters.'

'And who are they?'

'They are the honoured sons of Marcus Cornelius Bibulus, Governor of the Roman Province of Syria.'

A ripple of interest went around the assembled crowd and Cleopatra felt her throat tighten. She remembered Calpurnia mentioning that Bibulus had adult sons that very first time she'd met Porcia but what were they doing here? Was this what Servilia had been trying to warn her of? Bibulus had ridden into the East to steal Cassius' achievements and now he was sending his sons to Alexandria.

'Why do they seek audience?'

'On matters of urgent military business.'

The crowd's whispers turned to low mutterings and Cleopatra knew she had to act fast.

'Then send them in.'

The crowd parted as two men were let into the chamber and walked quietly towards Cleopatra and Ptolemy. Cleopatra felt Charmion tighten in at her right shoulder and Mardion at her left. Potheinos brushed something from his tunic and even Ptolemy looked up from his pet cat. The men were in warrior's tunics and simple boots. They had sword belts but had left their weapons at the door and, as they reached the dais, they bowed elegantly low.

'Marcus Bibulus,' one of them introduced himself. 'And this is my brother Gaius Bibulus. We come on behalf of our father to offer greetings to Egypt's queen and king.'

'That is most gracious of you,' Cleopatra said in Latin. 'I hear your father has had some success against the Syrians. An eagle standard re-captured, I believe?'

'Indeed,' Marcus agreed. 'He had some luck in finding it but luck is only of use to the man who seizes it.'

That much was true and Cleopatra said so at some length, very much enjoying Potheinos' frowns as he struggled to make out the Latin. The sun was heading downwards and she dismissed the rest of the petitioners until tomorrow and ordered refreshments for their Roman guests. She wasn't sure what they wanted, but she knew she must tread very carefully.

'Was it a hard journey from Syria?' she asked as Eiras served wine and sweetmeats.

The men exchanged looks.

'We've had easier,' Gaius told her, 'but it was worth it to see the beauty of Alexandria – and of her queen.'

He shot her a meaningful look and Cleopatra felt heat flood through her.

'My brother-husband and I are delighted to receive you,' she said formally, then felt ridiculously stiff and leaned forward to add, 'I met your father a few times when I was in Rome – his wife too.'

Gaius rolled his eyes.

'Poor you.'

Marcus nudged him frantically but Cleopatra seized on the

comment. It seemed these sons of Bibulus were not cut from quite the same cloth as their father.

'The Lady Porcia has very high values.'

'And loves to push them onto others,' Gaius agreed. 'She gets it from her uncle Cato who will never rest until all Rome is as tight-lipped – and tight-arsed – as he.'

'Gaius!' poor Marcus squeaked, but Gaius just grinned. It was an infectious smile and Cleopatra found herself returning it.

'Cato received my royal father and me on the latrine, you know,' she said.

'No!' Marcus looked shocked.

'The man is a boor,' Gaius told her. 'With so gracious a guest, he should have been on his knees wiping your feet, not his own arse.'

'Gaius!'

Cleopatra waved away Marcus' scarlet-faced protest.

'Fret not, please. Cato and Porcia are held in very rigid lines by their republican principles. I am sure it is most uncomfortable for them.'

Gaius grinned again.

'And for anyone near them. The other day, Marcus' wife offered Porcia a place on an outing to the astounding Hanging Gardens on the banks of the Euphrates. They are one of the wonders of the world, you know, like your Pharos, but Porcia refused the trip on the grounds that they are a "royal decadence".'

Cleopatra shook her head.

'Our line of Ptolemy is not the same as that of the Pharaohs who built the pyramids but that does not mean we cannot revere their achievements and embrace their legacy.'

'Well said, your majesty.'

'I trust your wife enjoyed the trip, Marcus?'

'She did, your majesty, very much.'

'And, er, your wife, Gaius? Did she go too?'

She felt foolish asking the question but Gaius held her gaze in his own, hazel-brown one and said, 'Sadly I have no wife – yet.'

Again, the hall seemed to gain in heat. Cleopatra stared at Bibulus' younger son. Was he flirting with her, the Queen of Egypt? She should be shocked at his insolence but it was far too pleasant to object. She glanced around and saw Arsinoë hanging off Achillas' arm. Her sister was always to be found with the general these days and recently a report had come in that his wife had died, apparently of a contagion. Achillas wore the dark tunic of mourning but seemed to derive much comfort from his pet princess and the pair were forever holding parties in the palace. Cleopatra would hear the revelry when she lifted her head from business at dusk, but was usually too tired to go and join in.

No doubt they talked about her in her absence but there was only so much she could manage and with the pressing matter of the famines to address, missing parties seemed the least of her worries. Suddenly, though, as she looked into Gaius' handsome face, she felt the sting of her solitary life. She was bound to Ptolemy-Theos but gained no company or support from him. Arsinoë grew daily more beautiful and more bold. Cleopatra had tried hard to marry her off to a suitably lowly man but she had resisted with heartfelt pleas.

'I am in love, Petra,' she would moan every time she made a suggestion, and whilst Achillas had been married, Cleopatra had thought that safe enough. Now, though, it was different. If, when Achillas' mourning ended, she sought permission to marry him, she could produce babies – powerful little Egyptian babies that, supported by the leader of the military, might suggest she were a better prospect for the throne.

Cleopatra shuddered. She was, it seemed, a prisoner of her non-marriage, although if she were to take a lover, she might gain an heir of her own. She looked again at Gaius. He was handsome enough, with an innate confidence that made him very attractive, and was here as her guest. If she issued an invitation to her bed, he was almost honour-bound to accept and then he would knock on her door and come into her room and he would take off his tunic and . . .

'All well, my queen?'

It was Charmion, leaning over to check upon her. Cleopatra shook the wanton thoughts away, horrified at letting herself wander with half the court watching.

'Quite well. Now,' she said, switching smoothly to Greek, 'you must tell us what it is that you seek in our kingdom?'

Gaius blinked but Marcus was swift to match Cleopatra.

'We come, your majesty, to discuss the recall of the Roman troops from Alexandria.'

Cleopatra raised an eyebrow. The courtiers, who had grown bored when Cleopatra and Potheinos had stopped fighting, suddenly looked up again.

'Just to be clear,' Cleopatra said carefully, 'by "Roman troops" you mean the Syrian and Judean soldiers that Aulus Gabinius brought with him when my father was restored to his throne three years ago?'

Marcus cleared his throat.

'I do. We have need of them on home soil for things are ... unsettled in the city.'

'So I hear,' Cleopatra agreed. 'Pompey and Caesar are wrangling for power.'

They shifted, glanced at each other.

'There is some lively political debate on various matters,' Marcus said eventually.

'And warring in the streets?'

'No "warring", Queen, but, nonetheless, more troops are required.'

'Which is why we are here. Gabinius' troops marched into Egypt as part of a Roman fighting force and were left here as peace-keepers.'

'They marched into Egypt as part of my father's fighting force and are paid from our royal treasury,' Cleopatra corrected him.

'A responsibility we will gladly relieve you of.'

He was quick, she'd give him that, but cheeky. With Caesar back in Gaul, Cato had led the senate in declaring the Egyptian mission illegal and recalled poor Aulus Gabinius to put him on trial for leaving his province to wage a private war. He was living in exile now but his troops – the Gabiniani as they'd become known – had very happily settled into the hotch-potch of Alexandrian life. Now there was a stir at the back of the room as Lucius Septimius, their leader, stepped forward.

'You can't make us go,' he said roughly. Cleopatra frowned at him and, with a shake of his head, he dropped to one knee and said, 'You can't make us go, your majesty.'

'You do not wish to be recalled to Roman service, Septimius?'

'No. And neither will my men. We live here. We have wives, children. We have been promised citizenship.'

That much was true. With no trouble from the mob, the Gabiniani had occupied themselves building homes in place of their military tents and finding local women for their beds. Three years on, they were as much a part of the city as the other immigrants who filled Alexandria with so much noise and colour. And yet, they were at least nominally here by permission of the Roman state so it was hard to know their exact status.

'What do you think, Potheinos?' Cleopatra asked, knowing that whatever opinion she expressed he would oppose. At least if she asked him first, he had to pin his colours to the mast.

'I think it is a matter of royal discretion, my Queen.'

Damn him.

'I see. Ptolemy – what do you think?'

Her brother looked up from feeding a poor spider to his cat.

'About what?'

'About whether the soldiers who came with Father and me to Rome should have to return.'

'To Rome? I don't know. If they want to, I suppose.'

'We do not want to,' Septimius said firmly.

'Then no.'

'But we want them to,' Marcus said, equally firmly.

Ptolemy considered him.

'Are they your slaves?'

'Not slaves, no, but servants perhaps.'

'Because you pay them?'

'No. *You* pay them, for now, but . . .'

'Well, if I pay them, then they are *my* servants. What will you want next, my crown? The clothes off my back? My cat?!'

'Oh no, your majesty,' Potheinos said slyly, 'we all know how Romans treat cats.'

The crowd tittered and Marcus and Gaius looked nervously at one another.

'My father gave specific instructions that the Alexandrian legion is to be recalled,' Marcus said to Cleopatra, his voice hardening. 'As this is a legion that was provided to your father in exchange for funds not yet repaid, it should be considered as collateral.'

'They are individual people, Marcus Bibulus, not simply "a legion".'

He frowned at her.

'In Rome, to be a part of a legion is considered a greater thing than to be an individual.'

'But these men are not in Rome any more. In truth, few of them ever have been. Septimius perhaps and, as you see, he likes it in the East.'

'And who can blame him,' Gaius said smoothly, half an eye on the burly warrior, who'd been joined by a number of his fellows. 'Perhaps this is something we could discuss when you have all had time to think about it. Tomorrow maybe?'

'Good idea.' To Cleopatra's surprise it was Arsinoë who stepped in. 'Sister?'

Arsinoë inclined her head graciously.

'It grows late in the day and no time for politics. Surely it would be better to hold an official meeting when all have had time to reflect on the situation?'

'I agree,' Cleopatra said cautiously.

Arsinoë offered her sweetest smile.

'We can surely accommodate these two young men in the guest rooms and they can dine with us tonight. It will be very pleasant to have some company, will it not?'

Cleopatra saw Achillas stiffen and realised that her sister's suggestion had nothing to do with politics and everything to do with making her lover jealous, perhaps to hasten his mourning period to its end. Well, fine – two could play at that game. She glanced at Gaius from beneath her lashes. He really was quite handsome, for a Roman.

'I shall have two of our finest chambers prepared this instant,' she said. 'If, of course, you are willing?'

The Bibulus brothers scrambled to confirm that they were, and Gaius favoured her with a slow smile that set something stirring in her belly, or perhaps lower. One word and he could be in her bed tonight. She was nineteen, she had been supposedly married for eight months, and she had never known the act of love. Rome had come calling and with cunning she could turn this to her advantage. She glanced to the statue of Isis – perhaps the Goddess had known what she was doing in bringing these men here after all.

'I am sure we can offer you an entertaining evening,' she said.

Gaius bowed low.

'You are too kind, your majesty.'

Cleopatra paced her bedchamber. She was all alone. Eiras had plaited her hair for the night and gone to her apartment with Cinna. Charmion and Mardion were in their own quarters, the two Ptolemies safely in their wing on the far side of the palace, and the Roman guests just down the corridor. All it would take was a word to one of the guards outside her door . . . She looked at the note in her hand.

Come and see me.

No more, no less. One night of pleasure, surely she deserved that? And this young man looked more than capable of giving pleasure. She pictured the gleam in his eye as he'd smiled at her and let a hand slide down her own skin, imagining it were his.

'Ridiculous, Petra,' she scolded herself, pulling it away. This was Bibulus' son; Porcia's stepson. He was a Roman and a cocky one at that, to be making eyes at a queen like herself. And yet ... No one need know. The men on her door were her sworn protectors and would guard her secrets, and if she had a child, well, it would be a happy miracle.

'What would Isis do?' she muttered.

She thought of Clodia and took a decisive step towards the door. At that moment, however, someone cried out from elsewhere in the palace. It was a yell of fear, bubbling into one of pain and was swiftly followed by a second. Cleopatra darted to the door but before she could get there it was flung open and her bodyguards were upon her, pushing her against the wall and forming a protective ring, swords poised against any attack.

'What's happening?' she demanded.

'We'll keep you safe, oh queen,' was the useless answer.

'Who is hurt?'

'Not you.'

They were single-minded in their devotion and she appreciated it, but she needed news. Someone else burst into the room and they lifted their swords.

'It's me!' the figure squeaked, high-pitched with more than just fear.

'Mardion!' Cleopatra reached a hand through the ring and, with a worried look at her burly protectors, he let himself be pulled through to join her. 'What's happening?'

He bit his lip.

'It's not good news, Cleopatra.'

'Ptolemy? Arsinoë?'

'No, no. Your royal siblings are all safe. It's the Romans, the two young envoys. They're ... they're dead.'

'What?!'

'Come and see.'

He ushered her along her private corridor towards the scene of the crime, the guards bristling protectively around them. She walked slowly, trying to compose herself, but the corridor had not yet been built long enough to prepare her for the sight that met her eyes when she stepped into the main courtyard. The two brothers were tangled together, their throats slit and their blood running across the tiles like an artist had gone mad.

'What happened?' she demanded furiously.

Mardion gestured to the general palace guards, huddled nervously on the far side.

'They say the Romans got aggressive, drew their swords, threatened them.'

Cleopatra turned her back on them to afford herself and Mardion a little privacy.

'And really?'

'And really Septimius' men must have got to them. Someone let them into the palace and someone lured the Romans out here. And now ...'

Cleopatra looked down at the slit throats and felt bile rise in her own. She remembered Achillas' dark eyes as Arsinoë had entertained their guests with her finest wit and most beguiling smiles and had little doubt who had let the murderers into the palace.

'Watch for snakes,' her father had cautioned on his deathbed and she had a horrible feeling that this dark night was stirring up the viper's nest. She had no idea if Achillas had acted from petty spite or wider treachery but one thing she was sure of – he had created trouble indeed. She clutched at Mardion's hand.

'These weren't any old Romans, Mardion. This wasn't some chance envoy kicking a cat in the street. These were important men, sons of an even more important man. Rome will not let this go. They are torn up by their own troubles and will seize on an external enemy, for little unites people more than a threat from without. If we don't act fast, Bibulus and Porcia will set the whole might of the Roman provinces upon us and Egypt will be sucked into the Republic before we can so much as bury these poor men.'

She looked to the bodies. Gaius' eyes were wide open, staring in horror at the gaping hole of the afterlife, but she could still picture them sparkling with mischief at dinner and sorrow flooded over her. If she'd only sent her note earlier, then he at least would have been saved this treachery. She stepped up to the guards.

'Are the palace gates shut?'

'Of course, your majesty. When an alarm sounds, they are barred immediately.'

'Good. Wake everyone in the palace. I want the murderers caught and I want them shipped to Syria to answer to their victims' father.'

'Cleopatra,' Mardion said, tugging at her arm. 'Are you sure that is wise? The men will be angry.'

Cleopatra shook her head sadly.

'Perhaps, Mardion, but not half as angry as the Romans will be and, trust me, we cannot afford to bring that upon us. Wake everyone in the palace – now!'

She felt furious that Rome had the power to disrupt her rule and that her own people were so willingly handing them the tools with which to do so. Footsteps sounded down the corridors of the palace as people began to emerge. Potheinos was first, Achillas at his heel, both of them rubbing apparent sleep from suspiciously bright eyes as they exclaimed loudly at the sight of the bodies in the heart of the palace. There was no sign of either of the Ptolemies, snoozing peacefully far from this dark tableau, but Arsinoë made her entrance, barefoot and lithe in a gauzy nightdress. Gasping theatrically, she fell into an elegant faint, conveniently close enough to Achillas for him to catch her before she hit the blood-spattered tiles.

Cleopatra looked around at them all and took a step closer to

Mardion. The dagger had found Roman hearts tonight but she feared their blood had only whetted its appetite. With Rome squabbling, the Nile at its lowest ebb, and the mob muttering about their grain, she must watch for snakes indeed.

Chapter Seventeen

FEBRUARY 49 BC

'Ptolemy! Ptolemy! Ptolemy!'

The crowds outside the palace walls were chanting louder and louder with every hour that passed and they were relentless. Last night they'd been rioting until the moon was almost heading to her rest and Cleopatra's ears were ringing with their calls for her brother – her useless, careless, self-centred brother. Potheinos' serpents had been crawling amongst them, spreading evil whispers about sub-standard grain and saying that the rest of Egypt was getting far better, and they had snatched on this unfairness like toddlers denied honey cakes.

They'd been ripe for rebellion and had risen up the moment Septimius, furious that she'd sent his murderous men for justice, had brought his Gabiniani out onto the streets. They were calling her a puppet of Rome, citing her Roman chancellor, her trip there as a child, and her 'many' Roman friends. If they met Claudia or Clodia, she'd thought, the first time she'd heard that particular accusation, they might realise they had little to fear, but Potheinos had been insidious in his propaganda and it seemed Berenice's long-ago coup still had the power to hurt her.

She'd tried sending out proclamations, addressing them direct and employing a few serpents of her own to spread positive counter-rumours but it seemed it was too late. She had foolishly assumed they would trust her to work for their good and had not asserted her position in time for them to be assured of it. She paced before her sister, who was reclining in the shade, seemingly oblivious to the hate echoing in over the high walls.

'How can I convince them I have their interests at heart?' she asked her.

Arsinoë waved a careless hand.

'Just sit tight, Sister, and they will surely come back to you. You know how fickle they are. Look at how they rose for Berenice and then, barely a year later, roared with joy at her execution.'

Cleopatra shivered at the memory.

'It was awful.'

'Awful,' Arsinoë agreed calmly. Cleopatra peered at her and she shrugged her slim shoulders. 'I was young. The memory has been wiped out by having your happy rule instead of hers.'

'Not so happy now,' she grumbled.

'They're just hungry. Pray Isis will cry her tears this year, for a good harvest will mean all is forgotten. Why not take that trip up the Nile you've always wanted? Is the new Apis bull not due for consecration in Memphis? That would be a noble duty for a queen and would give the tempestuous capital time to calm down.'

'Do you think so?'

'You are always telling me that you are Queen of all Egypt, Petra, so why do you only rule from Alexandria?'

Cleopatra jumped at her sister's criticism, but Arsinoë had a good point. If she took a trip up the Nile she could see the rest of her nation, and perhaps even meet her mother. It was an enticing thought, especially with the spoilt Alexandrians shouting her down at all hours.

'Could we prepare the royal barge?' she asked Charmion.

'Of course, my queen, though we may need the city to settle a little before we leave so as not to look unnerved.' Cleopatra nodded. It was such a wretchedly fine line between offending the mob and appeasing them. 'And I'm afraid there is another Roman envoy at court.'

'Another one?! Do I have to see him?' Charmion did not even grace that with an answer. 'Fine. Did he give a name?'

'Marcus Junius Brutus.'

Cleopatra gasped.

'Brutus?'

'You know him?'

'Very well. Is he alone?'

'He is, my queen.'

Cleopatra sighed. For a moment she'd thought she might see her dear Claudia but, no, it was just her friend's husband. What on earth could that mean? Suddenly she was keen to find out.

'Call him in.'

Charmion waved to the guards and she and Mardion came to quietly stand at her shoulder. Levi, calculating grain release at a table nearby, rose to join them. It was midday and the noise from the mob outside had dropped as everyone went to seek shade and sustenance but they would be back in full force once the sun began to dip. Cleopatra felt her ears ringing with their hatred and wondered how Brutus had got through their ranks – and what he would make of them.

'Brutus!'

'Cleopatra.'

He crossed the hall to stand before her and inclined his head but stood stiffly unbowed, a pose she remembered well from their previous encounters as the opposing forces of politeness and principle pulled him apart in her presence. Brutus was like a civil war within himself, so thoughtful that he could see the merit of every idea and philosophy and struggled to ever truly espouse one. She had seen him torn between Cato and the Claudii, between the Optimates and the Populares, between tradition and innovation.

'*Queen* Cleopatra,' she corrected him gently. 'Surely I am allowed my title on my own soil?'

'And surely, I am allowed to address you as a friend and not merely a ruler?'

She conceded the point.

'Wine?' She waved a server forward and Brutus took a cup and perched awkwardly on a couch. She took her own place opposite and leaned forward. 'Lovely as it is to see you, *friend*, I fear this is not just a social call.'

Brutus swallowed, his Adam's apple bobbing in his throat as if trapped.

'You have heard the news from Rome?'

'That she is tearing herself apart over politics as usual?'

'That she is at war.'

Cleopatra gasped.

'Truly?'

'Truly. Julius Caesar crossed the Rubicon river with his troops two weeks ago and marched on Rome. Pompey has disbanded the senate and fled to Capua, leaving all men to choose their side.'

'And all women to be stuck in the middle?'

'And all women to loyally follow their husbands.'

'Of course. So your mother . . . ?'

'Does as she pleases, as always.'

'Which is?'

'For now she is staying in Rome.'

'With Caesar?'

'Not with Caesar,' he said touchily, 'for he is chasing after Pompey. He has put his friend Marcus Aemilius Lepidus in charge of the city and Mother is, no doubt, helping him keep order.'

Cleopatra smiled.

'No doubt. And you, Brutus?'

He fidgeted with his wine cup, turning it round and round in his hands and peering into the ruby depths as if they might contain the answers he sought.

'I am here.'

'You are here for whom?'

He shuffled his feet like a child.

'I am here on Pompey's orders.'

'I see.'

'Although I will admit that does not sit easy with me. He killed my father.'

'I remember. It seems a strange recommendation for your loyalty.'

'He stands for the Republic. For order, for law.'

Cleopatra considered this.

'I met Caesar only once, Brutus, but he seemed to me a man most passionate about the Republic.'

'I know!' Brutus bleated. 'I know that. But he is the aggressor. He crossed the Rubicon. He marched on Rome.'

'Because they were denying him entry, despite his many years of service to the Empire.'

Brutus' eyes narrowed.

'How do you know that?'

'Oh Brutus, I am a queen, a ruler. It is my job to know what goes on elsewhere, especially when it is Rome, for her troubles rarely stay within her own boundaries.'

'That's not—'

'Why are you here?'

He drained the rest of the wine and sat up ramrod straight, like an actor on the stage.

'Pompey wishes you to loan him ships, and men to crew them. He wishes to remind you of his kindness to you and your father in your hour of need and asks that you repay that kindness in his.'

'With ships to sail against the man who allied with him in that kindness?'

'Caesar did not house you for a year.'

'True and I am ever grateful to Pompey and would gladly house him in return if he is in need. But I do not seek war and am reluctant to be dragged into another's conflict.'

Brutus cleared his throat.

'I was told to remind you that Egypt is still in debt to Rome to the sum of several thousand sesterces.'

'And these ships will repay that debt?'

'These ships will go some way towards repaying that debt, yes.'

'Unless Julius Caesar wins, in which case they will doubtless increase it.'

Brutus sighed. 'It is a tricky dilemma, is it not?'

'A tricky dilemma at a tricky time for me personally.' She gestured to the walls, beyond which the mob had returned, although the sun was still high. 'What's set them off again?' she asked Charmion.

Her vizier went up the side stairs to one of the many balconies that looked out over the city. She stared down a moment and then turned back in.

'I believe, my queen, it will be the three Roman galleons in the harbour mouth that have angered the people.'

Cleopatra looked to Brutus.

'You came with warships?'

'Of course. It's dangerous out there.'

'I know!'

Within the palace she could heard doors opening and closing, footsteps making hurried paths between the wings, and she knew that Potheinos would be quick to make the most of this precarious situation. She paced the room, trying to decide what to do and then, clear as a bell over the general roar, a voice called, 'Down with the Roman-loving queen!'

Cleopatra clenched her fists in a fury.

'You see!' she shouted at Brutus. 'You see what your arrival here has done to me. First Bibulus' damned sons and now you. I wish my father had never gone to Rome. I wish we'd never thrown ourselves on your calculated mercy.'

'And yet you did.'

'And it will be the death of me. Do you want that, Brutus? Do you want to tell your wife that your demand for ships for the man who killed your father, had her friend killed as well?'

Brutus sucked in a sharp breath and stood abruptly.

'I do not want that, Cleopatra, as I hope you know, but service of the Republic is about more than individual desires. It is about the greater good, the health of the whole. Julius has been too long in the dark lands and thinks he is a warrior-king, like the legends of old. That is dangerous and must be stopped, whatever the personal sacrifice.'

'You would have him dead?' He bit his lip but nodded. 'And your mother's heart broken?'

'Mother's heart is strong.'

'As is mine. What if I refuse you these ships?'

He shrugged.

'Then we shall take them anyway. And the rest of Egypt besides.'

Cleopatra shook her head slowly.

'And you say you came as a friend, Brutus.'

'It seems, Queen Cleopatra, that friendship is impossible in these times.'

'Not impossible, Brutus, if your loyalty is carved of rock not sand.' She strode across the room to stand between Charmion, Mardion and Levi. 'Take your ships, if you must, Governor, but know that when you sail them out of my harbour you are condemning me to sail from it too.'

'Because your people's loyalty is carved of sand?'

'Because I have not yet had time to turn that sand to rock and may now never do so. Give my love to your wife, Brutus, and ask her to pray for me – for I will need it.'

She swept to the door and he darted forward.

'Where are you going?'

'To my royal barge. Alexandria is no place for a "Roman-loving Queen" right now. Nor for that Roman either. Take your ships and leave.'

'Thank you.'

He bowed low and passed through the door as she held it open for him.

'Oh and Brutus . . .'

'Yes?'

'I fear you have chosen the wrong side.'

He frowned.

'My side has chosen me.'

'That is no excuse. Your precious Republic may be greater than the individual but the individual is free within it. That, Brutus, is democracy. Do not hide behind it.'

'No, Queen.'

He bowed, lower than she'd thought he knew how, and then was gone. She heard his feet rap across the courtyard towards the door and then a furious roar as he was let out. She hoped he had a good guard with him, or he would be dead before he could reach the water but, for now, she must look to her own safety.

'This seems to me to be a good time to visit Memphis, does it not?'

'An excellent time,' Arsinoë agreed. 'You will enjoy it.'

'You won't come with me?'

'To see your mother? No, Sister, but thank you.'

'It's not safe here.'

Arsinoë shrugged.

'It's not safe for *you*, Petra, but you need not worry about me. I have Achillas to keep me safe and I can keep reminding the people of your charms as their queen whilst you are away. *Temporarily* away.'

Cleopatra looked at her sister uncertainly. She did not want her suffering on her behalf but she had a powerful protector in the head of the army and, besides, she already knew from the set of Arsinoë's beautiful chin that she would not change her mind.

'Very well then,' she agreed, 'but you must join me if there is a threat to your safety.'

'It would be my honour. Safe trip, Sister, and I will see you soon.'

'I pray so,' Cleopatra agreed, keeping her voice calm, but as she followed Mardion towards one of his many tunnels, her legs shook more than they had done when she first fled the city seven years ago.

❖

She was on the deck of the great royal barge to see the first brand cast into the palace. She was high in the prow to watch the gates forced – with remarkable ease – and the mob rush in. She was in place to hear, on the still evening air, the cries of 'Kill the Roman collaborator,' and to watch with Charmion and Mardion, Eiras and Cinna, Levi and Sosigenes, as men with daggers stormed her home.

'They would have killed me,' she said, touching her fingers to her breast, feeling for the heartbeat beneath. She pictured the Roman she had seen torn apart as a child, she pictured Bibulus' sons, their blood splattered across her tiles, and she knew without a single doubt how this night would have ended had she stayed. The mob's cries tore through her, ringing with their brutal hatred. In Rome, she had sworn both to win Egypt back and to win her over, but although she had succeeded in the first, she had failed in the latter. No matter what clever machinations had stirred the Alexandrians up, the simple truth was that she had not been enough for them.

'Cast off!' Mardion was crying and, in the lower decks, her guards loosed the ropes that held them to the inland docks and long oars began to row them away from Alexandria.

Cleopatra watched the blazing lights of her home city and panicked. This was wrong. This was cowardly and selfish and not regal.

'I do not want to flee again,' she cried.

Charmion put an arm around her shoulders.

'You are not fleeing, my queen, but journeying. Your country is more than just its capital.'

Cleopatra suddenly remembered Berenice dismissing the 'hinterland' for being there only to provide 'grain and history'. She'd known her treacherous sister was wrong then, and now was her chance – albeit a bitter one – to prove her so. There was a reason she had learned Egyptian and she must use it to reach out to the rest of her nation. Pushing her chin up high, she set her face south to Isis, to Egypt, and to her mother.

Chapter Eighteen

MARCH 49 BC

They came to Memphis at dusk and the city rose up out of the waters of the blessed Nile as if crafted of purest gold. Cleopatra clutched at the railings of the upper deck and felt the Goddess within swelling to fill her soul. This was her mother's city; this was the ancient capital of an Egypt she had yearned to know, and it was beautiful.

The city walls stood white and clean above the river, the waters diverted to run around them like a verdant hem and within stood vast steps leading up to the famed Temple of Ptah. An avenue of sphinxes guarded the route and at the top, great colossi stood guard, faces glowing in the setting sun as they looked out from centuries of history and straight into Cleopatra's soul. The angry heat of Alexandria dropped from her and she felt a quieter warmth seep across every inch of her skin.

It had taken five days to sail here, the giant royal barge being too unwieldy to travel at any speed. The length of fifty men lying toe to toe, it had a lower deck for the rowers and staff and two floors for the bedrooms, living quarters and banqueting suites. On the main deck, where Cleopatra stood now, was a beautiful garden, with a shaded grotto, a viewing platform, and shrines to Isis and Osiris at either end. The bows were coated in polished ivory and black and white carved colonnades ran the length of the ship behind polished bronze rails. It was, she'd long been told, the most beautiful ship in the world and although she was unendingly glad of its comforts, she could see why her father had chosen to escape Alexandria in something less unwieldy for any smaller craft would catch them in moments.

Something less noticeable might have been wise too. All along their route, day and night, people had run to the banks to wave and cheer. It had been soothing to Cleopatra's soul, worn raw by the hatred of the Alexandrians, but had also meant that any pursuers on land would have little trouble in finding them. Cleopatra had spent the first day in an agony of fear, trying to smile and wave to the crowds, whilst scanning the lush horizon for any signs of Achillas or Septimius leading troops against her.

'No one would dare attack the queen in the royal barge,' Mardion had assured her time and again. 'The people would not stand for it.'

'The Alexandrians would.'

'We are not in Alexandria, my queen. You are amongst Egyptians now, amongst those who understand how to revere their pharaohs and keep them safe.'

As the hours had unfolded with no sign of pursuit, Cleopatra had started to believe him. Potheinos was happy to have driven her from the capital city and whilst she had no intention of remaining an exile, it was a problem to be resolved in time. For now, the people of Memphis were running to their elegant docks, calling her name to the golden skies and throwing flowers at the barge. Men were pulling leaves from palm trees to lay across the dock for her royal feet and the ancient city rang with joy.

'They love me,' Cleopatra whispered.

Below the barge, people were throwing themselves to the ground, forming a reverent human guard all along the route to the Temple of Ptah. The temple complex was built on the site where creation had begun, and was where pharaohs of old had been initiated with the double crown of Upper and Lower Egypt. The ancient name for the temple, Cleopatra knew from her studies, was Ai-gy-ptos: Egypt. She was at the very heart of her country and she raised her hands to embrace it.

Eiras was plucking nervously at her arm, muttering something about her hair, but Cleopatra didn't care for a group was emerging from the vast Temple entrance and processing towards the docks. The sliver of a Calends moon was rising in the darkening skies and they walked beneath large torches but the light was fickle and she strained to see if one of them was her mother.

'Cleopatra, please. You must dress to match the reverence of your welcome.'

She finally looked at Eiras, seeing the sense of this. The whole city was turning out to greet their queen and she must match their expectations.

'There's no time.'

'There's always time. You are the queen. Hurry.'

Cleopatra glanced once more to the procession. They were moving slowly, allowing those busy about the final tasks of the day to flock to the docks, and she let herself be hurried below deck. Eiras set about her make-up with lightning speed, whilst Mardion rummaged in the royal closet, drawing out her tightest, most traditional white sheath, and Charmion fetched a golden collar and belt.

Within minutes, Cleopatra was stood with her hair in an elegant roll at the nape of her neck and her simple diadem replaced by the traditional crown of sun disc, cobra-head and ox's horns. Cleopatra had only worn it a handful of times and it had always felt unwieldy but here in Memphis, towered over by ancient statuary and tombs, it was perfect, and she pushed her head up high as the frenzy of the crowds outside told them the procession was close.

'Will my mother be there?' she dared to ask Charmion.

'Not in the procession for she is sworn to dwell always with the gods, but in the Temple, yes. You will see her very soon. For now, though, your people await.'

Cleopatra nodded and headed for the doors of the great barge. She'd left Alexandria in fear, chased by shouts of hatred; she was arriving at Memphis to adoration. The guards flung the doors back and cheers rang out from the great crowds below and echoed off the dizzying heights of Memphis' vast monuments.

'Welcome, most glorious queen!' the High Priest boomed and she lifted her hands in acknowledgement and headed (slowly, for the sheath was impossible to move in and she dare not trip and spoil the scene) down the gangplank to join him.

The torchlit procession from barge to temple took a long time but Cleopatra gloried in it.

'How many people live here?' she asked the High Priest in tentative Egyptian.

He looked at her in surprise, then bowed low and replied in the same tongue.

'Six hundred and twenty thousand at the last count, my queen. Plus ten thousand within the temple complex.'

'Ten thousand?'

'The gods must be honoured.'

'Of course. I am keen to meet all worshippers, but especially . . .'

'The Priestess Safira?'

'My mother?'

'Your mother,' he confirmed softly. 'She will be with you shortly but first let us make our obeisance to the great gods who have brought you to us.'

He turned her gently at the temple entrance, sat her on a golden throne and led ostentatious prayers to more roars of approval. Cleopatra looked around her with tears in her eyes, but then a movement behind the myriad torches of the temple caught her eye. She thought at first there was a mirror behind the colonnades but

168

when the onyx-haired figure raised a quiet hand, she knew that this was the Priestess Safira. Raising a hand in return, she felt the Goddess swell within her once more.

Finally she was released and ran to her mother who rose to take her hands.

'You are so beautiful, daughter.'

Cleopatra tugged awkwardly at her headdress.

'I am not. You should see Arsinoë, she—'

'I am not talking of fleshly beauty, Cleopatra, but of your soul, which glows.'

'Oh. Oh, I see. You can tell that, can you?'

'Of course. I am a devotee of Isis, put on this earth to serve Her and she calls to me from within your person.'

Cleopatra put instinctive hands to her belly, wondering from whence the call came. Safira laughed and placed her own hands, fine and soft, upon Cleopatra's.

'She does not crouch in your stomach, daughter.'

'No. I did not think—'

'But infuses your very flesh.'

'Right.'

All her life she had been told that she carried the spark of Isis but never had anyone spoken of it with such genuine intent, never had anyone looked at her as if she were more than herself in the way that Safira was doing now. There was adoration, adulation, awe. In Safira's eyes she was holy and she suddenly felt desperately inadequate.

'I am sorry, Mother, that I have had to run here.'

'Oh, do not be. Isis will have called you to Herself for a reason.'

It was a consoling thought and Cleopatra looked up to the great statue and prayed that She would reveal that purpose. The Goddess looked coolly back.

'She will not be rushed,' Safira said gently.

'Of course not.' Cleopatra flushed. 'It's just that, the Romans are running rampant in the Green Sea and the Alexandrians are rioting at home. My brother has stolen my throne and if I am to take it back there is no time to lose.'

Her mother shook her head at her.

'The history of Egypt stretches across thousands of years, daughter. A few days will make little difference.'

'But the Romans . . .'

'Cleopatra, calm yourself. Relax. Worship. Isis will rule when she is ready.'

So Cleopatra tried. For days she walked with her mother. She prayed. She worked to wash the exigencies of the world from her soul and focus on the Goddess. It was easier here in Memphis where the Temples dwarfed everything and life swirled in calm spirals around their rituals, but however hard she tried, she could not banish the spectre of war further up the blessed Nile.

'How do you find Memphis?' she asked Eiras one evening when she was preparing her to dine with some foreign dignitaries.

'It's beautiful, my queen. Peaceful. And full of wonders. I have been introduced to a marvellous beetle.'

'A beetle?' Cleopatra squinted at Eiras, worried the mysteries of Memphis had gone to her head.

Eiras giggled.

'A cochineal. If you boil its scales in urine it makes the boldest red colour you have ever seen. Added to ochre, with just a touch of alum, I will be able to give you truly scarlet lips, my queen.'

'Boiled in urine?'

'It is a most useful substance. I use it for—'

Cleopatra put up a hand.

'I do not need to know, thank you, Eiras, but I am glad you like it here.'

'I do and Cinna is in raptures over its wonders. He writes verse day and night and says we are far better here than up north where the war is rampaging across every isle and shore.'

'How does he know what the war is doing?'

'He quizzes the traders at the docks.'

'So he is not writing verse *all* day and night . . . ?'

Eiras shrugged.

'He is still a little Roman, however hard he tries, and cannot resist news of the Empire.'

Cleopatra grabbed her arm, feeling as if a goblet of water had been offered her in a desert filled only with the richest wine.

'Ask him to come to me, Eiras.'

'Now?'

'Please.'

Eiras ran to fetch her husband and he came swiftly, Levi and Sosigenes at his shoulder. Sosigenes was as much in raptures over Memphis as Cinna, but for very different reasons. Where Cinna wrote verse to the beauties of the vast walls, Sosigenes persuaded engineers and architects to show him how they had been constructed. Where Cinna eulogised over the way the gods moved within the temple, Sosigenes climbed around the back and saw the pulleys constructed to shift their giant limbs and the devices set to make the fires in their hollow heads flare.

'Does it not spoil the mystery?' Levi had teased him the other day but Sosigenes had shaken his head vehemently.

'Quite the reverse, it enhances it, for what greater mystery is there than the workings of the human mind?'

Levi had thrown an arm around his shoulders and squeezed and Sosigenes had looked at him with such simple affection that Cleopatra had been taken aback. It was the sort of look she'd only seen between Pompey and his Julia, between Brutus and Claudia, or in Servilia's eyes when she spoke of Julius Caesar, the man causing 'chaos' in the Roman Empire.

Levi had seen her looking and leaped away from his 'friend' and Cleopatra had remembered him confiding about his mother turning on him for refusing to marry some girl called Sofia. It had been clear, now, why that might be and whilst she could see how a mother might be disappointed, she cared little. In Egypt, love was love, wherever it was found and she'd smiled upon them both and said that humans were a wonder themselves, especially in their infinite variety. She hoped Levi had understood and had even felt jealous of their closeness. But now was not the time for loving; now was the time for doing. As she summoned Cinna, she thought guiltily of her mother, enfolded within her Temple as if it were the very world itself. For Cleopatra, wonder needed focus – action.

'What news from Rome?' she asked eagerly.

'I am told Pompey has set his sons to rebelling in Hispania. Caesar has left Mark Anthony to amuse himself harrying the Pompeiians in the Aegean, and marched his veterans to crush them.'

'Caesar has marched all the way to Hispania?'

'It is nothing for a man like him. He strides the world as if it were a child's playground.'

Cleopatra looked out on the hallowed walls of Memphis and envied this Caesar his freedom.

'Might one get letters into the field?' she asked Cinna. He looked at her in some astonishment and she frowned. 'Is it such a curious request?'

He shook his head.

'Not at all, but you must have the Goddess strong within you, my queen, to think of such a thing for I have just this morning picked up this package of letters for you. They were bound, I am told, for Alexandria, but word has spread fast of your glorious passage down the Nile and a trader brought them here and passed them to me for a wily fee.'

'You will be reimbursed,' Cleopatra assured him, fixing on the package.

There were two scrolls, addressed in different hands, and she took them eagerly and pulled the binding loose.

'The dinner, my queen ...' Eiras said, glancing out the vast windows to where the sun was going down over the great walls of Memphis.

'Is not for ages. Come, Eiras, you made me ready to greet this city in barely twenty heartbeats, so you can surely afford me the time for two small letters?'

Eiras sighed dramatically but withdrew to start pointedly mixing eyeshadow and, with a smile, Cleopatra began to read.

To Queen Cleopatra of Egypt,

Greetings from Servilia of Rome. I hope you are well and that Egypt prospers. All is not so good in Rome. I am sure you have had news of the terrible conflict that is ripping the Republic apart, but believe me you cannot imagine the upset it is causing, not just for the men who are standing against one another but all those women and children pulled into their sphere. We have been scattered, Cleopatra, as the city has emptied and people have sought refuge in many different places.

I am still in Rome. It seemed wise to wait here for I have no husband to take me to any one camp and preferred to make my stance in my own home – though it looks and feels little like it these days with all the senators gone and only the normal, working people in the streets. Some of the poor have invaded the smart houses on the hills and are living there now, but who can blame them when their own tenements fall down regularly and these beautiful villas are empty? Almost no one has stayed to take care of them, so they must take care of themselves. More than one senator will return (assuming they do) to find his cellar drunk dry, but there is no destruction and if they are so afraid for their precious skins then they will not mind the cost of a little wine, however pricey.

Julius breezed through here for just eleven days before he was off making war again. I begged him to stay longer, to rest his head and gain strength before the travails ahead. It was not, after all, as if Pompey was doing anything other than retreating, but he would not listen. Men! They must ever rush to prove themselves on top when they would know, if they paused to hear their women, that all we want is simply for them to be there.

Ah well, he's gone and I can do little but rest in the empty city
and hope that, somehow, this bitter war comes to an end and we can
live again.

Yours with love,
Servilia

Cleopatra folded the letter, imagining Servilia writing it in the empty rooms of her beautiful villa. She could hear the loneliness in her words, as well as disappointment and anger at the actions of men. She understood that all too well. It was thanks to Potheinos' over-inflated ideas of his own worth and influence that she was now in Memphis and, although she loved it here, she would far rather have travelled in honour than fear. She turned to the second letter.

Cleopatra, queen, friend,

Oh, what an ungodly tangle this all is. How can Rome be at war,
and with itself too? Ridiculous! I know not whose fault it is. Some
say that Pompey imposed unfair sanctions upon Caesar and gave him
no choice but to cross the Rubicon, and some say Caesar is so hungry
for glory that he chose to cross it to win himself more. I have no idea.
I'd never even heard of the damned river before and now I am sick of
people going on about it.

The only good thing about all this, as far as I can see, is that my
Brutus got to see you. Oh Petra, would that I had been with him but
apparently it's too dangerous for women to go 'gadding about' the Mare
Nostrum, which is a nonsense when the really dangerous thing is all
these men fighting each other. Anyway, he says you looked very well and
your palace was beautiful. I begged him to tell me all about it but he
had noticed little save the shouting mob around the walls. Why do they
focus on soldiers when there are drapes and paintings and mosaics to
look at? The world is such a beautiful place, is it not, Petra, so why
can we not just relax and enjoy it?

I am naïve, I know. Brutus tells me so whenever I try and propound my simple theories, but I do not think that necessarily makes me wrong and, besides, he is always torn up with what to do for the best. He rarely stops weighing up who did what and when and in what way and, above all else, how their actions measure up to the precious rules of the Republic. The other day I dared to suggest that perhaps rules could be changed with circumstances, and you would have thought I'd served hemlock-pie for tea. I was subject to such a lecture on the importance of a constitution that I would honestly have leaped into battle myself to avoid all those tangled-up words.

Oh, but Petra, it does torture him so and I am sorry for that. I have told him that I do not think there is a 'right' side and that everyone should stop this ridiculous fighting but I do not think he values my opinion so I'm trying to keep it to myself. I will never have a baby if he is too cross to come close to me, though I begin to think I will never have a baby anyway. I tried that oil Eiras sent me, thank you, and I did conceive. I showered the Temple of Isis in gifts and, oh Petra, I was so happy for weeks but then my womb soured and I lost it. I wept for days. I wept far more than I have for Rome, but tears did me no more good than merriment and nowadays it feels as if I must just put one foot in front of the other and pray that eventually they take me somewhere nice.

I fear for all Romans, Petra, and I fear for you too. Brutus says that his demand for ships turned the people against you. I told him he should have retracted the request instantly for it is not fair that our squabbles should hurt your country, but he just said the Republic needed them and other such nonsense. I understand much of my husband's rants against royalty. I understand that privilege should be earned not born into, but I understand something else now – at least as a royal, a woman stands a chance in this world. I have only one hope in this unholy mess of men's making and it is that you, as a woman and a queen, have the freedom and power to work your own way through.

Yours in sadness,
Claudia

Cleopatra stared at the words, drinking them in. Her dear friend was not as naïve as she thought, nor as stupid as her husband told her. *You, as a woman and a queen, have the freedom and power to work your way through it.* Power with compassion. She had to act.

Rising, she went to the window to look out on the temple. Somewhere within the vast complex sat her mother, her hands folded in her lap and her eyes turned, as always, to Isis. Cleopatra sighed. The Princess Safira was a beautiful woman inside and out, but the only strength she knew came from the rich, safe walls of the Temple. Cleopatra could not live that way; her strength must be her own.

She could not leave her throne occupied by her lazy brother or her ungrateful capital to fall prey to his self-promoting vizier. She could not leave her army controlled by her sister's dark-eyed lover, or her country to be preyed upon by Romans. Let Rome suck the rest of the Green Sea into her power battles; she would not have Egypt whilst Cleopatra was alive to prevent it. She'd thought Isis would help but she did not need a Temple in which to hear the Goddess, for she dwelled within and spoke to Cleopatra not from her marble statue but through the traders' news and her friends' letters.

'Is all well?' Charmion asked.

Cleopatra shook her head.

'I fear all is ill. My friends are separated by place and by the sides their men are choosing in this bitter war stirring the seas. It is not right. We must get back to Alexandria and we must take it from Ptolemy, who does not know how to love the city or the country or anything but his own comfort, and we must shore it up against Rome.'

'You would go to war, my queen?' Sosigenes asked.

'I would go to battle. One fight, outside the city where no citizens can be drawn in – Ptolemy's men against mine.'

Charmion coughed awkwardly.

'You do not have any men, my queen.'

'Not yet,' Cleopatra agreed. 'But I have a people who love me and I am entertaining dignitaries from all over the East. Potheinos once told me I spoke in tongues; well, he is going to find out the value of that the hard way now. Who comes tonight?'

'King Antipater of Idumea,' Levi said. 'He is a young ruler, keen to prove himself and to gain honours for his Jewish people.'

'Excellent. Come, Levi, sit by me whilst Eiras finally gets her hands on my hair, and tell me of Jewish ways and customs. Eiras, your brightest eyeshadow; Charmion, your fiercest gown; Levi, all the information you can give me. There is war in the air and we must turn it to our advantage.'

She might be here on account of the machinations of men but she was not at their mercy and they would soon find her capable of a few machinations of her own.

Chapter Nineteen

Cleopatra stood tall within her chariot and looked out over her army of Egyptians and Idumeans to the massed forces of Alexandria a mere two hundred paces across the desert plain. To the north stood the border city of Pelusium, its gates firmly barred but its people lining the walls to study the opposing forces.

Tomorrow there would be battle and Cleopatra was ready, in her newly commissioned armour, to lead. She had been talked out of fighting – lacking the skill or strength to wield an effective sword – but she would address the troops before the horns were sounded. She had her words ready but still her heart quaked, not so much for the outcome as for the fight itself.

She could not think like that, she told herself sternly. She could not picture the sword strokes and dagger strikes, the javelins and spears. She could not picture the blood and the pain and the men crying for their mothers in the sand as they were trampled by those still fighting for their lives. She had, instead, to picture the victory. She had to focus on the end point – getting back onto the throne with as little loss of life as possible, not just for herself but for Egypt who, she was sure, would prosper more under her than under Ptolemy and his selfish cabal.

She squinted into the sand swirling between the two camps. Was she fooling herself? Was she every bit as power-hungry and selfish as them? She had done her best to keep the battle out of the cities and away from the normal citizens. She had striven to hire only professional mercenaries and not to force anyone into battle, but really, she was still asking men to put their lives on the line so that she could sit on a golden throne and call herself queen.

It had seemed so logical in Memphis where all was peace, but less so standing before the enemy camp five long months later, hearing them polish their weapons and shout taunts across the sand. There was much noise in the opposing camp and Cleopatra wished she were more skilled in warfare to interpret what it meant. She might have a fine chariot and a golden breastplate but she was no general, no Julius Caesar.

Cleopatra thought of the man she'd met in Lucca so long ago. She'd been on the cusp of womanhood and awed by the energy he'd radiated, but recently she'd been thinking about how that skill must translate into his leadership on campaign. It had to be formidable, for just two weeks ago word had come to her camp as it had set out from Palestine that, having quelled Hispania, he had won a great victory over Pompey at a place called Pharsalus in the Greek seas.

The messengers had been afire with tales of his tactics, of the way he had inspired the men, of the resounding victory against all odds, and the news had given Cleopatra hope. Caesar had been kept from his homeland like her and now he had seized it back; his victory surely presaged their own? But that had been at the start of their march, not stood across from the swords of the enemy. She must forget Rome's nonsense and focus on Egyptian affairs.

There was definitely something going on in Ptolemy's camp. Men were rising from their fires and gathering around their leaders. She fought to see more but the sand was obscuring the air between them. Glancing up to Pelusium, she saw that her citizens were leaving the walls, pushing down into the city and round to the other side. Her stomach swirled, as if it were full of the agitated sand, but there was no point in torturing herself with speculation. Someone was calling her name and she traced her way between the troops to find Levi talking excitedly with a pair of sweaty messengers.

'What is it?' she demanded. 'What's happened?' The men fell instantly to their knees but she raised them. 'I do not need your reverence, good men, just your news.'

They still seemed too awed to speak and Levi had to fill in for them.

'It is Pompey, my queen. He has, as you know, been fleeing for his life since his defeat at Pharsalus and these men tell me he has come to Egypt.'

'What?'

It was not a dignified response for a queen but it burst from her before she could stop it. Her mind raced. Why was Pompey come? And what did it mean for her own cause? He would be looking for shelter, labouring Egypt's debt to force her to accept him. But was that debt to Pompey, or to Rome? And did Rome not now belong to Caesar?

'King Ptolemy has gone to greet him. He is on the shores beyond Pelusium, waiting for Pompey to be rowed in.'

So that was where the inhabitants of Pelusium had gone – to see the show on the far side of their city.

'Is he with many men?' Cleopatra asked anxiously.

One of the messengers found his tongue.

'Only one ship, my queen. He will not swell the enemy ranks, I assure you.'

'Unless there are others behind,' she pointed out.

'We hear that all other Roman ships are either heading away from Caesar to hide, or straight to him to surrender. They are weary and afraid, oh Queen, and will have little interest in Egypt's internal battles.'

'They may have no choice,' Cleopatra said drily.

She doubted, though, that the Alexandrian force would welcome a defeated Roman general into their ranks and looked again to the enemy camp, which seemed to be in increasing confusion.

'We should attack,' she said. 'Now, whilst they are distracted.'

'Now?' Levi asked, looking nervously around to Appollodorus, the big Egyptian commander.

The man shook his head.

'It grows dark. Sending men into battle in this would be like sending them straight to the Field of Reeds.'

Cleopatra looked to the sky and saw the sense of his words.

'Trust the Romans to intervene,' she grumbled but now the men at the edge of the camp were jumping up and a noise was rising amongst them.

Charmion and Mardion materialised at Cleopatra's shoulders, Eiras and Cinna tight behind, but it was Sosigenes, eyes alight, who came bounding over with news.

'He's dead! Pompey's dead!' Cleopatra strained to hear him over the rising noise amongst the men and grabbed at his arms to keep him still.

'How, Sosigenes?'

'Your toe-rag of a royal brother betrayed him. Set up a welcome committee on shore, fetched him in a skiff and then set Septimius on him. The man cut him down in the shallows, dragged his body to the shore and cut his head off. Even now, Ptolemy is carrying it into his camp like a trophy.'

Sure enough, the noise from across the sands was louder even than that in their own camp. Someone, it seemed, was being borne into their midst, and Cleopatra could well picture her half-brother taking the adulation of his soldiers as he held the Roman head aloft, except that the blood would drip on his precious clothing and cut into his prodigious appetite. She'd been away from Ptolemy for over a year, but suspected he was every bit as spoiled as before and that it was Potheinos who was bearing the grisly trophy. Not that it mattered.

'Pompey is dead?' she said, fighting to take it in.

This was the man who'd received her and her father when they'd fled to Rome ten years ago, the man who'd been jibed by the Claudii, who'd fought a losing battle against the senate, who'd looked at Julia with such love. She had no fondness for him but it seemed a sorry end for a once-great man. Now, though, another rumour was shooting around the camp.

'He's coming,' people were whispering. 'Julius Caesar is coming to Egypt.'

Cleopatra groaned and looked to her massed army of carefully gathered supporters. She was all set to reclaim Egypt on her own terms and somehow the damned Romans were wading in again. What on earth did she do now?

❖

They woke the next day to find Ptolemy's camp had retreated back to Alexandria, presumably taking Pompey's head with them. Cleopatra wanted to follow immediately but her soldiers were nervous about marching into the Delta and Cleopatra understood; she was nervous about it herself. The last she'd heard of the Alexandrians, they'd been shouting 'down with the Roman-loving queen', and now, with one of those very Romans closing in, the situation was precarious. Egypt was technically still her own country but everyone knew that Rome controlled the Green Sea and Caesar controlled Rome so he had the power to arbitrate.

'We need to get to Caesar first,' she said to Charmion and Eiras as they sat eating the rough soup that they'd all got sadly used to on the road. 'If Ptolemy escorts him into the harbour and presents him with his enemy's head over dinner, he's bound to give him his backing.'

'I wouldn't be so sure,' Levi said. 'Romans may be happy to

slaughter each other but they don't like foreigners doing it. I don't think Caesar will be as pleased with your brother's offering as he expects.'

And so it proved. The news rippled through the camp a week later on a mocking laugh. The great Julius Caesar had been enraged at being presented with his arch-enemy's rotting head. He had publicly shed tears for 'one of my country's greatest ever generals' and sent Ptolemy and his cabal grovelling desperately before him. It was, of course, ridiculously hypocritical given that the man had been pursuing Pompey with the intention of killing him himself, so perhaps he was just sore at being robbed of the execution. Either way, it was funny, and, that night, the camp entertained itself with lively parodies of the imagined scene. Much beer was sunk and much amusement had, but they woke the next morning to find themselves still in the desert and Caesar somehow in charge of Egypt.

And then the summons came.

I, Julius Caesar, de facto leader of the Roman Republic and friend and ally to the Egyptian people, ask you, Queen Cleopatra, to come to Alexandria with all honour to resolve the disputes rocking your historic throne. Civil war is a bitter sorrow to a nation and I trust that between us we can stop it in your country with less bloodshed than has been needed for my own. I send an escort for your comfort and safety and look forward to meeting with you and your retinue in your own palace as soon as is practicable.

Cleopatra read the letter over and over, checking for tricks, but the scroll bore Caesar's official seal and his words were backed up by the arrival of her litter, richly arrayed and accompanied by one hundred Roman soldiers. She looked uncertainly to Charmion who was already having men inspect it in minute detail.

'It seems safe, my queen. You can take a hundred of your own soldiers besides these ones and we can come.'

'You would do that?'

'Of course.'

Charmion looked to Mardion, to Eiras and Cinna, Levi and Sosigenes. They all nodded and Appollodorus stepped up as well. Cleopatra pictured herself being carried up the Canopic Way and her heart ached for her home city, but as far as she knew the Alexandrians still hated her.

'Even if we make it to the palace safely, a public parley with Potheinos in full control is no good at all. We have to seize the initiative.'

Eiras stepped forward.

'Remember Lucca, my queen? He liked you there. Julius Caesar definitely liked you.'

Cleopatra remembered the twinkle in Caesar's eye as he'd quietly put down Cato at her side: *There are many horizons on this earth and it can be sadly limiting to see only one.* Now it seemed this Caesar, master strategist, was coming to her own horizon and she needed a strategy of her own to deal with him. She could not march through the mob, but there was more than one way into the palace.

'We will go,' she said decisively. 'Appollodorus, if you could ready a troop of good men to escort us?'

'Of course, my queen.'

'Thank you. I must prepare for the journey. Eiras, Charmion, Mardion – I would appreciate your help. And Appollodorus, if you could report to my tent when you have your men, we can be sure we are ready together.'

The big Egyptian bowed low and strode off into his camp. Cleopatra turned to the messengers.

'Please thank Julius Caesar, victor of Pharsalus, for his invitation. I am pleased to accept and hope to be with him within a few days. I will send ahead once we are close.'

The man bowed low and was gone, back to Alexandria on his swift horse. He would cover the distance at twice the speed of their own cumbersome journey but Cleopatra did not mind – it gave her time to plan. She tugged her friends into the tent and set about a loud chatter of women's matters but slowly, between talk of eyeshadows, gowns, and jewels, they carved out a plan. The royal litter would ride into Alexandria in state, but Cleopatra would not be in it.

Chapter Twenty

It was dark by the time Cleopatra and Appollodorus paddled up the marshy inland waterways to the palace. They tied up their little boat near the palace and tucked into a shadowed niche behind a thick jacaranda from where she could stare up at the white walls, picturing the familiar courtyards, corridors and rooms within. She could hear the gruff talk of the guards through the giant gates, the hum of dinner in one of the great halls, the chatter of householders strolling in the gardens after the heat of the day. She thought of the Museon, with the scholars working away, all but oblivious to who slept in the royal rooms as long as they could get on with their studies, and envied them.

Sosigenes, she knew, was eager to get back to his year-clock. His work with the Memphis engineers had sparked an idea for an improvement upon the intricate machine and he carried about an ever-increasing sheaf of papyri marked with sketches and calculations. He had lost much in following her from the city but, she hoped, gained much too, for he and Levi were ever together and she envied them their closeness. They had found a home in each other whilst she was left to try and sneak into hers like a thief.

'Is this madness, Apollo?' she whispered in Egyptian.

The big man patted her shoulder.

'It is,' he said softly, 'but it will work. Are you ready?'

She looked down at the bedroll he had laid on the floor and longed to say no. When she'd shared her idea to send Eiras in the litter as a decoy whilst she entered the palace unseen, Apollo had leaped at it.

'Bedrolls.' They'd all turned to him, bemused. 'Bedrolls,' he'd repeated. 'My family trade in them back in Memphis. Every day they are in and out of houses delivering rolls to people – new ones for homes, or hired ones for guests. Surely that must happen here too?'

'It does,' Charmion had agreed. 'The palace has a good store of them but if we host a large event, we hire extra. One of my first jobs when I came to the palace as a girl was to check them for bugs.' She shuddered. 'We had a terrible supplier back then. I was bitten head to foot on bedroll days and as soon as I was promoted, I made it my business to find a better one.'

'Our rolls have no bugs,' Apollo had said proudly, 'and neither, I assure you, will the one I will carry you into the palace in, my queen.'

'Carry me . . . ?'

It had not seemed a dignified way to enter but they'd raked over every possibility on the three-day procession to Alexandria and it remained the best. Now the litter and its guard were camped up for the night on the outskirts of the city and, thankfully, attracting much attention – far more than a couple sneaking around the back of the palace. Apollo was dressed in the stolen uniform of a Roman soldier and Cleopatra in the everyday robe of a house-servant, her queenly robes in a bag so she could change within – if they made it that far. Then, it would all come down to her persuading Caesar to back her and she had to pray that Eiras had been right about him liking her in Lucca. Back then, she'd met the famed Roman as an exiled princess; this time she would be an exiled queen. She prayed he would not think her cursed.

There was only one way to find out. At dawn tomorrow, the

royal litter would be carried up the Canopic Way in state, Eiras veiled within to stand as Egypt's queen, but, if this plan worked, Cleopatra would have had several hours to talk to Caesar in private before her official arrival at the parley. It would be a vital time to explain her own side of events and cut through the web of lies she knew Potheinos and Achillas would have weaved.

'I am ready,' she agreed and, clutching her bundle of royal clothing to her chest, lay down on the mattress.

'It will be cramped,' Appollodorus warned, 'and hot, but you should not be in there long.'

'However long it takes,' she said and braced herself as he began to carefully roll her up.

The noises of Alexandria were instantly muffled, her lights snuffed out. Cleopatra felt the big soldier lift her carefully and drape her over his shoulder, tight within the bedroll. He gave the roll a comforting pat and suddenly they were off and she was bobbing up and down with his big stride, the world in darkness. Fear welled around her, sucking the air out of the already tiny space and making her want to kick her way out, but she couldn't do that, not now. She would be killed and Apollo with her and that would be a poor end for sure.

She forced herself to think of Memphis, where this kind soldier's family delivered bedrolls to households all around the great city. He'd delivered to the temple as a child, he'd told her. He'd perhaps carried one for her mother to rest upon when she was first given to the Goddess.

What would Isis do? The question came to her in the cramped darkness and she smiled against the rough fabric at the sound of Clodia Metelli's lively voice in her mind.

'Isis would spirit herself into the palace without the need of a soldier's shoulder,' she muttered, then hushed herself. If she'd learned one thing in Memphis it was that she should rely on the Goddess within.

'Bedroll for the queen's party,' she heard Apollo say to the gate guards in rough Greek. She could not hear the answer but he spoke again. 'I know. Lazy bastards missed this one. Last thing I need, hoiking mattresses around, but I'm told it's for the queen's party. So much fuss, yeah. You love your royals, you Egyptians. Pretty, is she? Fair enough – I'll look forward to seeing her tomorrow, then. Make a change from bloody soldiers. Now, where shall I sling this?'

Cleopatra tensed at the word 'sling' but, after a rumble of an answer, Apollo started moving again, presumably into the palace. Straining, she could just make out the plash of the fountain in the first courtyard and her heart turned over. She'd done it; she was in. Now she just had to find Caesar.

''Scuse me, soldier – which way to Caesar's rooms? Bedroll for his guard.'

Whoever Apollo was addressing must have provided the information without demur for they were moving again and now a door was opening and she was being laid on the ground. Her heart pounded. Was she in Caesar's rooms? Had it been that easy? The mattress unrolled a little and she felt Apollo adjust it.

'Just leave it, man,' someone growled. 'Out of there now.'

Apollo gave her a quick pat and then he was gone. She lay very, very still. Footsteps echoed around the marble tiles of what was surely the best guest suite and then the door banged shut and she was alone. She lay a little longer in case there might be some attendant within but after an interminable wait, she thought it safe to move. Slowly, carefully, she unrolled, looked around and, finding herself safely alone, stood up.

It was clearly Caesar's room. A plumed helmet sat on the side table, a shield propped beside it, emblazoned with a picture of Venus Genetrix, his family's especial goddess. On the smaller table at the side of the bed sat a scroll and quill and Cleopatra yearned to read what he was writing, but she had a job to do. Ducking into the washroom, she softly closed the door behind her.

Moonlight flooded in through a large roof opening, casting a silvery glow across the basin and jug. She noticed a sharpened knife for shaving and a pot of hair oil and smiled at this small vanity from the great general but she had no idea how much time she might have before Caesar retired from the dining hall and could not afford to linger. Pulling off her rough robe, she took her favourite blue-green silk one from the bag. It was badly creased but that would drop out and the colour matched the eyeshadow Eiras had carefully applied in camp.

She pictured them all back there together, holding an ostentatious feast within the thin tent walls to offer the curious crowd the shadows of revelry around a queen who was, in fact, deep in the heart of the palace. Now all that queen had to do was to talk a great Roman general into backing her. She carefully tied her diadem in place, wishing Eiras were here to smooth her hair beneath it, but Eiras was playing queens whilst she went about the true business of royalty – securing power. She glanced in the little mirror, noting the shine of her lips, made scarlet by Eiras' new beetle friend, and the whites of her kohl-lined eyes in the low light. She looked a queen again at least. Now, all she had to do was wait.

It felt like forever. She hovered in the antechamber, afraid to sit in the main one in case servants arrived to turn down the bed or light lanterns but no one came. There was a comfortable chair but she could not relax long enough to sit in it and paced the tiles in her bare feet, feeling them reassuringly cool against the heat of her own nervousness.

Finally, she heard the main door open and a commanding voice say, 'No, no, no. I need no aid, thank you.' Then, more impatiently, 'It's very kind of you but I've slept in military tents for the last five years and think I can manage to remove my own garments. Good night.'

Despite her nerves, Cleopatra felt laughter bubble in her stomach and had to press a hand to her mouth to keep it inside. Her fingers, when she brought them away, were stained with Eiras' precious beetle-rouge and she bent anxiously to the mirror, dabbing at a smudge of red at the side of her lip.

'What on earth?'

She jumped as the door opened and there, before her, his tunic belt loosened and his hand rubbing sleepily across his face, was Julius Caesar. They stood a moment and Cleopatra fought for the right words to stop him calling for his guard but he showed no signs of doing so. Instead, he looked her carefully up and down and smiled.

'Queen Cleopatra – what a pleasant surprise.'

'I thought it might be good to parley less . . . officially.'

He looked around the little washing room.

'It could not be much less official.'

She shifted.

'I apologise, of course, for invading your personal area.' He raised an eyebrow and she flushed but pushed on. 'I know my brother's men of old and do not believe they would have been inclined to let me into the palace – *my* palace – without a little subterfuge.'

He looked around.

'How did you do it?' She pointed past him to the bedroll on the floor. He looked down at it, then back at her. 'Very enterprising – you had yourself delivered to me on a mattress.'

She bristled.

'It matters little how I arrived. I am here before you as a ruler of Egypt, come to reclaim her rightful role. It is regrettable that I have had to, to . . . '

'Invade my personal area?'

'Seek a private audience by unconventional means. But these are not conventional times.'

'Indeed they are not, Queen Cleopatra. We have both had battles to fight these last years.'

'And both against our own people.'

'Who would rob us of our right to titles justly earned.'

His eyes moved up to her face and she held them with her own, assessing him in turn. He must surely look older than when she had seen him Lucca seven years ago, but now she noticed less the lines around his eyes than the burning curiosity within them. She saw less the thinning of his hair and more the imperious curve of his brow, less the very slight stoop of his shoulders and more the forward thrust of his hips. Her body warmed and she bit at her lip, then cursed herself. She was here for politics not pleasure.

'I do not know what my brother's people have told you, but . . . '

'But I would be delighted to hear your side, ideally in comfort. Shall we . . . ?'

For a moment she thought he was guiding her to the bed but he was gesturing to the couches set at its foot and with a nod, she sailed past him as graciously as she could in her bare feet and took her place on one. He took the other but did not lounge back, rather leaning forward, fully alert.

'Please, tell.'

The room was lit by a single lantern the great general must have carried in himself and the flame caught in the golden edges of his shield, sending the lines of Venus Genetrix across his face as he waited for her to speak. She swallowed, seeking the words to convince this man to back her. In the end, though, she had nothing better than the truth.

'My brother is young and foolish and has been spoiled all his life so that he believes the world exists solely for his own comfort. It is not, perhaps, his fault for he has been schooled that way by Potheinos and Achillas, who prefer him docile so that they can take power for themselves.'

'And kill Roman generals at will,' he growled.

Cleopatra seized on his clear anger.

'Exactly. I know Pompey had become your enemy but he was owed the respect of a worthy adversary and you were owed a trial of his offence. These men are not rulers, Caesar, but chancers, petty officials who seek their own advancement and care little for the country they have worked so carefully to steal. They are not kings.

They do not carry the responsibilities of rule in their veins and will not work for the interests of Egypt as they should.'

He looked at her curiously.

'Because they are not royal?'

'Because they have not been bred to rule,' she said carefully.

'Or born to it? Do you think that fair, Cleopatra, that someone should rule by right of the womb they came from, rather than the deeds with which they prove themselves?'

She thought about it.

'They talk of you as a god, Caesar.'

'They do?'

His mouth curved sardonically and she felt a surge of energy run through her body.

'You know they do. Perhaps they are right. You have done heroic deeds, have won magnificent victories, have inspired the loyalty of many men and seized that of the rest by righteous force. You are, at least, god*like*.'

Again the smile.

'You are too kind.'

'You, as I see it, started out as a mere man but have worked to elevate yourself to something higher. That is commendable.'

'I'm glad you approve.'

'I, in contrast, was born godlike and must live up to that elevation. If I cannot prove that I deserve it, then I have failed.'

'I see.' He looked at her for a long time then, indicating her hand, asked, 'May I ...? She nodded and he took it, stroking a single finger thoughtfully up and down her palm. Her whole arm tingled at his touch but she forced herself to focus. This man was her tool, no more. 'I am a Roman, Queen Cleopatra, a coarse, simplistic Roman, brought up to believe in the Republic and eschew any right that is not won by popular vote. Royalty is anathema to me.'

'And yet are you not high born? Is it not because of your family's connections that you had the platform that offered you a chance to succeed?'

'It helped,' he agreed, and now his finger stroked at her wrist, tracing the blue bloodline that ran up her dark skin. 'We are all, perhaps, prisoners of our blood.'

'But servants of our minds.'

He laughed, sudden and loud.

'Yes! Servants of our minds, of our wills and our ambitions.'

The door flew open and a guard poked his head inside. His eyes widened at the sight of Cleopatra on the couch and she hastily dipped her head.

'Is all well, General?'

'All is very well, as you see, and I would appreciate not being disturbed until morning.'

'Of course. I understand, I . . . Of course, General.'

He backed out and Caesar gave another laugh.

'He thinks you are my—'

'I know what he thinks. And I am not.'

Caesar tipped his head on one side.

'Do you know, I don't think I've ever had a woman delivered to my chamber simply to talk before.'

'So I have heard. I hope you are enjoying the novelty.'

'I am, I think, though you are very beautiful, you know.'

'I am very well painted,' she said stiffly, refusing to be charmed by this notorious womaniser. 'I remember seeing you in Lucca, Caesar.'

'And I you.'

'You do?'

'Of course. No man who met you, Cleopatra, could forget it.'

He edged closer and she felt the heat of him ripple through her like a fine wine and fought to resist its pull.

'My father's will, officially ratified before the entire court – despite Potheinos' best efforts to have it suppressed – declared me as his heir, with my brother as co-consort. At the very least, I deserve to be restored and honoured according to his wishes.'

'You do.'

'Thank you. Are you prepared to say so in an open forum?'

'I am,' he agreed, adding, 'although I cannot, I fear, back you as sole ruler in the present, volatile times. Sharing power is not easy, Cleopatra, but it is better than no power at all.'

'And who knows how the wheel will turn. Charmion, my vizier—'

'You have a woman in charge?'

'I *am* a woman in charge, Caesar, and so know the value of others.'

He bowed his head with a wry smile.

'Of course, my apologies. As I said, I am just a coarse Roman. Please go on.'

'My vizier always told me that we cannot know the intentions of the gods and all we can do is be the best we can be so that if they come calling, we are ready.'

'She is a wise woman, and has raised another. And a bold one besides.' His eyes went to the bedroll again and he smiled. 'We are similar creatures, you and I, save, of course, that you are so young.'

'My body maybe.' She did not miss the way his eyes darkened as he looked back at her figure, much exposed in the gauzy silk, and forced herself to sit tall. 'But I am the product of an ancient lineage.'

'The Ptolemies? You are descended from a mere general, albeit one who had the sense to choose Egypt of all Alexander's countries, and to appropriate the great man's body to grace its capital. A chancer, for sure.'

'A victor,' Cleopatra corrected. 'Alexander the Great's body lies in state in the Serapeum at the heart of this very palace.'

He nodded. 'I have seen it. A great man.'

'A god perhaps?'

His eyes sparkled. 'But not a royal.'

'True, Caesar.' She touched her fingers to her diadem, feeling the silky touch of this simple statement of authority. 'But my mother, you know, is a priestess in Memphis, in the heartlands of a more ancient Egypt. Her ancestry can be traced way back into the great lines of the Pharaohs, into the pyramids and the royal tombs, into the very times of the gods.'

'You are, then, a true queen?'

'I am.'

'Hmmm.'

His finger traced the vein a little higher up her arm into the crook of her elbow.

'What are you thinking?'

'I am thinking,' he said, looking suddenly straight into her eyes so that she felt exposed before him, 'that I have never known a queen.'

'That cannot be ... Oh.' Realising what he meant, her words caught in her throat, as if it had suddenly swollen up.

'And I would like to,' he went on, his own voice hoarse now.

Every fibre in Cleopatra's body was straining to lean forward, to press her lips against his and let herself be initiated in the sensual mysteries of which she had heard so much, but she was here for Egypt, here for power. She met his eyes and held them.

'Then you had better, General, be sure that tomorrow I am made a queen once more.'

He gave a slow smile, traced his finger back to her wrist and then, dropping a light kiss on her palm, returned it to her lap.

'I had better,' he agreed. 'And for tonight, I shall take the couch.'

Chapter Twenty-one

Cleopatra stood with Julius Caesar just inside the back door of the great chamber, listening to the hubbub within. They were looking onto the dais where Ptolemy-Theos reclined in state and she regarded her half-brother in disgust. At thirteen, he had grown taller and wider too, his favourite sweet treats seeming to puff out his cheeks so that he could, himself, have been made of pastry. His younger brother, Ptolemy-Philopater, was sitting quietly at his side, absorbed by a beetle in a box. Past him sat Neferet, dripping with jewels, and to the other side was Arsinoë, Achillas hovering at her shoulder. Cleopatra fixed on her sister. She was safe and well then. She had no idea how deeply Arsinoë had been involved in the plots that had ousted her but any moment now she would find out.

All eyes in the hall, from the royals on the dais, to the crowds lining its length, were turned to the ebony doors at the opposite end. They stood open and beyond them the royal litter was set down with (though no one knew it yet) Eiras within. Cleopatra had hovered in Caesar's rooms this morning, listening to the roar of the crowd in the streets as the litter had processed up the Canopic Way and been soothed at the shouts of welcome. Some of the people at least, were happy to have her back and that would surely make the parley to come easier. Not that there would be much parley once Potheinos and his gang saw her enter at Caesar's side.

She glanced to Julius to see if he was nervous but he stood perfectly relaxed, his limbs loose and his eyes bright as he peered into the hall like a child watching the grown-ups at play. Cleopatra peeked around him as the litter was lifted and borne in, the linen curtains drawn across to obscure the figure within. She was, in her turn, veiled just enough to hide her features, but her bearing was strong, her outline regal, and the courtiers all dropped to their knees. Cleopatra saw Potheinos scowl and felt her heart rise.

'Your friend plays her role well,' Caesar whispered and she felt the warmth of his breath on her neck.

It had been a strange night, she in his bed, he on a couch, covered only by his cloak. She'd protested at that but he'd waved her concerns away, saying that his cloak had kept him alive across the snowy passes of the Alps so would surely suffice in the warmth of an Egyptian palace. And, oh, it had been warm. She'd scarce been able to sleep for awareness of him at her feet and had spent the long hours imagining what might take place tomorrow night. She'd thought guiltily of Servilia, lonely in Rome whilst her lover was here, winning Egypt for the price of a night between the sheets with her queen, but it was surely a small cost for a country. And it would be just the one night.

'Eiras is of a proud and elegant line of people,' she said, leaning around him to see as the litter was set down.

'I look forward to meeting her.'

'She is married to the Roman poet, Cinna,' she said, more hastily than was dignified.

'Is she indeed? I'm sure if she is even a tenth of the woman she is currently masquerading as, she will provide him with great inspiration.'

Cleopatra stepped back a little.

'You like to flatter.'

'I like to tell the truth,' he said, re-closing the gap between them.

'Beauty is not necessarily in the lines of the visage, Cleopatra, so much as the lines of the soul.'

'My mother said something similar to me.'

'She was wise. Your soul sparkles.'

'Sparkles?' she spluttered but the litter was reaching the top of the hall and the time for private conversation had passed.

'The Queen Cleopatra,' a herald announced loudly.

All eyes fixed on the litter but Eiras, within, did not move a muscle. Instead, Caesar took Cleopatra's hand and, holding it high, escorted her onto the dais. It took a moment for anyone to notice, then someone gasped, pointed, and suddenly the room was alive with voices speaking her name.

'How did you get there?' Ptolemy demanded.

He tugged furiously on Potheinos' arm, but Eiras was stepping from the litter carrying the dual crown, brought with them from Memphis, and all eyes were upon her as she set it on Cleopatra's head and bowed low. Caesar followed her example and hastily everyone else in the room – save Ptolemy – fell to their knees. Cleopatra looked around in awe but, before she could think what to say, Arsinoë was up and throwing herself on Cleopatra, sobbing prettily.

'Sister! I thought I had lost you. Are you safe? Are you well? How I have missed you.' Cleopatra let her own arms go round her sister, uncertain yet if she was pleased to see her, but very aware that the people loved her and this touching reunion would go well for them both.

'My heart has ached at our separation, Sister,' she said loudly. 'And I pray I will be restored to your company here in the palace.'

'I too,' Arsinoë agreed, then leaned closer to add, 'Ptolemy is a pig and Potheinos a bore. Even the mob tire of them and it's only my dear Achillas who has been holding things together in the palace.'

She glanced over to her 'dear' Achillas who gave her a melting smile.

'You are bedding him, Sister?' Cleopatra whispered.

'Every single night. It is marvellous – you should try it.' Involuntarily Cleopatra's eyes moved to Caesar and Arsinoë squealed girlishly. 'You have! Clever you.'

'I have not.'

'Oh. Well, you should. I hear he's an amazing lover.'

'Arsinoë!'

Cleopatra nodded to the courtiers, growing restless as they chattered, but Arsinoë just shrugged.

'They will wait. You are Queen, Cleopatra.'

'Not yet.'

But now Caesar was stepping between them, quietly drawing Cleopatra forward and nodding at Ptolemy-Theos to join them. Ptolemy looked furious at the summons but, at a stern nod from Potheinos, levered himself off the couch.

'I am grateful,' Caesar announced, 'to be present at this happy occasion and to see brother and sister reunited. The shadow of a civil war is long, as I should know.' His soldiers, crowded into the back of the hall, gave a guttural cheer, which he acknowledged with a small wave. 'So I am glad that Egypt, a country of most ancient and reverent culture and history, is not to be torn apart in a similar way to Rome. I trust that all parties are happy to ratify the sacred will of King Ptolemy XII and—'

But, at that, Potheinos stepped forward, simmering with rage.

'There has been no parley, Caesar.'

Caesar turned to him smoothly.

'Oh, but there has. I have spoken with King Ptolemy at length and last night I spoke with Queen Cleopatra.'

'Last night . . . ?!'

'Yes. It was . . . convenient. Does the timing matter? Both the royals consent to share the throne. Who else need I consult?'

Potheinos' mouth worked furiously but even he was not reckless enough to suggest himself. He looked to Ptolemy who looked helplessly back. Cleopatra could well imagine how easily Caesar had run rings around her slow-witted brother and was grateful for it. It rankled that the damned Roman felt he could step in and resolve Egypt's problems but she reminded herself that she must think of him as a tool in her own plans and use him to the best possible benefit. She could hear the courtiers calling approval, sense Eiras clapping wildly at her back, taste Ptolemy's ill-disguised petulance at sharing his crown once more, but feel – above all else – Julius Caesar's hand in her own, his fingers squeezing hers.

'I have not had a queen,' he'd said last night.

'Then you had better make me one,' she'd told him.

He had delivered his end of the bargain, so it was time for her to deliver hers. Nerves pulsed through her but she pushed them aside. She had waited too long for the act of love and was ready to be initiated in its mysteries. And if it won her a crown, then the pleasure would surely be so much more potent.

❖

'It will be slow,' Julius warned, lifting her up and laying her across the bed like a sacred offering. 'I wish to take my time over this treasure.'

'Good. I do not like my pleasure to be rushed.'

He raised an eyebrow in a gesture that was swiftly becoming familiar to her.

'I am glad you anticipate pleasure, Cleopatra.'

'Why would I not? I have heard too many praise the act of love to doubt it – and too many praise your own artistry to fear that I am in poor hands.'

He laughed.

'I forget you have been in Rome.'

Cleopatra's mind flitted to Servilia, to the yearning look in her eyes when she spoke of this man. It would be she, now, who he pleasured, and guilt quivered at the edges of her consciousness but Servilia was not here and she forced her thoughts elsewhere.

'Clodia Metelli told me she would love to bed you.'

'Did she indeed. I shall bear that in mind when I return, but for now . . . Where do you like to be touched?'

Cleopatra thought about it.

'I'm not sure. I like all massage but have no especial preference.'

He grinned.

'Then I shall have to experiment on every inch of you. I think you will find that some areas are more sensitive than others. May I . . . ?'

He lifted the hem of her dress and she nodded. All her life she had been used to people undressing her but never with such admiration, such appraisal, such hunger.

'You are like the Nile, Cleopatra – lush and ripe and waiting to be explored.'

'Not to mention fickle, unpredictable and full of crocodiles?'

He pulled off her dress and stood looking down on her naked body.

'You may bite me if you feel the need.'

'Is that likely?'

He grinned again.

'It is possible and what a joy it will be finding out.'

He cast off his tunic in one fluid motion and now he was naked too, every line of his body taut with muscle and so much of his skin marked with tiny scars and cuts that he seemed a map, each line a journey ahead of her.

'It will take time,' he said again, and as he knelt over her and licked his tongue with agonisingly wonderful care across her left ankle and slowly upwards, she arched back and surrendered to the sensations running out from him and all across her body.

Chapter Twenty-two

OCTOBER 48 BC

My dearest Servilia
Greetings, Servilia
To the Lady Servilia from Cleopatra, Queen of

Cleopatra cast the papyrus aside. This was hopeless. For days she'd been trying to find a way to write to Servilia but she could not even find the words to start, let alone to broach the huge topic that sat between them – that she was bedding Servilia's lover, and bedding him with rigorous enthusiasm.

She glanced over to the bed where Julius slept, the first rays of the autumn sun shining across the rumpled sheets. It was warm and he'd pushed the covers off so that the light danced across his bronzed skin, illuminating the many scars of a life lived hard and fast. Her eyes feasted upon him and she cursed her own greed.

This will be the last day, she told herself, as she'd done every morning for two weeks. She meant it each time, but each time her resolve wavered, and the moon had waxed from Calends to Ides with no move to stop their affair. Julius had only to walk into the room and her loins flared, the pleasure already rising at the mere anticipation of the places he might take her to once they were alone. It was wrong to be so in thrall to a man, especially a Roman. For now the mob were quiet but one false move and they would be up again. She must send him away. Today.

'What troubles you, my Nile goddess?'

She jumped.

'Business of state,' she bluffed, leaping up and wrapping a robe around herself, as if she might draw on her queenliness with its rich silk. 'I have a meeting with my dear brother and his advisors about this summer's grain harvest. Charmion is furious at the mess in which the royal barns have been left during her year away and is slaving to re-stock after the charitable distributions of the low years.'

That much was true. Potheinos might be good at seizing power for his pet king, but he was useless at wielding it effectively and the seed distribution and grain collection had become chaotic. Much of this year's harvest had gone into private barns and Levi and Charmion were combing the records to recall it to the royal store. She had taken the precaution of sending messengers out all around the streets to explain to the people that this was for their own benefit but she wasn't sure they understood the economics of reserves and there had been some trouble. Plus, Potheinos' officials weren't too happy about having a woman criticising them and the meeting ahead could be stormy.

'When do you start?'

'Once we have broken our fast.'

'Then there is a little time yet.'

His eyebrow arched invitingly and Cleopatra shook her head.

'For what, General? Are you wishing me to brief you on Egyptian grain harvests?'

He caught at her hand and kissed each finger in turn.

'I do not need that, for I trust your judgement implicitly. You might, however, brief me on the best way to pleasure the Egyptian queen.'

'I think you are already well briefed on that.'

'Ah no, Cleopatra, we are only just beginning and the ways are many and varied. I have not yet drawn your crocodile bite from you.'

He reached for her gown, pushing it aside and pressing his lips to the soft inside of her thigh, sending desire flaring across every inch of her skin – just as he knew it would.

'Isis take me,' she murmured, feeling herself melt beneath his touch, as if she were raw quartz and he a glass-maker, heating and reshaping her into something brighter and more beautiful.

'Maybe not Isis . . .' he teased, then pulled her gently onto the bed and pushed the gown away to continue the path of his lips upwards.

'Faster,' she panted but he resisted.

'No rush, Goddess.'

'There is! My meeting . . .'

'Can wait. You're the queen, remember.'

'I remember.' She sat up with a huge effort. 'And as queen I must be seen to respect my officials by valuing their time as much as my own.'

He paused, looking up at her curiously, then he gave her a quiet nod.

'You are right, Cleopatra. You are so right.' He pulled away and her whole body flooded with disappointment but then he gave a wicked grin. 'For once, we will go faster.'

❖

They made it around the city and into the royal granaries with moments to spare. Cleopatra was, she feared, more than a little flushed but she was here and that was what counted. Her brother was not and she turned to Potheinos, pacing irritably to one side.

'Where is the king?'

'He is busy.'

'With what?'

'With . . . important matters.'

'What could be more important than the grain distribution? It is core to prosperity for all our people. Have him fetched, please.'

'Why me?' Potheinos protested. 'He is *your* husband.'

She flinched but stood her ground.

'And your charge, by his own choice, until he comes of age.'

'Which is in three months' time. Perhaps then, my queen, you will take him into your bed as you should.' His eyes slid slyly to Julius. 'We would not want the Egyptian people denied an heir – an Egyptian heir.'

'A Greek heir,' she corrected. 'Is that not what you want, Potheinos? A Greek heir to the Alexandrian throne?'

'It is,' he spat, 'but you, it seems, for all your protestations of loyalty to your country, prefer Roman seed.'

Julius leaped forward but Cleopatra put an arm out to hold him. She could fight her own battles with Ptolemy's weaselly vizier.

'I am the queen, blessed and inhabited by Isis. My womb will nurture Her heir, whatever the seed, for I – unlike your lazy officials – know how to reap a fine harvest. Charmion, what news on the grain?'

Charmion stepped forward and led them deeper into the main granary. The vast wooden structure on the edge of the docklands was packed with people bringing in sacks of grain on carts and unloading them onto the long shelves. They had been all but empty until a couple of weeks ago, depleted from two years of low inundations and another of shameless corruption, but Isis' tears had been abundant at last and Charmion had been working day and night to correct the distribution of the resultant harvest. Now the barn was at least half full and the last of the misdirected grain was being brought in.

'As you can see,' she said, indicating a large wax tablet affixed to the wall, 'all shipments are carefully recorded with their weights and provenance to be sure that taxation is correctly re-calculated where there have been . . . errors.'

Julius stepped up to the board and examined it closely.

'Excellent. We have nothing like this in Rome.'

'Grain is centralised here,' Charmion said. She was still a little shy of the great Roman but this was a topic about which she was passionate. 'That way we can ensure all receive a fair allowance.'

'And that the royal coffers are correctly filled,' Potheinos said nastily.

'Of course,' Charmion agreed, 'so that we have money to improve the roads, collect the waste, light the streets . . . '

'I like your street lights,' Julius put in. 'We have nothing like that in Rome and the darkness of the streets means that many crimes are committed. I would be interested in meeting the engineers.'

'That can be arranged,' Levi said keenly.

'Thank you. Now, show me how you keep the grain fresh.'

Charmion happily escorted him to a side barn where giant clay vessels were filled and sealed with wax. Much of the grain was arriving already sealed as the harvest had been complete for several months now, but some of Potheinos' contacts had been unforgivably lax and the men were working hard to seal the rest before it germinated in the damp air of the inundations.

Cleopatra watched with pride as Charmion took Julius through the intricate process. This woman had risen from nursemaid to housekeeper to Vizier of all Egypt with consummate skill and without any of the treachery or trickery usually associated with such promotions. She was a marvel indeed and it raised Cleopatra's opinion of Julius that he was happy to draw on her expertise without question. She stood to one side, letting Charmion have the floor, and so was perfectly placed to see Ptolemy's face as he stomped into the barn, guards hovering nervously at either shoulder. It was a mixture of fury, contempt and utter bemusement.

'What on earth am I doing here?' he drawled, looking around the industrious workspace as if it were the worst slum.

Cleopatra took his chubby arm.

'We are here, my dear brother, to learn about grain distribution and storage.'

'Why?'

'Because it is vital to the economy.'

'Yes, but why do *we* have to learn? Aren't there people for that?' Cleopatra looked at him in disgust.

'There are "people" for everything, Ptolemy, but we are in central control so it behoves us to understand their roles and be sure that they are deployed effectively.'

He wrinkled up his pudgy nose.

'Sounds like a bore.'

'Sounds like our duty.' Cleopatra pulled him aside. 'Really, Ptolemy, it's important. Think about it. Potheinos has told you officials do all the work and you just need to be a figurehead, right?'

'Not just,' Ptolemy said petulantly. 'Figurehead is a very important role. I am the face of the government.'

'No.' She took his arm, willing herself to be patient. 'You are not the face of the government – you *are* the government. Do you know why Potheinos says that?'

'Because he has my interests at heart.'

She shook her head.

'Because if you are a "figurehead", he can run the country exactly as he wants to, with all the benefits for himself. How can you know if your officials are corrupt or inefficient if you never ask what they do?'

Ptolemy frowned and for a moment she thought she was getting through to him, but then he said, 'Potheinos has my interests at heart,' as if it was the only sentence he knew, which perhaps it was. It was clear that her father's vizier had been working on the young king for a long time and Cleopatra's only chance of bringing him round to fair rule was to get rid of his controller.

'Come, King Ptolemy,' Julius said, noting the tension, 'see how the wax is melted to just the right temperature to be moulded into the seal without defiling the grain.'

Ptolemy looked down his nose but Julius simply stood there, open and quietly determined, and eventually he shuffled over. The young man working the jar flushed with his important guests and bit on his lip as he concentrated on getting it just right. Julius kept asking him questions and even Ptolemy began to look slightly interested.

'Why don't you do the next one, your majesty?' Julius suggested.

'Me?' Ptolemy looked down at his perfectly smooth hands as if uncertain they would cooperate.

'Why not? You are a royal, a god, I'm sure you can seal a jar.'

If there was sarcasm in the words, then Ptolemy did not detect it. Nodding uncertainly, he let the workman heat him a pat of wax and place it in his hands.

'It's hot!'

'It's warm,' Julius said encouragingly. 'Here, press it to the sides as you saw this young expert do.' Ptolemy bent over the jar, focusing hard and began pressing the wax bit by bit around the neck of the jar. 'See, you're a natural.'

Ptolemy allowed himself a smile and looked around for Potheinos, but as he spotted him scowling by the wall, his hand wobbled and then slipped, squishing the wax and pushing it down into the grain.

'No!' he wailed, peering in after it. 'It didn't work. It doesn't like me.'

'It's not a problem, your majesty,' the poor workman was gabbling. 'I do that all the time, really, I . . . '

But now Ptolemy had spotted little lines of brown wax beneath his perfect, hennaed nails.

'Now look!' he wailed. 'Potheinos – look what it's done to me!'

'Horrible,' Potheinos agreed smugly. 'You never should have been asked to do such a menial task.'

'See,' Ptolemy said furiously to Julius. 'I don't know why I listened to you. You're just a rough Roman soldier with no idea of how to treat a king and I don't want you here any longer.'

Julius' eyes narrowed. He took three steps over to the furious young man, his body rigid with controlled anger.

'I am the ruler of most of the known world – a title I have acquired by daring, courage and sheer hard work, all qualities that you do not seem to have, *your majesty*. I'd be very careful, because if I decide I don't want *you* here any more, it won't take me long to turf you out.'

'How dare you? I'm the King of Egypt.'

'You are the *co*-king of Egypt and murderer of an important Roman general. If I issue the word, the might of the Roman army will be in your precious country within a month and then let's see how hard you can work in one of our labour camps.'

Ptolemy stood staring at him, his mouth working in furious indignation.

'Potheinos!' he eventually wailed. 'Tell him he cannot speak to me like that. Tell him how important I am.'

Potheinos shook his head sadly.

'He does not understand, your majesty. Romans have no culture.'

'And you,' Julius hissed, spinning to advance on Potheinos, 'have no manners.'

'Don't,' Ptolemy shouted, 'don't hurt him.'

He threw himself suddenly at Julius, fingernails first. One scraped down Julius' arm and Cleopatra gasped as it drew blood, but although the Roman was half the girth of his assailant, he had twice the strength and threw Ptolemy off with ease. The young king clattered to the ground, rolling awkwardly in the dust and chaff of the harvest before scrambling back up with a furious wail and running, limbs all anyhow, from the barn and into the streets of Alexandria.

Potheinos shot after him and his voice rang out around the docklands, loud and imperious: 'The Roman is taking our grain, and Queen Cleopatra is in his bed, encouraging him!'

It was an accusation perfectly judged to cut to the heart of all that mattered to the fickle Alexandrians and the roar of a response was immediate. Cleopatra looked at Julius in horror. Her lover might not know it yet, but that was the sound of the mob being whipped into an all-too-familiar frenzy. She had to act fast.

'Stop him,' she gasped, running to Julius' side. 'We need to get Ptolemy back and calm the mob. Fast.'

Julius nodded to the small guard at the door and several of them shot after the king as the rest barred the big doors.

'That's not enough men,' Cleopatra said.

She sprung after them to get back across to the palace and summon her army – if it was not gone already. It had been Achillas, she was sure, who had let the men in to murder Bibulus' sons, and Achillas who had led them against Brutus' demand for ships. Achillas and, perhaps, the woman in his bed. Her veins turned to ice and she yanked on the doors but Julius grabbed her around the waist.

'You mustn't go out there, Cleopatra. If the mob gets its hands on you, who knows what might happen.'

'And if I do not get to the palace, the mob *will* get their hands on me. Let me go!'

She fought furiously but he did not loosen his hold until Charmion came across and said, 'We have a special way for the queen.'

'Is it safe?' Julius demanded.

'Of course.'

Charmion nodded to Mardion who kicked aside some hay, and opened up a small trap door. Cleopatra gaped. That man had tunnels all over the place. How had she never found them as a child?

'Then that would be excellent.'

Caesar let go of Cleopatra and she rounded on him.

'I can decide what is safe for my royal person, thank you very much.'

He leaned in.

'I hope so,' he whispered, his lips so close to her own that she felt the very shape of the words. 'Because it is most dear to me.'

She stared at him, stunned, but then horns sounded out across the palace to raise the alarm and she swung back to Mardion. She could address the mob from the palace walls – once she had found Achillas.

'Let's go,' she said, letting him guide her down into the dank little tunnel, Charmion hot on her heels.

It wasn't until they were half way beneath the city that she realised it was just the three of them.

'Where's Julius?' she asked Mardion.

'He shut the trapdoor on us. Said something about "securing strategic positions".'

'What? No!'

She looked up the tunnel, wanting to rush back and take her own command but the distant clatter of feet on wood told her that the Gabiniani were into the barn and instead she let Charmion and Mardion hurry her on. Her first priority had to be to find Achillas, leader of her army – and Arsinoë. The tunnel sloped slowly upwards and eventually came to an iron door upon which Mardion banged loudly. Startled voices sounded on the other side, then the shriek of a rusty bolt being drawn and it opened cautiously, letting a welcome slit of sunlight flood in.

'Make way for the queen,' Mardion said imperiously, ushering Cleopatra out as if this were the entry to a state event and not an escape from a grain barn. She stepped gratefully through and found herself in a small chamber to one side of the Museon. A handful of bemused scholars bowed low as she walked past them, trying to look dignified.

'Queen Cleopatra is under threat,' Mardion announced, letting Charmion out too. 'We must seal the palace against traitors.'

He shot the large bolt back across the iron door and strode out of the Museon to ensure all guards were on alert. Cleopatra ran after him.

'What about Julius? We cannot leave him out there; they might tear him apart.'

'Or he them,' Eiras said. Cleopatra stared at her and she gave an easy shrug. 'If he wishes to fight for you, my queen, you should let him. Might it not, after all, be part of the bargain you have struck?'

Cleopatra shook her head, then laughed.

'You make a good queen, Eiras – perhaps a better one than I.'

'Oh no! You are the queen; I merely a shadow who can play the part on occasion. Shall we go onto the walls?'

'Shortly,' Cleopatra agreed, 'but for now I wish to know where my Captain of the Army is. And my honoured sister.'

'You suspect . . . ?'

'Do you not?'

Eiras glanced to Charmion but suddenly Arsinoë came flying out of the main palace buildings, crying fit to burst, and threw herself into Cleopatra's arms.

'He's gone! My Achillas has gone!'

Cleopatra put an arm around her sister as sobs wracked her lithe body.

'When did you see him last?'

'In my bed this morning. He mentioned nothing of this, Petra.'

'I do not think it was planned,' she said cautiously, 'but he must have been ready, for the mob rose too quickly not to be driven to it. Has he spoken for Ptolemy before? Or against me?'

'Oh no!' Arsinoë protested, clutching her tighter. 'But he would not, would he, for he knows how I value you. Oh, Petra – he has betrayed us both.'

She was sobbing again and Cleopatra could only pat her back and look to the others in horror. Somehow the city was at war again and, with her Egyptian army sent home and the Alexandrian one up against her, it was hard to see how she could win.

◆

All afternoon the battle raged in the streets of Alexandria. Cleopatra stood on the walls watching, Arsinoë clutched close, as

Achillas and the Gabiniani took on the Romans who had marched in with Caesar. The mob, initially excited by this new conflict, grew fearful and withdrew into their homes, leaving the streets to the soldiers, and Cleopatra absorbed it all with growing horror. She had worked so hard to avoid bloodshed but it had come anyway.

She saw a bold group of Romans make a break along the Hepstadion – the great breakwater that ran out to the magnificent Pharos at the harbour's edge – and thought she recognised the man at their head. He was dressed not in protective armour but in the everyday tunic suitable for a simple meeting about grain distribution, but he radiated strength.

She watched keenly as half his men formed into a tight tortoise of a shield-wall to hold off a succession of attackers, whilst the other half rolled stones from the breakwater onto its paved top to create a barrier. The attackers, infuriated, backed away and turned instead for the ships docked along the harbour's edge – the very ships that had been sent back by Pompey and arrived just two days ago. Fifty had survived their part in Rome's petty civil war and the Alexandrians stormed onto the first one, clearly set to attack the Hepstadion from the water.

'They will kill him,' Cleopatra gasped. She turned to Arsinoë. 'Your lover will kill mine if he gets to him.'

'And yours will kill mine if he gets there first.'

'Yours deserves it.'

That set Arsinoë crying again, but Cleopatra could not peel her eyes from the terrible scene to comfort her further. Caesar had already seen the danger and some of his men were rowing towards the great ships in one of the small skiffs moored along the Hepstadion. She watched, aghast, as they moved closer, seemingly heading straight into their own doom, but then those in the stern bent down and she saw that they had taken some of the torches set up along the road to the Pharos. They lit them with a flint box and tossed them, with daring accuracy, onto the ship's deck.

One, two, three brands flew through the air and caught in the waxed linen sail, sending it flaring furiously. Before Cleopatra could draw breath, the whole ship was alight and the Alexandrians screaming and casting themselves into the water. Several scrabbled to board the skiff but the Romans dodged them, heading straight for the stern of the burning vessel.

'Are they mad?' Arsinoë whispered.

It certainly looked that way but as the small ship nudged at the larger one, it caught the onshore tide, rocked, then tipped slowly and inexorably into the next vessel, sending it afire and into its neighbour. The Gabiniani on the docks backed off, watching in equal horror to those on the palace walls as all fifty of the beautiful Egyptian battle ships were caught by the increasingly excitable flames and began to burn. The tarred wooden jetties flared too and sparks flew into the air, acrid with heat as they caught in the breeze and were sent onto the wooden warehouses lining the dock.

Men spilled out of them, calling for help, and the city sprung to life again as people ran forth to try and stop the blaze before it engulfed their homes. Cleopatra clutched her hands into her dress, battling to stave off her own screams, as they formed lines, passing seawater frantically up in buckets to douse the flames wherever they caught. The end warehouse was already burning too brightly to stop and instead they focused on the second one, hacking down the closest wall to break the path of the fire and throwing more and more water onto what remained until, finally, the flames contented themselves with engulfing the first building.

Dusk was falling, not that anyone in Alexandria would know it as Cleopatra's navy burned brightly and, finally, sank into the harbour. The Gabiniani retreated to their camp whilst the Romans, driven on by their seemingly tireless leader, built more walls to block off the harbour and palace from the rest of the city and set up patrol points along them. Finally, with the area secure and the moon casting a silver shimmer across the burning remains in the charred waters, Cleopatra saw a skiff set off from the Hepstadion, a man stood at its stern in a simple tunic.

'A figurehead,' she muttered.

It was the word her feckless brother had used for his own role this morning before his tantrum had set Alexandria alight, but one that fitted Julius Caesar so much more perfectly.

'Surely you won't take him back?' Arsinoë said. 'He has burned up the city.'

'For me,' Cleopatra said. 'He has burned it up for me and he has come back. Has Achillas?'

'How can he?' Arsinoë snapped and ran from the walls, flinging herself into her own rooms.

Cleopatra sighed and considered following her volatile sister. She did not like being 'rescued' by Julius, however much she admired his courage, but she could scarcely refuse him entry after he had risked so much for her. Leaving her sister to sulk, she went slowly down to the side gate to meet Caesar. He looked weary close up, his face streaked with charcoal, his eyes red-rimmed and his shoulders hunched, but he smiled when he saw her.

'You are safe, Cleopatra.'

'Of course. The greater miracle is that *you* are.'

'That's not a miracle. That's just hard work. Now, can a man get some food around here? I'm starving!'

Cleopatra shook her head at the ridiculous normality. Her city was at war, she was prisoner in her own palace, and Julius was trapped in Egypt, but still the stomach called.

'Let's see what we can find,' she said, leading him inside.

Charmion and Mardion came running and they found Julius water to wash and summoned food from the kitchens. Eiras, Cinna, Sosigenes and Levi joined them and as Julius sank onto a couch and waved them all to do the same, Cleopatra found herself in a curiously cosy group.

'It's just simple meat and cheeses,' Charmion said apologetically. 'We did not know when—'

'It's wonderful. Thank you. Ah, King Ptolemy.' They all jumped as Julius waved to the door where the young king was furiously wriggling in the grasp of two large guards. 'How good of you to re-join us. Would you care for some food? No? A good sleep then. Guards – show his majesty to his rooms, will you? And see him well tended.'

Ptolemy finally found his voice: 'You will imprison me in my own palace?'

Cleopatra leaped hastily up before Julius could take control of her home as well as her city.

'We will secure you, brother, for your own protection against your treacherous advisors.'

Ptolemy howled in anger and Cleopatra signalled for him to be taken away, uncomfortable at aligning herself with the Roman impostor, rather than her own siblings, but what could she do? Ptolemy had turned against her and Julius had stood at her side. The Alexandrians might not like it, but the lines of loyalty had been drawn in the clearest of ways and if she was to win she had to accept and exploit them.

'I am sorry about your ships,' Julius said, pulling her onto the couch at his side. 'But there was no help for it.'

'A pity Pompey sent them back so promptly.'

'An irony. It seems Rome is fated to bring you only destruction, a tide I shall have to turn if I am ever to get home.'

'Wrong,' she said, stamping her foot.

He jumped.

'Wrong?'

'A tide we shall have to turn *together*, Rome and Egypt in concert.'

He nodded slowly.

'I have never had a woman as an equal partner before,' he said, looking her up and down like a curiosity brought for his amusement.

She smiled.

'We are not equal, General, but keep fighting and maybe one day you will come close.'

He gaped at her and she kissed him. This had been a violent

and frightening day and now they found themselves trapped within the palace. But it was, at least, *her* palace and even if he was conqueror of the known world, for now at least he would play by her rules.

Chapter Twenty-three

'A narcissus' Cleopatra exclaimed.

She reached into the royal flowerbed to stroke the tiny yellow petals as Eiras, Charmion and Mardion crowded round to see.

'Is it a special flower for you?' Julius asked, looking at the tiny bloom in surprise.

'It is the harbinger of spring,' Sosigenes told him, joining them with Levi. 'And almost as reliable as my year-clock. See, its petals are like the newborn sun rising.'

'How ... pretty?' Julius managed.

'How timely,' Cleopatra told him crisply. 'I have been thinking for some days now that we should shake off our winter lethargy and break this ridiculous captivity, but have done nothing.'

She tutted at herself. It had been a strange winter interlude, all of them locked in the palace by Achillas' army whilst life had gone on around them. Ptolemy-Theos had been kept under petu-lant guard in his rooms, whilst little Ptolemy-Philopater had run around chasing butterflies and digging up worms like a child half his age. Cleopatra feared his mind was too weak to be any use as a potential monarch but it made him pleasingly easy to amuse and

Cleopatra had seen him well looked after by kindly, insect-loving nursemaids.

Arsinoë, in contrast, had kept worryingly aloof. Once it had become apparent that Potheinos and Achillas had taken a permanent stand around the palace, she had come to join them at dinner, sliding in next to Julius and fluttering her beautiful eyelashes at him. Cleopatra had watched her sister with something dangerously close to hatred but Julius had batted her attentions aside and, in the end, Arsinoë had sulked back to her rooms where she largely stayed, locked up with her handful of ladies.

Not, she had to admit, her winter of captivity had been unpleasant. The palace was large, luxurious and well-stocked and, although she hated being separated from the city, her people had paid little attention to Potheinos' stand, and after a while she'd been able to relax and even rest. She and Julius had found a number of pleasant ways to make the time pass, and not just in bed. He was fascinated by all that Alexandria's scholars, working in the Museon at the heart of the palace complex, had to offer and been particularly drawn to Sosigenes, marvelling over his year-clock. The other day Cleopatra had found them in earnest discussion.

'The real problem,' Sosigenes had told him, 'is that the lunar calendar does not fit with the solar one. The turns of the moon do not match the turn of the earth around the sun.'

'The earth moves around the sun?' Julius had asked. 'How can that be?'

'We're not sure,' Sosigenes had admitted. 'But we know it to be true all the same. And it takes it exactly three hundred, sixty-five and a quarter days to do so, which is very awkward as it means the seasons can gradually fall out of alignment.'

'Which is exactly what has happened in Rome,' Julius had said excitedly. 'Usually, when we detect sufficient slip, senate votes to add in an intercalary month to get us back in line but with all the disruption over the last years it hasn't happened. We are celebrating the midwinter feast of Saturnalia in October at the moment and it creates much confusion.'

Sosigenes had chuckled.

'If you don't mind me saying, Caesar, that is a very antiquated system. The moon is a misleading planet. It is far better to have months of differing lengths to hit the end of the year at the same time and then, every fourth year, to add in an extra day to make up the stray quarters. The turning of the planets can be predicted with great accuracy – as, indeed, this little machine does. We set it going many years ago and it has never been out so you can be sure it will give you a year you can trust.'

Julius had shaken his head in admiration.

'Such precision is admirable. I would like to buy one for Rome, as a gift to the people – the gift of time. How much would that cost me?'

Sosigenes had looked nervously to Cleopatra.

'We will have to ask the scientists to do the calculations, Julius.'

The scientists had been happy to name a price and Julius prompt to accept, but what use was a year-clock if they were all frozen in time themselves? She stroked the narcissus petals again.

'This tiny flower is braver than I am.'

'Or I,' Julius said.

'Indeed.'

He blinked at her.

'You complained once, Petra, that I flatter too much but you, I would venture, flatter far too little.'

'I prefer truths plain. We have both of us taken our ease over the winter months and whilst we perhaps had need, we can claim that no longer.'

He clipped his heels together in mock attention.

'You are right, my Nile goddess. I shall shake off the ice and break us from this winter palace.'

'How?'

Again he blinked.

'I have people I can call on. I sent to Mithridates of Cilicia on the last boats of the season. He owes me troops and I confidently expect them to arrive within a few weeks. I am not, however, sure they will be sufficient and would, if at all possible, like to resolve this with debate. It is the most civilised way.'

'So true,' Levi agreed.

Sosigenes rolled his eyes at the earnest Romans and Cleopatra had to bite her lip to stop herself giggling. This was not a laughing matter. Julius did not understand the underhand ways of many Egyptians.

'Talks are good,' she said carefully, 'but only with armed back-up. I have sent for an army too and I think we should wait until they arrive before we attempt to negotiate.'

Julius stared at her.

'You have sent for an army?'

'Of course. I need force so I have sent for it.'

'Where from?'

He was looking at her with offensive astonishment.

'From the rest of my country, of course, plus my protectorate of Idumea. I had, if you remember, raised an excellent army to defeat my brother before we were deflected by the arrival of first Pompey and then yourself. I sent that army home, foolishly as it turns out, so now I have recalled them.'

'I see.' Julius walked in a slow circle around her as if she were a curiosity in a street show. 'You never cease to surprise me, Cleopatra.'

'It surprises you that I can command an army?'

'Frankly, yes.'

'I am Queen of Egypt.'

'True. I forget sometimes that queen is a true role, not one for my own titillation.'

'Julius!'

'I am only being honest. I apologise. It is foolish of me. I'm just not used to women having such autonomy.'

'Which is perhaps why Rome is in such a sorry state.'

He sucked in his breath.

'Rome would be in a far finer state if her leader were not trapped in an Eastern palace by an unruly mob.'

'Which is why,' she agreed calmly, 'I have sent for an army.'

He bowed his head.

'Then let us hope our forces meet on the road and can march together.'

'Better yet, let us organise it that way.'

She caught a strange noise that she suspected might be the great Caesar grinding his teeth and smiled. It had been a surprisingly pleasant winter trapped in the palace with her Roman lover but what had been meant to be one night had run into one hundred. This narcissus had broken from the cold soil and she must break out of this liaison before it became too hard to do so. It had served its purpose and delivered a bonus too.

Cleopatra placed a hand on her belly at the thought. Just this morning, Charmion had examined her and confirmed what she had suspected for some weeks – she was bearing Caesar's child. His only child. She remembered Servilia telling her way back in Rome that Caesar was desperate for an heir. It was why he had married Calpurnia not Servilia, but Calpurnia had not delivered. No one had delivered, save Egypt's queen. This baby, she swore, would be a Horus, a son of Isis but it would not hurt him to have a foot in Jupiter's camp as well.

She turned back, finally tuning in to Julius' discussions with Levi and realised to her horror that he was proposing they invite Potheinos and Achillas to dine with them.

'Here?' she gasped. 'Julius, are you mad?'

'What harm can they do in the palace? We will demand they leave their swords at the door and have guards everywhere. They are just two men, Petra.'

'Two Egyptians,' she said darkly. 'My father told me on his death bed to watch out for snakes and those two slither through the undergrowth like no other.'

'So let us force them into the open.'

Cleopatra considered. She looked to the narcissus. If it was spring then the seas and roads were open once more.

'I agree,' she said. 'But only when we are ready.'

❖

'Cleopatra, may I talk with you?' Eiras came sidling into the bedchamber just as Julius was wrapping himself into his nonsensical toga for the negotiation dinner.

'Of course. What's wrong?'

'I have word of treachery.'

Julius was across in an instant, toga forgotten.

'What word?'

'I was cutting some of the men's hair this afternoon. There is no barber in the palace so I have been standing in and you would not believe what people tell you when you are tending to their comfort. One of them said to the next that he had heard Potheinos was going to, to kill you tonight, Caesar.'

'Kill me? How?'

'They weren't *that* open, but there were some very lewd jokes about the man having a "working dagger" beneath his tunic for once.'

'I told you inviting them in was a bad idea,' Cleopatra said, horrified, but Julius just smiled.

'On the contrary, it was an excellent one. What better excuse to kill someone than because they tried to kill *you*?' He clapped his hands, apparently delighted at the impending assassination attempt. 'Well done, Eiras – very well done. Now we just need to draw Potheinos' dagger out at our own time, not his. How do you fancy a little flirtation with the enemy?'

'No,' Cleopatra said, standing up. 'I do not want Eiras in danger. And, besides, Potheinos is a eunuch. He doesn't do flirtation.'

'Potheinos is more than capable of getting an ego hard-on.'

'Julius!'

'Well, he is. All Eiras need do is tell him he's wise, get close and stroke his thigh to find the knife.'

'What if he draws it upon her?'

'Then we will be ready. But he will not. It is me he wishes to stab and me he will lunge for if forced. Then we will have him.'

'But—'

'I'll do it,' Eiras said.

'Eiras, please. You do not need—'

'I'll do it,' she repeated, calm but firm. 'You do not deserve to be held captive in this ungrateful city, my queen, and getting rid of Potheinos is key. So, I'll do it.'

'And I will ensure you are protected,' Julius agreed.

After that there was little Cleopatra could do but find a dress. Arsinoë was nervous too and paced at her side in the hall. She was painted to perfection to face the man who had escaped the palace without her and wearing, Cleopatra noted with a start, a familiar golden collar.

'Is that the collar of the heir?'

Arsinoë touched immaculate fingertips to the gleaming jewels.

'It is. Am I not your heir?'

'I suppose so, yes.'

'So it is mine to wear, is it not?'

'I suppose so,' Cleopatra said again. She had not formally presented it but that was as much her fault as her sister's.

'It shows my bond with you,' Arsinoë assured her. 'It unites us against any enemies.'

She cocked her pretty head to the noise from the mob, who had gathered like violent lambs to someone else's slaughter. Cleopatra heard her name cursed but also caught grumblings against the 'wobbly boy-king' and prayed the balance of opinion could be tipped in her favour.

'Should I address them?' she asked Arsinoë.

'Best not. Let us conclude the talks first, then we will better know what we have to say.' She took Cleopatra's arm and squeezed it. 'All will be well, Sister.'

'I fear treachery.'

'And you are right to. This is Egypt, after all. But you have many friends and I will be near you. Come – let's get this over with.'

Cleopatra nodded but she was nervous all through the meal, taken on carefully separated couches in a large circle in the great hall, with many soldiers stood around the walls and swords laid ostentatiously either side of the door. Everyone was tense, not least Arsinoë who sat tightly opposite Achillas, glaring at him like a very Medusa from across the circle. Finally, cheeses were brought and sweet wine poured. Cleopatra felt her stomach churn as Eiras slid onto Potheinos' couch and began murmuring away to him. She looked to Julius and saw he was watching her friend like a hawk but was little comforted.

'So how can we resolve our differences?' he asked suddenly.

All eyes turned his way. Potheinos sat up.

'It is very simple,' he said. 'King Ptolemy XIII is fourteen now and by the terms of his father's will should come to his majority and rule as King. Cleopatra can, of course, remain as queen-consort but should be allowed to step back, take her leisure and fulfil her destiny as mother of Egypt's future rulers.'

Cleopatra's hand twitched to her belly but she forced it away. Now was most certainly not the right time for an announcement.

'It would seem a shame,' Julius said mildly, 'for Egypt to lose all Queen Cleopatra's experience and wisdom.'

Potheinos' nose wrinkled but he kept his composure. Cleopatra saw his hand shift to the hem of his tunic but Eiras did too.

'Of course,' Eiras said smoothly, 'we must not underestimate the experience and wisdom of King Ptolemy's advisors either.'

Potheinos looked at her and visibly swelled. Ego hard-on, Julius had coarsely called it earlier and although she'd objected at the time, Cleopatra could see exactly what he meant. She tried to look relaxed but could feel every fibre of her body straining. Achillas was sitting up straighter too and Cleopatra spotted Mardion and Charmion slide round behind him. She set down her wine glass. If Eiras could do this, then so could she.

'You think Potheinos wise, my lady?'

'Oh yes,' Eiras agreed, reaching out a hand to touch his knee. 'The very first time I came to the palace I recognised him as a man with command of a room.'

'You did?' Potheinos asked.

Eiras dipped her head and looked coyly up at him through her dark lashes but it was not until Cinna gave a low growl and took a few steps forward that the eunuch smiled and leaned in to her.

'But then, sadly, the mob descended and I had to leave with my mistress so I did not get to know you very well. It seems a shame to me that has happened again.'

Cleopatra watched, transfixed, as Eiras' hand crept up Potheinos' thigh. Achillas, more alert, got to his feet and, dead opposite, Arsinoë did the same. Julius sat forward and Ptolemy looked around, confused by the tightening of the atmosphere.

'I don't see why I should share power with anyone,' he objected.

'Not even your marvellous vizier?' Eiras asked. 'Look how ...' Her hand completed its journey to the top of his thigh and she pounced. 'What is this?!'

She almost got the dagger but the sheath presented it more easily to a hand from above than below and Potheinos was swift to move, leaping up and pushing her to the floor as he drew the thin blade and threw himself at Julius.

'No!' Cleopatra shrieked and dived into his path.

She saw the blade flash close to her face and was knocked to the floor but when she rolled around, it seemed she'd done enough to give Julius time to grab Potheinos' wrist. The guards leaped forward, severing the treacherous eunuch's head from his shoulders in vicious hacks. Achillas tried to go to his friend's aid but hesitated at the arc of blood and Mardion, moving with his usual deceptive speed, caught at his ankle, knocking him to the ground and sitting on his back. Cleopatra pulled herself slowly up and looked around in astonishment. They'd done it; they'd bested them. She put a hand to her cheek and felt blood spattered across it, warm and wet.

'Cleopatra!' Charmion shouted.

'I am well,' she called. 'Fret not.'

Too late, she realised it was not concern but warning. Cold steel kissed her throat and she froze.

'No silly movements, Sister dear.'

'Arsinoë?!'

Her sister gave a low chuckle.

'Surprised?' Her voice hardened. 'Back, all of you. And let him go.' She gestured to Achillas. 'Now!'

Mardion squeaked and leaped from Achillas' back, yanking Charmion away with him. Achillas clambered to his feet and ostentatiously brushed himself down.

'Magnificent,' he said adoringly to Arsinoë.

'Competent,' she said scathingly. 'Unlike you. Anyone would think you'd never seen blood before.'

'He was my friend.'

'He was a snivelling low-life, good only as the bluntest of instruments. He will be no loss to my government.'

'Your . . . ?' Cleopatra tried to twist in Arsinoë's arms but for so slight a woman she was surprisingly strong. 'You would be queen?' she stuttered.

Arsinoë rolled her eyes and touched her fingers to the heir's glittering collar.

'Of course I would be queen, Petra, my poor dear innocent. It is what I was born to, what I was bred for. You're not the only one with the Goddess within, you know. And I will offer Isis a so much more pleasing shape upon the throne.'

Cleopatra pursed her lips.

'Beauty comes not from the fleshly form but from the soul.'

'Is that what your precious priestly mother told you? Sweet.

228

But wrong. Listen.' She cupped an ear towards the low rumble of the mob beyond the gates. 'The people are far too rough to see a queen's soul. They note only the curve of her breasts, the sweetness of her smile, the pretty sorrow of her tears.'

'You do those all so well, Sister.'

'Thank you.'

'And entirely for your own benefit.'

Arsinoë shrugged.

'I do not see that your self-righteous care has got you very far, Petra, but I'm sure it will keep you warm in the afterlife.'

She dug the tip of the knife into Cleopatra's flesh and she felt the sting of its bite and the sticky warmth of her own blood.

'No!' Charmion cried and Arsinoë glanced her way.

'It's not very well brought up to murder your sister, is it, Charmion? My apologies but it turns out we are not such sibling-loving gods after all.'

'Arsinoë?' Ptolemy-Theos stuttered.

She sent a beaming smile his way.

'Not you, sweetheart. No one will hurt you. In fact, if you're really lucky, I will marry you.'

His eyes widened.

'I would love that, Arsinoë. But I am married already.'

'Not for much longer.'

Cleopatra's heart thudded.

'You would kill me?'

'*Execute* you, my queen, as you did Berenice. For the people, of course, to rid them of your poor rule. Oh, don't worry, I'll do it with dignity, not like those poor Romans. Heavens, they were surprised when I asked them to meet me in the main courtyard but they came like lambs. My nightdress was, of course, particularly see-through that night.'

'You?' Cleopatra gasped. 'You lured Bibulus' sons to Septimius' men?'

'Of course. Achillas was not sure about it at all, were you,

229

Achillas? Something squeamish about honour amongst soldiers. Men are so stupid.'

'Honour is not stupid.'

'Tell that to Bibulus' sons.'

Cleopatra looked to the army chief in confusion.

'Is that why Achillas left you here when Ptolemy had his tantrum?'

'In the granaries? Isis wept, no!' She reached out her spare hand to stroke the big man's cheek. 'He had long since crept back into my bed by then, had you not, Achillas? He left me here because I told him to. We needed someone to keep an eye on you and, oh, it was a tedious winter. You and Julius wimping around looking at clocks and calendars and street lights. I've never been more bored in all my life. Let me tell you now, Sister, that once I am queen, scholars and musty old engineers will be banned from the palace and it will be filled with musicians and dancers and people who know how to have fun.'

'Ruling is not about having fun, Arsinoë.'

'Well, perhaps it should be. It might make your precious soul a little brighter for the people to see. Berenice was far better at that than you.'

'And look where it got her.'

'Because you brought Rome to Egypt. And you have done it again. It's pathetic, Petra. Egypt was a great country millennia before the first Romans were running around in loin cloths and She can be a great country again if we stop pandering to them and look to our own business. That is what I will offer Egypt as queen, that is what the people want, and that is why your time on the throne is over.'

'You think?'

'I know.'

'You are clever, Arsinoë. Father told me to watch for snakes, but he did not warn me they would come in such beautiful colours.'

Arsinoë preened and Cleopatra felt the knife slip against her throat but the moment she tried to move, it was back.

'I told you, Sister, no silly movements. You and I are going to walk out of here. No one is going to touch me or you will die. We are going to stroll to the gate and we are going to let in Achillas' lovely army and then … If you are good, I might let you go into exile but, either way, I will be queen.'

'I see.'

Cleopatra glanced to Mardion. He was as white as the marble of the palace walls but he stared at her with intent and cocked one ear towards the mob, just as Arsinoë had a moment ago. Forcing her heart to still enough to listen, Cleopatra caught new sounds on the air. There was fighting outside. Either the army had grown impatient and were attacking the palace of their own accord, or new troops had arrived. There was only one way to find out.

'Come then, Sister, let us take this walk,' Cleopatra said. Arsinoë looked at her suspiciously. 'But you should know, before you dig your pretty knife into my flesh, that it will kill not one person but two.'

That, at least surprised her.

'You are … ?'

'Pregnant?' Julius finished on a gasp.

'I am.'

She should have told him before, when they were alone and could rejoice in the news, not fear its import, but if she were to die, she wanted him to know.

'Excellent,' Arsinoë said. 'You have given me the perfect reason to kill you, for who wants a queen with a Roman bastard in her belly? Go!'

Cleopatra's legs shook as Arsinoë pushed her out of the hall and across the main courtyard. The others followed, herded by Achillas, as the palace guards watched helplessly. Was this how it was all going to end, her life cut out by her own sister?

I'm sorry, Father, she thought as they made for the great doors. She heard the merry plash of the fountains, smelled the rich scent of the incense-infused candles, saw the sun-bright petals of the many narcissi which had sprung up to join their first bold comrade in the royal flowerbeds. It was a beautiful day to die, if die she must.

'Open up,' Arsinoë ordered, shoving her at the large wooden doors onto the street, the knife at her back.

'With pleasure,' she agreed.

She glanced to the sky, looking for Isis, but Isis was within and, placing one hand on her belly, she reached for the giant bolt with the other, drew it and stepped back. The doors flew open and there, bristling with swords and fury, was the army. *Her* army.

'Apollo!' she cried. 'Perfect timing.'

'No!' Arsinoë shrieked but her fury was muffled by Apollo knocking the knife from her hand and seizing her as the army of Upper Egypt stormed in to defend their queen. His men grabbed Achillas and disarmed his few men, and the palace was secure. Julius rushed to Cleopatra's side.

'Are you safe?'

She put a finger to her throat and drew it back with a bead of her own blood on its tip. It glistened, rich and red and pulsing with life.

'I am safe.'

'And the baby?'

'Is safe too.'

He held her close, and she leaned into him. His arms were so strong around her, the way he cradled her against the chaos in the palace so tender, that for a moment she found herself wondering if they could be together as Eiras and Cinna were together, as Levi and Sosigenes were together, as Servilia and . . . Her heart snagged. She was not a commoner to marry at will but the Queen of Egypt. She stepped away from him and looked around.

'Where's Ptolemy?'

Apollo cringed.

'I saw him grab a sword and run out into the crowd, my queen. It was bravely done but I fear he will have been no match for my soldiers.'

Sure enough, a messenger rode in, head low as he reported that the young king's first and last fight had not lasted long. The wobbly fourteen-year-old, fighting without the trappings of a king, had been cut down and thrown into the marshes.

'Are you sure?' Cleopatra demanded.

'Quite sure, my queen. I'm sorry, we did not realise—'

She cut him off.

'Bring me his body.'

Bring . . . ?'

'I need to see it. He needs a royal burial.'

'Cleopatra,' Julius said, 'he's a traitor to you and—'

'And the Alexandrians need to see he is gone and I am sole queen.'

He bowed.

'Of course. Clever.'

'Experienced.'

'And this one?' Apollo demanded, shoving Arsinoë before her. 'Does she get a royal funeral too?'

Cleopatra looked down on her sister, crumpled and weeping.

'Please, Petra,' Arsinoë begged, wrapping her arms around her legs, 'you can't kill me. I did it for love. You understand, surely? You must know how that feels.'

'I know how it feels to be betrayed by my siblings,' she shot back. 'I know how it feels to have a knife at my throat and I never want that again.'

Julius pushed Arsinoë roughly away from Cleopatra.

'We should execute her.'

'No!' Arsinoë wept. 'I was foolish, that's all. Weak and foolish. I am just a woman.'

'Your sister is "just a woman",' Julius retorted. 'And she is every bit as wise and strong as a man. I see no excuse. You should hang.'

'No!' Cleopatra said.

The spectre of Berenice's kicking body still haunted the far reaches of her mind and she did not wish to add a second sister into that dark space.

'She does not deserve to live, Petra.'

'And I do not deserve to have her death hanging over me. Prison,' she told Apollo.

'Are you sure, my queen?' Charmion asked. 'Here? Where any disaffected Egyptian might seek her out?'

She had a point but what other solution was there?

Julius sighed.

'If you insist on being merciful, Queen, let me take her to Rome. Our prisons are dark and secure and far from any traitors.'

'Rome?' Arsinoë gasped. 'No! Oh, Petra, please not Rome.'

Cleopatra looked down on her, pitiful in her pleading. And endlessly calculating.

'Rome,' she agreed. 'I had to flee there whilst you played at flattery with Berenice so it seems a just destination.'

'But you hated it!' she wailed.

'Not as much as you will,' Cleopatra told her darkly. 'And remove that now!'

For the second time it was Eiras who took back the heir's collar and handed it to Cleopatra as Apollo yanked Arsinoë away. She took it weakly and looked down on the glittering symbol of succession and, it seemed, treachery.

'You did well, my queen,' Charmion assured her.

'Very well,' Eiras agreed. 'It is more than she deserves.'

'You can always, you know, come and visit her,' Julius offered.

Cleopatra forced a laugh, though she was not entirely sure he was jesting and it was a troubling thought. Rome was a good place for a prison, not so good for a queen. No, her interlude with Julius Caesar was over in the harshest of ways and she must let both him and her treacherous sister go and concentrate on winning Alexandria back to her side as sole head of a united Egypt.

Chapter Twenty-four

Cleopatra stood on the palace wall, watching as the royal barge was prepared for departure. Julius had been called to Pontus and she had offered him her own ship to see him down the Nile to Giza from whence he could cross into Palestine and march north. King Mithridates was facing rebels and, as his army had helped break them out of the palace, Julius was honour bound to go to his aid. And thank Isis for that. She'd been beginning to think he'd stay forever. And beginning to like it.

She pulled her eyes away from the barge and let them sweep across the city, thankfully quiet at last. She had given Ptolemy a quiet but dignified funeral, in the golden armour he had not worn in his brief, helpless fight, and had made it clear to the subdued Alexandrians that she was now their only option. So far they were quiescent. Cleopatra had offered civilian accommodation to Apollo and those of her army who wished to stay in the city, and their presence was helping to keep order and to enforce the idea of Egypt as a country not just a city. She was slowly building bridges but she had to get Julius away as soon as possible to be sure of continued loyalty.

She watched as her lover emerged from the palace and strode down to the royal docks to supervise the packing of his horse and armour. The animal looked nervous of the great boat and Cleopatra saw him step close, caress her muzzle and talk to her until he could, personally, lead her on board. She sighed. The man was a constant contradiction. How could a general hard enough to smash his way through Gaul to the wild shores of Britannia, have it in him to be so gentle? How could the man who had torn Rome in two, spend a winter so happily in the company of scholars and engineers? And how could a soldier who would execute beautiful Arsinoë without a moment's hesitation, caress her in bed with the devotion of an artist. Her resolve faltered.

'Julius!' He looked up from on board her ship and waved. 'I am coming with you.'

At her side Eiras raised a single eyebrow.

'You are?'

She turned away to hide her blush.

'I have a letter I must send with him and have not yet had time to write it.'

'Not had time or not found the words?'

'Both.'

'I see.'

'And, besides, I think it best I see him off Egypt's shores, do you not?'

'Oh, I do. A noble motivation, my queen.' Cleopatra grimaced at her and Eiras grinned wickedly back. 'Have fun.'

❖

Three days later Cleopatra looked up from her papyri to see the sun dropping over the great pyramid of Khufu just beyond the royal barge in her docks at Giza. Julius was on deck outside the doors of their chamber and she should join him before Isis painted the sky in her most glorious colours but she couldn't resist one more read over her words. They'd taken so long to write and were still so very imperfect but tomorrow Julius would ride for Palestine and she would return to Alexandria. Time was running out.

Servilia,

 I write to you from Egypt where I have been sorely beset by my own people but have finally triumphed with the help of your own Julius Caesar. He has proved himself a most able general and we have worked well together to secure my throne. There has also, I confess, been more to our relationship and I am carrying his child.

 I have no need to tell you of his charm. I do, however, feel the need to tell you that I am sorry, because I know how much he means to you. This was not the same. We were thrown together as rulers in a very specific, very precarious set of circumstances that were best fused with . . . well, you know. Those circumstances are now past. He returns to Rome and to you.

 As for me, the baby is mine, and Egypt is mine and I hope, Servilia, that you can find it in your heart to understand and forgive and wish me well in caring for both.

Yours with love,
Cleopatra

'Petra!' Julius was at the door. 'What are you writing?'

'A letter to a friend,' she said, dropping wax hastily onto the join. 'Could you carry it to Rome for me?'

'To Rome? To whom do you write?'

Cleopatra swallowed.

'To Servilia.'

'Servilia?! Petra, you know that she and I—'

'Of course I know. Why do you think I write?'

'What have you said?'

He peered curiously over her shoulder but she snatched up the scroll and pressed her royal seal into the wax.

'Women's business – mere trifles.'

Julius shook his head.

'I have been with you long enough, Queen Cleopatra, to know that women's business is never mere trifles. Why are you writing to my . . . '

'Lover?'

'Former lover.'

'I hope not.'

'You do?'

'Of course. Ours has been but a dalliance, a fusion of, of purposes in a very . . . a very specific set of circumstances.'

'That's how you see it?'

'Do you not?'

'It has been a fusion of something for sure.'

He kissed her and she felt the heat of them but time was running out.

'I am not writing to *your* lover,' she said, trying to writhe away, 'but to *my* friend. It is not all about you, you know.'

He held onto her, his grip firm and sure.

'I bet you wrote just a little bit about me though, didn't you?'

'I wrote about my baby.'

'*Our* baby. I wish I could stay to see it born.'

'Rome is a cruel master.'

'And Egypt an enticing mistress. Oh, but look . . . ' Isis, bless her, had chosen this moment to cast her colours across the vast desert sky and Julius pulled Cleopatra onto the deck, leaving the scroll thankfully forgotten on her desk. 'Is it not beautiful?' he murmured.

'The sky or the pyramid?'

'Both. When was the pyramid built?'

'The fourth dynasty,' Cleopatra told him. 'That's twenty-six centuries ago.'

'Twenty-six . . . ?' He shook his head. 'And we revere Romulus and Remus for founding Rome seven hundred years past.'

Cleopatra gave a modest cough.

'I'm sure they were very clever men.'

He laughed.

'Don't patronise us, Petra.'

'It can be very hard not to when . . . ' She indicated the stunning monument and he nodded.

'I see that.' He took her into his arms, smiling down at the press of her belly between them. 'You will come to Rome, Petra?'

'Why?'

'You know I wanted to stay for the birth of our child.'

'But duty calls you.'

'Try not to sound so relieved.'

He looked genuinely hurt and she kissed him.

'I *am* relieved, Julius. This has been wonderful, truly, but it cannot last and we both know that. I do not want it to end in regrets or arguments. I will send you news of the baby when he or she comes and I hope you will be glad of it but they will be heir to Egypt.'

'And perhaps to Rome – if you come and visit.'

She shook her head.

'Rome would never accept a prince as its heir.'

'She might, if I ordered it.'

'Oh Julius, you forget I have been there. I have met Cato, I have wrangled with Brutus, I have seen my father forced to enter a party over the back wall. If I came to Rome, I would not even be allowed past the precious run of stones that marks your sacred border.'

'Things are going to change once I'm back.'

'Not that much. Now hush and enjoy the final blessings of Isis on your visit.'

She pointed to the sky, lighting the pyramid blood red before them but already Julius' arms were snaking around her bulging waist and he was pulling her back into the cabin.

'Surely not Her *final* blessing,' he said and, as his lips found hers, she surrendered. After all, time was running out.

Four weeks later, she gave birth, up on her knees like the monkeys that ran amok in Alexandria's streets, pushing out all her frustration and fear with the child of her womb. Eiras stood before her, her forehead against Cleopatra's own as she urged her to strength, and Charmion and Mardion stationed themselves at either shoulder, fetching cloths and drinks and sweet treats to keep her energy high. Sosigenes and Levi stood at her feet, firmly turned away, and the court officials and ambassadors paced and murmured in the antechamber beyond. At first Cleopatra felt she should be contained, dignified, but as the pains grew, she cared not.

What would Isis do? she asked herself and the answer came through the haze of pain, as if from the Goddess herself: *Do not men in battle utter war cries? Roar, Cleopatra — roar like a queen and like a mother and let everyone know this, my precious child, is coming into the world.*

So Cleopatra roared and she pushed and finally, on a rush of blessed release, the baby burst from between her legs and gave a fierce cry all of its own. Cleopatra looked down and there, lying on the bed before her was the reddest, gunkiest, most wrinkled creature she had ever seen. She loved him instantly.

'A boy,' she breathed, gathering him into her arms, the pulsing cord still linking them together. '*My* boy.'

If she had thought her feelings for Julius an instant storm, they were not a patch on the tempest whirling through her now. This was her son, her own tiny Horus, heir to Egypt.

And maybe Rome, a treacherous voice whispered in her head, Isis perhaps, playing mischief with her, for they both knew that could never be. *Should* never be. Cleopatra shook it away and, as Eiras cut the cord, she lifted him high to the courtiers. The news whistled down their ranks and out to the mob beyond who roared, finally, with hard-earned approval. She had, perhaps, won her throne by being the last of the not-so-sibling-loving gods standing, but now the work truly began. She could replace that precarious, rivalrous little net with a single, strong rope that the mob could grasp with confidence. Never again, she swore, would she share her power with any bar her own son. She was Egypt's queen and that was enough. Surely, that was enough?

PART THREE

Rome, 46 BC

Chapter Twenty-five

Queen Cleopatra,

Greetings from Rome. The city is in great excitement about your visit, as you can imagine. Rumours abound about your son who is, variously, endowed with dragon's scales, the size of Hercules, definitely Caesar's, definitely not Caesar's and even half boy, half crocodile. The things people will believe of the East! It is good to be back, I suppose, although Rome simmers with tension, as you will see for yourself.

Julius, at least, is holding it together. He smashed the rebels at Pontus in just three hours you know. As he said himself, he came, he saw, he conquered, and he seems a man truly energised. I cannot think why – perhaps it is your Eastern sunshine ...

I was so grateful when he pardoned my dear husband who, after all, was only fighting as ordered by his direct superiors. There is talk of him being given the governorship of Cisalpine Gaul, which is horribly far from Rome, if you ask me, but Brutus says beggars cannot be choosers and says it so darkly that I know better than to object.

His mood has not been improved by the death of Cato, though if you ask me Rome has been. Porcia is whining a lot, which is irritating. She is a widow now as Bibulus went down with his poorly managed ships in the Greek seas, and is more bitter than ever. She seeks another husband, and Isis help whatever poor man she gets her claws into for they are sharper than ever. It's Cato this and Cato that, as if he were a martyr not a traitor but I tell you, without him and Pompey bullying senate they are much less obstreperous. They have appointed Julius Imperator for ten years, which means dictator and makes him as good as a king if you ask me, though I haven't said so to Brutus who is dreadfully touchy. He whines nearly as much as Porcia.

Cato, of course, could not just go quietly like so many other servants of the Empire. Oh no, the gruesome man tore his own guts out with an eating knife rather than surrender to Caesar. He was holed up in Africa and the quacks there stuffed his guts back in and sewed him up but he ripped them open a second time and barricaded the door so they could not prevent him bleeding out. Why he could not just slit his throat and be done with it, I have no idea, but it certainly makes a gory story for Rome's gossips and it is tearing poor Brutus apart. He feels that suicide is dishonourable, but still reveres his uncle so has no idea how to interpret it or who to blame. It is not good for him at all and there is me, his wife, still unable to cheer him with a child.

But that is not your concern. I am so glad you finally agreed to come to Rome again and cannot wait to see you. It will be quite like old times!

Yours with love,
Claudia

Cleopatra had read the letter so many times it was worn around the edges but she needed her dear friend's easy enthusiasm to smooth out her own severe reservations about this damned trip. She had not wanted to come, had not intended to come – and yet here she was.

It was her own fault really. She had vowed that once she was established as Queen of Egypt she would listen to her subjects and she had, setting up councils, touring, and asking advice, and everyone wanted their precious new prince formally acknowledged as Caesar's son. They called him Caesarion – little Caesar – and delighted in the jewel that heirless Rome must surely covet. And who could blame them? They had all been too ravaged by the Republic not to value such a hold over them. It was still, however, Cleopatra who had to face the damned city, not to mention its glorious leader.

Carefully folding up the letter, she tucked it into the small travelling case at her side in the carriage. Rome was approaching and soon she would be back, ten years since she'd last been here. It was a nerve-wracking prospect and she glanced out the window to check that the closely guarded cart full of treasures was still with them. Egypt had always been able to dazzle with Her riches and Cleopatra had every intention of showing these coarse Romans what true cultural history looked like. Amongst other treasures were a pharaonic death mask from the nineteenth dynasty, a half-sized obelisk from the twenty-sixth, and a shining new statue of Isis, coated in solid gold and bearing Cleopatra's own face to show the divinity within her.

At her side, her son stirred in his sleep, then his eyes suddenly pinged open and, just like that, he was wide awake. Ptolemy-Caesar looked around him and let out an angry cry to see that he was still in the carriage in which he had spent most of the day as they rode north from the port. A month after his first birthday, he was an avid crawler and straining to walk, spending most of his days edging himself around any surface to steady his chubby legs. Confinement in a carriage, however luxurious, was not his idea of fun.

'There, there,' Mardion said, leaping to attend him. The eunuch had fallen in love with Caesarion nearly as hard as Cleopatra and was there to tend to his every need. 'We're nearly there, look. We're nearly in Rome.'

He drew back the curtain, holding tight to the little boy as he strained to lean out and see, though in truth Mardion was leaning nearly as far. Cleopatra heard him grunt and then mutter something to Caesarion before he turned back into the carriage with a shocked 'Is this it?'

Despite her nerves, Cleopatra giggled.

'This is it,' she agreed. 'This is Rome.'

She leaned out of her own window, looking down the Appian way, past the rows of sombre tombs that stood sentinel to the city gates. They were close enough to see the piles of leaning buildings that formed the ramshackle *Subura* and Cleopatra was sharply reminded of her first sight of the city.

'It's so scruffy!' Mardion said as they reached the gates and hit the uneven cobbles of the maze of streets. He snatched Caesarion back in as beggars leaped to the side of the carriage, and pulled the curtain firmly shut. Cleopatra patted his knee.

'It's not all like this,' she reassured him. 'The Forum is quite impressive, though not a patch on our own government buildings.'

Mardion grinned at her and reached into his case for a honey cake to keep Caesarion amused a little longer. Across from them, Eiras stirred from where she'd been napping on Cinna's shoulder as the poet jiggled, excited to be in Rome once more.

'You like this place?' Mardion asked him curiously.

'Of course,' Cinna agreed. 'It's home. I have friends here and the city has many surprises if you know where to look.'

Mardion tilted his head.

'Then I hope you will show me.'

'It will be my pleasure. I know all the best parties!'

Mardion cheered up and Cleopatra looked happily around the carriage, grateful to have her friends with her. Only Charmion was not here, claiming she was too old to travel, so Cleopatra had appointed her Ruler of Egypt in her absence, Levi volunteering to stand as her deputy. Sosigenes, sat on Eiras' other side, had tried to persuade him to come home but Levi had said he felt ten times more at home in Alexandria than in Rome and refused even his dear partner's pleadings. Sosigenes had taken consolation in the completion of Julius' year-clock which he held clutched on his lap like a baby, ready to be presented and put to use on Rome's struggling year.

'We're not going into the centre?' he asked, edging the curtain open again as the carriage took a sharp turn left to cross over the Tiber.

'No,' Cleopatra confirmed. 'We're not allowed to. Or at least, I'm not. Rome is allergic to royalty.'

Sosigenes shook his head.

'How tolerant. So where are we going?'

'To the Horti Caesaris, Julius' villa on the other side of the river where we cannot infect the Republic with our Eastern decadence.'

'Bet we can,' Mardion said, 'if Cinna's parties are half as good as he claims.'

'Oh, they are,' Cinna assured him. 'Wait till you meet Clodia – you'll love her!'

Cleopatra thought that was probably true and her heart warmed at the thought of the extravagant woman who had once stood as her friend and hopefully would again.

'What would Isis do?' she muttered, looking down at her gown.

She had changed at the last stop into a pristine Isis costume, with Caesarion dressed as the goddess' blessed son, Horus, to show their ancient lineage, and was determined to enter Rome as a proud Queen. Her face was painted with Eiras' boldest cosmetics and she was dripping in gold. Let them rail against royalty if they must, but they should know its power.

The carriage turned over a bridge and headed down a long driveway, lined with elegant Cypress trees before pulling up outside a low, white villa. Sweeping steps led up to an arched entrance and at the sound of their arrival people spilled excitedly out. Caesarion tugged at the curtain, wriggling excitedly as the great figures of Roman society pointed and waved at him.

'Let the games commence!' Cinna cried and threw back the door, leaping out and flinging his arms wide.

There was an audible ripple of disappointment and he grimaced but turned good-naturedly to hand down first Eiras and then Sosigenes. The crowd pressed forward. Cleopatra felt her legs shake and pressed her hands on her knees to still them. She was the Queen of Egypt, Isis incarnate; these people held no fear for her. Did they?

And then she saw him.

He stood, calm and relaxed at the top of the steps and as his eye caught hers and he raised a wry eyebrow, her whole body stilled. He was here, Julius was here, and he was waiting for her. She could not help the rush of lust that surged through her body and was annoyed with herself for it. She had taken the precaution of marrying a second brother-husband before she came. As little Ptolemy-Philopater remained interested only in insects, it had been purely ceremonial but she had thought that being married might shore her up against Caesar. She could see now how foolish that had been.

She cast around for Servilia but could not see her in the crowds surging to the steps so there was nothing for it but to face him alone. Hitching a wriggling Caesarion onto her hip, she rose, drew a deep breath and stepped out. A surge of noise met their appearance and she fixed on a smile as she made her way steadily through the crowd towards him. His eyes moved from her face to his son and he took an involuntary step forward, giving her further courage. At last she was opposite him.

'Greetings Cleopatra, Queen of Egypt and honoured friend and ally of the Roman people. We welcome you.' The crowd cheered and, under cover of the noise, Julius leaned in to offer her a formal kiss of peace and whispered, 'I, in particular, welcome you.'

Her body filled with instant warmth but she angled herself determinedly away and addressed the crowd.

'I am pleased to be in Rome once more, and my son, Ptolemy-Caesar with me.'

They gave a delighted little gasp at his name and, if Julius was cross at her refusing his intimacy, he did not show it. Taking his namesake into his arms, he stared into his face as if he would absorb every last inch of him and, despite herself, Cleopatra's heart swelled at the public acknowledgement of his son. She could hear the Romans hissing and whispering and wondered if they were upset at the lack of dragon's scales or crocodile's teeth on her bonny son. Oh, she hoped so. No one else had given Caesar a son. No one but her. The bounties of the East were rich and she intended to show that to Rome now that she was here in state, so, taking Julius' arm, she strode with him into the villa, all society trailing eagerly behind.

For a little time, they trod the room together but greetings were self-consciously formal and she was relieved when Julius was claimed by a pair of sycophantic senators and, with Mardion taking Caesarion, she was able to step away for a moment. Almost instantly, Clodia swooped in.

'Cleopatra! Sorry, *Queen* Cleopatra. It's so wonderful to see you again. You look so well, so ripe and luscious and elegant.'

Cleopatra smiled.

'Hello, Clodia. You look well too.'

It was true that Rome's wildest woman was still wonderfully willowy in the brightest gauzy fabrics, although Cleopatra had to hide her shock at the lines around her stunning eyes and the mottling of the skin on her elegant hands.

'I look old,' Clodia said, as if reading her mind, then she leaned down and winked, adding, 'luckily I don't feel it. Or behave it either. There's nothing like a younger man in your bed to rejuvenate you.'

Cleopatra laughed; she wasn't changed much then. And now Fulvia was coming up at her side, glamorous in her favourite red.

'I was sorry to hear about Clodius' death,' Cleopatra said to her.

Fulvia gave a small shrug.

'It was bound to happen one day, the way he lived.'

Clodia leaned in.

'Fulvia is all set to marry again – to Mark Antony.'

Cleopatra vaguely recalled the kind-natured, blond-curled man who'd stood as Gabinius' lieutenant against Berenice.

'Congratulations.'

'Thank you. He's a good man and better at staying alive than most.'

'Praise indeed.'

'Oh, we understand each other. He says he's marrying me so Porcia doesn't get him whilst he sleeps.'

Clodia and Fulvia laughed wildly and gestured to a nearby woman who turned and glared at them. Cleopatra's heart sank.

'What are you saying about me?' Porcia's familiarly whiney voice demanded.

'We're just wondering what lucky Roman might get the chance to wed you.'

Porcia stuck her nose in the air.

'I am still grieving for Bibulus.'

'No one could grieve for Bibulus,' Clodia said.

'A good wife should always observe a decent mourning period and not go jumping into the first bed she can find,' Porcia shot back with a snide look at Fulvia.

'Oh, I don't know,' Fulvia countered. 'I think it depends on whether you can find a bed to jump into.'

Cleopatra hid her smiles as Porcia bristled.

'There are plenty of men wanting to marry me, but I value myself enough to wait for the right one. Unlike some, who will bed any man who comes riding into their city.'

Now she cast her sly look Cleopatra's way. Cleopatra stared her down.

'Are you talking about me?'

She waited for an answer but Porcia, looking nervously around Julius' villa, chose evasion.

'I suppose at least our own dear Caesar wasn't summarily murdered in Alexandria, unlike my poor stepsons.'

'That was unfortunate,' Cleopatra agreed smoothly. 'I was very sorry that the Roman soldiers camped outside the city saw fit to murder one of their own and sent them for swift punishment to your husband.' Porcia gave a strange little growl in the back of her throat. 'I'm also so glad to hear your concern for your "own, dear Caesar",' Cleopatra went on, warming to her onetime favourite pastime of Porcia-baiting. 'I'm sure his welfare was top of your list when your husband was sailing his ships against him.'

'Bibulus was acting as ordered, just like Brutus and Cassius and all the other soldiers Caesar has pardoned since Pharsalus.'

'As was your father, the honourable Cato, when he continued to oppose him from Africa?' Clodia suggested.

Porcia sucked in her breath and Fulvia pulled at Clodia's arm. It was a low blow and Cleopatra almost felt sorry for Porcia as she battled for composure.

'My father was a principled, high-minded, courageous man,' she spat.

'He certainly had guts,' Clodia countered and this time Fulvia did pull her away.

Cleopatra stood opposite Porcia who looked lost suddenly amidst the turning crowd.

'I'm sorry Cato died,' she offered.

Porcia looked up, eyes shimmering, but then forcibly hardened her gaze.

'At least he kept his principles,' she spat, 'unlike some who are happy to sell them for their own gain.'

She gave a curt nod to Caesarion, playing in a circle of courtiers, and all Cleopatra's sympathy drained away.

'Life is hard enough, Porcia,' she said, 'without hiding from happiness when it is offered.'

Then she spun on her heel and made for her son, but before she could get there she was ambushed by a flying head of curls.

'Cleopatra! It's so good to see you.'

Claudia flung her arms around her and, laughing at the simple warmth of this greeting, Cleopatra hugged her back.

'You too, Claudie. How are you?'

Claudia pulled back.

'Oh, you know me. I'm fine. Well. Too well.' Her eyes clouded and Cleopatra felt a sharp pang of sorrow for this good-natured girl who so deserved to be happy. So many Roman women, it seemed, struggled to conceive.

'I'm sorry.'

Claudia leaned in.

'Me too. Brutus is so down, Cleopatra. I mean, he's happy to be pardoned obviously and very pleased to be governing Cisalpine Gaul. No complaints there, oh no. We're very lucky and all that. But he's still torn up by the very fact there was a civil war at all and goes over and over what went wrong until I swear he will drive himself mad with it. And that's before he even starts on Cato and his self-seeking suicide stunt.'

Cleopatra blinked.

'That's a little harsh, isn't it, Claudia?'

Claudia sighed.

'Probably, but it's sent poor Brutus into such a spin and I could do without it. Why couldn't Cato just have been killed in battle like anyone else? Some artist is painting a picture you know – all knives and guts and blood. Why? What's the point in dragging it all out?'

'Absolutely,' Cleopatra agreed. 'I've spent the last year working to bring Alexandria back to harmony after our own ... disputes. Luckily the harvests have been good, my officials are now all loyal, and the birth of Caesarion has distracted everyone.'

'He's so cute, Cleopatra! Quite the handsome lad and there's little doubting who his father is. I bet there'll be no gossip on that score now that everyone has seen him, for he's the image of Caesar.'

'Do you think so?'

'Oh, yes. Julius could see it straight away, I could tell.'

'Julius had no reason to doubt it.'

Claudia bit her lip.

'No, no, no. Of course not. I didn't mean ... '

Cleopatra hushed her.

'It's fine, Claudie. People gossip. Now, I'd really like to talk to Servilia. Do you think she'll let me?'

'She'll have to,' Claudia said, 'you are the honoured guest. Come on.'

She took Cleopatra's arm and steered her expertly between the crowds and suddenly there was Servilia, standing talking to a small group with her back to them. Cleopatra felt the vast villa close in on her, but there was no stopping Claudia.

'Aunt Servilia, look who is here.'

Servilia turned, saw Cleopatra and stiffened. She gave an exaggerated bow.

'Your majesty. Did you have a good journey?'

'Yes, thank you,' Cleopatra said. 'Did you get my letter?'

'Yes. Thank you.'

'I really am—'

'There is no need to explain yourself to me.'

'But I wanted to.'

'And you did. Thank you. Is there anything else?'

There was, Cleopatra thought, there was so much else but it was clear that Servilia did not wish to talk about it, or to address Cleopatra at all and the only gracious thing to do was to bow her head and excuse herself.

'Well, that was fun,' Claudia said brightly.

'Does she see Caesar still?' Cleopatra could not stop herself asking.

'Not in private.'

Isis help her, but Cleopatra was glad at that – though it could, of course, be because he had a new mistress. She glanced around the villa and found him standing stock still, staring straight at her. As he caught her eye, he gave her a slow, deliberate wink, hardly appropriate for an honoured guest but, to her shame, all the more enticing for it.

She looked to the large doors and saw that the sun was dipping so low towards the trees that its light was slanting almost directly into the villa. People would start to leave soon, for no one liked to negotiate the streets of Rome in the dark. Perhaps once Julius had Egyptian-style lamps put in, it would be a different but, for now, thank heavens, the pickpockets could roam freely and the rich would seek the safety of their homes before the sun was below the horizon.

'You are wishing us gone,' a low voice said and she looked around to see Brutus.

Claudia was talking with Fulvia and for the moment they were alone.

'Of course not,' she said and then, feeling false, gave a little shrug. 'I admit I am tired from the journey.'

'You crave your bed?' he asked slyly and she rolled her eyes.

'Not you too, Brutus? I am here as Egypt's queen.'

'And mother of Caesar's child.'

'Mother of my own child.'

He drew in a deep breath.

'True. I am sorry. You are lucky to be so blessed.'

'And I am sorry you have not been. Perhaps now you are back in Rome . . . ?'

'I have been married to Claudia for eleven years, Cleopatra, and the gods do not see fit to bless us. What does that mean? You carry Isis within, do you not, so what is She saying about my marriage?'

Cleopatra put her hands up.

'It's not like that, Brutus. I am not some sort of oracle.'

'Then what are you?'

'A queen.'

'Hmmm. It seems a waste of a goddess to me.'

'Thank you very much.'

'Oh, not you personally. I'm sure you're very good, as royals go. Just, you know, philosophically.'

Cleopatra had forgotten the abstract nature of her friend's husband, but Claudia said he was troubled and that was sad.

She remembered him coming to her in Alexandria, working on Pompey's mission but so very unsure if he should be. The civil war had torn more than just Rome apart and some rifts would take longer to heal than others.

'I'm glad you are back in favour, Brutus,' she said gently.

'Should I be, though? I was Julius' enemy. I chose my side and it was the wrong one – as you told me it would be. Why do I deserve to be allowed to change?'

'Because it was a strange set of circumstances, I suppose. There were arguments in favour of both sides.'

'As there always are. But when a man chooses—'

'He has the right to admit his mistake.'

'And a woman?'

'Sorry?'

'I hear your sister is imprisoned beneath Rome's streets.'

'Because she tried to kill me.'

'As I did Caesar.'

'With a knife direct to his throat?'

'Not personally, but the Republic is greater than the individual so, in effect, yes.'

She stared at him, her head spinning.

'You think I should give my sister a second chance, Brutus?'

'Not necessarily. I am simply saying that it is the same idea, philosophically.'

Cleopatra's brain hurt. Conversations with Brutus were often like this.

'I don't know. Arsinoë's was a personal vendetta not a political struggle.'

'But philosophically . . . '

'Oh, Brutus,' Claudia said, coming up and wrapping her arm around his waist, 'not philosophy again.'

For a moment he looked furious but then he controlled himself and dropped a gentle kiss onto her forehead.

'I'm sorry. Come, we should get home before it is dark. Good evening, Queen Cleopatra. I shall look forward to talking to you again.'

'And I you,' Cleopatra agreed, privately hoping that next time she was a little fresher to handle his endless questions.

Philosophically, did Arsinoë deserve another chance? The thought had not even entered her mind before but it was a spiky one now it was in there and she rubbed at her temple.

'Are you well, Petra?'

Julius was close up behind her and her body flared. The guests were flocking from the villa as fast as the sun was dipping and they were all but alone.

'Is Arsinoë still in Rome, Julius?'

'Arsinoë? She is deep in the prisons where she belongs. Why?'

'Oh, no reason.'

She didn't want to think about it right now and looked around for Caesarion who was cooing happily in Mardion's arms as three young women kissed him goodbye.

'He likes the ladies already,' Julius commented.

'Just like his father.'

'Not any more.' His voice was hoarse.

'You have given up women?'

'I had. Today, though, I feel my resistance crumbling.' He stared at her so intently that she felt the villa sway and had to clutch at him for support. He looked down at her hand on his arm and then placed his own very carefully over it. 'You must be . . . ready for bed.'

'*Must* I?'

He checked himself.

'Might you be . . . interested in bed?'

Her loins throbbed.

'How far away,' she asked carefully, 'is bed?'

'Too far,' he moaned and the next thing she knew, he was snaking an arm around her waist and pulling her backwards into the villa, away from Mardion and Caesarion, away from the last of the guests, away from the public spaces and through the nearest door. It was a linen cupboard, small and utilitarian, but neither of them cared. Twisting into his arms, she kissed him hungrily, the rest of the tricky world melting away in the heat of his passion.

'Julius,' she moaned against his lips as he hitched her up onto the shelf, scrabbling at her skirts, all his customary composure gone. And then he was kissing her again, and pushing himself into her and she clutched her hands tight around his neck and rained alternate blessings and curses on Isis for bringing her back to him.

Chapter Twenty-six

My dearest Cleopatra, my queen,

You ask me if you should speak with Arsinoë but I know not what to advise. You are sisters, so should stand together, but Arsinoë, I fear, has always preferred to stand apart. She never liked the attention to be on anyone else and I worry that she has grown into a woman who understands loyalty only to herself. If she was prepared to kill you once, she will be prepared to do so again, by whatever means she can find.

You told me, dear one, that your royal father cautioned you against snakes and I fear that this most beautiful of royal reptiles is also the most deadly. If you must go, tread with the utmost care.

With love,
Charmion

'Down here?' Cleopatra looked uncertainly at the rickety stone steps, worn smooth by centuries of feet and echoing with cries of despair.

'It *is* a prison, your majesty,' the guard said apologetically.

'Of course,' she agreed, feeling foolish. 'Mardion?' Mardion came rushing forward to offer his sturdy arm and she felt instantly better. 'Is this madness?' she asked him in a whisper as they headed downwards.

'She is your sister, my queen. I think you would feel unhappy if you did not at least try to speak to her.'

Cleopatra nodded and focused on the steps. They passed cage after cage, some large and filled with a roiling collection of men, some tiny with just a lone figure inside, hunched up in miserable resignation or throwing himself against the bars in perpetual fury. Cleopatra's skin crawled. She'd thought she was being merciful sparing Arsinoë's life after the rebellion but perhaps she had in fact been condemning her to something worse than death.

When they finally passed through an iron gate, however, she was surprised by a sudden flood of light. Stepping nervously through she found a sealed room, freshly tiled and swept clean, with a barred window high up in the bright walls to let the sunshine in. The bed was large and comfortably furnished with a feather mattress and soft furs and opposite it was a small oak table and two padded chairs. In one of them sat Arsinoë, her dress clean, her hair plaited and her face a stonily beautiful mask beneath her diadem. She did not get up and after a moment's hesitation, Cleopatra edged forward.

'Sister.'

Arsinoë stared at her, cold and unblinking.

'How good of you to come, Cleopatra.'

'I wanted to see you, Arsinoë, to talk to you.'

'How lovely. I'm a little busy at the moment, as you see, but I'm sure I can fit in someone of your great importance.'

She did not offer Cleopatra the second seat but Mardion pulled it forward and she sunk into it opposite her sister.

'This is not so bad,' she tried, gesturing around.

'Not so bad? Did we, or did we not, Cleopatra, grow up in a palace the size of a small city? A palace with courtyards and gardens, with a renowned centre of learning, a theatre and beautiful temples, with its own harbour and three banqueting halls.'

Her eyes bored into Cleopatra, deep with loathing.

'And did you not, sister, attempt to kill me within it?'

Arsinoë tossed her head.

'It is no more than you have done. You stood at father's side whilst he hung Berenice. You let Ptolemy-Theos go to his death against a Jewish army brought in by you, his co-regent, to drive him from his own city. You can claim righteousness, Cleopatra, but you are the traitor. You are the whore who sold Egypt to the Romans for your own gain and it is *I* who end up in this shit hole! Clever, sister, very clever.'

She spat the last words so viciously that saliva flew into Cleopatra's face and she recoiled. Mardion stepped protectively between them and Arsinoë let out a manic laugh.

'Ah look, how sweet – your pet eunuch is protecting you. Do you shag him too? Do you take his floppy, disconnected little dick into your queenly mouth and make him—'

The slap rang out around the cell, cutting off the coarse words. Arsinoë put her hand to her cheek and Mardion looked down at his own as if unable to believe himself capable of what he had done.

'You were right, my queen,' he said thickly, 'this was a madness and we should go. Now.'

He hurried her away, Arsinoë's taunting laugh following them back up the tunnels to the teeming streets. Cleopatra went with her cheeks burning. This had been a foolish idea indeed. What had she been looking for – Reconciliation? Contrition? Absolution? When would she learn not to be so naïve? There were no sibling-loving gods and the sooner she accepted that, the better. She stalked back to Julius' villa, determined to be glad of her sister's incarceration, but Arsinoë's bald defiance still niggled at her and when Julius welcomed her back as his 'little queen', she snapped.

'There is nothing little about being a queen, Julius.'

He threw up his hands.

'Of course not. Apologies.'

'Just because you Romans hate them.'

'Not hate, Petra. We started out with kings, you know – smart, dignified kings with golden thrones and red boots.'

She squinted at him, confused.

'Red boots?'

'So the artists would have us believe – long, red boots. I've always thought they looked rather smart. They'd go well with the uniform but no one is allowed them because ...'

'They're a symbol of royalty and you hate royalty. Maybe you're right.'

He grabbed at her hands.

'What's wrong, Petra?'

She looked out the window to the roofs of Rome. Somewhere beneath those – far beneath – Arsinoë was spitting fury.

'My sister says that I am a whore who has sold Egypt to the Romans for my own gain.'

'Your sister?' He pulled back. 'When did you see her?'

'Does it matter?'

'It does, yes. Who gave you permission to visit?'

She stared at him, shocked.

'Do I need permission to see my own sister?'

'A prisoner of Rome.'

'A princess of Egypt.'

'Who betrayed you, Petra.'

'Which is why I wanted to see her.'

'It obviously went well.'

His sarcasm stung and she yanked away from him.

'That is Egyptian business.' She looked around the beautiful Horti Caesari and suddenly it felt almost as much of a prison as Arsinoë's cell. 'I need to make arrangements to go home.'

He caught at her hand.

'Don't be petty, Cleopatra. I'm sorry. It *is* Egyptian business but it is unpleasant and I only wanted to spare you it.'

'I do not need sparing, Julius. I am a queen, a ruler.'

'I know. I am trying to accept it. You are a very good ruler.'

She shook her head.

'How do you know?'

'Because you rule me.'

He reached for her other hand and, exhausted, she let him take it. It had been a long, confusing day and she did not want to argue any more.

'I will see your sister punished for her cruelty,' he said.

'No, Julius! *I* will.'

'Of course. Sorry.' He banged his head against a column, drawing a reluctant laugh from her. 'Don't leave, Petra. We have so much to do.' He kissed her, long and deep. 'I gained more than a spoiled prisoner of a princess in Egypt, you know. Last winter in Alexandria was the happiest and the richest of my life. I learned so much that can benefit Rome. I am to take Sosigenes into senate next week and—'

'Ah! It is my engineer that you wish to keep, not me.'

He kissed her quiet.

'It is you, Cleopatra. The gods help me, but it is all you.'

Chapter Twenty-seven

'This machine is truly a marvel. The senators were astounded by it, were they not, Sosigenes?'

Sosigenes gave a modest smile that was fooling no one and patted his year-clock like a fond parent. Cleopatra pushed herself up off the day bed where she had been taking some valuable rest whilst Caesarion slept and went to meet her engineer. He and Julius had spent a long morning in the senate-house and for once Cleopatra found herself pitying the poor senators who must have had their brains tied in knots by her engineer's calculations. They would usually be fanning themselves with Baiae's sea breezes in this sultry month of August but Julius was too keen for reform to let anyone holiday this year.

'The session went well, I think,' Sosigenes said.

'Well?!' Julius clapped him on the back. 'It was stupendous. You dazzled them.'

'Befuddled them more like,' Cleopatra said in an aside to Eiras who smiled.

Sosigenes had been unimpressed with Rome and appeared to be on a one-man crusade to, as he put it, 'drag them into the modern era'. He'd been taking various poor senators through his ideas and was ever off around the city. At times he was rather evasive about where he'd been and Cleopatra worried he'd get himself into trouble but he was a grown man and it was not her place to probe, however much she longed to.

'The senate have voted for my proposed calendar reforms, Petra,' Julius told her. 'And not a moment too soon. Can you believe this year needs four extra months?'

'The Republic does seem to have got rather out of kilter.'

He gave a low laugh.

'You can say that again, but now we can start afresh with a calendar that truly works.'

'And a permanent extra month named for you, hey?'

He blushed, making her laugh. Having the additional month named for Julius had been Sosigenes' idea but apparently the senate had embraced it.

'It will mean my name will stand after I am gone,' he said.

'As it should, for it is you who has freed Rome from the madness of tangled time. But you will not be gone, I hope, for a long time.'

He laughed and kissed her as Sosigenes melted away, leaving them alone.

'I hope not too, for there is much to do. We will make Rome a better place, won't we, Petra?'

'We?'

'Yes – we. I need you.'

'For all that Egyptian advances can do for the Republic?'

'In part. I am having street lights installed and people are hailing them as a miracle – save the thieves and gangs, which is exactly as it should be. I have architects drawing up plans for a library and am putting out feelers all across the Empire for great manuscripts with which to fill it. I am working on a way to develop the harbour at Ostia along Alexandrian lines and I'm considering setting up a competition to design an eighth wonder of the world.'

Cleopatra burst out laughing.

'Oh Julius, you were doing so well.' He frowned. 'An eighth

wonder of the world? The *ancient* world? You cannot just build a new one.'

He pouted.

'I don't see why not. It's all right for you with your Pharos and your pyramids but if we do not have an "ancient" wonder, then why not a new one? I am thinking of a stadium right in the heart of Rome, bigger than any that has gone before and with a giant colossus guarding it.'

'This is, then, a very open competition . . . ?'

'It still needs to be designed, thank you very much.'

She gave in.

'It is a fine idea. And you are right – everything has to be new at some point.'

'And will be ancient in its turn, just like us.'

'*You* will be ancient way before me.'

'How dare you!'

He made a sudden lunge, grabbing her and casting her onto the day bed, pinning her hands to the cushions in a way that made her heart race. It was so easy to be with this man. He was the first, bar her snaking siblings, to truly stand as her equal and neither of them needed to be on their dignity with each other. Oh, she loved her friends dearly but to them she would always be a queen first and a woman second. With Julius it was the reverse and she revelled in it.

And feared it.

'It is time, I think, for me to start planning my return, Julius.'

'Not this again? You have barely arrived.'

'It is but a visit.'

'An enjoyable one, I hope?'

'When I am with you, perhaps, or with the Claudii, but the rest are so . . . supercilious. I swear they see me simply as a Roman prize, like my year-clock or my scrolls or my statue. And I swear you like it like that.'

He squirmed.

'It is but a game, a political game, as well you know. I rescued your throne for you and Rome must see a benefit from that.'

Furious, she took advantage of his discomfort to spring herself up, pushing him onto the bed and straddling him.

'I was rescuing my throne perfectly well myself, thank you very much.'

He tipped his head up at her.

'We don't know how that would have gone, do we?'

'I think we do. It was my army that came and rescued both of us after a winter under siege.'

'It was *both* our armies.'

'But . . . '

'And that is the best way. We are a partnership, Cleopatra.'

'One in which you must be seen to be superior to me?'

'Only here in Rome.' He reached up for her shoulders and shook her gently. 'It would be the reverse were we in Alexandria.'

'True, but we are not in Alexandria, and everyone here is so overbearing. And so damned contradictory.'

'Contradictory?'

'You are Imperator, correct? A dictator, free to act in whatever way you choose without any of the constitution's obsessive checks and balances?'

'Correct, I suppose.'

'And that is a power far greater than any royal, who must always consult with his – or her – learned advisors.'

'Well, yes, but—'

'But Imperator is still apparently within the treasured constitution it overrides. And still better than being "king".'

'Rome is a complicated place, Petra. You know that by now. Her lines are rigid and do not accommodate a relationship of equals such as ours. Can we not, simply, give them a show they can understand and then pursue the truth of the matter between ourselves?' Cleopatra sighed. 'Or do you want to marry me?' he pushed on. 'Is that it? Do you want me to divorce Calpurnia and cleave to you?'

268

'No! I am married too, Julius.'

'Symbolically. In a show that your people can understand whilst—'

'I pursue the truth of the matter with you,' she allowed reluctantly.

He smiled.

'Exactly! We understand each other. I need you and Rome needs you too, though she may never understand how much.'

'And you should not try to make her.'

'Pah!' He waved this away. 'The people trust me and why would they not? They have little to lose. It is those whose small portions of power I have taken who I need to watch.'

'Porcia,' Cleopatra said, pulling back to look into his eyes.

'Sorry?'

'You need to watch Porcia.'

'A woman?'

She squeezed her thighs so tightly into his sides that he yelped in pain.

'Of course a woman. Have I taught you nothing? You do not need to stand on a platform in the Forum to influence people, Julius. There is more real talk done in the parlours and the dining halls, in the bathroom and the bedrooms. Above all, the bedrooms.'

'You are right.' He ran a slow hand over the curve of her breasts. 'The toga is not the ultimate symbol of power, is it?'

'No. Why do you think Egyptians worship Isis above all others?'

'Because they do not have a Jupiter?' he tried, already wincing in anticipation of the squeeze she duly delivered.

'Because they know that true power comes from giving life, not from taking it away.'

He smiled.

'You have taught me much, Cleopatra.'

'And will continue to do so. Oh look!' She pointed to where a gecko had popped its head out of the wall next to them, its eyes alert as it darted glances around the area, assessing it for safety. 'My father used to call me gecko.'

Julius squinted at her.

'And that makes you smile?'

'Oh yes. He said geckos were nimble and sharp-witted and clever.'

Julius looked at the little creature and for a moment it seemed to look back at him.

'I can see that,' he agreed. 'Only, I'd say that you, my fiery, fearsome Cleopatra, are more dragon than gecko – bold and proud and beautiful.' The gecko made a dart across the tiles and into the greenery beyond. Cleopatra sighed and Julius snaked his hands across her hips to rub at the small of her back. 'You are, you know, already a far better ruler than your father ever was.'

Cleopatra thought of Ptolemy-Auletes and remembered his big, loose body clambering eagerly over Servilia's wall to attend her reception for Cato. She wasn't sure whether to laugh or cry at the memory of that strange year in exile here in Rome. For her it had been a curious type of freedom, but for King Ptolemy it must have been agony. He had, perhaps, grown into a decadent ruler but he'd cared about his country with a passion, and he'd wanted her to rule it. She hoped he would be proud.

'I really should make my preparations to head home,' she said, moving to climb off Julius, but he grabbed at her.

'Why?'

'Because the autumn will soon be upon us and the seas will close. I would be trapped here over winter.'

'As I was trapped with you.'

'That was different. We did not have to go out in public.'

'True.'

'Or have philosophical debates with the likes of Brutus about the nature of royalty.'

Julius pulled her gently down on top of him.

'He's been at it again?'

'Always. He is tormented by Cato's death. He was his uncle after all.'

'And a self-righteous boor of a man, as I will show all Rome.'

'How?'

'Oh, I have my ways. It is not only you who can do show, my Nile goddess. Brutus needs to see that Cato is, indeed, a coward for killing himself rather than a hero for refusing to bow to anything that threatened the principles of his precious Republic.'

'Have you not threatened that, Julius, by bringing in a queen – and the son you share with her?'

'I have brought in many riches from Egypt, as the people will see in my Triumph.'

She sat up.

'Your what?'

'My Triumph – the parade to celebrate my victories over Gaul and Hispania and, and . . .'

'Egypt? You had no "victory" over Egypt.'

'Of course not. But I had a victory *with* Egypt, which is precisely why I have invited you here, to, to share in it. And precisely why you must not go home.'

'You are trying to entice me to stay with promise of a parade?'

'Do you have any better ideas?'

'You could formally declare Caesarion your son.'

'My heir? I'm not sure—'

She put up a hand.

'Not your heir, Julius, your son.'

'That is what you want?'

'It is what my country wants. It is why I came.'

'For your country? Not for your handsome Imperator? For the lure of his bed? Or the pleasure of his company?'

He looked so despondent that for a moment she thought him genuine, then she shook herself free of her naïvety. He was teasing her, as he always did.

'There is some pleasure to be had in both his company and his bed,' she allowed, 'but certainly room for improvement.'

'You ...!'

Then he was grabbing her and pressing his lips to hers and for a fleeting moment she wished she could be trapped here with him all winter long, but that would be madness. She would make her plans to leave and pray that, when the time came, she had the strength to see them through because, Isis help her, this man was far more enticing than he should be.

Chapter Twenty-eight

Cleopatra paused at the entrance to the thronged grandstand and looked around, disconcerted to find no central throne awaiting her but, of course, this was Rome where glory went to soldiers and senators and she was pointedly made to fit in with everyone else. Everyone else with money, that is. For all its snobbery about royalty, Rome had far more social distinctions than Egypt and, with the city out for the ten days of Caesar's Triumphs, it was achingly obvious. The poor lined the streets, packed in with their food, their children, and their latrine pots whilst the rich could afford seats on the grandstands.

Those lucky enough to have apartments or villas lining the way could view from their windows, although they usually invited so many friends that they were every bit as crowded as on the street below. Yesterday one packed tenement had collapsed, taking out a float of Gaulish wine so that the street had run ghoulishly red with the pulp of grape and human intermingled and – apparently more to everyone's concern – the parade had had to be hastily re-routed.

Cleopatra had never seen anything like it. They had parades in Alexandria, of course, but they were spectacular, mystical, religious processions, not these martial 'Triumphs'. Even the name told you all you needed to know about Rome's obsession with victory and inflated sense of pride. They did it well, there was no doubting that, but it brought normal life to a standstill for far too long and she was grateful that this, at last, was the final day of the non-stop gloat of a party.

'This way, my queen.'

Mardion shouldered the crowds aside and led her and Caesarion to a seat near the centre, placing a richly embroidered cushion ostentatiously down, before taking his own seat with Eiras and Cinna behind. She thanked him, glad to settle Caesarion who was heavy on her hip and desperate to get down. He had chosen the inaugural day of his father's Triumph to take his first steps.

'A natural politician,' Sosigenes had said wryly but it had certainly charmed Julius, who'd sat on the floor in the flamboyant purple and gold toga that was the preserve of a triumphant general to encourage him and been late to his own reception as a result.

Julius was very taken with Caesarion, coming to find him at least once a day, between his duties in the city or with his dull Roman wife. He would chatter away with his son and bring him gifts – building bricks, a toy chariot, even a tiny sword. Cleopatra had sucked in her breath at that but he had kissed her and said, 'the child will need to learn to fight' and, given the evidence of both their lives to date, there was little refuting that.

Caesarion, of course, loved the weapon and the poor plants in Julius' pretty gardens were savaged to bits from his eager swipes. His delighted father had commissioned him a tiny belt and scabbard and he was wearing it now. Cleopatra feared for the heads of the people in front of them and hoped that today's parade was suitably distracting. For herself, it might prove too much, so for today Caesar was celebrating his victories in Africa at the end of the civil war and there was a palpable tension in the grandstand.

'Why would you do that?' Cleopatra had asked him when she'd

first seen the plans. 'Why would you parade a victory over half the men in the audience? And over me, your "honoured guest"?'

He'd repeated his assertion that her presence here implied her share in the victory but if that were true then surely she would be on horseback at his side, not stuck in the stands with the vanquished. Half the senators were marching in the parade as the victorious army, and the other half were pardoned but palpably not a part of the celebrations.

As if to exemplify this, Claudia slid in on her right with Brutus, stiff-backed and tight-lipped. His mood was clearly dark and Cleopatra sought for something to say to ease it, but now more people were arriving in the seats below them and Cleopatra realised in amazement that they were Porcia, Servilia and Calpurnia. Were they friends now? United in a common enemy – herself?

'Good morning, Servilia,' she said.

The older lady turned.

'Good morning, Claudia,' she said pointedly. 'Ah, Brutus, are you well?'

'Wonderfully well, Mother,' he agreed bitterly. 'There is nothing I like more than spending the day having my poor choices paraded across the city.'

Claudia gave a little sob and Cleopatra saw Brutus battle to compose himself but now Porcia was bending around, smirking at Cleopatra and pointedly stopping her children from playing with Caesarion. Cleopatra glanced to her son's sword belt and, for once, hoped he drew it out.

'It's just not dignified,' she said pompously. 'You should not have to sit through this, Brutus. You are a man of great honour who only did what you thought best within the Roman constitution.'

'Thank you, Porcia,' Brutus said.

'The civil war cost many precious Roman lives,' she went on piously. 'They should be buried with honour not turned into the symbol of another man's success.'

Cleopatra stared at her in disbelief.

'You think only Roman lives are precious, Porcia?'

'Well, no, but . . . '

'It's fine, is it, to turn Parthian lives into symbols of success? Or Grecian lives, or Syrian or Jewish or Egyptian? It's fine to celebrate those deaths as mere paving stones on the way to Roman expansion, not husbands and brothers and sons of women left grieving in their own countries?'

Porcia turned puce.

'All death is a sadness, of course, but that is a matter of national pride.'

'Oh, of course. And the Republic is far greater than any individual?'

'Yes.'

'In which case, this Triumph is surely celebrating its survival and no individual should concern themselves with their own personal losses or gains?'

She was not doing herself any good, she knew, but Porcia's ridiculously blinkered view of the world drove her mad.

'You make a fair point,' Brutus said tightly. 'I shall try to look on today as a celebration of the Republic.'

'And not of the man who would be its king,' Porcia sniped.

'Porcia!'

Servilia clamped a hand over her niece's mouth and looked nervously around. Luckily, the first floats of the parade could now be heard on the bright morning air and the chatter of the crowd below rose to sufficient volume to drown out Porcia's treacherous choice of word. It was ridiculous, Cleopatra thought bitterly. 'King' was just a title, much like 'Consul' or 'General' and far less loaded than 'Imperator' or, indeed, 'Triumph'.

The crowd was up on their feet and she only just spotted Sosigenes as he squeezed into a seat behind her with Cinna, Eiras and Mardion. He looked flushed and untidy and she regarded him suspiciously.

'Where have you been, Sosigenes?'

'On private business, my queen.'

'With whom?' He tried to look away but she was having none of it. She'd got enough on her plate dealing with underhand Romans, without being unable to trust her own people as well. 'With whom, Sosigenes?

He swallowed and fidgeted with his robe and she feared the worst, but his answer, when it came, was not what she'd expected at all: 'With Levi's mother.'

'His mother?!'

He shrugged awkwardly.

'I've been looking for her. Levi was coy about his home address so it's been hard but the Jewish community is a close-knit one and people have been kind. Today, at last, I found her. I spoke to her.' His face softened into a smile and he leaned forward. 'She misses him, my queen. I think she regrets their arguments. I told her I, I love him. I mean, I love him like . . . '

'I know how you love him, Sosigenes, and I think it's wonderful. I was afraid you were cheating on him.'

'On Levi? Never! I just wasn't sure you—'

'Could spot true devotion when I saw it?'

'I have been stupid?'

She laughed.

'You have been stupid – wonderfully, sweetly stupid. Do you think they can be reconciled?'

'She needs time but maybe she will come round. I hope so for I know the rift in his family creates a rift in the centre of Levi too.'

Cleopatra felt tears prick at her eyes and wiped hastily at them lest they should spoil the sparkling paint that was her mask on this most difficult of days.

'Families are complex,' she managed.

Images flashed across her mind of her elder sister dangling on a rope and her younger one spitting fury below Rome's streets and she shivered, despite the relentless heat. She was feeling increasingly adrift here. Julius had been too busy in these last ten days of his 'Triumph' to spend much time with her and it had confirmed how little, other than him, Rome had to offer the Queen of Egypt. And how much priority he gave to the selfish, demanding city.

But now the parade came trumpeting around the bend, squeezed tight into the narrow space, and all craned forward to see the first exhibit – a terrifying run of African animals. At the front, a pair of lions, one male, one female, were being slowly trundled in a cage that, to Cleopatra, did not look sturdy enough for the fury into which the shouting crowds were sending the poor beasts. The female was pacing up and down, her amber eyes assessing every leaping bit of prey close enough to drive her carnivore's nostrils wild with hunger. The male, meanwhile, was throwing himself against the bars, mad with constriction after the plains of his homelands. Cleopatra's heart ached for both of the beautiful creatures.

Behind them came hyenas and ostriches, cages of leaping monkeys, striped zebras and elephants being ridden by acrobats. It was clear that many of the crowd had never seen such creatures and they pressed forward, reaching out hands to touch them until one of the hyenas took a bite at a tantalisingly chubby finger. The man howled and the crowd drew back, jeering at the animal as if it was wrong to follow its natural instincts and chew on the food it had been offered.

'It ate him!' one of Porcia's children cried gleefully.

'He was stupid,' Brutus said crisply and Cleopatra was glad that someone in Rome still had sense.

But now the final animal was coming and a sort of awed hush fell over the crowd at the stately creature with a patterned neck so long it stretched way above the cage in which it stood.

'What is it?' Claudia gasped.

'A cameleopard,' Porcia informed her.

'It's a giraffe,' Cleopatra said.

'No it isn't. It's a cameleopard. Cicero told me.'

'And Cicero lives in Africa, does he?'

'You know he does not, but he's a very learned man.'

'And *I* live in Africa. It's a giraffe and it's far too beautiful to be stuck in a cage parading through a city. It should be running wild in the savannah.'

'Tell that to your lover, Cleopatra,' Porcia shot at her, though at her side both Servilia and Calpurnia sucked in their breath and she looked momentarily ashamed. 'Don't worry,' she said to Calpurnia, 'she may have his bed but you have his name.'

'And me?' Servilia snapped. 'What do I have? You speak too wildly today, Porcia.'

Porcia shifted uncomfortably and Cleopatra was glad to see it but Servilia's words had made her squirm too and she clutched Caesarion close and looked down the interminable run of floats. The sun was heading to the top of the sky and it was hot and muggy packed in with so many people. On the first day of the Triumphs, Julius had ordered the stands draped with canopies of tinted linen. Everyone had sung their praises, until they had learned they were an Egyptian idea and then there had been foolish mutterings about Eastern extravagance and someone had torn them down, leaving everyone stuck out in the sun again.

Cleopatra yawned as carts full of gold ambled past, closely guarded. Even the poorer people were shifting, worn out by so many riches. Claudia's head dropped onto Cleopatra's shoulder and, with a smile, she put an arm around her friend, pleased to see her rest after what had obviously been a hard morning with furious Brutus. She was even more relieved Claudia was asleep when Porcia's daughter climbed across Servilia and onto her uncle Brutus' knee.

'She does love you,' Porcia said smugly. 'And you're so good with her, Brutus.'

Cleopatra stared. Was Porcia flirting?

'That's disturbing,' she whispered to Eiras, nodding at the irritating woman.

'That's dangerous,' Eiras hissed back.

'Porcia and Brutus?' Cleopatra gasped. 'No! He's married.'

Eiras sighed.

'Cinna says that marriages in Rome are never as binding as they should be.'

'But surely Brutus wouldn't do that? He prides himself on his honour.'

'And is desperate for children.'

Cleopatra looked past sleeping Claudia to where Brutus was offering Porcia's daughter a chain from around his neck and felt even hotter than before. Porcia was a widow, a high-born widow with proven fertility. But she was Porcia!

'He'd have to be *very* desperate to marry her,' she whispered to Eiras who gave a wicked laugh that dropped away as Claudia stirred at a new noise from the crowd.

It was less a cheer than a sort of hiss and suddenly everyone on the grandstand was on alert. Cleopatra strained to see what was coming. It looked to be some sort of giant rectangle, held upright by wires and stays.

'Is that a painting?' Sosigenes said from his vantage point above her. Then, 'Jupiter jumps, who would paint that?'

Eiras leaned forward.

'Don't let Caesarion see,' she hissed and, as the float drew level, Cleopatra could see why.

Her blood ran cold. What had Julius done? What on earth had the fool man done? The painting on display was the much-discussed one of Cato, his face pale and turned to the gods in clear agony, his hands to his stomach which was jaggedly cut open to let his guts spill into the forefront of the scene. Cleopatra pressed her hands over Caesarion's eyes and closed her own but it was too gruesome to resist and she opened them again to take in the painstaking detail of the death of one of Rome's most treasured senators.

'Has Julius gone mad?' Claudia gasped over the hiss of the crowd.

Cleopatra could find nothing to say. She remembered him saying he wanted to show Cato up as a coward not a hero but she'd never thought him stupid enough to put him on display in all his martyred glory.

'My uncle,' Brutus gasped, pain rasping through the words. 'My poor, brave uncle.'

Claudia fumbled for his hands, tears springing anew to her eyes as she blinked back into consciousness, but he was standing, turning this way and that, as furiously trapped as the poor lions. Porcia leaped up.

'And my poor, brave, honourable father,' she said. Then loud and clear, she cried: 'Shame!' The people below looked up. 'Shame!' she shouted again and they seized upon the word, bellowing it louder and louder until all of Rome seemed to rock with it and the crowd stormed forward. They trampled the guards and pulled the painting down, ripping it into tiny pieces and scattering them in the air where they were caught by the breeze and blown across the rooftops.

Porcia gave a satisfied nod then, taking her children's hands in her own, marched from the stand. Brutus stormed after her, Claudia running frantically in his wake, and everyone else watching in prurient delight. Cleopatra saw Servilia take a step or two to follow and then stop and ostentatiously settle herself, staring hard ahead as soldiers ran in to clear the chaos on the street. Slowly the rest of the stand followed her example. Cleopatra longed to lean over and compliment her onetime friend on her composure but dared not risk any more upsets.

But there was upset to come all the same, for at the rear of this final parade came Julius' Egyptian triumph and Cleopatra had to sit, as rigid as Servilia, as the treasures of her dear country were trawled through Rome. She tried not to look at the stunning golden cups that had once graced her table, the ancient tablets inscribed with hieroglyphs that looked as out of place here in Rome as the giraffe, and even the golden statue of Cleopatra as Isis, as if it were a trophy of war, not a gift of love.

'How dare he?' she muttered but there was more to come.

The year-clock rolled past, encased in glass but shaking on the rough Roman streets, and Cleopatra heard Sosigenes gasp in horror behind her.

'What's that?' she heard someone ask and then the reply, 'It's some Egyptian machine to steal time.'

'Steal time?' Cleopatra burst out, standing and pointing a furious finger at the astonished man. 'It is the most sophisticated machine anyone in this backwater city will ever have seen and it is to *regulate* time so that you useless Romans can keep your seasons in balance with your calendar and not let it run away from you like a mangy dog.'

The man gave a low whistle.

'Keep your hair on, sweetheart.'

Mardion leaped forward.

'How dare you. That's the Queen of Egypt you're addressing.'

'There are no queens in Rome,' came the insolent answer.

'There won't be for long,' Cleopatra agreed darkly, pulling Mardion back. 'Ignore him,' she urged. 'He's an ignorant fool and not worthy of our attention. He's ... '

But now the crowd were hissing again.

'Who's that?' they cried, clutching at one another. 'For Isis' sake, who is that poor child?'

Cleopatra knew before she turned who was eliciting such pretty pity and sure enough there, walking down the centre of the street in heavy chains, her hair loose around her face, tears falling down her smooth cheeks, and her white dress artfully torn, was Arsinoë.

'It's the Egyptian princess,' the crowd muttered in glee. 'The poor thing, she's just a girl, just an innocent girl.'

Arsinoë turned shining eyes to them all, perfect in her sadness, and Cleopatra ground her teeth in fury. There was nothing innocent about her sister and every tiny detail of her perfectly crafted sorrow was designed to illicit just the sympathy it had done. This was the final straw. How dare Julius take *her* prisoner and parade her as a symbol of his own victory? That was an insult to Cleopatra as both his lover and, far more importantly, Egypt's queen.

'Shame!' the cry went up again and her sister's eyes found her, sparkled in momentary triumph, and were turned to the hissing crowd once more. Julius was bringing up the rear, dressed in his ridiculous purple toga, but she did not even look at him. He had gone too far and the moment she could safely get out of here, she was sending for her ship.

❖

'Cleopatra, please. Don't go.'

'Don't go?' Cleopatra glared at Julius as he stood before her at the bottom of the gangplank, crumpled and gasping from running. Someone must have tipped him off that she was at the docks and he had made it to the ship just before they cast off. 'Why would I stay, Julius? You have humiliated me before the whole of Rome. You said you brought me here as an honoured guest but you put the treasures of my country on display, including the statue that I gave you as a private gift, as if the good will of the men in the street matters more to you than I.'

'It wasn't meant that way. I wanted only for everyone to see the riches of Egypt, to appreciate them as I do.'

'To appreciate you for winning them, you mean. And then you put Arsinoë before them and they saw her so carefully beautiful in her suffering and they blamed me, as I could have told you they would if you'd only thought to consult with me. But no – you knew best. You tell me I am wise, Julius, and then you treat me like a fool. I've had enough of this so-called partnership.'

'I apologise, truly. I've been the fool. Don't go.'

He looked so earnest, so desperate and her heart thudded as if trying to reach out for him but Cleopatra was not having that.

'I am your lover, Julius, mother of your child, but have seen little honour for it. I have put up with not being allowed into the city, put up with being patronised by the likes of Porcia, put up with being treated as a second-class citizen because I am a queen – a queen, Julius, ruler of a beautiful, rich country with a history rooted so deep into the earth that it makes your precious republic look like a weedy little sapling.'

'That's true, my Nile goddess. That's—'

'Don't call me that. I am not your Nile goddess. I am Egypt's ruler, bearer of Isis for my country, not for any man.' She shook her head, furious at herself. 'Perhaps you were right to treat me as a fool, Julius, for I have most certainly been one. Goodbye.'

'Cleopatra, no. What of Caesarion?'

'What of him?'

'I can make him my heir, future ruler of Rome.'

'Too late, Julius. Caesarion is *my* child, my Horus, born of my Isis-blessed womb. He will be ruler of Egypt and that will be more than enough. You once told me, way back in Lucca, that the roofs of Rome were not as fine as you thought before you left their confines but it seems to me that they confine you still. I wish you the joy of your little city, Caesar. Now, goodbye.'

She pulled away from his grasp and turned to mount her ship.

'Petra,' the name came out of him on a sob and almost she turned.

But then she looked up and saw Caesarion with Mardion and Sosigenes, Eiras and Cinna, a wall of kindness waiting to support her, and, pushing her head high, she walked steadily up the gang-plank towards them. She was done with travel, she was done with Julius Caesar and she was done with Rome. Forever.

Chapter Twenty-nine

Cleopatra paced the upper deck of the royal barge, desperate to shake off the restless energy that seemed to course through her these days. Life was good. Egypt prospered. She'd just come back from seeing the new Nilometer, a smart building on an island at the base of the Delta. It was Sosigenes' new project, a spiral of brick stairways, plunging down into the earth to pick up the earliest indications of the levels of the great Nile and today those indications had been excellent. Isis was pouring her tears into the river at its mysterious source and the inundations would be plentiful. Charmion's granaries would be packed before the year was out and the people would be happy.

It was simple really. Cleopatra could work hard to listen to her people, to create public buildings in which they could meet and worship, to improve their lot with better lighting and hygiene. She could attract the finest scholars, maintain good relations with her neighbours, and keep the Romans at bay but still, if the Nile did not flood and there was no food, her reign would be a failure. She was in the hands of the Goddess and must pray she pleased Her.

Turning her gaze south to nearby Memphis, she wondered if it was her proximity to her mother that was making her feel unsettled. The Priestess Safira had not been the powerforce she'd hoped but she had been good and gentle and calm and those were things a queen needed too. *Power with compassion.* The words came to her in a new voice and she shuddered. Servilia. It had been hard seeing her in Rome, hard having her turn away. She remembered the kindly woman taking her into her house the day she had come to womanhood. Servilia was the only person in Rome who had ever truly cuddled her – the only person in the world, bar Charmion – and Cleopatra had betrayed her.

She let out a strangled yelp and clapped her hand to her mouth, furious with herself for her lack of control. Perhaps it was the time of her moonblood? She fought to remember but was sure it had not been long since the last. She had hoped, on her return from Rome, that she might be pregnant again. Another prince or princess for Egypt would have been a fine reward for a visit that had not, otherwise, been worth the making, but her womb had emptied within days of her return and continued to do so with precision ever since. It was probably for the best. One child of Caesar's was trouble enough, two would be worse.

Cleopatra kicked at the railing and then looked guiltily around in case anyone had seen her behaving like more of a toddler than Caesarion. The guards probably had but they were looking studiously into the middle-distance. It was lonely sometimes. There was no one to truly talk to, no one to truly understand the pressures upon her. Even her sisters had taken such a different slant on rule that they had been little comfort and now Berenice was dead and Arsinoë reportedly despatched in disgrace to some Greek island by a contrite Caesar – the only one who had ever truly understood . . .

She stopped herself furiously. There was no point in thinking of him. He'd sucked her in with his power, his interest in the world and his damned skills in bed, and then he'd treated her like a bauble to be displayed to his precious Roman people. It was insulting and cruel, and no number of grovelling letters would ever suck her in again.

She glanced inside. She had kept his letters, every one. They were in a casket on her desk. She didn't read them. Well, not often. Perhaps occasionally, in the night, when she couldn't sleep and needed something laughable to distract her. They were full of stiff apologies:

Julius Caesar, Imperator of Rome, begs Cleopatra, Queen of Egypt, to understand the high regard in which he holds her.

Then:

You, of all people, must understand the pressures of rule, the expectations of a nation.

And finally:

I invite you, as my honoured guest, to visit the opening of my new library. It was inspired by your great centre of learning in Alexandria and it would grace Rome to have you there and help her to understand what we can learn from such an ancient culture as Egypt.

Oh, he was clever. She'd nearly fallen for that one. She'd imagined herself standing at the door of his new library, cutting a ribbon, perhaps, to let the people inside. She'd imagined Caesar telling the gathered crowds of his visit to Alexandria and how it had inspired him, and then she'd imagined him being unable to resist adding the details of him fighting on the Hepstadion or of his damned army arriving to break him out of the palace, never mind that it had been her army that had got there first and she, at knifepoint to her own sister, who had let them in. She would not give him that satisfaction. Not again.

The sun was dropping now. It would be time to dine shortly. She should call Eiras and Charmion, take a bath, pick a fine gown and her most golden eyeshadows. That would make her feel more like a queen and less like a weak little girl. She turned to ask a guard to summon them but then saw the sky, streaked with pink, as if Isis were blushing above, and froze. She watched, transfixed, as the sun sunk towards the horizon and the heavens turned from pink, to orange to deepest blood red, pulling her back two years to when she'd stood on this very spot with Julius. The same light had burned across them as his arm had snuck around her waist and he'd pulled her into her cabin and . . .

'Stop!'

'My queen?' The guards darted forward, terrified.

She groaned.

'Fetch me Eiras and Charmion. Now.' She checked herself. 'Please.'

'Of course, my queen.'

And they were gone, grovelling their way thankfully from her grumpy presence. Charmion, however, was not given to grovelling.

'What have you done to the guards?' she demanded, striding into her chamber. 'They look terrified.'

'So they should be. I am Isis in her great and magnificent glory, am I not?' Charmion raised an eyebrow and, despite herself, Cleopatra laughed. 'Is a queen not allowed to have a bad day?'

'Of course. But Levi has something that might cheer you up, if you will permit him entry?'

'Of course. I'm not that grumpy.' She beckoned Levi inside, Sosigenes in his wake, but when she saw what he was holding up she groaned. 'Maybe I *am* that grumpy. Why does he write again?'

'Perhaps,' Levi suggested, 'because you are the one he wishes to be with at the end of every day.'

Cleopatra scoffed.

'Perhaps because he wants me to take Caesarion back to Rome as proof of his damned manhood.'

'Or perhaps because he wants to see you?'

'Oh Levi, you're such a romantic.'

'Yes,' he agreed easily, 'I am. And if you wish to go to Rome, my queen, I will happily accompany you.'

Sosigenes put out a hand.

'I'm not sure the queen wishes to return to a city that reviled her most unjustly.'

Levi flushed.

'No. No, of course not. I apologise.'

Cleopatra waved this away.

'Please don't worry, Levi. If I were to go back to Rome you could of course come, though last time you did not care to return.'

He flushed deeper and she looked at him curiously.

'Levi has had a letter from his mother,' Sosigenes said proudly. 'She has written to tell him that she loves him and that she is happy for me to love him too.'

It was said so simply that Cleopatra's heart squeezed. Sosigenes and Levi were an unusual couple but their affection for each other was so genuine that no one, surely, could deny them the right to it.

'That's wonderful news,' she said. 'I'm very pleased for you, Levi, and of course if you wish to travel to Rome, I would happily release you from service for the time your trip took.'

At that, though, Levi shook his head.

'I thank you, but there is no rush, my queen. If you change your mind though ...'

'Levi!'

Sosigenes nudged at him again and Levi lost his balance and toppled against him. Sosigenes hugged him close and murmured something to him. No doubt, Cleopatra thought grumpily, it was something about having to understand that not everyone had a partnership like theirs. Which was true. She looked at the letter in her hand but to her surprise saw that the writing on the outside was not in Julius' hand. Her eyes widened.

'Claudia?!'

Eagerly, she snapped the wax. A letter from her friend always cheered her up and she sank onto the couch, ignoring the glow of the pyramid as the sun threw out the last of the day's rays from behind it.

Petra,

Greetings to the queen and all that, but truly I write to you not as any person of power or influence – though of course you are both – but as my friend, for I am in sore need of friendship. Oh Petra, Brutus has asked me for a divorce. A divorce! He worries that the gods have not smiled on our union and has asked me to leave his house. Can you believe it? My Brutus, to be so cruel. But he is not, it seems, mine any more and I can do nothing about it. Fulvia is furious, Servilia too but he will listen to no one. He talks only of Cato and the Republic and divorce.

Oh Petra, I am miserable indeed. Clodia says that she believes you might, one day, return to Rome. She said something I did not understand about what Isis would do, but if it is true, Petra, if you think you might, then I would welcome you indeed for right now I feel so very, very alone.

Claudia

Cleopatra stared at the words. They seemed to morph on the papyri and she could not quite take them in. Brutus? Divorce?

'The bastard!' she burst out and the others looked at her in shock. 'It's Brutus – he's divorcing Claudia.'

Eiras ran forward.

'No! I remember their wedding so well – the roses on the water, the Claudii all dressed up in rainbow colours, and little Claudia so beautiful in white. Do you remember, my queen?' Cleopatra closed her eyes. Of course she remembered. 'They had that peculiar ritual where the men came marauding in to capture the bride.'

'As if women will only go to them by force,' Cleopatra said darkly.

Eiras placed a soft hand on her shoulder.

'It is a mistake they make again and again.'

They shared a look but Cinna had come up behind his wife and made a rare interruption.

'But one that comes less from an arrogance about your willingness and more from an underestimation of our own worth in your eyes.'

Cleopatra gaped at him.

'You're saying all this posturing is a sign of, of insecurity?'

'Women are, you know, very scary creatures.'

Cleopatra stared at him and then tossed her head.

'Nonsense. Brutus is clearly not afraid of Claudia if he is putting her through such pain.'

'Perhaps,' Cinna said, 'he is more afraid of someone else.'

Cleopatra glanced at Eiras and knew that her friend was, like her, remembering the way Porcia had flirted with her cousin at the Triumph, the way they had stormed from Cato's brutal painting together. Her stomach contracted. That would be bad news for Claudia and bad news, too, for Julius. She went to the window but the sun was gone and the great pyramid was just a shadow against the purple blur of the horizon.

Levi coughed.

'There is a second letter, my queen.'

She spun back.

'Julius?' She groaned. 'It can wait.'

'Of course, my queen.'

He placed it delicately on the side and bowed away. Eiras picked up her make-up brushes and Cleopatra settled herself at the mirror but she could see the scroll in the corner of her eye, the wax seal catching in the candlelight and seeming to wink at her. She closed her eyes to be painted but before the brush could even touch her skin, they flew open again, seemingly of their own accord.

'My queen, you must—'

Charmion interrupted her. 'Just read it, Petra.'

Cleopatra looked to her, then back to the scroll, then at herself in the mirror. She looked tired. Her skin was grey, her eyes had bags that would take all of Eiras' skill to cover, and her hair hung limply in the damp air of the delta.

'Fine,' she snapped and, whirling away from the dressing table, flung herself onto the bed and cracked open the wax. 'Though it will just be more about his "glorious" battles in Hispania, and his "intrepid" march back to Rome and his damned heir.'

'*Your* "damned" heir,' Charmion reminded her, then she and Eiras retreated into a corner.

'Cowards,' she threw after them but the letter was open now and, despite all she had said, she could not resist the curl of his familiar hand.

To Queen Cleopatra from Julius Caesar, Imperator,

Greetings. I trust you are well and that and your son thrives and your country prospers. I wish to … Oh, Jupiter be done with this. I cannot write to you as one ruler to another any more, Petra, for although I know you to be a wise and great queen, for me you are first and foremost a woman. And a woman I long to hold in my arms once more.

I am tired, Petra. I have finally put down the rebellion by Pompey's upstart sons but I have lost my joy in victory. Will they never let me alone? All I want, all I have ever wanted, is to work to further Rome's interests, but always She resists me. They have paused the building on my library whilst I am away, you know. It makes me furious. This will be my fifty-fifth year on this earth and I should be at home, working on the many projects you were kind enough to encourage me in, instead of treading the plains of Hispania.

Still, I am nearly done. Old age makes me more impatient than ever and I have smashed my troops into the rebel lines and decimated them. I have shown little mercy, I'm afraid, for I tried that after the civil war and look where it got me — booing in the streets of my own Triumph and the loss of the finest woman in the known world. Truly Petra, I curse myself every day for the foolish actions that drove you from me. I told you once that I am only a coarse Roman

and it remains true. You are too refined for me, too beautiful, too
very special.

Please come back to Rome. I will be there within the month and I
yearn to see you. I want to apologise in person. I want to show you, in
word and deed, what you mean to me. Our son too, but above all you. I
would gladly come to Alexandria, for my winter there was the happiest
of my life, but I am not so good a ruler as yourself and my country is
too volatile to leave for much longer.

Come to Rome, Petra, I beg of you, not as a ruler, not as mother of
my child, but as yourself – the woman I love.

Julius

Cleopatra stared at the words in disbelief. She read them over –
and over and over – but still they shifted and shook on the page,
all save the last four: *the woman I love.* She wanted to tell herself that
he didn't mean it, that it was mere flattery, but that would be an
insult to the heartfelt confession. Could she do it? Could she return
to Rome and be with him? Could they try, amidst this chaos of
countries and battles and governance, to be a simple couple, like
Eiras and Cinna, like Levi and Sosigenes . . .

Like Brutus and Porcia, an evil voice whispered in her head but she
ignored it. If those two married, it would be a partnership based
on mutual hatred, not on shared love.

Love.

Was it possible?

She glanced to the window. The skies were inky black now but
the moon was rising, casting an ethereal line down the pyramid
like a silver thread into her future. She leaped up, scroll in hand.

'Tell the men to prepare the barge. Tonight we sail back to
Alexandria. And from there . . . ' She swallowed but the silver line
led her on. 'From there to Rome.'

Chapter Thirty

The sound of music woke Cleopatra first – a haunting melody from a single pan pipe. She shifted, curious to know which part of the Claudii villa it was coming from but then Julius draped an arm over her, pulling her close, and she snuggled down once more. Sea mist drifted into their chamber on the first threads of thin winter light and she settled into the warmth of his arms to listen to the music drifting across them like a blessing.

These weeks in Baiae for the midwinter festival of Saturnalia had been a blessing indeed. She'd made it to Italy on the autumn winds and had been living on the fringes of Rome ever since. Eiras and Cinna had headed into the city but Cleopatra had stayed in the Alban hills. Claudia had joined her, hiding from Brutus and his new wife, Porcia, and, even better, so had Julius. He had, however, been back and forth, pulled by the eternal demands of Rome, and it was a relief to escape to Baiae for the holy days. Out here, in the company of the liberal Claudii, they need be neither queen nor imperator, but just themselves and for perhaps the first time, Cleopatra could feel what that self was without the need for performance, duty or self-defence.

The notes from the pipes rose, enticingly jaunty, and she slid out of bed. Pulling on a robe, she padded out of their shared chamber and down the tiled corridor, relishing the feel of the pipe-warmed tiles on her bare feet. The music was coming from the main atrium and, as Cleopatra stepped out, she gasped in delight. The huge room was decked in the green swags that had been there for all twelve days of the Saturnalia festivities, but for Sigillaria – the final day celebrating the birth of Mithras, the sun god – someone had clipped candles to every branch so the whole place seemed to dance with tiny lights. Each one flickered in personal greeting to the sun as it crept over the horizon and sat in the middle, cross-legged and wearing nothing but loops of ivy, was Clodia, her beautiful face turned to the sun in quiet contemplation. Cleopatra stood very still, not wanting to break this unusual peace from her lively hostess, but Clodia must have sensed her.

'Come and join me, Petra.'

Cleopatra sunk down at her side thinking Clodia brave to be so lightly clad. Winters in Italia felt very chilly to her Egyptian skin and she was glad to see Claudia pad out of her chamber wrapped in a blanket and even gladder to snuggle under it with her.

'Rebirth,' Claudia said softly.

'Rebirth,' Clodia agreed. 'The end of a dark year, sweet one, and the start of a better.'

Claudia nodded and laid her head on her aunt's shoulder and together the three of them watched Mithras rise from the waters. It would be a good year, Cleopatra was sure. Claudia would find a new, more straightforward husband, Julius would tame Rome and she . . . She put a hand to her belly. All the signs were that the gods had blessed her with a second child and surely this meant Rome and Egypt were destined to work together for the prosperity and advancement of both.

The three of them sat perfectly still until Mithras was fully up and the rest of the household began emerging. Then Clodia stood, stretching out her lithe body.

'A swim?' she suggested.

Cleopatra looked at her in horror.

'It's far too cold to swim!'

'Nonsense. It's good for the blood.'

'I can think of other activities that are better,' Julius said, coming into the room and dropping a kiss on Cleopatra's neck.

'Maybe you're right, Julius,' Clodia agreed easily, 'but Catullus has had me at those activities half the night and I need a rest! Coming, Claudia?'

Claudia shook her head and pulled her blanket tighter but Fulvia and Mark Antony came bouncing out of their room and Cleopatra, Claudia and Julius went out onto the balcony to watch the three of them run naked down to the Claudii's private beach and straight into the icy blue sea.

'Mad,' Julius said, his lips dipping to Cleopatra's collar bone. 'Now, about that other activity . . . '

Cleopatra looked awkwardly to Claudia but her friend waved her away.

'Don't mind me. I'm going to find Mardion and work on my costume for later. Yours better be ready.'

'Oh, they're ready,' Cleopatra confirmed.

Tonight, for the Sigillaria feast of reversals they were to dress up in ways that turned their roles in life upside down. Cleopatra had had a tiny Isis costume made for Caesarion and a Horus one for herself and as Julius tugged her back to their chamber, she remembered something.

'I have a gift for you, Julius.'

'Is it your beautiful body?'

'No.'

'Shame.'

'For that is yours to take at any time.' He raised his eyebrow in the gesture she had grown to love and she laughed and changed it hastily to, 'Any reasonable time.'

'Is this a reasonable time?'

'Shortly. First, your gift.' She slid away from him and dug under the bed for the package she'd hidden when they'd first arrived. 'Here.' She'd meant to present it in grand style but, suddenly nervous, she simply bundled it into his hands. He looked curiously down, turning it over and over.

'What is it?'

She threw her hands up.

'If you open it, Julius, you will find out. That's how gifts work.'

He gave a little laugh and sat on the side of the bed to untie the ribbon and release the linen wrappings. Cleopatra watched with baited breath. Julius was to go to the feast tonight dressed ironically as Romulus, the first King of Rome and, remembering a previous conversation, she'd been struck by one particular detail.

'Boots!'

Julius lifted them up, turning them in the light to see more clearly. They were long, almost up to the knee, and made of the softest leather dyed an exuberant scarlet. The dye had been expensive and was a ridiculous extravagance for a party costume but Cleopatra had remembered Julius talking fondly of red boots and decided it was worth making. Looking at his face now, she was glad she had.

'You like them?'

'I love them. Oh, Cleopatra, truly I love them. They're so soft. And so red!'

'And so royal,' she teased.

His face fell and for a moment, wicked as it was, she enjoyed toying with his mind. Julius had come to understand much about royalty, but he was still at heart Roman and his childish delight in this regal trapping amused her more than it perhaps should.

'They are just for tonight,' she said, feeling mean. 'Just for fun.'

'Of course.'

He relaxed again and bent to pull the first one onto his right foot. To her relief it slid on perfectly and as he hooked the catches into place, the leather upper clung elegantly to his calf. The left one followed equally smoothy and he strutted happily up and down their chamber.

'What do you think?'

'I think,' she said, reaching out as he passed and tugging at the cord of his robe, 'that they would look twice as fine without this.'

And they did.

❖

That night the Claudii and their friends outdid themselves. Everyone had dressed as something contrary to their own nature and the results were magnificent. Sosigenes came as an abacus – a nod to Levi's work in accounts – in an elaborate set of wires and balls that could be actively moved across his body. Levi, in contrast, was dressed as one of Sosigenes' precious clocks, with working hands coming from his belt and a full hoop of numbers. The pair of them found it almost impossible to move in their grand concoctions but were very pleased with themselves all the same.

Mardion, in a joke on his eunuch-status, had come as Jupiter, King of the gods, renowned for his vast number of children. These he'd represented with stuffed poppets tied on strings around his waist and Caesarion chased delightedly after them, stamping on dangling limbs and screaming with laughter. Caesarion himself looked wonderful in his little Isis costume – a tiny gold dress, dark wig and sun-disc headdress that continually fell askew as he ran after Mardion. Soon he would be big enough to support the bejewelled collar of Cleopatra's heir – and support it, pray Isis, with more integrity than its last two bearers – but for now he was happier in a pair of blue wings that he could flap as he went. It was as it should be and he was told far more times than was good for him that he looked adorable.

Cleopatra missed Eiras, who was with Cinna's family for the festival, but had a blue and gold Horus headdress, topped with the eyes and beak of a falcon instead of fancy make-up. She'd chosen to take a leaf out of Clodia's book and go daring in the simple kilt of a god with nothing on top bar a golden collar. It had dipped below her nipples in the original fitting but now seemed to sit just above them. She must, indeed, be with child for her breasts to have rounded out so far, but Julius' eyes when she'd stepped from their washroom had persuaded her to be brave enough to wear the costume out. It was only the Claudii after all and she would most likely look tame next to them.

Sure enough, Clodia made her ironic appearance as Vesta, goddess of the hearth and patron of the vestal virgins, a costume that should have been modest, save that Clodia had chosen to represent the story of her miraculous impregnation by a phallus appearing from the hearthfire in an exceptionally graphic way. Catullus, dressed as the Roman centurion he would never be, followed her around with his tongue scraping the floor. Fulvia and Mark Antony had swapped sexes to be the married couple Venus and Vulcan. Fulvia wore two pieces of red and orange fabric, wrapped between her legs and up across her breasts as the god of fire and Mark Antony was eye-popping as the goddess of love in a long wig and three artfully arranged scallop shells.

It was Claudia, however, who stole the show as Juno, goddess of marriage. Cleopatra admired the boldness of her choice and even more so the beauty of her costume – a gauzy white dress, topped with a stunning peacock cape. It was not as daring as some of the others but the colour of the peacock feathers brought out the blue of her eyes and the white of the dress made her look appealingly vulnerable. The young men of the party flocked to her and Cleopatra smiled to see her open up in their attention like the pomegranate flowers woven into her dark curls.

As they gathered, Clodia called the whole household into a circle, slaves joining their masters as equals on this upside-down night. The food was laid out already, jugs of wine alongside, so that no one need do anything but enjoy themselves. First though, Clodia announced, the mock-king must be chosen.

'Mock-king?' Cleopatra queried.

Many of the decorations and rituals of this Roman Saturnalia were identical to the Egyptian midwinter feast, but this was unique. She looked to Mardion with an eye-roll; trust the Republicans to have to have a mock-king.

'Or mock-queen,' Clodia said hastily. 'They rule for the night and get to wear the crown of feathers and do whatever mischief they wish.'

Again Cleopatra grinned at Mardion. As far as she could see, the Claudii did more or less what they wished every night, but who was she to question such a game?

'How do we choose?' she asked.

In reply, Clodia waved Claudia to lift a platter of cakes from the table and offer them around.

'Let the game commence!' Clodia said gleefully and everyone took a tentative bite.

Cleopatra looked nervously at hers. What was in these little treats? They looked pleasant enough and smelled enticingly of lemon but there must be more to it. Did they have cola nuts in them? Or poppy pods? She'd seen Fulvia and Mark Antony drinking cretic wine, made from the Opium poppy, and it had done very strange things to their eyes and made them giggle endlessly. Not that that sounded so bad. She nibbled at the edge; it tasted as good as it smelled.

'Take care,' Julius said, leaning in, 'in case you bite on metal.'

'Metal?' She pulled the cake away from her mouth and he laughed.

'One of the cakes has a coin within. If you get the lucky cake, you are the mock-queen.'

'I do not need to be a mock queen,' she retorted but at that moment Julius yelped, put his fingers to his mouth and drew out a coin, small and bright from the lemon-juice and with his own profile stamped upon it.

'Julius is mock-king!' Clodia cried and, snatching up a strange feathered headdress, planted it firmly on his head and kissed him smack on the lips. 'What sort of mischief will you get up to, oh king!'

Cleopatra's heart pounded. *That* sort of mischief? Surely not? She remembered Clodia talking to her about bedding Julius back when she'd first met her in Rome – was that, then, what this mocking was meant to do? But Clodia, spotting her face, whirled round and kissed her too, harder and longer than Julius.

'Fret not, my *real* queen, I will not take your mock one from you. Indeed, I do not think I could.'

'If anyone could, it would be you, my beautiful hostess,' Julius said, bowing low, his feathers tickling Clodia's chin, 'but you are right – I am all for Cleopatra.'

The pounding in Cleopatra's heart slowed as Julius struck a pose, both ridiculous and glorious in his Roman tunic, long boots and bobbing crown. Caesarion ran to him and he swept him into his arms.

'See, Caesarion, we both have feathers. Let us fly.'

He began bounding around the room with Caesarion held high before him, flapping his wings and squealing with delight and Cleopatra thought she might burst with joy. This truly would be a very happy new year.

❖

The party, as ever in Baiae, was long and merry. The wine flowed, the musicians played their fastest tunes, and the Claudii gave themselves to the dancing with an abandon that Cleopatra had only otherwise seen in the East.

'Are you sure your family are not Egyptian?' she asked Claudia, when they both collapsed onto a couch after yet another fast-turning reel. But Claudia was prettily flushed and sending coy looks to the young man she'd been partnering and she was up again without answering. Cleopatra smiled and took the chance to lie back a moment. The party was joyous but, oh, she was tired.

'Are you well, my queen?'

Cleopatra felt feathers tickle her cheek and reached up to loop her hand round Julius' neck.

'A little tired, that's all.'

'You have danced a great deal?'

'I have.' She tugged him round next to her. 'But it is more than that.'

His eyes filled with dismay.

'Are you ill?'

'No. No, I'm not ill.'

'You have had bad news then?'

'No! I have rather, Julius, had the best of news.' He stared at her, his eyes confused and his crown askew. Cleopatra shook her head at his slowness. 'It is simply, my mock-king, that your Isis will soon give you another Horus.'

Still, he looked befuddled. The mock-king had, it seemed, been drinking an unusual amount for a man who was normally so careful. He frowned in concentration at her falcon-head then down to her swollen breasts and suddenly the pieces seemed to lock into place in his mind like the cogs in Sosigenes' clock. 'You are with child?'

'Yes, Julius.'

'My child?'

'Of course.'

'My child!' He leaped onto the couch, pulling Cleopatra up with him and calling the room to attention. 'Cleopatra is having my child! My second little Horus. A tiny mock-king.'

'A tiny *real* king,' Cleopatra corrected but no one heard her over the cheers, and the party reels turned louder and faster.

❖

Cleopatra must have slept for she came to sometime later to find most of the guests gone, the musicians playing soft half-tunes, Caesarion curled up against her, and her friends sitting around her feet, costumes askew but smiles still firmly in place. Julius was leaning forward, his crown bobbing as he addressed his little audience.

'What would a perfect world look like, do you think?'

'Pink,' Claudia said drowsily, leaning into the arms of her dancing partner.

'No. Really.'

Julius had obviously danced himself sober and his eyes burned with the intensity Cleopatra loved. She pushed herself up, careful not to wake Caesarion.

'People would be allowed to love who they wished,' she offered with a glance to Sosigenes and Levi, curled up together in a tangle of wires and numbers.

'Agreed,' Julius said. 'Thank you, Petra. What else?'

'People should write what they choose,' Catullus suggested, 'without fear of censure.'

'And should have their words kept safe,' Fulvia added.

'In great libraries,' Julius enthused. 'Of course. Not just poetry but history and science and philosophy. For what use is learning if you cannot pass it on to those yet to come into the world?'

Cleopatra stared at him.

'That's so true,' she said. 'Take Eiras – she knows so much about herbs and medicines and cosmetics. That should all be written down.'

'Of course it should, for it is research of the best kind, tried and tested in real life.'

'Scholars should, then, be allowed time and money to research,' Sosigenes suggested.

'Museons in every city,' Julius agreed, 'developing and sharing ideas in universal scholarship.'

Everyone gave a sleepy cheer, but now Levi was sitting up.

'A perfect world is not just about learning,' he protested, 'but living. Rulers should make sure their people – *all* of them, not just the rich ones – have somewhere safe to live and enough food to nourish them through the year.'

'And there should be beauty,' Clodia cried. 'A perfect world cannot just be learning and facts and food. There must be beauty to sustain the soul.'

'Art,' Cleopatra agreed. 'And sculpture. Intricate jewellery and grand buildings. Wonders to reach a little way up to the gods.'

Claudia gave a hiccup of a laugh.

'These gods here tonight do not need much reaching up to,' she said, indicating the dishevelled costumes of Venus and Vulcan, Vesta and Juno, Isis and Horus. But at that Julius leaned forward.

'That's not true, Claudia. These are exactly the gods we must reach – not just the eternal ones in the netherworlds, but those residing in our minds. In Egypt they recognise the Goddess within their wonderful queen.' He smiled at Cleopatra. 'But maybe there is a little bit of godliness in us all if we can just dig around enough to find it.' He shook his head and leaned back on the couch. 'Oh, I don't know. It's late and I am speaking nonsense.'

'No, Julius,' Clodia said. 'You speak more sense than you know. For if we cannot imagine a perfect world, how can we strive to create it?'

Julius smiled. Then he laughed.

'True. That is very true. Clodia Metelli, you are wiser than you let anyone know and I thank you for it.' He bounced up into the space between them all. 'This year I will improve Rome, however she kicks against it. There are many wonders in the world, not the least of them its people – its scholars and artists, its chefs and lawyers—'

'Not the lawyers!' Mark Antony protested and everyone laughed.

'Very well, not the lawyers. But the doctors, the priests, the bakers, the slaves and the, the . . . '

'Kings,' Claudia finished, reaching out to stroke his red boots. He frowned and she added hastily, 'Including its mock ones.'

Cleopatra sat up.

'Imperators for sure. And is that title not, after all, greater than king?'

'Greater?' Julius looked at her in confusion.

'It implies, does it not, that you have power over everything? And have not the senate voted you Imperator for life? And more or less granted you the opportunity to choose your heir? Is that not, then, royalty?'

'It is security,' he said carefully.

'It is sense,' Cleopatra told him. 'The problem with Rome is that it gets so tangled up in who is going to hold power that half of every year is wasted in choosing – campaigning, electing and voting.'

'That's true,' Mark Antony agreed. 'And during that period nothing gets done bar whispering and bribery. Even once the consuls are elected, they're too busy choosing policies that will get them elected again to do anything useful. Rome has been improved ten times more under your sole care, Julius, than ever before.'

'I thank you,' Julius said solemnly. 'But I am not a king.'

Cleopatra laughed.

'You *are* a king, Julius, and any other place but Rome would have the sense to acknowledge it.'

He looked at her, confusion writ large across his previously smiling face, and she rushed to kiss him. These Romans! Even the cleverest, boldest, sharpest one of them was too blinded by the illusion of his precious republic to see that it had long since outgrown the possibilities of true democracy. It was simply too hard to rule a sprawling Empire that way. But now was not the time to probe further.

'Let's just say, that you will always be a king to me, my love.'

He kissed her back but, thoughtful now, moved towards the balcony.

'Look – Mithras is returned to scold us for not being abed and Saturnalia is done.'

Lifting the crown from his head, he tossed it into the bay below. It caught the winter winds and they all rose to watch as it landed on the water and bobbed there, no longer a crown but simply a collection of feathers heading gently out to sea.

Chapter Thirty-one

The mists were rising off the Tiber, wreathing Rome in a chill haze, and Cleopatra hunched gladly into Julius' warm cloak. He'd finally persuaded her to come to the city but she'd not imagined her entrance to be via the back streets.

'You are smuggling me in, Julius?'

'No! I am proud to have you here with me, my son too, but I wanted this first step to be for us alone.'

'Where are we going?'

He laughed and tugged her onwards. The bakers were stoking their ovens, sending warm patches of light through the fog, and a few people were stumbling sleepily to work, but other than that they were alone. Two men bearing shovels nodded a sleepy hello and then did a visible double-take.

'Here.' Julius stopped in a small square and pointed down. Cleopatra saw a rough white stone at their feet and, to their left, another – the Pomerium. 'I have thought much about your words on Imperators at Saturnalia.'

'You have?'

'And you are right. We are too rigid in Rome, too bound by

titles and honours, by simple words. A truly imperial city should let anyone in. To refuse to do so is insular, paranoid and lacking in dignity.'

'I believe so,' Cleopatra agreed, 'but it is not my place to decide how another race chooses to live.'

'Nor I. This city, Petra, glories in being at the head of a great Empire but it doesn't understand it at all. Few people here have been more than twenty miles from Rome, and fewer still out of Italia. They have no grasp of how different life is at the further reaches of Hispania, Gaul or Britannia. They think they can put square walls around such countries, like those of the Forum, and make them all conform but that is neither possible, nor desirable.'

Cleopatra grasped his hands.

'I have the same issue in Egypt. The Alexandrians cannot understand the needs of wider Egypt and it is only very, very slowly that I am able to make my council see that we are not just a city but a nation.'

'Exactly! Oh Petra, I am so glad we met, for no one else sees the world quite like you and I. Rome has conquered so much and she can improve life for so many of her new subjects but only if she is flexible to their needs.'

'And respectful of their ways.'

'Exactly! And we take the first step right here, right now.'

She looked at him in confusion and, with a smile, he slid an arm around her waist and took an exaggerated step across the invisible Pomerium. Cleopatra resisted at first but he was insistent and, giggling, she let herself step across. Nothing happened. Of course it did not. But her body thrilled with the import of the gesture, as they reached the far side of the square, she grabbed him and pushed him up against the wall, kissing him hard.

'Get a room,' someone grunted from a doorway and they both burst into helpless laughter.

'Come on.'

Julius was off again, deeper into the city. Rome was beginning to wake now, the early light turning from subtle pink to brash daytime yellow and burning the mist off the streets so that the rough, tumbled buildings came more clearly into view. For once Cleopatra didn't mind them. For once she didn't shake her head at their twists and turns, at the temples and tenements crammed into every space, or the stuck carts and the crush of humanity. To be in Rome with the real people of the city as they woke to their everyday business was to feel Julius' energy tenfold, and she was almost sorry when they traced their way out of the *Subura* and into the more self-conscious centre.

He bought her a pastry at a small stall, winking at the astonished seller with ready ease, but already it was getting busy around the Forum as would-be senators began setting up their platforms in the best places to impress the inevitable crowds. They would not stay anonymous for long. She saw several people nudge and point, saw messengers go scrambling, and knew the Forum would fill fast this morning.

'Are you sure this is a good idea, Julius?' she asked nervously.

'Very sure. You may not be mine according to the self-conscious laws of Rome ... ' He waved a dismissive hand around the grand Forum. 'But you are mine all the same, and I yours, and I wish them to know it. You may not be my wife-in-law, Cleopatra, but you are most certainly my wife-in-love.'

Wife-in-love! The title thrilled through her. It was so exactly right. She and Julius were bound to others and bound, too, to their countries. Those ties were inextricable and defined their lives but there was room, if you looked, for bonds that ran between those seemingly rigid threads, for a union that was as definable as the morning mists but that no sun could ever burn away.

Taking courage from his fierce pride, she stood tall at his side as the crowds began to flock in. Today there were not just senators but their wives, dragged from household duties for the sight of royalty standing rudely in their midst. Julius stood with her, his head high, making conversation of which she heard not a word over the buzz of gossip as the worker bees crowded round the queen they reviled. For some time no one dared strike openly, but then she heard a shrill voice.

'Queen Cleopatra, you're back! And in the heart of Rome too. How ... bold.'

Porcia was hanging onto the arm of a red-faced Brutus, and Cleopatra gladly squared up to her.

'As far as I can see, Porcia, the city has not cracked open at the sacrilege.'

'You think so? Hmm. Have you met my husband?'

She tugged Brutus forward.

'Of course I've met your husband, Porcia, though as I recall he was someone else's back then.'

She felt Julius' amusement shudder down his arm and saw Porcia's eyes narrow.

'The world cannot stand still.'

'Not with you agitating it, certainly. Congratulations. You must be very proud.'

'I am very happy,' she said primly. 'It is what my father would have wanted.'

'And he was always a man of such perfect taste.' Cleopatra saw Brutus squirm at Porcia's side as a crowd drew in and raised her voice. 'Did I ever tell you how I first met Cato? It was on Cyprus. Do you recall, Brutus? I'm sure you do. A memorable reception.'

Brutus' eyes flickered wildly from Cleopatra to Julius and back.

'Queen Cleopatra, let's not ... '

'He received my father and I sat on the latrine, did you know that, Porcia? Sat on the latrine with his toga bunched around his waist, emitting foul odours even as he spoke to us.' A murmur of pleasing horror ran round the growing crowd. 'I was a girl of fourteen. It stuck with me, as you can imagine, and I am obviously delighted, therefore, that you feel he has set an appropriate stand-ard for your marriage.'

Porcia's mouth worked like a fish but for once she could find no words and, flushing even more furiously, Brutus dragged her away. Cleopatra turned to speak to Julius but he'd been claimed by sycophantic senators. He'd recently proposed a new invasion of Parthia – ever Rome's most sparkling and impossible enemy – and all were keen to lead it. They flocked around him, leaving her at the mercy of the crowd, and she was relieved to spot Claudia and Fulvia.

'Porcia is as vile as ever, Claudie,' she said as they slid into a quiet corner.

'Isn't she just? I don't know what my poor, dear Brutus thinks he's doing. It's Cato. He's been obsessed by the man ever since that damned painting was paraded through the streets. He used to have such life about him, you know, such light, but Porcia is shutting that down.'

Fulvia leaned in.

'Someone told me they've had a huge death mask made of Cato and that every day they bow before it, as if he were some sort of god. That cannot be healthy, can it? And then they go down the line of their shared ancestors until they get right to the start – right to Lucius Junius Brutus.'

'Who's he?'

Claudia rolled her eyes.

'I thought you knew Rome, Petra. He's the man who threw the tyrant kings out. His statue stands at the end of the ones of the first seven kings, like a giant full-stop.'

Cleopatra remembered now. It was a classic piece of Roman confusion to have statues to the royal founders of the city alongside one of the man who'd got rid of them.

'Well,' she said crisply, 'he doesn't need to throw *me* out because I would go with pleasure. I am only here for Julius.'

'And it is clear he is glad of it,' Fulvia said. 'I just hope he stays that way.'

'Fulvia!'

'Oh, not because of you. It's clear he adores you. It's what Rome makes of such adoration that is the problem. He is breaking the sacred laws of the city for you, and people will ask what more he might do to win your favour.'

Cleopatra grabbed her arm.

'I am not asking anything of him.'

'Yet you are here.'

Cleopatra stared at her old friend in dismay.

'What are you saying, Fulvia?'

Fulvia sighed.

'I'm not sure. It is just, I suppose, that the civil war was horrible for Rome. All our petty divisions were wrenched out of us and put on display in the harshest possible way. Men stood against their friends and women were dragged along with them. I never want to see it again. Never.' She shook her head. 'But listen to me being so negative. Enjoy Julius, Petra, enjoy Rome. But not for too long.'

And then she, too, was gone into the crowd, leaving Cleopatra feeling suddenly vulnerable. This morning, creeping across the Pomerium amongst the workers, she had almost seen the magic of this upstart young city but it had been an illusion. Julius' vision was certainly right for Rome; the question was, would they ever accept it?

Chapter Thirty-two

The next day, Julius was up with the first light, letting a cold draught under the covers. Shivering, Cleopatra burrowed down and thought longingly of Alexandria's clear skies. What on earth was Julius doing going out with the sky still dark and the earth hard with frost? One thing she did know as she watched him dress with military efficiency – he couldn't do it wearing those.

'Not the boots, Julius.'

'I like the boots.' He stroked the red leather as he fastened the clasps. 'They are comfortable and warm, and you gave them to me.'

'For Saturnalia, Julius, as well you know. They're costume boots.'

'They're far too good for that. Saturnalia is long gone, Petra, but these boots will last all year and are quite the finest footwear I own.'

'And the brightest. You know what they symbolise, Julius – you know they will annoy people. Let me, at least, have them dyed brown again for you are not, you know, actually Romulus.'

'I know!' he snapped. 'And do not try to be.'

She flinched at his sudden anger, but this was important. Perception was all. Had she not learned that early in life? First Berenice and then Arsinoë had cared for nothing but their own advancement and yet they had somehow persuaded the

Alexandrian mob that she, not they, was the enemy to their prosperity. She did not want to see that happen to Julius.

'*I* know that, my general,' she said carefully, 'but it is important that everyone else does too.'

'Everyone else should worry less about what I look like and more about what I do. I am going to make Rome great for them and if I choose to do it in red boots, that's my business. Goodbye, Petra.'

He strode to the door, not even kissing her.

'Will you be back later?'

'I'm not sure. Rest well.'

And then he was gone, the boots tapping out a stern departure across the mosaic of his pretty villa. Cleopatra burrowed beneath the furs, put her hands to her lightly swelling belly, and sighed. He had a point, and she totally understood that someone who worked so hard for the good of everyone around him should not have to put up with their petty censures but sometimes people were hard to help.

How she wished she'd never come up with the stupid gift.

◆

She didn't know he was back at first. She was playing with Caesarion in the lovely room at the rear of the Horti Caesaris where the pipes from the adjacent bathhouse ran under the tiles, like in Clodia's Baiae home, to make them glow blissfully warm. She was happily absorbed chalking pictures on stones with her two-year-old when Mardion came in.

'Julius is returned, my queen, and he looks a little . . . '

'A little what, Mardion?'

'A little . . . shaken.'

She stared at him. That was not a word she ever associated with the bullish, energetic Imperator. Handing Mardion the chalk box, she picked up her skirts and ran to find him. He was sat in his private office, not at the desk, but in a window arch, his feet drawn up to his chest in a strangely childlike pose and his red boots on the floor below him.

'Julius? Are you well?'

He looked over.

'Quite well,' he said but his eyes were cloudy and his words seemed to come from outside of him.

'Has something happened?'

He nodded slowly.

'Something has happened, yes.' He put out a hand and she took it and sat on the window seat beside him. 'You were right, Petra. They do not like the boots.' He pointed to the discarded footwear, then suddenly slammed his hand into the cushion between them. 'Why, Petra? I give them so much – new countries, new buildings, new riches – and all they care about is the colour of my boots.'

'What happened?' she asked.

He pressed his head against the glass, peering out at his gardens, then the dark Tiber and the tangled streets of Rome beyond. For a long time she did not think he was going to speak but suddenly the words came pouring out of him.

'We'd been up to the Temple of Jupiter for the Latin festival. It's a small event but important to some. Important, actually, to me. Jupiter is King of the Gods, as you know, and . . . ' He stopped himself. 'King!' he groaned. 'That bloody word. The festival matters little; it is what happened on the way back down that was so frustrating. A crowd had gathered, the way it does. There were petitioners as always and people shouting for attention. It was nothing new.'

Cleopatra shuddered but knew better than to comment. She hated the way the Romans were allowed to batter their precious senators with demands wherever they went. It seemed dangerous to her but it was part of the Republic's treasured 'openness' and she could as easily damn the Nile as stop the flow of people in Rome's streets.

'Did someone hurt you?'

'No, nothing like that. A man just shouted, "Hail Caesar, Imperator, God . . . "'

He stuttered to a halt and she looked at him curiously.

'That does not seem so bad.'

'Rex!' He spat the word out. 'He hailed me as Rex, Cleopatra, and so did others.'

'They want you to be king?'

'I know not. There were just as many protesting at the title as calling it and we were close to riot.'

'What did you do?'

'I made a joke of it.' He wiped a hand across his brow. 'I shouted, "I am Caesar, not Rex." It was a poor joke but my men knew to laugh loudly and it calmed things.'

'Caesar not Rex?' She didn't understand.

'Rex is a family name for some. A simple word, no more dangerous than Metelli or Claudii or Brutus.'

Cleopatra's eyes narrowed.

'Oh, I think Brutus is far more dangerous, or, at least, Porcia Brutus is. She's poisonous and she's poisoning he husband too. You should send them away. Put him on the Parthian campaign, get him out of Rome.'

But at that Julius shook his head.

'I have promised him the role of Praetor Urbanus and cannot take that away without causing offence. I might send myself to Parthia.'

'What? Julius – no!'

'Why not? I can leave Brutus and his self-righteous friends to run Rome, and ride for the East. I am a general at heart, Cleopatra. I work best with soldiers who will respect me for making hard choices and tactical decisions and will not care one iota if I choose to wear red bloody boots.'

'But it will be dangerous and, forgive me, Julius, but you grow old. Do you really want to live in an army tent again?'

He looked around his luxurious office and gave her a sad smile.

'I'm not sure, Cleopatra. Tents are rough but they are, at least, truthful. And the weather is surely far better in Parthia than here?'

He nudged at her and she smiled, glad to see him a little restored.

'The weather is certainly good in the East,' she said, 'but it will improve here soon?'

'I hope so,' Julius said, looking down, 'because it seems it is time to dig out my sandals again.'

She reached for the boots, stroking her hand across the soft, red leather.

'Rome needs you here, Julius, and – for now at least – she needs you as Imperator.'

'Should I, though, bow to the whims of the mob?'

Pictures flashed across Cleopatra's mind – the Alexandrians storming into the palace on her fourteenth birthday, ugly voices baying for Ptolemy as they were twisted against her, being chased away on her own royal barge in fear of her life.

'Don't, perhaps, bow to them, Julius, but be wary of them. They do not understand how you see the world, but perhaps you do not understand how they do either?'

He sighed.

'Perhaps. But, oh Petra, they are such lovely boots.'

'Maybe,' she suggested, moving closer, 'you can save them to wear in the bedroom?'

His eyes lit up and, delighted to see it, she took his hand and led him through. Rome was in a ferment over the idea of royalty and her presence was as inflaming as the damned red boots. She must make her preparations to return to Egypt as soon as the seas were open but for now, how could she resist just a little more time with the man that, Isis help her, she truly loved.

Chapter Thirty-three

'They coming, Mama. They coming.'

Caesarion strained so far forward in Cleopatra's arms that she feared he'd topple them both onto the platform where Julius was sitting on a golden seat to watch the Lupercalia. This peculiarly Roman festivity celebrated the suckling of Romulus and Remus – founders of the city – by a wolf and, for reasons best known to themselves, involved the sacrificing of goats and dogs and the running of flayed strips of their poor hides around the city by near-naked young men.

Women crowded to be whipped as they passed, believing this would make them fertile, and Claudia had excitedly informed Cleopatra that she was setting out early for a prime spot. Quite how she intended the bloody flesh to work its miracles without a husband, Cleopatra wasn't sure, but she knew better than to say so. She would have avoided the whole event, but Caesarion had been desperate to see the 'wolves' so here she was, hiding in the wings of the platform to watch. She wasn't risking being seen in public, especially not with her son, and she looked gratefully back at Mardion as he encased them both in his broad arms to hold the prince back.

'There!'

Caesarion squirmed, pointing, and sure enough, the 'Lupercali' –
several young men wearing nothing but tiny leather loin
cloths – came bounding through the crowd, whooping and
whipping up a frenzy with their strips of hide. At the front was
Mark Antony, broad chest oiled to catch the weak February sun.
Handsome, gregarious and easy-going, everyone seemed to love
him, and the crowds cheered wildly as he frisked amongst them,
drawing closer and closer to the platform.

'I wolf!' Caesarion cried ecstatically, tugging at a lock of
Cleopatra's hair as if it were a strip of hide and making her cry
out in pain.

The shouts of the crowd luckily drowned her out and Mardion
quickly plucked a long-stemmed flower from a nearby pot and
handed it to Caesarion. The release on her hair was welcome but
he waved the stalk with such exuberance that the flower crashed
across her face, sending petals everywhere and clouding her eyes
as Mark Antony sprung up onto the platform before Julius.

'The Imperator doesn't need fertility!' someone cried over the
roar of the crowd.

'Ask the Egyptian queen!' someone else shouted. 'Her belly
swells with another little king!'

Cleopatra cowered into the shadows. Caesarion batted crossly
at her but she didn't care; her son's safety was worth more than his
view of this peculiar ritual.

'How do they know?' she asked Mardion.

She was not showing yet and had told no one bar the Claudii
who, for all their personal indiscretion, knew how to keep important secrets.

'Gossip?' he suggested. 'Speculation?' He was right, of course.
This riotous crowd was spouting tittle-tattle from the salons of
Rome's finest ladies and, no doubt, one in particular.

'Porcia.'

There was no time to dwell on what this meant, for Mark Antony

318

was kneeling before Caesar and offering him something. The crowd roared and she strained to see but it wasn't until he moved to place the offering on Julius' head, that she made it out clearly – a plain white diadem, the undisputed symbol of royalty.

'No!' she cried but the noise was deafening. Some were shouting 'Yes,' and 'Rex,' others crying 'Shame!' Julius pushed the diadem away. Mark Antony offered it again, and once more Julius refused. His gestures were wide, grand – designed for effect – but if he intended to publicly convey his refusal, it was lost in the confusion of calls. Cleopatra watched the man she loved hesitate as Mark Antony offered the diadem for a third time. She peered into the crowd and saw the ordinary people cheering wildly. Was Mark Antony right? Did they, after all, want a king?

But then her eyes turned to the senior senators and their wives, gathered in a prim white mass on a stand to Julius' left, and saw their pursed lips and narrowed eyes. They were watching as intently as hawks and there, prime amongst them, was Brutus, his eyes fixed on Julius in a stark mixture of desperation and hope. She'd heard that there was graffiti all over the city glorifying the name of his ancestor, Lucius Junius Brutus, slayer of kings. It called on him to be a 'new Brutus' and she could not imagine the pressure that was putting him under, especially with Porcia in his bed instead of sunny Claudia. His tortured mind must be given no more fodder to oppose Caesar.

'No!' she cried again. 'Julius, no!'

A month ago he'd tried to tell her that 'Rex' was a simple word, carrying no inherent danger, but she could see from the hysteria of Rome that, on the contrary, it was the most dangerous weapon in the city. Julius glanced her way and, shoving Caesarion into Mardion's arms, she stepped into the light, willing him to see her shake her head. His eyes met hers and he looked at her with something like longing – did he, then, truly want to be king? Surely not?

Please, Julius, she willed him, *do not risk all on a simple title.*

Perhaps he heard her thoughts, or perhaps they simply mirrored his own, but either way, he took the diadem and dashed it to the ground.

'Take that to the statue of Jupiter,' he cried, loud and clear, 'for He is the only King in Rome.'

Mark Antony bowed low and whipped the diadem away as the crowd went wild. On the stands, Brutus seemed to crumple in relief and Porcia clutched proprietorially at his arm. Cleopatra scurried back into the shadows, leaning against Mardion and feeling herself shaking all over. The crowds thankfully turned to follow the Lupercali and, after sitting rigid for some time, Julius finally rose and slid out to join them.

'Did you know he was going to do that?' Cleopatra demanded, still shaking.

'It was discussed,' Julius said tightly.

'Why? What were you hoping to achieve?'

'Mark Antony said we should test the waters.'

'Well, the waters turned out to be far too hot to touch.'

'As we saw, Cleopatra, and as we dealt with.'

'You think that was dealing with it? You think that little show will calm Rome? Do you know how gossip works, Julius?'

'Why would I?'

'Because it is lethal. It is your enemy's sword and spear, their battle-plan and their supply chain, and you need a far greater shield against it than some ceremony no one will remember clearly by tomorrow. Do you think that word will spread of your grand refusal? Or do you think that people will, rather, grasp onto the clear image of the diadem, the word "Rex", and the simple associations of the two with you, Julius Caesar?'

He stared at her, as the whoops of the crowd receded behind them, then fell suddenly against a pillar. Cleopatra darted forward in alarm but he waved her back.

'You are a wise woman, my queen.'

'Wiser than you,' she agreed curtly.

'It seems so. I wanted to stop them saying it. I wanted to stop them calling me that.'

She reached out and stroked a loving hand down his worn cheek.

'I'm not sure it worked.'

'No.'

He took Caesarion into his arms and the little boy, still caught up in the ceremony, batted happily at him with the remnants of his flower-whip. Cleopatra swallowed. She so loved seeing them together but it was not safe in Rome.

'I think, Julius, that I should take Caesarion home. I need to travel before I grow close to my birthing and—'

'You will not have the baby here?'

'No, Julius, I will not have my baby here. He or she belongs to Egypt and must be born in Her waters.'

'You will sail for the East?'

'I will.'

He caught at her hand where it still rested on his cheek and kissed it.

'As I said, you are a wise woman. I will too.'

'What?'

'I will sail across the Mare Nostrum with you and on to Parthia.'

'But, Rome, Julius—'

'Rome rocks with the word Rex, Petra, and you are right – no gestures or words, however grand, will stop that. I need to get out and let the city settle. If I win in Parthia, I will bring Rome back riches enough to settle all Italia. I will bring monies to feed every man and house him in safety, to build libraries and fund scholars, to commission art and sculpture and show them what the perfect world can truly look like.'

'You can do that here, Julius. If I am gone, they will forget.'

'You are not the problem, Cleopatra.'

'I am as much the problem as the red boots and the diadem and the Republican obsession with titles they do not understand. I will go and you will rule.'

'Without you?'

'We can write.'

'We can write,' he agreed. 'You will find me in Parthia.'

'Julius—'

But his face was turned firmly to the East and, with the wolf-packs of Rome baying at the base of the Palatine Hill, Cleopatra could not find it in her heart to blame him.

Chapter Thirty-four

Cleopatra, my queen,

I write, I am afraid, with sad tidings. Your brother-husband Ptolemy-Philopater took with a sickness and has gone to the gods. It was a peaceful passing. He talked through his fever to butterflies only he could see and, in the end, I think, they escorted him to the Afterlife where I trust he can rest in eternal meadows. His sweet presence is missed but his influence, as you know, was little.

In truth, you have been sole queen for some time and now all must acknowledge it. I thank Isis for you every day and beseech her to look over you. Take care in Rome, for I fear that paltry city does not understand you, nor care for you as we do, and I wish to see you home safely.

Yours in love,
Charmion

Cleopatra's eyes went to the scroll sat on the side of her bath as Julius paced the room, spouting something dull about troop movements. Now he was set on conquering Parthia, preparations were moving apace and before Cleopatra's eyes he had turned into the soldier of whom she'd heard so much. He wished to sail just after the Ides of March and already seemed consumed by the petty details of campaigning.

She reached for the pot of Dead Sea salts to smooth her skin, smiling as her belly broke the surface of the water. Eiras had added milk to help loosen her skin and stop the baby stretching ugly lines into it, and watching the swirls of the green salts in the white liquid was far more absorbing than listening to Julius. He no longer had time for philosophy or ideas, but only for logistics, maps and plans. He was up early every morning and back late at night and some days he did not return at all. There were generals and senators to meet, and Rome's elite preferred to dine on Calpurnia's prim couches than with a decadent foreign queen. Cleopatra had thought she would lose Julius to war, but already she was losing him to his wife as he was sucked back into the rigid routines of Rome.

'Are you listening, Petra?'

'Not really,' she said, rubbing at her belly.

He put furious hands on his hips, looking momentarily so like a scolding fishwife that she only just stopped herself laughing.

'Why not?'

'Because I am tired and the baby is kicking at me and, frankly, I lack interest in the toilet arrangements of a legion.'

'The baby is kicking?'

'They do that.'

He strode over, thrusting a hand onto her belly with none of the usual care or tenderness she was used to, as if their child was just one more logistic. She flinched back, sending the milky water splashing over the edge, and he looked at her crossly.

'What's wrong?'

'I have something to tell you, Julius.'

'You do? What is it? Is it the baby?'

'No. It is my husband.'

'Your . . . ? Oh, the boy king?'

His easy dismissal stung. Ptolemy-Philopater had been a gentle soul and the palace would be a poorer place without him chasing insects around its beautiful gardens. Plus, however simple, he was an Egyptian royal and deserved to be mourned.'

'King Ptolemy is dead.'

'Dead? I see. I'm, er, sorry. Oh, but – does this mean you are free now? You can rule alone?'

This eagerness stung too and she pushed herself up and stepped crossly from the water, grabbing at the bathsheet on the side before he could pass it to her.

'I have been ruling alone for years, as you well know. It does, however, make me a widow.'

He froze.

'What do you mean by that?'

'I *mean* nothing. I simply state the facts.'

'I am married.'

'I'm well aware of that, thank you. You spend enough time with her.'

'I have to, Cleopatra.'

'Because that is the way Rome wants it?'

'Yes.'

'Fine then. If they matter more to you than me, I'm glad I'm going home.'

His body went rigid and she saw him adjust his face into something that she presumed was meant to look like care.

'Now, Cleopatra, look . . .'

He reached out for her but she ducked away, dripping water as she went.

'No, Julius, you look. You look to your plots and plans and do not come creeping to me with shallow promises. I am not a little wife to be soothed with lies. I am a queen.'

'Do I not know it.'

'I think you should go now.'

'Cleopatra, please—'

'I need to dress and it is clear you do not care for me at the moment so please go.'

He gave a deep sigh.

'Of course I care. I'm just busy. I thought you of all people would understand the demands of rule.'

'"Rule" does not demand you lick the arses of all the men you purport to despise.'

'It does if I get what I want from them.'

'A ticket out of the city?'

'For now, yes.'

'And a ticket back in once you return with Parthia in your pocket? Do you really think you will do that? Do you really think you will conquer the unconquerable?'

He stared at her in shock.

'Do you not?'

'Have you been to Parthia, Julius?'

'You know I have not. Yet.'

'Have you, then, read the reports of the other Romans who sought to defeat her? Have you read the numbers of men lost? Of generals taken prisoner? Have you read of Crassus having molten gold poured down his throat by the Parthian king? What makes you think you will be any different?'

He glared at her.

'What makes you think I will not? Have I given you any cause to doubt me? Did I not free you from imprisonment by your own people?'

'No! How many times must we go over this? You fought well, yes, but not alone. My army was first to the palace gates.'

His body went rigid.

'You think I will be defeated then? You think I will be captured and executed and my men left to limp home with nothing but their injuries?'

'I think it is a possibility – and Julius, it fills me with true dread every minute of the day.'

That silenced him.

'Dread?' he asked eventually.

'Yes, dread – because I cannot, now, imagine the world without you in it.'

He stared at her and she tucked the bathsheet closer around her.

'You do not need me,' he said, low-voiced.

She considered this carefully.

'I can live without you,' she agreed. 'I can live for my son and for the new baby, for my friends and for my country. I can, and will live but, Julius, it would be like battling through the grey clouds of Britannia instead of basking in the glorious sunshine of home.'

'Oh.'

He stood there, mouth gaping, and she wasn't sure if she wanted to hit or kiss him. She grabbed at his hand.

'War is not the answer, Julius. Go to Syria, shore up your borders, hold talks with the Parthians. Diplomacy is all that is needed. It will calm the East and it will calm Rome and, most important of all, it will keep you safe.'

'What if I am bored of safe?'

'Then I cannot help you. No one can.' She looked at him standing there in his soldier's tunic, his hands full of maps and charts, and felt anger rise from somewhere deep beneath his second child.

'Is this truly you, Julius, this soldier-boy, keen for sword-glory? You say you want to rule. You say you want to work for the improvement of your nation, you want culture and technology, great buildings, art and theatre. You say your people are small-minded and cannot see the scope of what is possible but neither can you. You cannot settle into everyday rule because you cannot see past the simplistic release of a battlefield victory. It's so ... so stupidly male.'

He drew himself up tall.

'Perhaps, if I disappoint you so much in my masculinity, you should find a woman with whom to share your royal bed.'

'Perhaps I will.'

His eyes darkened but she turned away. He had told her once that he had trouble remembering she was a queen for more than his titillation; clearly the same went for the simple fact of being a woman. He was, it turned out, as disappointing as his cocky little city.

'Go, Julius. Go back to Rome and back to Calpurnia and back to your precious army. I will move to the coast tomorrow to be ready for the first sail home.'

'Cleopatra, I . . .'

But she'd heard enough and strode from the room before she could weaken, head high despite her nominal covering. The clouds, it seemed, were gathering and the best she could do was to accept them with dignity.

'Eiras!' she called. 'Mardion! We must pack and prepare to leave Rome. Now.'

Chapter Thirty-five

Cleopatra stood stiffly at the top of the Temple steps and tried to ignore the whispers below. The invitation had arrived the morning after their argument, a formal one from Imperator to Queen, and she had not dared refuse it and leave Rome. She was still an official guest in Italia and even if their personal relations had soured, their diplomatic ones must be kept strong. It was most uncomfortable.

This was to be the grand unveiling of the statues within the Temple of Venus Genetrix. The temple was Caesar's own special commission and beautiful in an orderly Roman way. Perfectly square, it sat on an unusually high plinth with long steps all around and eight columns on every side. The entrance was apparently at the rear but no one was allowed inside before him so she was stuck in front of everyone until he chose to show up.

To one side, Claudia caught her eye and gave her a cheery wink but, as she was standing next to an iron-backed Servilia, it was little comfort. The older lady had offered Cleopatra only the stiffest of acknowledgements since her return to Rome and Cleopatra did not blame her. She hated the thought of Julius in Calpurnia's bed, despite his assurances that it held no allure for him, so how much must Servilia hate knowing that he'd chosen to defy Rome to be with her.

'He hasn't,' she reminded herself.

Their stinging argument last week still rang in every fibre of her being, thrumming painfully through her veins, puddling sourly in her stomach and battering at her womb. The babe within seemed to kick it off with casual ease and Cleopatra envied it.

She shifted. Where the hell was Julius? It was unfair of him to keep her standing here, toppling under the weight of his child with the spring sun shining directly down. Her belly had swollen this week, as if sick of hiding away, and she had chosen a sheath dress that emphasised its curve. Let Rome see her in all her royal, fertile glory. She was everything they hated but she was not going to let that cow her any longer. Isis help her, though, she would love a chair.

At last, the trumpets sounded and Julius arrived in a flurry of attendants, pursued by an eager crowd of everyday Romans. Beaming round, he strode up the steps, took Cleopatra's hand and kissed it with studied flamboyance. It was all she could do not to snatch it back but he was already turning away and flinging his arms wide to the crowd.

'Good people of Rome, we are here today to unveil a new statue of Venus in her special temple, to honour her as goddess of love and fertility, and to commemorate her importance to my family. The temple is intimate, so not all will be able to see the unveiling, but rest assured it will be open all day so that everyone who wishes can stand before her beauty and know what she means to me. Shall we?'

He offered Cleopatra his hand and, puzzled, she took it. This was the first time she'd seen him since she'd dismissed him from his own villa but he was acting as if they'd just risen from the sheets together.

'Julius . . . ' she hissed.

'Cleopatra?' he said blithely.

'What are you doing?'

'A little patience please. It will be worth it. This way.'

He ushered her round the back and through an arched doorway.

The entrance was dim but when they stepped into the *cella*, light flooded in from windows high up around the vaulted ceiling, shining on the elaborate carvings of dolphins and shells in the frescoes and falling on the central altar, behind which stood a statue, draped in linen.

'If you would stand here, please.'

'Julius, what are you playing at?'

'Here, next to the statue. That's it.'

'Julius!'

But now the rest of the guests were fanning out around the *cella*, eyes fixed on the masked carving. Cleopatra leaned against the altar and prayed for the strength to see this Roman nonsense through. Julius stepped into the centre, the light falling onto him as if he'd been sent down on a sunray. He took hold of the linen to whip it away and everyone in the temple gasped. The sound ricocheted around the circular room and Cleopatra felt herself sway as she gazed up at Venus, her lines carved out in Egyptian gold and unmistakably those of Cleopatra herself.

'My statue,' she gasped.

The last time she had seen this it had been paraded before her as a spoil of war, but now here it was, set up high above the whole city in Julius' own temple.

'Where it deserves to be,' he murmured in her ear, 'dedicated to the goddess I know you are. Egyptian Isis transformed into Roman Venus – what could be more perfect?'

'But it's so clearly me, Julius.'

'Which is what's so glorious about it.'

She looked nervously to the crowd, their whispered comments echoing in slivers of delighted disapproval around the tight space of the temple.

'What do you think they're saying?'

He shrugged.

'I expect they're saying that I am besotted with you. And they are right. I am sorry, Petra. I was arrogant and foolish. I angered you with my lack of care and I hope this goes a little way to showing you how important you are to me. You are my wife-in-love and all should know it.'

Cleopatra looked up at the statue in awe. It was an astonishing, personal gesture and yet, seeing herself in gold in the very heart of Rome sent a dark chill right through her.

'Julius—'

'Hush, my Petra. You said I did not care; now you know that I do.'

'Now I do,' she agreed, looking up into his dear face.

She was touched, of course she was, but she was scared too. Today was, perhaps, the first time she'd had reason to regret the skill of Egyptian craftsmen, for there was no doubting the likeness to herself, or the angry comments that was attracting. Julius stood fiercely below it, daring anyone to complain, and they did not – to his face.

But as Cleopatra stood with him, watching Servilia and Porcia and their thin-nosed friends troop past this show of his devotion to his foreign queen, she feared he had misjudged it. Truly, a private apology would have been sufficient but, oh no, he must parade his devotion before all like a pair of red boots, glorious but misplaced. Men had ever been deaf to the whispers of 'gossip', and blind to its power, and she prayed he would not come to regret this flamboyant gesture.

One more week, she told herself as she plastered a smile onto her carefully painted face and dared the Roman crowds to be rude. It was one more week to the Ides and then the seas would be open and they could sail away. She still feared for Julius in Parthia but it seemed that even those fierce warriors might be less dangerous to him than his own people and she was counting the days until they could escape.

Chapter Thirty-six

Two more days.

Cleopatra reached out to cross 14 March off her calendar. Tomorrow was the Ides and, the day after, she and Julius would ride for the port. She could not wait to taste the salted air of the Green Sea and its alluring promise of home.

'Can I come?' someone asked and she spun round to see Claudia standing in the doorway.

'To Alexandria?'

'Yes. Why not? I'd love to see it and there's little for me here.'

Cleopatra went over to draw her friend into the room and noted the red rims of her eyes. It was an all-too-familiar sight these days.

'Brutus?' she asked gently.

Her friend shrugged but the tears were rising again and Cleopatra tugged her down on a couch.

'I never see him, Petra. Oh, I know that's to be expected. We are, after all, divorced—' she shook her head as if the word had lodged like a stinging creature in her hair '—but it does not feel that way to me. I miss him. I miss cuddling up to him, I miss eating with him, I even miss talking with him, for all that I was useless at that.'

'You were not useless, Claudia. It is simply that Brutus does not wish to listen to any opinions other than his own.'

'He listens to Porcia's.'

'Because she offers him no choice; that is not truly listening.'

Claudia huffed miserably.

'I hear he's very grumpy these days.'

'I'm not surprised. If I was bedding Porcia, I'd be grumpy too.' She clapped a hand over her mouth. 'Sorry, Claudie.'

Claudia gave a sad little attempt at a laugh.

'He was always so lovely in bed. Such strong hands. And he used to look into my eyes when . . . Well, you know. I can't bear the thought of him doing it with that cow.'

'Oh, he won't,' Cleopatra assured her. 'He'll bend her over so he can't see her face and get on with it.'

'Petra!' Claudia protested, but the laugh was more genuine this time.

Cleopatra hugged her.

'Don't worry, Claudie, you're not the only one whose man is in another's bed. Julius is staying with Calpurnia every night until we leave.'

Claudia hugged her back.

'Horrible, isn't it?'

'Hmm,' she agreed, though she tried not to think about it and, in truth it was she who had urged him to stay with his wife after the debacle at the Temple of Venus.

He'd been confused. 'I did this to show you how much I care for you, Petra.'

'And I truly appreciate it, Julius. It was a noble gesture and a brave one too.'

'Brave?'

'Did you see Porcia's face? She was furious.'

'Women's foolishness.'

He did not understand.

'I am touched by your care, Julius, truly. And I am asking you to stay with your wife to show the same care in return.'

He'd frowned.

'I thought it was me staying with Calpurnia that angered you.'

'I know you did ...' She'd stopped herself again. 'It is simply that, much as I want to invite you into my bed, I do not want to invite the assassin's dagger as well.'

'You think ...?'

'Call it women's foolishness if you will, Julius, but it is only a few more days. Once we're at sea, we can be together without boundaries.'

'Like we were at Saturnalia.'

'Exactly like that. I can wait a few days if you can?'

'I'm not sure,' he'd said, kissing her again, but then some general had arrived and he'd been forced to step away and she hadn't seen him since.

Two more days.

She blinked herself from the future and back into the present.

'Is there anything I can do to help, Claudie?'

'Well, now you mention it, is Eiras here?'

'She is. Do you want me to call her?'

'If you don't mind. I really need her to do something with my hair. Servilia's grandson is getting his toga virilis tomorrow so there will be a procession to the senate house.'

'And you wish to look beautiful for that?'

She flushed.

'Brutus will be there.'

'Of course.'

Cleopatra wondered when Claudia might give up trying to impress the man who'd divorced her, but she rang the bell and Eiras appeared almost instantly.

'My queen?'

'Claudia asks if you would work your magic on her hair?'

'Of course! Shall we go to your chamber?'

They settled in, Claudia before the mirror, Cleopatra reclining to watch her precious companion at work. Cinna had been drawn into the political morass of the city, so Eiras was with her most of the time

335

and she was grateful. She could still remember the very first day her dear companion had arrived in Alexandria, sent up the Nile by her mother. It was the greatest gift – after her own life, of course – that the Priestess Safira could ever have given her and she sent up prayer of thanks to Isis.

'Do you know what I heard yesterday?' Claudia said, as Eiras smoothed oil through her hair. 'I heard the Senate are going to vote to make Julius King of Rome so he can beat the Parthians.'

'That cannot be true,' Cleopatra told her.

'It is. Well, it might be. There's a prophecy, you see, that only a king can defeat the Parthians, so they're going to vote to make Julius a king.' She caught Cleopatra's look of horror and her voice faltered. 'But only out of Rome. Only, you know, in the East. Only . . . What?'

'Only with his corrupting Queen of Egypt?'

Claudia fiddled with her neckchain.

'They don't like you much, do they, Petra? I stand up for you though, I promise. I tell them it's not you influencing him.'

'And do you believe you?'

'Of course they don't,' Eiras said. 'They only believe the bad stuff. The other day someone asked Cinna if it was true that he was proposing a bill to senate to allow Julius to take two wives.'

She and Claudia both laughed but Cleopatra sat up, alarmed.

'They really asked that?'

The other two, catching her sharp tone, stopped laughing.

'They did,' Eiras agreed cautiously.

'Because they believe he wants to marry me too?'

'I suppose so, now that you are . . . '

'Widowed.' Cleopatra leaped up. 'That's dangerous, Eiras. They can just about tolerate me as a mistress – a symbol of all that is wicked and decadent in the East – but as a wife . . . Oh, Isis help us, we have to leave Rome.'

'Two more days,' Eiras reminded her but suddenly it felt like far too many.

She paced the chamber.

'Porcia will love this. She'll be spreading it like poison to every senator's wife and from thence into their gullible ears.' She grabbed Claudia's arm. 'Do you think Brutus would believe that?'

Claudia swallowed.

'I think he might,' she said in a small voice. 'It is the sort of concept he can understand – marriage as, as . . . '

'Power,' Cleopatra filled in. 'Power without compassion.' She sank wearily back onto the couch. Oh, I wish you could have Brutus back, Claudie. Things were so much better when he was with the Claudii.'

Claudia grimaced.

'You never know, Porcia might die.'

'Only if you take a dagger to her treacherous heart and probably not even then. It would be far too hard to pierce.'

'Petra!'

'What? I bet she's behind this damned rumour. She's evil.'

'You can't say that,' Claudia objected weakly.

'She can.'

They all jumped at a fourth voice in the room – a low, melodious, authoritative voice. Cleopatra recognised it immediately and didn't quite dare turn around.

'Servilia!' Claudia leaped up. 'What are you doing here?'

'I'm not sure, but it's important.' She looked at Cleopatra. 'Can we speak?'

Cleopatra flushed and levered herself off the couch.

'Of course.'

Servilia put a gentle hand on her shoulder.

'Here will do. You should rest in your condition.'

'Servilia, I'm sorry, I—'

'I know you are. I've known it for ages. I still have your letter and if I ever forget, if I ever get angry or upset, I read it again. Some of the words are too worn to see but I know it by heart anyway. And I understood it all even before I read them. How could I not? I was once every bit as in love with him as you are now.'

Eiras and Claudia had backed away and it felt as if it were just she and Servilia in the room, as if they were right back when she'd tumbled into her house with her first bleed, twelve years ago.

'I didn't mean to hurt you.'

'I know. And, let's face it, it wasn't you who hurt me but Julius. He chose you, Cleopatra, and who can blame him. You two are a perfect match – as fiery, intelligent, exciting and capable as each other. We may, once, have ruled a bed together but you pair, you can rule the whole world. How could I ever compete with that?'

'You overestimate—'

'I do not. But, listen, I'm not here to rake over the past. Something is wrong in Rome.' She beckoned the other two in again. 'I know this city. I know every street and every building, every crooked corner and every twisted square and right now they are seething with trouble. Where is Julius?'

'Julius?' Cleopatra's heart spiked with fear. 'I don't know. He's with Calpurnia. Eiras?'

'I believe Cinna said that he was dining with Lepidus this evening. They're preparing their final demands for the senate tomorrow.'

'Lepidus is good,' Servilia said tightly. 'He can be trusted. I think.'

'Who cannot?' Claudia demanded. Servilia stared at her, clearly uncomfortable. 'Aunt Servilia, who cannot be trusted?'

She bit at her lip.

'Brutus.'

'Brutus? Our own Brutus?'

Servilia's eyes narrowed.

'He is no longer our own, my dear, as you know all too well. Porcia has taken him. She's taken him and wrung him out and poured her own brand of poison into what remains. Cleopatra is right – she is evil. And she's plotting.'

'Against Julius?'

'Perhaps. Perhaps they all are. I have questioned everyone that I know – and that is many – and they seem to me either as ignorant as I, or pretending to be. I don't like it.'

'But what can they do?'

'I'm not sure. This meeting in the senate tomorrow seems loaded.'

'Loaded?' Cleopatra asked hoarsely but it was Eiras who had the courage to speak their darkest fears.

'You suspect treachery?'

Servilia wrung her hands.

'It's a possibility. The senators have been very keen to get Julius into the house. They have switched from grumbling endlessly about the Parthian campaign, to singing his praises for taking it on. They are promising many honours and privileges and wish to ratify them all tomorrow.'

'You do not believe them?'

'It is a mighty turnaround, especially from men whose opinions are usually grooves in granite. I do not like it.'

'Which is why you are here,' Cleopatra said softly.

'Some things are more important than personal differences. Julius' life is one of them.'

Cleopatra grabbed at the arm of the couch as her chamber seemed to spin. She looked at Eiras.

'Remember Potheinos?'

Eiras nodded grimly. Cleopatra closed her eyes a moment, recalling that dread meeting three years ago when Potheinos and Achillas had come into the palace under pretence of amity, with daggers concealed against their thighs. It had been 'idle gossip' in the barber's queue that had alerted them to the danger that time; was it to be similar now? She stood up.

'He cannot go to that meeting.'

Servilia clutched Cleopatra's arm.

'Agreed. You have to keep him in the house tomorrow. You have to stop him going to the senate.'

'Servilia, I can't.'

'Of course you can. Seduce him . . .'

'No, you don't understand. I can't because he's staying with Calpurnia.'

'Oh. Oh, I see. Horrible that, isn't it?' Cleopatra felt as if this strange conversation was turning in circles, or maybe spirals, inwards and inwards to who knew what terrible end.

'We have to go and see her,' she said. 'Now.'

'Calpurnia?' Claudia squeaked in astonishment.

'Calpurnia,' Cleopatra confirmed.

❖

Julius' wife was not pleased to see the queen of Egypt standing in her atrium.

'What are *you* doing here?' Her eyes flicked to Servilia. 'And what are *you* doing with her?'

'It's Julius,' Servilia said. 'He's in danger, Calpurnia, and we need to keep him safe.'

'We?' she spat. 'We – his wife, his former lover and his Eastern whore?'

'Yes,' Servilia agreed calmly. 'We three, who love him best.'

'But, but . . . ' Calpurnia looked from one to the other in confusion but must have seen the fear in all their eyes for with a sigh she ushered them inside. 'What must I do?'

❖

It was impossible to sleep. Cleopatra tossed and turned, trying to picture Julius in Calpurnia's bed and wishing he were here instead. Many times during her stay in Rome she had wished the same but never with such intensity. Never with a such a sense of fear. It griped low in her swollen belly and ached across her limbs and, when first light finally came, she rose gratefully and went to Caesarion's room to watch him sleep. His delighted face when he woke to find her at his side was cheering and she crawled in with him, hugging him close.

'Pray for Papa, Caesarion,' she told him and Caesarion dutifully got down on his knees by his bed and raised his hands to the skies.

340

'Isis, lady of the Nile, look after Papa.'

Cleopatra could only pray Isis was listening and rang for breakfast. Caesarion tucked in with his usual gusto but Cleopatra felt too sick and sore to eat and sipped at warm *calda* – more wine than milk this anxious morning – as first Mardion, then Sosigenes and Levi joined her around the breakfast table. Eiras had gone out at first light with Cinna and they all sat tensely waiting until finally they heard footsteps hurrying across the marble floor of the atrium. Eiras burst in and thrust a note at Cleopatra.

'From Calpurnia, my queen. She passed it out of the window.'

Cleopatra scrabbled the tiny papyri open and read:

I have convinced Julius the omens are poor and he is to stay at home.

'Praise Isis,' she muttered.

Caesarion was leaping impatiently around and she took him into the garden. Sosigenes had hung a swing in the trees and now he and Levi took him off to play on it, leaving Cleopatra free to look across the Tiber to the tumbled roofs of Rome. Somewhere out there Julius was in his home, with his wife.

'I thought it was me staying with Calpurnia that angered you?' he'd said to her after the day of the statue.

She'd told him she'd only asked it to show her care but it had been a topsy-turvy idea then and it was a topsy-turvy one now. Why would he stay in with Calpurnia? She felt another pain in her belly and curved her hands beneath it.

'I think we should go into Rome,' she said to Eiras.

Her friend shook her head furiously.

'Not today. It's tense there today.'

'Exactly! Julius is in danger.'

'And you have done what you can.'

'I have not!' Cleopatra grabbed her arms. 'If it were Cinna's life under threat, would you leave it to someone else to prevent him coming to harm?'

Eiras swallowed.

'Not if I thought I could help. But I am not a queen. I do not have duties to others, to my country. It matters little to any but those close to me if I die, but you ...'

Cleopatra screwed her hands into her eyes. Eiras was right, damn her. Cleopatra had come back to Rome for love, nothing more or less, and for a few short months at the back end of last year it had felt like enough. At Saturnalia she and Julius had been happy together, but almost from the moment this new year had begun, their duties as rulers had intruded and never more so than today. Cleopatra could not pick up her skirts and run to Julius, for she would carry too many others into danger with her.

She plucked nervously at a rhododendron bush, pulling off a rich pink flower and fraying its petals as she paced.

'Cinna is there,' Eiras told her.

'He is but one man.'

'Among many. The senate love Julius.'

'Not all of them.'

Cleopatra thought of Brutus and how the civil war had turned him from an open, earnest young man into a tortured, angry one. She pictured his face when he'd seen the portrait of Cato paraded in the street and the quick way Porcia had fuelled his ire with her catcalls. Julius had had no idea of the effects of his stupid Triumph.

'Rome is not his usual battlefield,' she moaned, her eyes fixed on the road to the city.

There was a messenger riding up it at some speed and she snapped her fingers for one of her men to greet him. He brought a new note bearing Servilia's seal and she tore it open.

My grandson is home, splendid in his toga virilis, bless him. He says the senate want to wait for Caesar. He says Brutus is most insistent he comes. I'm scared, Petra. I'm going to see him. I'm going to try and keep him at home. Stay there and stay safe.

Cleopatra stared at the words. So now Julius' former lover was joining his wife to shield him from harm whilst she – the woman he had taken so many risks for, the woman whose very presence here was a danger to him – sat across the stupid, sludgy river and did nothing. It was ridiculous. She turned slowly, looking at Caesarion playing on the swing. Mardion had stuck himself in front so that the boy's foot could connect with his substantial behind as he swung forward and Caesarion was helpless with merry laughter. The sound pulled a small smile from her, despite the anxiety cramping across her body, and she forced herself to go back to her own.

These were the people who mattered now, the people she would be on the boat with in two days' time, the people who would help her rule Egypt. But still her gaze strayed to Rome. She had let herself love Julius. She had known it was an indulgence but she'd been unable to resist and she wanted him on that boat too. Was it so much to ask?

There was another messenger pounding up the road to the villa and she ran to meet this one herself. Her name was scrawled on it, barely legible, and it was sealed so clumsily that it had to be from Claudia. She ripped it open.

Porcia has collapsed in the street. I saw it myself. Quite the scene! Someone was calling that she was dead, but it was all an act, if you ask me. The only thing I don't know is why. She demanded a message be sent to Brutus but perhaps if he has to come to her side, the senate will disband and we can breathe again.

Cleopatra certainly hoped so. Her chest felt constricted and the pain in her belly was now too great to be ignored. Was she losing the baby? She felt tears prick but could not let them fall, not when so much seemed to be at stake. The sun was rising fast now, shining down on the city, and surely every fingerspace it moved upwards reduced the chance of senate staying in session. She would send to him, tell him to leave by the back way, tell him she would meet him on the road and they could ride south to the port, to the sea, to the East.

'Watch Caesarion,' she threw at her friends, though she knew already that they would.

Darting indoors, she snatched up her writing materials and began to pen the missive. There was no time for pretty words or clever arguments and she stated her plan baldly, praying to Isis that he would trust her. He could surely put out word that he had been called to the many troops already amassing at the southern tip of Italia. It was the sort of thing that generals did all the time, was it not?

There was a disturbance at the door and Cleopatra looked up in alarm as the guards cried out. A man was trying to run between them, making straight for her. She leaped up but her men grabbed the impostor just in time, throwing him to the ground and yanking his hands behind his back. Cleopatra's heart pounded.

'Let me go!' the man shouted. 'I come with an urgent message for Queen Cleopatra from the Lady Calpurnia.'

'Calpurnia?' Cleopatra gasped. 'What says she?'

The man craned up at her from his position on the floor.

'She says Caesar has gone to the senate. She says his own lieutenant came for him, sent by Brutus to escort him personally. She could do nothing to stop him but she says the man is loyal to Julius and all must surely be well.'

'No!'

Cleopatra's hands flew to her mouth. She should have brought Julius here. Or failing that, she should have gone to his villa, got into bed with him and Calpurnia if she had to. Anything to stop him walking into that lion's den.

'I have to go,' she said.

She threw the letter down and made for the door as the others came running inside. She was a queen but she was also a woman and right now that was all she could feel.

'I have to go,' she repeated. 'I have to go to him.'

The messenger, eyes wide, proffered his horse and, with a nod of thanks, she swung into the saddle. It was a rough, scrawny creature, a far cry from the fine mounts she was used to, but she cared not.

'I'm coming!' Eiras cried, running after her and grabbing at the bridle.

There was no time to argue so Cleopatra reached out a hand and swung her into the saddle at her back, but even as they pounded down the elegant drive from Julius' villa, they heard a roar rend the heart of the cursed city in two.

'No!' Cleopatra cried.

'Go,' Eiras urged. 'It may not be too late.'

Cleopatra prayed she was right but as they pounded into the Subura, the chaos in the streets belied all hope. The ordinary people were scrambling for their homes, fear in their eyes as they slammed their flimsy doors on the city.

'What's happened?' Eiras cried down to one woman, who was limping past with a babe on each hip and another clutching at her skirts.

'They've stabbed him,' she wailed. 'They've stabbed Julius Caesar.'

Cleopatra felt the words cut through her as if it were she who had taken the blade. Tears blurred her eyes and she furiously blinked them away, trying to find a path through the mass of panicking people. Screams filled the air as riots broke out and smoke began to rise where looters were swift to seize the chance of gain. Cleopatra pushed on, carried inexorably towards the Forum on a wave of angry people, thankful for the thin back of the poor horse to keep them above the worst of the violence.

'We have to get away,' Eiras said, clutching at her waist. 'If someone works out who you are, we're dead.'

The stark truth pierced Cleopatra's fog of grief. Thankfully she had run out in just her house-dress and simple sandals and on the messenger's poor horse there was little to identify her as a queen but they were close to the Forum now and someone might recognise her. She remembered Claudia's note saying that Porcia had collapsed in the street. That had been by design, she was sure, and the evil woman might still be abroad. She would not hesitate to point the finger and the hysteria in the crowd would do the rest. Cleopatra grabbed the reins and turned the terrified horse into a side street. She had not ducked being torn apart by the Alexandrian mob to die at the hands of the Roman one.

The side street was a little clearer and she guided the horse gratefully away from the crowds but then, glancing back towards the cacophony of noise, caught a glimpse of a man stood high on a platform in the centre of the Forum. He held a dagger over his head and the fresh blood upon it glimmered red in the sun.

'Brutus!'

She could not hear what he was saying over the roar of the crowd but caught odd words about tyranny and liberation and the restoring the Republic. They were predictably idealistic but were not being well received and already his personal guard was hustling him away. She watched, sadness filling her heart. Claudia's once happy husband had murdered the greatest man this damned Republic had known for the sake of a dead ideal. It would be laughable if it wasn't so terribly sad.

'Down there,' Eiras was urging. 'If you take a left and then a right, we will be close to Calpurnia's house.'

'Is that wise?'

'It is where they will take him, dead or alive.'

Cleopatra nodded, though she had little hope of there being breath still in Julius' dear body. She'd seen his blood glittering on the traitor's knife and even Julius Caesar, for all his energy and spirit, could not live without blood in his veins.

'Who goes there?'

The guards at Calpurnia's door were aggressive and who could blame them. Cleopatra slid from the horse and ran forward.

'A friend.'

'Friends cannot be trusted in Rome right now. We must keep . . .'

His words died in his mouth as he looked over her head and, turning, Cleopatra saw a sight she knew she would not forget for the rest of her life. Three servants, heads low and eyes pinned to the cobbles, were hefting a litter on which a dark shape lay, covered in a red cloak. One corner drooped where they were missing a fourth man and from beneath the cloak, an arm dangled.

'Julius!'

Cleopatra ran forward, clasping the hand. It was white and limp and, as the poor servants let the body drop to the ground on the doorstep, she pulled back the cloak to see his dear face, glassy-eyed and staring into eternity. His toga was slashed at many points, blood caking the white fabric in a dirty brown so starkly different to the scarlet on Brutus' dagger. Brutus' blood was the showy glare of principles but this, this back street stain, this broken body of a man who had lived hard and well, was the truth.

Cleopatra fell to the ground, pulling the husk of Julius Caesar into her arms and pressing her lips against his as if she might breathe life back into him, but it was useless. Even the Goddess within her could do nothing now for he was gone.

'Two more days,' she moaned as the door opened and Calpurnia and Servilia came tumbling out. 'That's all we needed, my love – two more days.'

The boat for the east would sail and she would be on it, but on it alone.

'Come, my queen,' Eiras whispered, tugging her away. 'Come with me.'

Not, then, quite alone. Cleopatra stumbled back from the remains of her lover, leaving the Roman women to pull him into their villa, to call their doctors and their undertakers, to perform their oblations and mourn their loss. She would mourn hers in the blood-red glow of the great pyramids where once he had pulsed with such life.

'Take me home, Eiras,' she moaned. 'Please, take me home.'

Epilogue

'Land, my queen! Look – there is land!'

Cleopatra grabbed Caesarion and scrambled to the bow of the ship to peer across the deep green waters. Rising up from the shimmering horizon was land – *her* land.

'Egypt,' she breathed.

'Me see!' Caesarion demanded and she lifted him high in her arms, pointing to the unmistakeably proud outline of the Pharos, soaring upwards as if it might touch the gods and lifting her spirits with it.

It had been a long, hard month. They had fled south for the port with Rome in fire and fury, information following them as fleet messengers carried the shocking news around the country. They said Julius had been stabbed twenty-three times and so 'few' only because many of the sixty men who had collaborated against him had not been able to get close enough to deliver their blow before he died. Brutus had been first, followed in a heartbeat by all of Julius' closest men, lost in petty self-interest and navel-gazing philosophy and believing their bold leader was the root of their problems. Fools.

It had not turned out well for them. They had taken a stand on the Capitoline Hill, preaching about the Republic, but the people, it turned out, were happier to give their loyalty to an inspiring man than to an ideal. Or perhaps the people, unlike their senators, had already known that the Republic was dead.

Mark Antony, at least, had stood loyal to Caesar. It had surprised Cleopatra, for she knew him as a man of spirit and fun, but not so much of principle. He had proved her wrong, refusing to bend to the conspirators and turning Caesar's funeral into a riot, parading a waxen image of his body marked with the twenty-three wounds, and delivering an oration that had stirred the masses to hysteria.

Claudia, it turned out, had done better from her sad divorce than she could ever have known, for the conspirators were gone now, fleeing their precious city in shame. Caesar's will had been read in public with many of those who had turned their daggers on him being honoured as beneficiaries. Brutus, she'd heard, had wept. But that was Brutus for you – ever indecisive.

Porcia had fled Rome too, but not with the husband she'd led so deliberately into bitterness. Cleopatra wondered if Brutus' philosophising was doing him any good now and hoped not. He should suffer. The conspirators should all suffer, for they had robbed the world of a man who made it a better place – and robbed her of the man she loved.

Tears bit, as they so often did these days, and she reached out a hand to Claudia, who was rubbing sleepy eyes and staring in joy at Alexandria.

'You are glad you came?'

'Very glad. This city will be a new beginning for me.'

'For us all,' Cleopatra said sadly.

She had lost Julius' baby in the flight, as if her body had no strength to hold it without him in the world. It had been a second wound digging into the still gaping one of his loss and had left her weak and awash with tears. She wanted this new beginning just as little as Claudia, but they had no choice and could, at least, hold their heads up high to step into it.

The boat, sensing harbour, picked up speed and she let her tears flow and mingle with the spray flying over the railings. The others joined her and she felt their friendship at her back, like a sail to blow her onwards as Alexandria's glittering white buildings grew clear before them.

'Those Romans,' Mardion said, shaking his head, 'they have no idea of beauty.'

'Nor of loyalty,' Levi added darkly.

Cleopatra sighed.

'Egyptians can be treacherous too. I have fled this city twice in fear of my life.'

'Only because of the machinations of those who wanted power for themselves,' Sosigenes said.

Cleopatra grimaced.

'So, quite like Rome then?' She sighed. 'There is no excuse. I have learned, the hard way, that it is a ruler's job to explain their actions with sufficient clarity to carry the masses. Not doing that was perhaps Julius' only failing and it cost him his life; I will not let it take mine.'

She looked up as the ship reached the Pharos and passed through into the Great Harbour. The wind stilled, the waves calmed and Cleopatra felt the warmth of her home city on her face and its delicious smells in her nostrils. A crowd was gathering on the dockside and she could hear voices shouting up the perfectly straight streets of Egypt's capital: 'The Queen! The Queen is here! The Queen is home!'

More and more citizens were coming, glorious in their myriad different shades, outfits and languages. Cleopatra drunk in the sight of them, then spotted a lone figure standing right on the very tip of the dock and felt her heart swell. The captain steered the boat in to dock and Cleopatra stepped eagerly back onto Egyptian soil and straight into Charmion's arms.

'Cleopatra, it's so wonderful to see you. Alexandria has pined for her queen – and I with her.'

Cleopatra hugged her close as Caesarion squirmed in to join

the cuddle and the others gathered round. Soon she would have to turn, put her head up and be queen for her people, but for just a moment more she could be herself, Petra, with the people who truly loved her.

Three times she had returned to this city: once to watch Berenice hang; once to see Ptolemy-Theos drown in the marshes of the delta; and once running from Arsinoë's taunting tears. Her father was long dead, her mother locked away in her temple, and even her simple little brother had gone to the eternal meadows. She had no blood relatives around her and yet in these loyal servants and friends she had all the family she would ever need.

Cleopatra closed her eyes, picturing poor Julius' dear face as those closest to him drove daggers into his big, visionary heart, and she felt pain ripple through her. Then, with a last squeeze to her family, she pushed her head up high, stepped out of their embrace and stood before her people, Egypt's queen, now and for always.

Acknowledgements

This book has been a long time in the making and it could not have been done without the help of a great many people. First off, a huge thank you to my wonderful editor, Anna Boatman, whose astute editing and profound encouragement have helped shape this book into far more than it would otherwise have been. Congratulations, Anna, on the birth of your own little princess, and thank you to Rebekah West and Kate Byrne for picking up the threads so admirably and getting this book out into the world. A big shout out must also go to Eleanor Russell, the clever person who pointed out to me that Cleopatra is closer in history to the iPhone than the Great Pyramids and sparked off this entire novel. Thank you, Ellie.

A special thank you to my agent, Kate Shaw, who has championed my work on Cleopatra, and the two amazing women who will follow her in this series. You always push me to do more than I know I can, Kate, and I couldn't have got this far without you. Thank you.

This book took a great deal of research and I would like to take this chance to record my gratitude to the British Library. I have spent many productive and happy hours in the reading rooms in St Pancras over the last few years and have recently discovered the wonderful 'northern branch' at Boston Spa. The library has enabled me to seek out so many texts that I wouldn't have found elsewhere and certainly wouldn't have been able to afford and we are very lucky, in this country, to have such an amazing institution.

On the same note, a big thank you to Cambridge University Library, who are also a wonderful research resource. I returned there for the first time since leaving the university in 1994 and felt quite nostalgic. I even cycled to the 'UL' to complete the feeling of time-travel – though not, in my advancing years, from my college room, but from our motorhome! I loved it just the same, and will be back.

This novel is dedicated to my good friend Johanna, who has backed me from the days when I was knee-deep in rejection letters and who so proudly goes into Waterstones to buy my latest novel every single time. I hope you enjoy buying this one, Johanna, (even though you definitely deserve a free copy) and that you know how special you are.

Thank you, as always, to my family. Some of you have more creative input than others. Stuart, you are my most loyal and bravest beta reader (I challenge anyone to try reading an author's manuscript sat in bed next to them!). Others of you (you know who you are . . .) haven't read a single one of my books, but the love and joy of having every one of you in my life gives me the strength to sit down and rip stories out of myself and I cherish you all.

Finally, a huge wave to my readers, without whom this novel would be just a load of scribbled-on pages! Thank you so much for reading and do get in touch as I love to hear from you.

Historical Note

My interest in Cleopatra was first truly aroused when someone smarter than I am pointed out that her reign is closer in history to the iPhone than the Great Pyramid at Giza (built c 2500 BC). The Ancient Egyptian Empire flourished from around 3000 BC and, with Cleopatra taking the throne in 52 BC, close to the birth of Christ, she actually belongs far more in the biblical world, with the Romans and the aggressive, Mediterranean-focused politics of that time, than in the mythical age with which I think many of us tend to associate her.

That interest was hugely heightened when, with just a little basic reading, I discovered an intelligent, bold and popular ruler who held her country steady through very difficult times, being the only leader in the Mediterranean and Near East to resist the ravenous Roman Empire. She was also an intellectual, documented as being able to speak at least nine languages with ease, and author of a treatise on potions that almost certainly included the asp-poison she used to kill herself (a sophisticated distillation, rather than the more basic but, clearly sexier, notion of putting the actual snake to her breast).

The final piece in the inspiration for this novel was the intriguing fact that Cleopatra was in Rome – indeed, living in one of Julius

Caesar's houses with his only son and a second child on the way – when he was assassinated. The Roman near-pathological obsession with royalty as evil was played out in the tragic killing of one of history's great rulers and just a little research left no doubt in my mind that Cleopatra's relationship with the great dictator was a key part of his downfall. It was not, however, part of hers.

This is a woman who, like so many others in history, has been thrown from the justly-earned podium of 'good leader' and relegated by male historians to one of their favourite and least subtle tropes – whore. History is written by the victors and in this instance the Romans were ashamed at the idea of not just one but two of their great leaders having a relationship with the sophisticated, elegant Queen of Egypt, and chose to write this off as seduction (which, if you ask me, is as denigrating to Julius and Mark Antony as it is to Cleopatra). I wanted to present her as the complex, complete person she clearly was, whilst also exploring her relationship with Julius Caesar as a meeting of both minds and hearts.

The historical details in this novel are as accurate as it has been possible to make them, but I felt there was room here for a little expansion on a few points, and explanation of any creative licence taken.

Historical Background

The Greek leaders of Egypt.

In the novel, the Egyptian royals are very aware of their 'superior' status as Greeks and scathing of the 'coarse' Egyptian language. Cleopatra really was the first of a line of Ptolemies stretching back to 305 BC who learned the native language, but how come these royals were Greek at all?

In truth, most rulers in the Mediterranean and near East area were Greek in this period and it's all thanks to Alexander III of Greece and Macedonia, who marched out at the head of 40,000 troops in 334 and rampaged through the east. Pausing only to marry Roxane, daughter of an Iranian chief, he pushed to the very edges of India, only turning back when his army refused to go any further. Alexander the Great was preparing to go East again when he died of a fever in the summer of 323. He was 32 and had only ruled for ten years, but left an empire stretching from the Adriatic to India, over which inevitable scraps immediately began. With no man strong enough to take and hold the whole, it splintered into various countries who were at war with each other for the next hundred years.

One of Alexander's seven key commanders, Ptolemy, however, made the canny move of heading to one of the Empire's furthest-out provinces, holding Egypt as a royal representative and soon taking it for himself, ruling as King Ptolemy I from 305-282 BC. He also cunningly kidnapped Alexander's corpse and had it installed in Alexandria, setting up a cult religion around it that helped the city prosper and Egypt thrive. A succession of Ptolemies would succeed him, of which Cleopatra was the thirteenth and the last.

Egyptian geopolitics

It would be a mistake to think that Egypt's separation from conflict made it a simple place to rule, not the least because of a problematic split between Alexandria and the rest of the country. The inhabitants of most capital cities see themselves, in my opinion, as something special – note Romans, Parisians and Londoners today – but the Alexandrians almost thought of themselves as their own country. Indeed, the royals ruled 'Alexandria and Egypt', and the inhabitants of the modern capital (built in 300 BC, rather than the 3000 BC of more ancient cities like Memphis) were an unruly lot, very prone to rebellion, as shown in the novel.

To add to this there was also a split between Upper Egypt (which, confusingly, is in the south – but "up" the Nile) and Lower Egypt around the Nile delta. Again, this is far from unusual (note the UK's continuing North-South divide) but exacerbated because the Nile is over 4000 miles long. Most of the vital agriculture of Egypt took place along the fertile banks of the great river, whilst Alexandria was entirely a service economy of traders, accountants, bankers and public services. The Alexandrians were fed from the countryside and assumed, as so many such people have, that they had a greater right to the corn than those who harvested it. Cleopatra, whose mother does seem to have come from Upper Egypt, had a far greater sympathy with the rural populations outside of the capital – and could speak their language – and, as shown in the novel, used this to her advantage when she was thrown out of the perfidious capital. She then worked hard to unite the country as a whole to stand strong against the Romans.

On top of being rich in natural minerals, Egypt had the Nile to provide an excess of corn to trade with less fertile countries – winning her the name, 'bread-basket of Europe' – and gain the vast wealth for which she was known. However, the harvest depended utterly on the twice-yearly inundations to provide crops with water and nutrients from the rich delta soil to thrive. The royals, revered as living gods, were expected to commune with Isis to ensure that She wept her tears onto them, and any failures in the inundations were therefore considered to be a sign of ill-favour and very dangerous to the monarch. Alexandrians were quick to rise up at any time, but hungry Alexandrians were even quicker! One of Cleopatra's great skills was as an administrator and, after the first few tricky years of her reign, she and her team seem to have excelled at storing excess to cover loss in lower years and, therefore, create both economic and political stability.

Royalty vs Republic
It was Alexander the Great who introduced the concept of modern kingship into the Mediterranean regions, and what a problematic introduction it was, especially once the Romans countered with their republic. Rome was founded in 753 by two kings, Romulus and Remus (who they still, ironically worshipped in Caesar's day)

but after problems with 'tyrant' kings, they chucked them out and, in 509, set up the republic with elected leaders. The concept was good – two men in charge, re-elected every year and reporting to a senate, also elected, to keep them in check. As with all such purist concepts, however, it rapidly became corrupted, with elections being mainly won by those with the money and status to command votes.

The republic had also, by Caesar's time, become a victim of its own success, growing so large that it was almost impossible for central administration to stay in command. The Romans were consumed by their own petty politics, whilst the men clever enough to get governorships in the wider Empire could rule as they wished. The only way, it emerged, to hold this together was with a single, strong leader – a king!

Julius Caesar was the man with the vision to see that, and the charisma to fulfil the role but the rest of Rome – notably the purists around Cato and, later, Brutus – were not ready. It is true that royals were not allowed within the 'Pomerium', the boundary of the ancient city, and to Romans they had become a form of wicked monster to be feared. Clearly, the presence of a queen – and a 'decadent, eastern' one at that – in Caesar's bed seemed to them to underline his corruption. Brutus and his fellows' Republican ideals meant more to them than their practical application and that was, ultimately, Caesar's undoing. It is a dark irony that Octavian, Julius' successor after the rebellion, was the man who swiftly became Augustus (meaning majestic or venerable) and Emperor – a king amongst kings!

Character Questions

The Outrageous ones
Several of my characters may seem, to some readers, to be exaggerated or even fabricated and I would like to take a moment to assure them of the veracity of several of the more outrageous ones.

The Claudii may seem overdone in the novel but I can assure you that I have, if anything, downplayed their outlandish stunts and liberal attitudes. Clodia was openly the lover of the poet Catullus and known for her risqué clothing and loose living. Clodius was similarly flamboyant and the scene where he baits Pompey over his young wife is taken from true reports. The Claudii were classic rich-kids playing at being poor, though also, I think, motivated by a genuine desire for a more open, free society, and they would certainly have been companions who appealed to an Egyptian princess.

Cato was one of the staunchest defenders of the republic and was as stern and unbending a man as shown in the story. The scene in Cyprus, for example, is based on a real report from Plutarch that he received King Ptolemy sitting on the latrine to show his disdain for royalty. Roman latrines were often out in the open, so it is not beyond the bounds of possibility. The padded stick with which he wipes himself in the scene was a known cleaning method and I can only imagine the impact this act of total disrespect would have had on King Ptolemy and the young Princess Cleopatra.

Porcia is a character rarely mentioned in the much-told story of Caesar's assassination but I would like to assure readers that, although this is not based on documented evidence, it is created from a web of facts and, indeed, speculation from the time, that make it highly plausible.

Cato was Porcia's father and Brutus' uncle and instrumental in their upbringings. It's clear from Brutus' published writings and actions how great an influence Cato was on him, and I honestly believe that he killed Caesar - his great supporter, and his mother's long-term lover – because he was convinced he wanted to be a king and bring down the sacred idea of the republic (as discussed above).

It is notable that Brutus started to turn against Caesar once he'd divorced Claudia – one of the liberal Claudii – and married Porcia.

Although he fought with Pompey in the war, that was mainly because he felt he was the elected Roman leader at the time and he was swift to come back to Julius' side afterwards, begging for forgiveness and working hard for him for several years before he turned against him.

Roman women were expected to stay in the home, but we know that they were hugely influential behind the scenes. Both Servilia and Fulvia are key figures in political shifts and Servilia is documented as offering wise advice to a huge range of senators, so it would not be a surprise if smart, determined Porcia drip-fed ideas into her husband's brain. Brutus was an intellectual, a deep-thinker, easily tortured by right and wrong, and I am convinced that his new wife's certainty that Caesar was harming Rome would have been a critical part in the decision to assassinate him.

The missing ones

Readers who know the period well may also have noticed the absence, or near-absence, of several significant figures at the time and I would like to explain why I did not include them in the novel.

Crassus. The meeting in Lucca was between Caesar and Pompey, as shown, but also a third man, Crassus. These three formed the first triumvirate, some years before the more famous one of Octavian, Lepidus and Mark Anthony. It was Pompey and Crassus who went on to be tribunes in 55, with Julius Caesar still governing (and conquering) Gaul but behind much of their power. Trying to explain all this, however, clogged the story unnecessarily so I chose to leave poor Crassus out.

Cassius and Decimus. Servilia mentions Cassius in passing as the hero of Parthia and indeed he offered Roman soldiers a great service in removing them from peril when Crassus (above) attempted an ill-judged invasion. Cassius was, in fact, Servilia's son-in-law, married to her third daughter Julia Tertia, known as Tulla. In an original draft, Tulla was friends with Cleopatra and Claudia but, with the novel already heavily populated, it confused the narrative too far and she had to go. Cassius, along with Decimus, were also key figures in Caesar's assassination, but including them and the tangles of their personal and political lives would have doubled the size of this novel so, sadly, I could not feature them fully.

Curio. I show Fulvia as moving from marrying Clodius to marrying Mark Antony but in fact she had another husband in between – Gaius Scribonius Curio. They were only married a short time before he was killed, like so many, in the fighting between Pompey and Caesar, and it was simpler to leave him out of this particular story.

A few points of detail

Titles. I spent some time agonising over how to have Cleopatra addressed by her subjects. It was vital, given the theme of royalty vs republic, that I used a title that distinguished the queen clearly, but modern forms of address were not in use at the time. In medieval Europe, a king would most usually be addressed as 'your grace' or possibly 'my liege' or 'sire' (or other language equivalents).

The title 'your majesty' was introduced by Charles V when he became Holy Roman Emperor in 1519 and taken to Britain by Henry VIII. The term 'your highness' arrived even later, in the seventeenth century as a way of highlighting the superiority of certain ruling families, so clearly none of these were correct for a Queen of Egypt. The Egyptians would, of course, have had their own term in Egyptian – or, indeed Greek – but as I was writing this novel in English, I had to choose something that reflected a reader's concept of royalty so went, in the end, for 'your majesty'. I hope I am forgiven the anachronism.

Royal headgear. Although monarchs in this period had very beautiful crowns, they wore them only – as now – for ceremonial occasions. The rest of the time, Greek monarchs wore a diadem. This was, as shown in the novel, a very simple piece of white ribbon but it was a sacred symbol, worn by no one else, so when Mark Antony offered it to Julius at the Lupercalia, it would have been a gesture understood by all.

The calendar. It is absolutely true that, by the time of Julius' rule, the Roman calendar was four months out of alignment with the seasons. This was because extra weeks to balance the lunar and solar clocks had to be voted in by senators and they were usually too busy fighting for more power to pay it enough attention. Julius Caesar is famed, among other things, for his Julian calendar, which he most definitely nicked from the Egyptians.

The year-clock shown in the novel really existed and if you search the Antikythera mechanism on the internet, you will find pictures of a recreation of the most beautifully intricate device that was, thankfully, recovered from a shipwreck off the coast of the Greek island of Antikythera in 1901. This enabled the Egyptians to very accurately calculate leap days and years, and Julius was quick to see its potential for Rome, installing a stable calendar in 46 BC, which included the extra month, July, named for himself. It is, therefore, anachronistic of me to use our modern months in the chapter headings of the novel, but for the sake of comprehension I decided it was clearest.

Infertility in Rome. There are several Roman women in this novel who suffer from being unable to conceive, notably poor Claudia, whose childlessness gave Brutus the excuse to divorce her (not that Romans needed much excuse!). Evidence suggests that this was a common problem in ancient Rome and a theory has been put forward that the lead in the water from the Romans' legendary and otherwise very efficient plumbing systems, made many women – and/or men- infertile.

Name of the Mediterranean: The ancient Egyptian name for the sea bordering Alexandria was Uat-Ur. This translates directly as 'the Great Green', but I chose to use the Green Sea for clarity. The Romans called it 'Mare Nostrum' – our sea – which classic piece of arrogance, I was pleased to retain.

Historical Licence

I have played with history just a little in a two key places in order to ease the flow of the narrative:

Cleopatra's initial stay in Rome. King Ptolemy XII was, as shown, restored to his throne in the Spring of 55 BC, but it is likely that he was actually away, staying in both Rome and Ephesus, for three years, having fled in 58 BC after the Romans took Cyprus (Cato was governor there 58-56 BC). There is some evidence that Cleopatra – a favourite of her father's - may have either gone with him or joined him, but three years was a protracted stay that strung-out the narrative unappealingly so I chose to make it a one-year exile.

Brutus' visit to Egypt. There is no evidence that it was Brutus who came to ask Cleopatra for ships to support Pompey in the civil war. It was more likely Gaius Pompeius – one of Pompey's elder sons – but that meant introducing another character and, as we know that Brutus was in the Mediterranean at the time, it did not seem unreasonable to make this small narrative leap and allow him to meet with Cleopatra at this critical point.

There is no way of knowing what Cleopatra thought and felt, so it is perhaps with her character that I have taken the greatest historical licence. It is, however, the task and privilege of the historical novelist to attempt to convincingly enter their protagonist's persona and present them to the reader as a believable figure and I have worked hard to do so. Cleopatra is not an unknown persona, like many of the women about whom I have previously written, but she is one who has been presented by historians and storytellers throughout history – not the least those in Hollywood – as a far less subtle and interesting woman that she truly was. I hope this novel has gone some way to correcting that.

It is exceptionally annoying that Cleopatra is known mainly for her ability to seduce Romans when she was in a fact an intelligent, skilled and politically astute ruler. What's more, she wasn't even a serial seducer, having just two long-term and very loyal 'marriages' with men who also happened to be Roman leaders. Under her rule Egypt prospered and, if she kept Rome at bay by consorting with the 'enemy', I strongly believe that she did it for her country.

That is not to decry her relationship with Julius Caesar. Her more problematic romance with Mark Antony is a much-told story, but I genuinely believe that she and Julius were a meeting of bright, focused minds and a true love. Both were sharp, charismatic people who loved life and wanted to drink deeply from its cup. They were also both passionate about the countries they ruled and isolated at the top of them, and they found solace and refreshment in each other. It is their tragedy that they were on either side of political schisms too deep to resist.

Can't get enough of
Joanna Courtney?

**Keep reading for a sneak peek
of *Blood Queen* . . .**

Available now at

PIATKUS

Prologue

I did not ask to be queen. I did not look for gowns and crowns
and the weight of a country upon my shoulders. I wanted only to
join my hand to that of the man I loved and be Lady Macbeth.
I wanted only to be a wife and mother and to build a contented
home upon the welcoming shores of the Moray Firth.

Or did I? I fear maybe my heart was not forged so simply. Yes,
I wanted love – what girl does not? – but I wanted more too. I
wanted position, pride, achievement. My blood is royal and royal
blood is a prickly fluid. It does not run as freely as that of normal
men and women. With such blood in your veins you are a recep-
tacle not just for your own life but for so many others, past and
present, whose hopes and duties and privileges you perpetuate. I
did not ask to be queen but I did look for the *right* to be so and the
way the times turned around me, it amounted to the same thing.

Did God intend me for the throne? It would be comforting to
say so but I'm not sure God thinks that highly of me, or of any
of us. Alba's kings and queens are inaugurated on the Stone of
Destiny but they have to seize that stone first – they have to *make*
that destiny for themselves. They have to climb the Hill of Belief
to sit upon that stone and it is not so named for nothing. I did not
ask to be queen but I believed I could be.

And she, the other one – Lady Duncan – did she believe so too? She had no royal blood, nor Alban blood neither, but she took to our country as if she had been waiting for such a gift all her life. She had her own destiny to chase and it was perhaps just an accident of fate that she was chasing it in the same time and space as I. The threads of our lives, in the end, crossed in so many places that they became almost a single chain – a chain to hang around Alba's neck and decorate her history.

My heart was not forged simply but it was forged strong and it beat out a rhythm I can never regret. I did not ask to be queen but neither did I refuse. I made my destiny and I followed it all the way across Alba to its throne and its tomb. I was Lady Macbeth and I was Queen and I can only hope that in some small way Alba was richer for it.

Chapter One

Cora

Inverness, August 1025

Cora MacDuff stared contentedly up at the soft Moray sky. The patch of vivid blue directly above her was framed all around by waving bulrushes and marked by a single small cloud which, if she half-closed her eyes, looked very like a beating heart. A smile fluttered at the corners of her mouth but then, ashamed of her foolish fancy, she exhaled and the bulrushes surrounding her sighed in protest.

'What are you sighing about, Cora? Not me, I hope.'

Macbeth raised himself up on one elbow to look down at her and, despite herself, she smiled.

'No, not you, Macbeth.'

How could she sigh over him? With his mop of blond hair and dark brown eyes, he was a fair sight for any lass and somehow he'd turned that fine gaze of his on her. He made her ridiculously happy and *that* was the problem. She didn't want to be happy; she wasn't *meant* to be happy. She was meant to be angry and resentful and full of hate, not mooning around in bulrushes cuddled up to handsome young Mormaer's sons as if all was right with the world. For it was not; it was not at all.

Cora had arrived in the northerly province of Moray a few months ago after a desperate flight from the vicious enmity of

King Malcolm's men. The king was their father's first cousin but had seen their shared blood as a threat not a tie. She grasped at one of the bulrushes, welcoming the sting of its sharp-edged leaf against her skin as she forced herself to picture the desecrated body of her father, Mormaer Lachlan, cut down in his cornfields and then hacked apart like an animal. They hadn't needed to do that. He'd been dead at the first stroke, or so she prayed. The rest had been the king's cruelty.

Not that King Malcolm had killed his cousin himself, nothing so crude, but what king did his own dirty work? She'd known it was a royal edict the minute she'd looked up from her father's rich Fife farmhouse and seen the armed men crashing towards it through the corn. It hadn't taken Lachlan's hoarse cry of 'Run!' to tell her the mortal danger they were all in, for she had seen it written in the line of raised swords.

She and Kendrick had run for the woods beyond their estate, trusting to their knowledge of the paths to help them evade their father's murderers. But it had been clear as they'd huddled deep in their favourite cave that they couldn't go back. For them the comforts of home had been curtailed as surely as their father's life and that very night, in just the clothes they stood up in, they'd turned north.

Cora released the bulrush and lifted her hand to stare at the thin line of blood it had left across her palm. Macbeth flinched away and for a moment she felt sorry for shocking him but he should know what he was getting into. She was no forlorn exile who needed soothing and looking after. She was a woman with a purpose and it was best that he realised that and turned his damned kisses elsewhere. Though they were such lovely kisses . . .

'Cora?' His voice was soft – too soft.

He was always so wonderfully gentle but she couldn't let him soothe her too far. Her hurt had to stay raw to keep her purpose alive. She sat up, pulling away from him.

'Why do you bother with me, Macbeth?'

'Why?' He looked surprised but gave the question careful thought before he replied. 'You intrigue me, Cora MacDuff. You're different.'

'Different? That's it?'

Amusement sparked in his chestnut-coloured eyes.

'Wrong answer, my sweet? Then I'll try again. How about the fact that I love your dawn-red hair and your sun-freckled skin and your wishing-pool eyes?'

'Wishing-pool eyes? Really, Macbeth?'

She looked towards the pond they were lying by, which was indeed as pure green as her eyes. Local legend had it that in the morning mists you might catch a glimpse of the faeries bathing here, but right now the sun had chased the mist away and the pool was good only for cooling their bare toes. Cora pulled hers back, hugging her knees against her chest.

'I'm not looking for empty compliments, Macbeth.'

'They're not . . . '

'Keep them for your Moray girls. I'm sure pretty words will please them well enough.'

'True. See – you're different.'

She rolled her eyes.

'Of course I'm different. I'm from Fife. We have villages of more than three crofts and roads you can actually drive a cart on and we can attend court whenever we wish. We don't just wander about herding sheep and watching dolphins dance.'

Macbeth grinned.

'You love the dolphins.'

Frustratingly, that much was true. Cora had been astonished the first time she'd seen the great fish leap from the waters of the Moray Firth, twisting and turning for the pure joy of it. But life wasn't about joy, or at least hers wasn't. Not anymore.

'I won't stay long.'

'Fair enough. It must be nearly dinner-time anyway.'

'Not at the pool, Macbeth. I mean here, in Moray. I won't stay long.'

At this, at least, he looked hurt.

'You don't like it?'

'It's very nice, very pretty. It's just so far away.'

He frowned.

'No, it isn't. It's right here. See.'

He reached out and flicked pond water into the air. It danced in sparkling droplets between them but Cora turned her head from the pretty sight.

'Not far away from *us*; far away from important things.'

'Like?'

'Like the throne.'

'Ah. And is that more important, then, than us?'

'Well, of course it is.' He nodded back at her. So calm, so thoughtful – so irritating. Cora leaped to her feet. 'You don't understand, Macbeth.'

She turned to walk away but he was up too, remarkably quickly for such a big man, and clasping her against him. Cora felt her blood pulse and struggled to fight its petty impulses.

'I don't,' he agreed, 'but I'd like to. I like *you*. To me, you resemble a piece of iron – whenever you get near the slightest heat, you spark like crazy and that fascinates me.'

His face had dipped closer to hers. His brown eyes were fixed on her 'wishing-pool' eyes and somehow, just like that, he seemed to suck all the hatred out of her and make her long to reach up and press her lips to his and lose herself in his dolphin-like joy in her. But what use would that be?

'Iron?' she choked out and he pulled back a little. 'You're right – I am iron. I must be iron. I must make of myself a sword to avenge the wrong done to my father by his own blood.'

Macbeth took her hands, rubbing them gently between his fingers.

'I know that, Cora. I know what King Malcolm did to your father and I swear I will help you find vengeance. All Moray will help you.'

'When, Macbeth?'

'When the time is right.'

She smiled at him bitterly.

'It is kind of you to say so but the time will *never* be right, not for your father's men, and why should it be? This is my problem; mine and Kendrick's. We are grateful that you have sheltered us, truly, but this is not a fight for Moray.'

She felt Macbeth release her. He turned away and she longed to go after him but she mustn't. He wanted to heal her with gentleness and love but it couldn't work that way. Could it?

'Macbeth . . .'

He turned back.

'Marry me, Cora.'

'What?'

The soft meadowland seemed to shift beneath her feet.

'Marry me. Be my wife. I love you, Cora. I love your passion and your determination and your damned ferocity. I want your fight to be my fight and I want to help you win it. Marry me, please.'

She stared at him. There was a word fighting its way up her throat and biting against her tongue to be let out. 'Yes,' she wanted to shout. 'Yes, yes, yes.' Macbeth was like no one she'd ever known. He was so easy in his skin, so at one with the world. He took her every raw argument and considered it with a care and logic that reduced it to something so much easier to cope with. He made her feel comfortable and safe and, yes, happy. But she wasn't meant to be happy. She was meant to be angry and resentful and full of hate.

He came closer again, a new, more serious light in his eyes.

'I have a claim too, Cora.'

'A claim to what?'

'To the throne. My father spoke of it with me last night. My family are the last of the line of Aed.'

Cora's eyes widened. He spoke true. There were two royal

lines in Alba – descending from Aed and Constantin, sons of the first king, Kenneth MacAlpin – and under the rules of alternate inheritance the lines were meant to take turns upon the throne. King Malcolm was a Constantin, as was she, and he had plans to put his grandson, Duncan, on the throne after him. The Aed line in the south had died out, leaving him unchallenged, but up here in Moray there was a second line, a line that dwelt quietly beyond the sheltering crags of the Mounth – the fearsome mountain strip cutting Alba in two – or who had done so far.

'You have a claim too,' Cora repeated hoarsely.

'And if we married and were lucky enough to have a child, he would combine the two royal lines for the first time ever. He'd be Constantin and Aed: the ultimate heir.'

Cora stared up at him. He'd thought hard about this – of course he had – and he was right.

'With such an heir we could challenge King Malcolm. Or at least Prince Duncan.'

'Yes!'

'And then you would have your vengeance.'

Cora shifted her feet. It sounded so cruel.

'Restitution,' she corrected. 'I want restitution for the injustice done to my father by his own vicious brother.'

'And would his grandson being crowned not be a fine way to achieve it?'

She nodded slowly.

'It would take time though, Macbeth.'

'So impatient, my sweet? We *have* time. We are young. You and Kendrick can grow strong here in Moray and gather support. And meanwhile I'm sure we can find something to do to while away the hours . . .'

He ran a finger lightly up her arm and across her neck, sending shivers of wanton delight through her body and drawing her irresistibly towards him.

'What did you have in mind?' she murmured.

In response, he kissed her long and deep and all his gentle strength seemed to surge into her with his embrace. She'd come to Moray lost and hurt and torn apart and somehow God had blessed her with the love of this man. How could she refuse it?

'So, Cora MacDuff,' he said when they finally pulled apart. 'Will you marry me?'

'Yes,' she gasped. 'Oh, Macbeth, yes.'

And then he was kissing her again and she was clinging to him and praying he was right and that restitution could be found, not just with the piercing immediacy of hatred, but with a care and deliberation that might build her and Kendrick and all of Alba a better future than the one afforded it by murderous King Malcolm.